CW01373923

OVERGROWTH

OVERGROWTH

MIRA GRANT

Daphne Press

First published in the UK in 2025 by Daphne Press
www.daphnepress.com

Cover design by Jane Tibbetts
Typesetting by Adrian McLaughlin

A CIP catalogue record for this book is available from the British Library.

Hardback ISBN: 978-1-83784-094-6
eBook ISBN: 978-1-83784-097-7
Starbright edition ISBN: 978-1-83784-098-4
Australian TPB ISBN: 978-1-83784-108-0

The authorised representative in the EEA is Authorised Rep Compliance Ltd
71 Baggot Street Lower, Dublin, D02 P593, Ireland.
Email: info@arccompliance.com

Printed and bound by CPI Group (UK) Ltd, Croydon CR0 4YY

1

For Merav.
I told you so.

SEED

Yet across the gulf of space, minds that are to our minds as ours are to those of the beasts that perish, intellects vast and cool and unsympathetic, regarded this earth with envious eyes . . .

—H.G. WELLS,
THE WAR OF THE WORLDS

Sometimes I wonder if pollution isn't humanity's way of denying how hard it is to build a wall against the stars.

—STASIA MILLER

Fermi's Paradox, named after the esteemed physicist Enrico Fermi, asks an essential question about the existence of extraterrestrial life: namely, where is it? Given a universe the size of our own—functionally infinite when compared to something as small as a human being—and the number of planets we have already discovered which are potentially capable of supporting life, it seems impossible that we have not yet been visited by our neighbors. Yet conclusive proof of alien civilizations has not been found. Every sighting can be explained; every abduction can be swept away. We are, for all intents and purposes, alone.

Either life is vanishingly rare in the universe, or some other factor is at play. Perhaps intelligence is the rare quality: we may be surrounded by living worlds whose occupants have never risen above the level of common beasts. Or perhaps something, some great and terrible thing, prevents life from developing beyond a certain point. Perhaps we are alone, not because evolution has shown us any great favor, but because we have yet to come to the attention of that which keeps our skies devoid of company.

—FROM *THE FERMI PARADOX AND THE MILKY WAY*,
BY ANTHONY VORNHOLT,
ORIGINALLY PUBLISHED 2030.

Anastasia has a vivid imagination and does not shy away from sharing her fantasies with the rest of the class. She needs to learn restraint, and when it's time to put pretend away and focus on the real world. It is slightly concerning how detailed her imaginary scenarios can become. She rarely deviates from the details of her make-believe once she has settled on them, and will argue with other students who attempt to contradict her.

It is not yet a problem for Anastasia to have such a rich fantasy life; at her age, this is fairly common. She should still be monitored in case of future issues telling the truth from fiction, as she will be expected to focus more on her studies as time goes by.

—LETTER HOME FROM MS. ANNE O'TOOLE,
KINDERGARTEN TEACHER.
SENT NOVEMBER, 2002.

THE STORY

1.

This is a story. It can't hurt you anymore.

It's still important that you listen, because I am going to tell you things you need to know, and it will be easier for you to understand what's happening if you pay attention to me now. But if you get scared, or if you wonder why I'm making you listen to this, just remember that this is a story. There was a time when it could hurt you, but that time is over and done. You're safe. I'll protect you, I promise. I really, really do.

This is a story. You need to know how it starts.

It can't hurt you anymore.

2.

Like so many things, it begins with a seedpod, large and thick-skinned for protection, irregularly shaped to ease its passage through the air. It isn't aerodynamic, but where this seedpod floats, there isn't any atmosphere to pierce. It travels through the depths of space at a speed that no Earthly seedpod has ever approached, trapped in the frozen heart of a comet, followed by a bridal train of stardust and ice. It goes where gravity and orbital forces take it, and it knows nothing of where it is or where it came from. It is not aware.

In the beginning before the beginning that matters to us, this seedpod was one of dozens scattered through the same fertile cloud of icy planetesimals, left by a fruiting body long since passed. Ice and debris swirled around the seedpods, slowly coalescing into comets, which broke loose from their nursery and began their long, uncharted trek through the cosmos. Some of them died before they could finish forming, never quite hardening, their cargos destroyed and undelivered. Others crashed into lifeless moons or were pulled into blazing suns, the ice melting in an instant, the seedpods crisping and dying only a moment later. But some . . .

Some, like this one, managed to soar on gravitational lines, dancing through the sky on their unknown and unknowable errands. One by one, this seedpod's fellows have dropped away, even the survivors, leaving it to chart its course alone.

The planet that lies ahead of it is blue green and bright, glowing with points of artificial light. The seedpod has passed it a dozen times before, but this time, ah. This time, there is debris in the air around it, artificial structures and satellites scattered through low orbit. This time, radio signals flutter and flash through the air. Something deep within the seedpod—something less organic than the seedpod itself, something less casually grown than the comet that protects it—sparks and flares to life, recording those signals, picking them quickly to pieces, like a centipede slicing up its prey with the ends of its razored legs.

The signals are good. The signs are good. The comet, which has flown past the planet so many times before, shudders, orbit suddenly adjusting from within rather than from without. It tilts, bending toward the gravitational field. It shakes, spinning wildly, shedding chunks of ice in all directions.

It is not a large comet. Not the sort of thing that attracts admirers or ends epochs. Only a few astronomers on the planet below notice its odd behavior. They take pictures, excited to capture a comet breaking up so close to the atmosphere; they notify their friends that something exciting is going on. They don't think any more of it. Why should they? Comets die all the time. The sky is a living thing, a void filled with points of slow, deliberate vitality.

The comet spins one last time and plunges below the orbital horizon. Gravity takes over, greedily grabbing for the projectile, like a child snatching the first pieces of candy out of a broken piñata. The last of the ice is ripped away. The surface of the seedpod bulges and contracts, exposed to the elements for the first time since it was nestled in its icy nursery.

The skin, a deep, pitted purple the texture of fruit leather, begins to crack. Gravity continues to pull. The skin splits, a seam running from one end of the seedpod to the other. And then, with no further ceremony or incentive, it falls away entirely, scattering seeds in its wake.

They are surprisingly small, these interstellar wanderers, each about the size of a withered apple or a squirrel's skull. They are wrinkled like walnuts, labyrinthine in their folds and channels. They fall, surrounded by bright coronas of fire as the friction of their descent ignites the thickening air around them, burning away the top layers of their protective skins.

The wind catches some of them, blows them across oceans and over continents. See how they fall, these travelers, these seeds of something new! They drop out of the sky in fiery halos, and people make wishes on them, call them shooting stars, delight in their presence and their novelty. Astronomers make notes. Some of those astronomers will talk during the weeks to come about the rare and beautiful comet that died in their sky, and none of them will wonder what it carried in its belly.

The seeds fall, in ones and twos and dozens. Some of them drown in the deep oceans. Others land in inhospitable soil, in frozen tundra or burning volcanos. A few even fall on city streets, to be swept up as refuse or collected by curious children who will never recognize them for what they really are. So many opportunities, even now, for discovery, and one by one, they pass by untaken. No one questions the comet. No one slices open a seed found on a sidewalk. No one looks. No one *learns.*

One by one, they fall, and one of them falls in a green forest on a green continent. It lands in rich and fertile soil, still smoking with the heat of its long journey. No one sees it fall. No one comes to collect or quarantine it. Still, it sits fallow for a full turn of seasons, slowly adjusting to the weather, to the conditions around it.

A year after the comet died above the Earth, the first seeds crack their shells and send down thin, waxen roots, piercing deep into the ground beneath them. They begin to draw water and nutrients from their surroundings. They begin to *grow.* Inch by inch, cautious to the last, they begin to grow. Some sprout in sun and some in shadow. One grows in the heart of a desert, sending its roots spiraling deep in the quest for water.

Still they are not noticed. Still they are left alone.

At the end of a week, there is a sprout where each of the surviving seeds had been, their green skins underlaid with a thin sheen of blue, like the shimmer of a beetle's wings. Half the seedlings die before they pass this stage, swallowed by grazing animals which follow them into death a heartbeat later, collapsing into anaphylactic shock.

At the end of a month, each sprout has become a stalk, unfurling delicate, fernlike leaves covered in stinging hairs similar to a jellyfish's nematocysts. Another quarter of the seedlings die entering this stage, collapsing under their own weight as they fail to properly account for this new world's gravity.

At the end of a month, buds form atop the strengthening stalks, purple and white and red, streaked and gory. Each bud opens on the third day after its formation, turning a sightless eye toward the heavens, almost as if they can remember coming from those vaunted heights.

Silent, patient, hidden, the flowers wait.

They are very good at waiting.

3.

The seedpod isn't our only beginning: that doesn't suit the lifecycle we're chronicling here, which has many parts and many players. It also begins in a hospital, in a small town in Washington State, where a woman—call her Caroline; say that she is pretty and she is tired and she is trying very hard, even though she is very frightened—has just given birth to her daughter. See her now, sweat matting down her hair, tears on her cheeks, cradling the small, screaming creature she has made with her own body, fueled with her own blood. Is it any wonder she loves and fears it in equal measure, this tiny thing that can cause her so much pain and bring her so much joy at the same time?

The nurses take the baby away. Caroline, exhausted, uncertain, goes to sleep.

When she wakes, her parents—her frustrating, beloved, infuriating parents—are in the room. Her mother is holding the baby. Her father is sitting next to the bed, holding her hand. For the first time, Caroline is struck by how much he looks like she feels, how much parental love transcends generation and gender and even estrangement, even if she can't quite remember what made her decide she needed to do this on her own.

"Before you get mad, your sister called us," says her father. "She said that no-good boyfriend of yours ran out as soon as he heard you were in the family way."

"He didn't want to be a family with me, and good riddance," says Caroline. "I don't need him. I can be a family just fine on my own."

"Not entirely on your own," says her father, with a meaningful glance toward the tiny bundle still cradled in her mother's arms. "What are you going to name her?"

This feels like a test. That was part of what drove her away, she remembers that now: the way her father always seemed to be testing her, the way she could never be sure she had the right answer. It wasn't comfortable. It wasn't *fair.* Caroline takes a breath.

"Anastasia," she says. "Like Grandma."

Now her mother looks up, surprised and pleased and smiling. "You're naming her after my mother?"

"I miss her," says Caroline, and that's the reason "away" could never quite be forever, could never come with changing her name or moving to another coast. Family is where you keep the pieces of yourself that need to be shared with someone else if they're going to have meaning, the memories that must be seen from three or four different angles at the same time before they find their context. She's been circling her parents since she left, never coming close enough to catch, never stepping far enough away to escape, because these are the people who remember where she comes from, who understand who she is when she's alone.

"I miss her too," says her mother, and then, "I miss *you*. We both do. I'm sorry we aren't always perfect together. Do you think we could try again, for your sake? For Anastasia?"

Caroline hesitates.

She's tired. She's tired of couches, and shitty little apartments with roaches in the walls, and motels that are as happy to rent by the hour as they are by the week. She doesn't mind the sex workers—they're sweet ladies, for the most part, and some of them have kids of their own; she's made her rent more than once by providing babysitting services to glamorous escorts in mended silk skirts and sky-high shoes—but the druggies, they're a problem. She doesn't want them around the baby. And how many couches are going to be open to her now that her daughter is out in the open, wailing and puking and messing her diapers, instead of peacefully tucked away inside her belly?

I should have kept you inside forever, where you'd be safe, she thinks, and she's righter than she will ever have the chance to know.

"It can't be like it was," she says. "Not this time. I'm a mother now. I have to be allowed to know what's best for my little girl."

"As long as you'll let me help," says her mother. Her father, who has no competition in sight for the position of most important man in Anastasia's life, says nothing. This part of the conversation isn't for him, and he's a clever-enough man to know it, to understand that sometimes the right thing to do is stand back and hold his peace.

"I think I could use some help," says Caroline, and holds out her arms, asking for her mother, asking for her daughter, asking for her family.

Renee Miller, who raised three children of her own, only to lose them all—one to a war, one to the other side of the country, and one, her precious baby girl, to her own stubbornness—walks her granddaughter across the room, and it's like she's coming home, and it's like she never left.

Caroline takes Anastasia in her arms, and everything is perfect. Everything is just the way it's supposed to be, forever.

4.

The Millers live in a small town in Washington State, surrounded by trees on all sides, with the mountains misty in the distance, playing hide-and-seek with the shadows cast by clouds. It rains less often than people from out of state assume, more often than Caroline, cooped up in a three-bedroom house with an excitable toddler, would prefer.

Whenever the sun is shining—and sometimes when it's not—Anastasia is outside, tearing around the yard, kicking her little wheeled scooter down the driveway, chasing the squirrels that cluster and chitter in the nearby trees. Their street doesn't get much traffic, and they know all their neighbors; it's as safe here as it could be anywhere. That's enough to make up for the boredom, Caroline thinks. Her daughter is safe.

Anastasia has only three rules for playing outside. Don't go into the street; don't go down the sidewalk unless her mommy or one of her grandparents is in the yard to watch her; and don't go into the trees. The woods are very big and she is very small, and she would be lost very quickly if she strayed too far.

She doesn't *want* to go into the street. She saw one of the squirrels after it had gone into the street, and it was flat like a pancake, or like one of the paper dolls her gramma cuts out for her. Only it wasn't a paper doll, and it wasn't a pancake, it was D-E-A-D, dead, and it was never going to chitter at her from the trees ever again. She doesn't want to be flat and quiet forever, so she doesn't want to go into the street.

She doesn't *want* to go down the sidewalk when there's no one to see her. She has a feeling, vague and unfounded but solid enough to haunt her dreams, that sometimes people go down the sidewalk and they don't come back. All the other kids she knows have mommies *and* daddies. They aren't always in the same combination—Shawna has two mommies, and Mark has two daddies—and they aren't always around—Alison's mommy drives a big truck, and she's gone for weeks sometimes—but they exist. No one ever talks about her daddy, or says where he is, but sometimes her mommy looks at the sidewalk with a great big sadness in her eyes, like everything is wrong. Anastasia's daddy must have gone out when no one could see, and he couldn't find his way back to home. She doesn't want to get lost forever, so she doesn't want to go down the sidewalk.

But the trees . . .

The trees are where the squirrels live, and the deer, and the big old owl that goes who-who, who-who at night outside her window. She saw it once, all feathers and silence, flying across the yard like a dream, and she wanted to go with it, with the owl, off into forever. Going into the woods isn't like going into the street, and it isn't like going down the sidewalk when there's no one to see you. Going into the woods is going to see the owl. It's going to dance with the deer. It's all good things, and no bad things at all.

Anastasia is three and a half years old, and she wants the woods like her lungs want air. She wants the woods so badly that some nights all she can dream about is what it must be like, out there in the trees, surrounded by rough brown trunks and soft green needles, with the sound of owls all around her.

Her mother knows she wants the woods, and most days, Caroline watches her like a hawk, ready to swoop in and carry her back to safety. But this day is different. This day, her mother is on the phone in the kitchen, distracted, saying things Anastasia doesn't understand and doesn't really care about. This day, her mother isn't watching. Anastasia takes a few steps toward the edge of the wood and pauses to look back, gauging her mother's distraction. All she can see through the kitchen window is the back of her mother's head, brown-blonde hair tangled carelessly, like she hasn't even bothered brushing it yet this morning.

Anastasia turns and runs, not aware that she will never see her mother again. She is consumed by her wanting for the woods, running as fast as her legs will carry her, and she imagines she's faster than the wind, faster than the owl with its great brown wings, faster than anything has ever been or will ever be. She is a child racing toward the end of her own life. She is the only thing that has ever mattered, or ever will matter. She is a universe unto herself, and up until this moment she has been expanding, stretching toward infinity.

Her legs carry her past the edge of the trees, past the twilight zone of underbrush and fallen branches where she has played before, under the careful supervision of an adult, and into the woods proper. She stops, stunned, looking around herself with open-mouthed wonder.

Sunlight pierces the air, refined into tight golden shafts by the interplay of shade and open space. The ground isn't only ferns; it's mushrooms and fallen logs and everything a fairy tale forest *ought* to be. She feels like she's walking into one of her picture books, and she doesn't think about how she's getting farther away from home with every step she takes, or how her mother may be worried about her. She only wants to see what's past the next tree, what's over the next little rise in the ground. She only wants to find the owl.

She thinks she could be happy never going into the woods again, never doing anything forbidden ever again, if only she could see the owl.

So she walks, and she walks, and home dwindles behind her, forgotten, forsaken, until something bigger than she is rustles in the brush to her left, and she jumps, startled, and realizes she has no idea where she is.

Anastasia is three and a half years old, which feels very grown-up and mature when she's explaining to her grandfather how she absolutely deserves extra ice cream, and which suddenly feels very small and very young and very alone.

"Mama?" she says.

The woods answer with the rustle of branches and the call of small, distant birds.

"Mama!"

Not once in Anastasia's life before now has a sincere cry for help gone unanswered. But this time is different. This time, she has wandered past the edges of what is allowed. She has gone too far to be heard.

Crying now, Anastasia starts to run. She isn't the fastest thing in the world anymore. She's the lostest, and all she wants is to be found. She's also running the wrong way. She runs and runs until her foot finds a shallow root, and then she's tripping, she's falling, she's rolling down a hill, and there's mud in her hair and moss in her mouth and she wants . . . she wants . . .

"I wanna go *home*!" she wails, sitting up and drumming her heels against the ground.

She smells something.

It smells like . . . like popcorn and cookies and grass that's just been cut and watermelon and sugar candy. It smells like all the good things in the whole world, all jumbled up together. She sniffles, tears stopping, and thinks about candy houses in the middle of the wood, the kind with gingerbread walls and sweet frosting eaves. She doesn't think about witches, or the kind of things that might use a candy house as a lure. She's still too young to take the dark messages from the fairy tales she listens to at bedtime, and all she's thinking of is candy.

Anastasia gets to her feet and starts following the smell. She's more cautious now that she's fallen, now that she has scrapes on her knees and on the palms of her hands. They sting and ache and bleed, but they're not as important as the possibility of candy.

She comes around a corner. There's no candy house, and she's briefly disappointed, but then she sees what *is* there, and she stops, eyes going wide with awe and delight.

It's like a flower, if flowers were made entirely out of dragonfly wings. The insectile petals glitter in the sunlight, breaking it up into little rainbows. If she were older, she would call them "prismatic," but she's not older, and so all she thinks is "pretty" as she walks toward the flower, eyes still very wide.

If she were older, she might be wary of something that doesn't look like anything else she's seen since she stepped into the trees, of the way the curling vines around the base of the thick, fleshy stalk that supports the massive bloom—it's almost as wide across as she is tall, and the stem is thicker than her arm—seem to twitch in anticipation as she approaches. But she's not older. She's just a lost little girl looking at the most beautiful thing she's ever seen and wanting to possess it with all of her half-formed magpie heart.

All the good smells are coming from this flower. She knows it, even though it's impossible, as impossible as the flower itself. It is miracle and living rainbow and candy house, all rolled into one, and she keeps getting closer, and the vines keep twitching, and this is inevitable. This has *been* inevitable for thirty years, since her grandparents bought the house on the edge of the woods, since the comet with a heart made of alien seeds turned its sightless eye toward the distant blue shadow of the Earth. Everything she has done in her short life has led her here, away from safety, away from the life she might have lived, away from home.

Look away, if you must. What comes next is part of the story, but it is not as important to witness it as it is to know that it has happened: that it was inevitable. That it could not be run from, or avoided, or escaped.

Anastasia climbs onto a fallen branch, adding a few more precious inches to her height. Even so, she has to strain to touch the tips of her fingers to the center of the flower, which is hard and bumpy and feels like the gravel-rich dirt that forms along the edges of the sidewalk. The bumps are regular, and if she were older, she would associate the feeling with sunflowers, the way they push their seeds up against the surface.

The dragonfly wing petals vibrate, tapping against each other in silent staccato. The bumpy center seems to pulse, growing warm under

Anastasia's fingers. The vines twitch and tangle, drawing closer, drawing tighter together. Suddenly, and without warning, she is afraid, her deeply buried animal instincts rising up to protect what's already past protecting. She tries to pull her hand away.

The flower holds her fast.

There is no sensation of stickiness, but her fingers refuse to budge from the surface all the same: it's as if she has become bonded to it, glued down so suddenly that there was never any chance to break the seal. She takes a step backward, and drops abruptly as the log rolls out from under her feet. Even that isn't enough to sever the connection between fingers and flower, only to wrench her arm from its socket, leaving her dangling and terrified and in pain. She opens her mouth to scream.

She never sees the vine begin to move, not until it slithers tight around her face and neck, cutting off her air, cutting off the sound before it starts. The rest of the vines are close behind, binding her, cocooning her, until all that remains is a tangled knot of vegetation, bucking wildly as she struggles.

Inside the vegetable cocoon, thorns as fine as threads are pushing out of the vines, piercing her skin, slithering into the meat of her. They begin pale as bone and quickly brighten to a deep, arterial red as they drink and drain, drowning themselves in blood.

Bit by bit, the struggle stops.

Bit by bit, the heart of Anastasia Miller stops with it.

5.

Caroline hangs up the phone harder than strictly necessary, taking some satisfaction from the act of slamming it down into the cradle. Then she picks it up and slams it again, wishing she could hang up more than once.

"Asshole," she mutters before looking around guiltily. Little pitchers have big ears, after all. But there's no sign of Anastasia: her transgression has gone unwitnessed. Normally, she would be concerned. Right now, she's just relieved. Ana didn't need to hear that. Ana didn't need to hear *any* of that.

Where does he get off? Alan walked out on *them* when he heard she was pregnant, not the other way around. Alan said he didn't want to be a father, that he had *never* wanted to be a father, and he never *would* want to be a father. Now he's hunting her down and demanding to be a part of his daughter's life? Now he's acting like he has a say in where she lives, what she does, how she raises Anastasia? No. It doesn't work that way. Once you run out, you don't get to swagger back in like the running was nothing. You just don't.

You don't.

Slowly, her chest unclenches and the blood rushing in her ears quiets. The courts will find for her, if it even gets that far—which it won't. There's no way Alan will actually press the issue, not once he realizes she's not simply going to roll over and show him her throat. He only likes things when they're easy. For whatever reason, he thinks walking in and becoming a father to a three-year-old girl he's never so much as seen before will be easy. Well, it won't, and neither will she.

The thought of Anastasia makes her realize, all too abruptly, how quiet it is in the house. The air has the particular stillness that means she's alone, which isn't right. Heart sinking, she tries to remember whether she heard the front door close while she was on the phone with her ex. She did, didn't she?

Well, that's all right. Anastasia is allowed to play in the yard, as long as she stays on the grass and in view of the windows. Everything is fine. She's sure that everything is fine. She rushes to the window. She looks out.

There is no little girl on the lawn.

Caroline's heart sinks deeper, a rock dropping through her chest. She forces her steps to stay light as she walks to the door, opens it, and steps onto the porch. As long as she doesn't panic—as long as she doesn't lose her cool—nothing will be really wrong. As long as she doesn't admit the possibility of true crisis, everything will be fine.

She's there, she thinks, and the words are half to reassure herself and half a plea to a distant and possibly imaginary God. She's aware that bargaining with the divine is a bad habit to fall into, but she doesn't see another option. She lost focus. She got distracted. She didn't pay attention. She did all the things she's not allowed to do, all the things that would make her a bad mother, and now . . . and now . . .

For just a moment, when she opens the front door, she sees Anastasia sitting on the lawn, playing some complicated and incomprehensible game with her eternally expanding stable of plastic horses. For just a moment, she can see the sunlight shining off her daughter's hair, hear the soft mutter of instructions conveyed to imaginary equines, and everything is going to be okay, everything is going to be *fine*. For just a moment.

Then the moment breaks, and the sunlight is shining down on nothing but empty grass. The horses are there, a few of them, but they lie discarded, not held tight in loving hands. There is no sign of Anastasia. No sign at all.

Caroline is very quiet, and very still, like she's waiting for God to realize that this is wrong; like she's waiting for God to take it back. God does no such thing.

Caroline begins to scream.

Within the hour, everyone on the street is out and searching for the missing child. Every house has been checked, every duvet pulled back and every cupboard opened. Anastasia is not in any yard, not watching television in any babysitter's living room, not asleep in any bed. Anastasia is *gone.*

Within two hours, the street is crawling with police. Search parties, hastily assembled around powerful flashlights, have begun combing the woods. They call Anastasia's name, over and over again, until the crows roosting in the trees take off, startled into frenzied motion.

And Anastasia is gone.

Some of the searchers come within feet of the green bundle deep in the trees, but they take no notice of it. There is no enticing smell, and the flower—the bright, impossible, obviously alien flower—has closed its petals as the plant it grew from devotes all its energy to the task of germination. The inevitable has happened. What comes after might still be avoided . . .

But they do not noticc, do not see. They scream the name of a little girl and walk past her resting place at the same time.

The search continues, and Anastasia is gone.

6.

Three days. That is the amount of time required to drain a body dry, to render it as frail as a cicada's discarded exoskeleton or an empty seedpod. When the tendrils of the green, green vines finally unwind from their prize, what they drop to the forest floor bears no more resemblance to a human child than it does to a lizard's shed skin. It is already crumbling, falling apart, dissolving into the dust that birthed it.

Anastasia's clothing remains surprisingly intact, torn in a few small places, stained in a few more, but not even as dirty as it should be after three days in the depths of the wood. The impossible flower has collapsed inward on itself, dying, drying up, until no one but the canniest of botanists would be able to tell that it doesn't belong here.

The stalk, meanwhile, has thickened, grown gravid with the great seed that is its life's work and purpose on this world.

The seed pulses ripely, almost obscene in its vitality. It pulses again, and then it splits, green giving way to membranous gold and finally to the pale pink of a child's skin, the cornsilk pallor of a child's hair. Anastasia Miller—but not Anastasia Miller, no, Anastasia Miller is dead and gone and lost forever—tumbles into the watery sunlight that filters through the trees, naked, as are all things at the moment of their birth. She blinks at the brightness of it all, and she at once recognizes the light and knows she has never seen it before. Everything is familiar. Everything is new.

Carefully, remembering without really knowing how, Anastasia stands. Her knees, new-formed and unsteady, wobble. She spreads her arms to steady herself. The wind blows around her, and her skin prickles in response to the chill. Her clothes, discarded on the ground, are suddenly tempting. She picks them up, one piece at a time, and puts them back on. Only then does she look back at the plant that is her parent and was her prison.

It is dying. The stalk, burst by her emergence, is withering into brown mush. The dragonfly petals have fallen from the flower's face and lie scattered amongst the withering vines. There is no going back. Only forward; only out.

She picks up a petal, admiring the prismatic beauty of it for a moment before it crumbles into dust between her fingers. For a moment, she feels obscurely sad, like something has been lost forever. Then she turns, suddenly sure of which way is home, and begins to walk.

Three days and six hours after Anastasia Miller disappeared into the woods, something that looks just like her walks back out.

Anastasia's mother has been weeping all that time, stopping only when drugged into a light and useless daze. She is weeping when the little girl walks across the lawn, reaches for the doorknob, and lets herself inside. The sound of the door swinging shut shocks her out of her tears. Her parents—Anastasia's grandparents—are supposed to be at the police station, following up on a possible lead. Alan, her ex, has been brought in for questioning. Every avenue is being explored. No one should be opening that door.

The little girl steps into the doorway. Caroline's heart lurches in her chest, almost returning to its place between her lungs, protected by the birdcage of her ribs. She's halfway on her feet before she registers the intent to move, stumbling toward the little girl, toward *her* little girl, toward hope, toward salvation.

"Anastasia," she breathes.

"No," says the child, because she isn't, because she's too fresh off the tree to understand the need for subtlety. That will come much later, if it comes at all. "The aliens came and took your real baby. They left me. I'm sorry."

The only words she has for this world are the ones harvested from the real Anastasia Miller. The only vocabulary she can use is the one she's stolen. Learning the rest of the patterns of this planet will take longer, assuming she's allowed the time. So many invasions fail right here, with defenseless seedlings meeting the species they have come to study, being recognized, being destroyed.

Caroline barks laughter through her tears as she drops to her knees and takes the child who is not her daughter into her arms.

"You be an alien if you want to, baby," she says. "As long as you come home."

The police will comb the woods again, this time looking for a kidnapper, someone who would steal a little girl only to return her, disoriented but unharmed, to her home.

Anastasia's kidnapper does not exist, and will never be found.

Neither will Anastasia.

7.

This was a story. It can't hurt you anymore.

But you needed to understand before I could tell you what happened after.

ROOT

Then came the night of the first falling star.

—H. G. WELLS,
THE WAR OF THE WORLDS

Humanity is sort of a mess, I guess, but I think we're doing okay. We're pretty cool. I like us.

—STASIA MILLER

When discussing the paucity of life in our local universe, the question of hostile invasion always seems to arise immediately after noting how quiet it is among the stars. Are we isolated because something—some great, predatory force—is using the space around us as a hunting ground, picking off our neighbors before they have the chance to find us? If so, do we have a responsibility to reach the stars as quickly as possible, in order to join this ancient, life-threatening fight? Or should we, as a species, agree to keep our heads down and our skies closed, hoping to avoid the notice of something great enough to silence civilizations?

The probability of alien life is high enough that we must question its apparent absence. The probability of any specific trait appearing in that alien life is, in contrast, vanishingly small. When we finally do meet our neighbors, it is no more likely that they will come as a conquering horde than it is that they will come in peace and plenty, intending to uplift humanity to join them among the stars.

In short, when it comes to what we can expect to find out there, it makes as much sense to flip a coin as it does to make guesses. We can't change the nature of our neighbors either way.

—FROM *THE FERMI PARADOX AND THE MILKY WAY*,
BY ANTHONY VORNHOLT,
ORIGINALLY PUBLISHED 2030.

It is an absolute delight having Anastasia in my class. She has an agile mind and a seemingly limitless hunger for knowledge. She does not participate in class discussion as much as I would like, seemingly afraid of being labeled a "know-it-all" by her peers. Assuring her that no such teasing will be tolerated in my classroom does not appear to make much of an impression. I am concerned she will not be able to reach her full potential if she does not learn to express herself in front of the other students.

It is my recommendation that Anastasia be considered for the Gifted and Talented track, where she is more likely to be challenged, and may—in the presence of other children performing at her level—find the courage to emerge from her shell and begin to truly bloom.

—LETTER HOME FROM MR. MICHAEL WILLIS,
THIRD-GRADE TEACHER.
SENT NOVEMBER, 2005.

1

SEATTLE, WASHINGTON: JULY 13, 2031
TWENTY-FIVE DAYS PRE-INVASION

1.

My alarm went off promptly at 6:02 a.m. I sat upright in the dim light of my bedroom, gasping and clutching the blanket to my chest. My curtains glowed like jewels under the pressure of the sunlight trying to break in from the outside. Dropping the blanket, I slapped at my phone until my finger managed to slide the alarm notification over to Ignore—more out of luck than anything intentional on my part. The sound silenced, I staggered out of the bed, tripping on my own dirty laundry and nearly stepping on the cat. He gave me a dirty look as he moved aside. I didn't care. I was focused on getting to the window, on opening the curtains.

Sunlight flooded the room as I pulled them open, shocking the last of my exhaustion away. I closed my eyes and inhaled, breathing in the faint, sweet scent of *morning*, and everything was fine. Everything was *amazing*.

I love the summer. Most of my friends grumble about the way climate change has rearranged the Seattle seasons. "If I wanted to see the sun every damn day, I'd live in California," they say, and then they huff off to get their sunscreen and their sunglasses and their sun-sun-go-away goth T-shirts, and I guess I can feel sorry for them, even as I feel totally happy for me. I'm a sunshine girl. Always have been. They've had decades of Washington tailoring its weather to them, and it's only fair that I should have a few years of the weather tailoring itself to me.

Sure, rising sea levels and declining air quality mean my time in the sun—ha-ha—will probably spell the end of life on Earth as we know it, but at least I'll be warm until the giant tsunami comes and sweeps us all away.

Besides, I never wake up properly when my alarm goes off before the sun comes up. I don't mind clouds. Sunlight is better than rain, but the sun is always there, even when the sky is a blanket of gray. I *do* mind darkness.

I breathed in sunlight and breathed out wakefulness. The cat twined around my ankles, chirping his weird, breathy chirp, and by the time I opened my eyes, I was ready for the day. Outside my room, I could hear my housemates going through their own morning routines. For Mandy, that involves singing in the shower, even though she sounds like she's gargling bees. For Lucas, it means cooking something way too elaborate for the hour, so he can pretend he's the master of his own schedule, and he doesn't care about needing to do dishes as soon as he gets off work. Now that I was paying attention, I could smell frying eggs and sweet baking waffle batter. If I hurried, I might be able to get him to share. He always makes too much, never having quite gotten the hang of portion control.

I stayed where I was. The cat gave another turn around my ankles and I bent to scoop him into my arms, letting him slam his furry head into the bottom of my chin so hard my teeth clacked together from the impact. He settled down to purr. I watched the sunlight filter through the trees in the backyard, and tried—as I did almost every morning—to remember my dreams.

Trees. Screaming. The flower with the dragonfly petals I used to see everywhere when I was a little girl. Something in the air, the taste of copper, the feeling of lightning in my veins. The same jumble of unconnected images that haunted me most nights, as formless and fading as they always were. My therapist says the key to my depression is hidden somewhere in my subconscious mind; I'm supposed to write down my dreams for her. My dream diary is like a checklist of the same elements, over and over again, a tidy recipe for making me slowly lose my mind.

When I was three years old, someone snatched me off the street in front of my grandparents' old house near Mt. St. Helens. They kept me three days before bringing me back unharmed, still wearing the same dress and little sweater I'd had on when they'd taken me. Then they'd disappeared, fading back into whatever nightmare they'd slithered out of. They were never caught. They were never identified. For all I know, they're still out there somewhere, snatching happy little girls and hauling them away for whatever reasons seem to make sense to them.

I got lucky. I came home. Dehydrated and confused, but still, I came home. Mom can even laugh about it now, the way I came out of the woods and told her the aliens had stolen her real baby.

Grandma never learned to laugh about it. There had still been shadows in her eyes when she died a decade ago, more than twenty years after I'd been taken, and she was never easy with me the way she was with my little sister. It was like, by being hurt, I had become an invitation for the universe to do more harm, and she couldn't let herself love me out of fear that the next time something happened, it would be the last time.

I miss her. I never understood her, but I miss her. She never understood me either, but in a way, I think she understood me better than my mother did, because she realized I wasn't kidding. She *did* need to worry about the aliens.

"Stasia?" Lucas's voice was accompanied by a light knock on my bedroom doorframe. I turned away from the window with only a faint pang of regret. The sun and I would see each other again. The sun and I always did.

Roommate number one, and the owner of the house: Lucas Evans. Tall, skinny, with a collection of vintage cartoon T-shirts only a geek could love, and a girlfriend who kept her apartment on Capitol Hill more out of the love of lizards than any other motivation. He was holding a plate that I found honestly way more interesting than his face, because the plate was covered in waffles, and the waffles smelled amazing.

"For me?" I asked.

"You're still in your pajamas," he said.

"That's good. I can get syrup on my pajamas and be on time for work without needing to change my clothes twice." I held out my hands, opening and closing them in the classic "gimme" gesture. "Waffles."

"Don't you need to be at work soon? You should probably put clothes on."

"*Waffles*," I repeated, with more urgency. I opened and closed my hands with more vigor. "Mars needs waffles. Give me the waffles."

"Put on your clothes," Lucas countered, and shut my bedroom door, the waffles still in his hand, but now shut out in the hall where I could neither see nor smell them.

"Asshole!" I called amiably, and went digging for clothes.

Like most of the people I know in Seattle, all three of us work in tech. Sort of. Mandy is a project manager, keeping people doing things and controlling her team with a terrifying iron fist out of proportion to her pixie-scale body. Lucas is a programmer, which is how he's able to afford silly things like "an actual house," even if he needs the rest of us to feel comfortable with his ability to pay the mortgage. Me, I'm in customer service. I answer phones, answer email, and get yelled at for a living, usually by people who don't understand how not paying their $25 bill for four months results in them owing more than $100, or how a tree falling on the phone lines means their internet stops working. It's an endless grind, but it pays. Quite well at this point, since I've been there for more than five years, while most customer service drones quit after two, if they make it that far.

As the lowest-tier worker in the house, I'm also the only one who has to go into the office, which makes no sense to anyone other than the corporate overlords who get paid for timing my bathroom breaks.

I like solving problems. There are so many problems in this world that can't be fixed. At least when somebody's cable goes down, I can generally make it better, or dispatch a technician who can. My call times aren't the best in the company. My customer satisfaction scores, on the other hand, are through the *roof*. Best of all, my job doesn't come with a dress code. I can wear whatever I want.

Today, as with most days, "whatever I wanted" was jeans, a nerdy T-shirt—this one with a silhouette of Audrey II from *Little Shop of Horrors* and the slogan "Don't feed the plants"—and a pair of comfortable shoes. Mandy and Lucas worked from home but still had to buy nice shirts for their many videoconferences. I may not make as much money as either of my housemates, but what I don't get in my bank account is more than balanced by not being forced to wear business formal five days out of seven.

I followed the smell of waffles down the hall to the dining room, where Lucas had cleared half the miniatures from the previous night's *Pathfinder* game out of the way in order to set up the plates. Mandy was already planted firmly behind hers, a plastic bag tied around her neck to protect her dress as she mowed through her breakfast like she thought the meal was going to be canceled.

"Morning, Mandy," I said, walking past her to the beverage fridge in the corner of the room. Lucas didn't like having our sodas and Brita filters getting in the way of his precious trays of cold cuts and marinating meats. The solution? Mandy's old dorm fridge, which was continually packed with everything from her real-sugar Coke—imported from Mexico—to Lucas's insulin.

She grunted her response, far more interested in inhaling waffles and bacon than in talking to her housemate. I didn't hold it against her. Talking to Mandy before she's had enough calories to fuel somebody five times her size is generally pointless.

Roommate number two: Amanda Reyes. Five-foot-one in her stocking feet, and incredibly fond of shoes with heels that add eight inches to her height and make her walk like she's slightly drunk at all times. Her wardrobe consists almost entirely of cute dresses, demure, plain-colored ones for work and wild, extravagantly patterned ones for play. She likes to refer to herself as a manic pixie nightmare girl, which is not inaccurate. She also likes to talk about how her existence as a smart, successful, educated Mexican-American woman in tech makes her a unicorn, which is another way of saying "a horse with a giant fucking knife stuck to its head."

I have good roommates.

Pitcher of water in hand, I returned to the table and reached for my own plate. I was cutting my waffles when Lucas emerged from the kitchen and took his own seat.

"Morning," I said.

"You found clothes," he said.

"I don't spend *all* my time in my pajamas."

"You would if you didn't have to leave your room in order to get paid. One day you're going to find a job that lets you telecommute, and you're never going to get dressed again."

"Sounds good to me," I said, and speared a chunk of waffle. "I could be a houseplant."

"How's the invasion going to like that?" asked Mandy.

I shrugged. "Probably not that well, but hey, if they wanted me to do something specific, they should have left instructions. Pass the butter?"

She did.

When I came back from whatever terrible, traumatic thing happened to me in the woods—a thing I have never been able to remember, no matter how much time I spend talking to experts on childhood memory recovery—I came back claiming the aliens had abducted the real Anastasia Miller, leaving me in her place. My last therapist said it was an attempt to disassociate myself from the terror of abduction, using a narrative framework I had probably picked up from something I'd seen on TV. It's unusual for a three-year-old to come back absolutely convinced of her own inhumanity, but as it never seemed to really *bother* me, they eventually stopped trying to change my mind.

I told them I was an alien, and when they refused to believe me, I told them it didn't matter, because the invasion was going to happen anyway: believe it or not, I was telling the truth, and when our motherships darkened the skies, they would have to deal with the consequences of their disbelief.

Not that I can prove it. I said I was the vanguard of an invading species of intelligent alien plants—I've always been very clear about that—and yet I looked human, sounded human, walked like a human, and had human bodily needs. I ate, I slept, I caught colds and twisted my ankles and did everything else a real human would do. I couldn't even photosynthesize, despite spending the entire summer when I was ten trying to figure out how. I'm an ordinary thirty-five-year-old woman. I just happen to be an ordinary thirty-five-year-old woman who's been talking about the alien invasion for the last thirty years.

As personal quirks go, it's not the strangest. And it means I always have something to talk about at parties. Lucas thinks I'm a little nuts, but his girlfriend lets her lizards roam freely through her apartment, so he tries not to judge. Mandy doesn't care one way or another. I think she's hoping I'll be proven right one day, just so she can see the looks on everyone's faces when they realize they had thirty years of warning, and chose to do nothing.

The waffles were delicious. It was time to get ready for our day.

2.

Being the vanguard of an invading species of alien plant people doesn't get me special privileges on the bus. I sat crammed between a man who seemed to think he needed to occupy my seat as well as his own, and a teenager who was trying to cover up their lack of a shower with about a gallon of cologne. I sneezed, earning myself a dirty look from the man with the spreading knees, as if I had done it solely to annoy him. I smiled sweetly in his direction.

"Don't worry," I said. "I'm only allergic to manspreading."

He moved his knee away from mine.

That helped. I was still way too confined, but at least now I wasn't fighting a losing battle to retain my seat.

The tech industry had already put Seattle in the middle of a massive population boom when the rising ocean levels became less something for pundits to argue about and more the reason San Francisco was experiencing sudden, catastrophic flooding events. They didn't have enough rain in California, but they had tsunamis washing into the Financial District. Silicon Valley fared better but still had to contend with rising temperatures—a new record every summer, as the previous summer faded from "the hottest on record" to "I wish it could be that cool again"—and constant wildfires.

Humanity had two choices: try to clean up their mess and undo the changes they had already made to their home planet, or run for someplace that wasn't in quite as bad of shape. Naturally, they'd gone with the latter. Seattle and its environs were growing fast enough to put kudzu to shame. Almost everyone I knew with a spare room was renting it out, even the people who would have been happier living on their own, because there was no housing. The former Californians complained constantly, about everything from the rain to the buses to the state of the roads. None of them offered to go home. For better or for worse, climate change and the tech industry had given us a glut of people, and they were our problem now.

I hugged my purse against my chest, trying not to pay too much attention to the people around me. Most of them were ignoring me as fiercely as I was ignoring them, eyes fixed on their phones or closed entirely as they focused on the songs playing through their headphones. It seemed like the more people we packed into a small space, the more time everyone spent trying to pretend no one else was real.

My therapist calls that "disassociation," and says it's part of why I continue to say I'm an alien. Whatever happened to me during those three days, it was bad enough to make me disassociate from my *species*. It was the kind of trauma most people will never have to deal with, and I should feel lucky that a little disassociation was the only thing I'd come away with.

Well, that and the nightmares, and the flower with wings for petals, like some hybrid of plant and insect, impossible, incredible, blooming just out of reach. No matter how many times I dreamt of it, I could never reach it, never pluck it and have it for my own. I wasn't worthy. Maybe no one was.

Or maybe it was the flower that would destroy the world.

The bus turned onto the company campus where half these people worked, myself included. I sat up straighter, checking my things. Supposedly, the bus company had a lost and found service. Functionally, anything left on the bus was likely to disappear, even among a crowd like this one, well paid and supposedly cared for. I could have something worth taking. Gas coupons, for example, or a valid Canadian shopping license. If I left my purse or my backpack, I would never see them again.

The brakes hissed as the bus pulled up to my stop. I rose, timing the motion to the sway of the vehicle, and let myself out through the back door. A few others followed me. I knew some of them, and we exchanged weary nods as we turned toward the boxy building that would be our home for the next nine hours.

Customer service jobs used to be largely outsourced to countries where it cost less to staff a call center, India and Mexico and China and even Brazil. That changed shortly after the tech industry shifted its heart to Washington. Now, any company that wants to be considered for tax breaks under American law must be able to prove at least sixty percent of their staff is employed in North America. Some companies staff their centers in Canada, but that's less about tax breaks and more about fear of the weather continuing to shift, forcing the companies to move again, over the border, into the great thawing north. Most companies wanted to be able to continue saying they were American—go patriotism, go marketing—and so they brought their call centers home, eating the cost of domestic labor in the pursuit of future profit.

Thankfully, American call centers came with American unions, and unions came with the kind of demands unions have been making since they first began. When the call centers came back, they weren't the horror-story factories we'd heard of from older friends and relatives. We still spent our shifts yoked to phone, email, and chat, but we weren't subjected to "open floor plans" that seemed like genius to management looking to be sure we weren't playing online during work hours, but which had turned even the briefest customer interaction into a struggle not to piss off our coworkers. We had reasonable attendance policies and benefit packages, and a glorious lack of dress codes.

I approached the front door, swiped my badge, and got the brief green light that signaled my permission to be in the building. I stepped inside, my coworkers repeating the procedure behind me, and smirked. It's always amused me, the way green equals "go" in American culture. That whole "secretly a plant person" thing.

Well. Not so secretly. Despite years of therapy as a child, and several managers telling me the joke has gotten old and I'd have an easier time getting promoted if I'd knock it off, I've never been able to swallow the urge to tell everyone I spend any extended period of time with that hey, by the way, I'm here because the invasion is coming, and people should probably know. It's like a nervous tic. Hi, nice to meet you, my name's Anastasia, I'm secretly an intelligent alien plant and one day everything you love will be devoured.

Mostly people are pretty cool about it, because mostly people don't believe me. It's funny how that works.

Half the cubes in my section were occupied by the time I reached my seat. The cube walls were a compromise between the union's demand for privacy and sound baffling and management's need to hold us accountable for every second that we spent on the company clock. When unoccupied, the walls were solid white. As each cube's occupants arrived, they would hit the button next to their nameplate and the walls would turn translucent, allowing us to be monitored without sacrificing the sound-muffling effects of the material. The walls could be set to solid again during breaks and lunches, when we were free to surf company-approved websites, deal with personal email, and otherwise goof off.

It's not a perfect system. I'm not sure there *is* such a thing as a perfect system. Everything has its flaws, when it's looked at from the correct angle. Why should someone who makes their productivity targets and doesn't goof off be subjected to the same degree of monitoring as someone who never does what they're supposed to be doing? Why could some people get away with dozens of violations before they got so much as a note in their files, while others got fired after their first actionable offense? It didn't make sense, because nothing really makes sense if you dig deeply enough.

Take my coworkers. Some of them liked me, because I worked hard and was happy to answer questions. Others thought I was a stuck-up jerk, because I'd refused multiple promotions and preferred to spend my time at work *working*, rather than socializing. In the words of the old reality-show classics, I wasn't there to make friends. Friends were a nice bonus, if they happened, but really, I was happier just knowing I had a job I could leave behind at the end of the day.

You'd think—or at least, *I* would think—they'd be grateful to have someone who kept her head down and the team's numbers up. Instead, I was subjected to a continual low-level hazing, like being perpetually, casually cruel would one day cause me to go, "Oh, wait, I was wrong, I really *do* want to go out drinking with you at the end of my shift." As I hit the button to clarify my cube walls, it became painfully clear that today was going to be no different.

Working in a cube farm doesn't leave many opportunities for self-expression. No more than ten percent of any given wall can be covered, either with personal items or work-related paperwork—after all, what's the point in having walls you can see through if people persist in blocking your view with nonessentials like the escalation phone list? But people are people, and people will always find a way to mark territory. Little toys, potted plants, even the occasional low-maintenance fish, they all have their place in the ecosystem of the office, allowing each cube's resident to feel as if they have some control.

In my case, that control took the form of a picture of my cat, Seymour; a small potted succulent that had proven functionally unkillable, surviving three desk moves and an accidental week without water when I was out with pneumonia; and a retro motorized piggybank shaped like an off-brand Audrey II. It made a cute snapping sound when I fed it coins, and it never had more than fifty cents in its belly, to avoid tempting people to break it open in order to buy a candy bar.

And it was gone.

I stood there for a moment, looking at the place where it should have been, then looking to either side, in case I had somehow moved an eight-inch-tall chunk of plastic without noticing. No bank. I stepped into the cube and opened the drawers of the filing cabinet next to my desk. Sometimes people would hide things in there, thinking they were funny, or the custodial staff would move things during the cleaning process and forget to put them back again. No bank.

According to the clock on my computer, I had five minutes before the official start of my shift. That was five minutes before I would have to explain my tardiness to my managers. They were sympathetic people, for the most part, and accustomed enough to the socially awkward people who gravitated toward support work that they would probably understand when I said my bank had been missing. Of course, this would be the third time in a ninety-day period that the disappearance of a personal effect had resulted in my clocking in late. That could be a problem.

I don't like problems. Problems spawn solutions, and solutions are almost always worse than leaving things the hell alone. Putting my purse carefully on my chair, I stepped out of the cube, back into the aisle. Everyone I could see was focused on their computer screen, but very few of them were on calls, and I couldn't shake the feeling that they were watching me, waiting to see how I was going to react.

"I seem to have misplaced my bank," I said, voice clear and calm and barely shaking. Lucas would have been proud to hear me talking to people that way. He'd known me since the idea of public speaking would have been enough to send me crying into the nearest bathroom. "It's really too bad, because I love that bank. I'm going to sign in and then go deliver my vacation request to my supervisor. I hope my bank is back when I start taking calls. I'm pretty sure if I have to tell management someone took it, we're all going to get another six-month ban on personal items at our desks, and that would be a real shame."

No one said anything, but a few sets of shoulders tightened, and a few heads turned in my direction, like their owners were trying to gauge my seriousness with a sidelong glance. I didn't say anything else, only turned on my heel and walked away.

I was halfway to my supervisor's desk when I realized I'd forgotten my paperwork. Dammit. I clenched my teeth and kept walking. Much as I wanted my bank back, I didn't want to catch the thief or thieves in the act of returning it. It wouldn't do me any good to know, and I've never been good at pretending to be okay with someone when I'm not. If I knew who kept messing with my things—instead of just suspecting—I wouldn't be able to treat them the same way. That could be a problem. A "we involve HR, because you're not acting like a team player"–level problem. I hate dealing with HR. They always look at me like I don't know how to person right, and they're going to have to grade my performance.

I don't know how to *human* correctly. But I'm pretty good at being a person. I have thoughts and feelings and opinions, and that's enough to qualify. Right?

Scott looked up when I approached his desk, a frown already on his face. "Ana?" he said. "What's wrong?"

"Nothing," I said, too quickly. I'm Ana at work and Stasia at home, and Anastasia on the rare occasions when my mother calls to ask for money. Compartmentalization is good according to my therapist, who says having a name for every major role I play lets me keep things straight in my head. I say that eventually I'm going to run out of names, and what's going to happen then?

"Uh-huh." His frown faded, replaced by a look of understanding sympathy. "You know if you're having trouble, you can tell me. I'd be happy to have a talk with the rest of your team."

"I know that if I tell you something, you're required by law to act on it. Which means you'd *have* to have that talk with the rest of my team."

"Yes."

"Nothing's wrong." I put on a bright, sunny smile, trying to believe it enough that he could pretend to believe it too. "I was going to bring you my vacation paperwork, but what do you know? I left it at my desk."

"Uh-huh." He glanced at his screen, where the team-monitoring software would tell him what state we were each in. "Your shift starts in two minutes. I'll log you in and put you into not-ready, since you were talking to me, but next time, remember the paperwork you're supposed to be delivering, all right?"

"Yes, sir," I said, before turning and scurrying back to my cube.

My coworkers were focused on their screens, on their customers, on their *jobs.* My bank was sitting in front of my keyboard, where I couldn't possibly have missed it before. I picked it up. It was light enough that I knew my fifty cents in pennies and nickels had been stolen, along with the AA batteries that made its snapping mechanism work. That didn't matter. I put it to the side and sat down, reaching for my headset.

Time to get to work.

3.

By the end of the day, I was starting to seriously reconsider my desire to maintain gainful employment. Maybe Lucas would let me live in the house without paying rent if I agreed to do the dishes.

Or maybe he'd get tired of the fact that I have no real skill when it comes to cleaning, and he'd throw me out, and I'd wind up working somewhere even worse. Someplace where the people would be just as unfriendly and willing to tease, but with stricter hours, or even—horrors—a dress code. I don't even own a business casual wardrobe. I'd need to get a job to pay for dressing myself for my job. No. I needed to stay where I was, to keep enduring the teasing and blowing the bell curve all to hell.

Besides, I actually sort of liked my customers. They were each a puzzle to be solved, and once it was untangled, they went away forever, fading conveniently into the low background roar of experience. That wasn't something to give away without a fight.

My remaining coworkers wouldn't meet my eyes as I gathered my things and walked for the door. I could hear them whispering behind me, and no matter how hard I tried to convince myself that I was being paranoid, I knew full well that if I turned around, I'd find them artfully not looking. They didn't like me, thought I was weird and standoffish and a know-it-all, and maybe they were right about all those things, but that didn't make it okay for them to treat me the way that they did.

"See you Monday, jerks," I muttered, and left the building.

Home was calling, and I was ready to answer.

2

SEATTLE, WASHINGTON: JULY 13, 2031
TWENTY-FIVE DAYS PRE-INVASION

1.

Lucas was waiting at the park and ride. That was nice. I can drive, but I don't own a car, and taking the bus home takes forever and isn't much fun. All my complaints about riding the bus to work are tripled when I have to ride the bus home, with a heaping side order of feeling like a terrible person due to not wanting to be around strangers. I'm not misanthropic. I just don't like people. They're not quite the same thing.

Similar. But not the same.

It was the misanthropy that made me stop, nearly stumbling, when I got closer to the car and realized the front passenger seat was occupied by a tall woman in a Rat City Roller Girls T-shirt, her head crowned by a mass of corkscrew curls dyed in all the shades of sunset. She was as indie-looking as Lucas was corporate, and the main reason I hadn't noticed her sooner was that she was halfway into his seat, the fingers of one hand threaded through his hair, the fingers of the other hand wrapped tight around his tie.

Roxanna. Oh, joy.

It's not that I don't *like* Roxanna. On paper, we should be the best of friends. She's quirky at best, eccentric at worst, with a passion for reptiles that I honestly respect, even if I don't understand it. She works at the university, helping them keep their bio department from bursting out of confinement and eating everyone, which I assume is what poorly tended bio departments do. She's been dating Lucas for almost five years. Mandy and I both expect to be evicted one day so he can give our rooms to her lizards.

As long as it makes Lucas happy, we'll go. We won't be happy about it, and we'll complain constantly, but we'll go.

Roxanna let go of Lucas's tie when I opened the door and climbed into the back. She twisted in her seat to give me a serpentine smile, keeping her fingers threaded through his hair. I was used to that. She worries Mandy or I might make a play for him one day, using our proximity to establish a sort of, I don't know, home-team advantage. The fact that Mandy doesn't think of Lucas that way and I've been in a relationship for years doesn't seem to strike her as a factor.

"Hi, Ana," she said brightly. "Isn't it nice how we were able to come and get you?"

Subtext: be grateful, because she could have convinced Lucas not to pick me up, even though our schedule for the week had been arranged since the first of the month. Roxanna thinks schedules and plans are things that happen to other people. Mandy calls her "the wrecking ball" when Lucas isn't around, and she's not wrong. Roxanna never met a social construct she didn't feel the need to challenge, if only to show that she considers herself above such petty ideas.

Sometimes I want to drop six of Roxanna's own lizards down the back of her shirt and watch her dance around the house until she figures out what she's done to piss me off.

Lucas looked abashed, although that may have been as much over the fact that he doesn't like PDAs as anything else. "How was work, Stasia?" he asked.

"Same old, same old," I said. "I think I'm going to clean out my desk."

"Oh, no," said Roxanna, all mock concern. "Are you getting fired?" She lowered her voice on the last word, almost whispering, like it was some sort of delicious secret.

Lizards. In her pants. "No," I said, focusing on buckling my seatbelt, not allowing myself to look at her. If I didn't look at her, I could pretend she was one of my phone customers, too distant to be worth getting mad at. "My co-workers keep messing with my stuff. I've talked to my supervisor, but I can't prove exactly who's doing it, and I don't want to go to HR, because they'll like me even less if I get the whole team in trouble. So I may bring my things home, to make it easier."

I could keep the picture of Seymour taped to the edge of my monitor. No one ever messed with that, maybe because they understood that defacing family photos, even pictures of pets, would make HR intervention inevitable. Besides, they'd just find a new way to torment me if I took everything home. I knew that. But I wouldn't worry about my toys disappearing anymore, and I wouldn't start every morning in my cube feeling like I'd been violated.

Roxanna made a noise that I would have read as sympathy in anyone else. From her, it sounded like a trap. I tensed, waiting for it to snap shut.

I didn't have to wait for long. "You know, I can sort of sympathize with your co-workers," she said, earning a sharp look from Lucas as he pulled out of the parking lot. She gave him a soothing pat on the arm. "Sorry, Luke, but you *know* she's weird. You know you're weird, Ana."

"I do know I'm weird," I allowed. I didn't bother correcting her on my name. It wouldn't do me any good.

"Maybe if you stopped introducing yourself to people as a space invader, they'd be, I don't know. Nicer to you. Or less inclined to mess with you for fun. You could make this stop."

"You realize she'd have to change jobs," said Lucas. His voice was flat. They were going to have a fight tonight, I realized, and while he might never say explicitly that it was about the way she'd spoken to me on the ride home, that would be the cause.

Roxanna knew it, too. She twisted again, shooting me a quick, sharp glare—as if I'd been the one to start this—and said, "That doesn't make sense. She likes her job."

"Uh-huh," said Lucas. "She likes her job. She doesn't like her coworkers, because they don't like her. They don't like her because . . . ?"

"Because she won't stop saying that weird alien crap," said Roxanna. Then she paused, sitting up straighter. "Oh."

"Yeah," I said loudly, in case they'd forgotten I was in the car. "Oh."

Not telling people seems like a logical idea. That's what people have been suggesting since I hit third grade and having what my teachers always termed a "rich fantasy life" went from being a good thing to being a sign that something was seriously wrong with me. Who cares if I think I'm an alien plant person? That part's fine. Everyone has their little delusions. The trouble is the way I keep saying it out loud.

It's funny how everyone who suggests that sort of silence seems to think they're the first ones. Like everyone else I've ever known has thought, hey, who cares if she runs around telling people she's not from this planet, at least she knows how to floss. I've been told to keep my mouth shut a thousand times, and I tried it for maybe the first hundred, biting my lips and smiling blankly until I wanted to scream.

It never ends well. Every time, I slip, or I run into someone who knew me before the latest attempt at silence, or I finally decide I can trust my new friends with something more than the glossiest, most marketable version of myself. Belief in my own alien nature aside, I've never been able to stick to a story for long, and eventually it just seems easier to tell the truth as I know it. And you know what?

It's worse. Every single time, it's *worse.*

When I tell people right out the gate, they can decide that I'm quirky or decide that I'm deluded, and either way, they build their mental models of me with that particular trait in place. When I don't tell them . . .

When I don't tell them, I'm messing with them. Or I'm not just deluded, I'm dangerously disconnected from reality, since apparently I know I'm not normal and I chose to hide it for as long as I could. Or they laugh at me. That's almost the worst. People who find out I'm an alien as soon as they meet me, even though I can't prove it and I look human and I've been on this planet for more than thirty years, which seems like a long time for an advance scout, they sometimes laugh. But it's a short laughter, a disbelieving laughter, the kind of laughter that's waiting for a punchline. The people who find out later laugh like I *am* the punchline, like there's no point in pretending I'm ever going to be anything else.

I wasn't dismissing Roxanna's idea because it came from her, or because I didn't like her and knew she didn't particularly like me. I was dismissing it because it had come from my mother, from my therapist, from my favorite English teacher, and from myself. Because it had come from virtually every person I'd ever trusted, and if it hadn't worked when it was born from a place of love and compassion and genuine concern, it certainly wasn't going to work when it came from a place of "you're weird, stop being weird."

The strangest thing about Roxanna was how such an enormous weirdo could survive being continually judgmental and abrasive, yet not see how these two sides of her personality were in conflict. Lucas and Roxanna would never have met if not for the overlap in their respective weirdnesses luring them both to Burning Man, where love on the playa had blossomed into love in my living room three nights a week. But she sure did feel like she was entitled to judge Mandy and me.

Lucas pulled into the driveway. I waited exactly long enough for the engine to turn off, and then I was out of the car, leaving the two of them in my dust. I heard Roxanna shout something. I didn't slow down enough to find out what it was. I wanted my bedroom, safe and secure and full of things that belonged to me, and more, I wanted my *door,* solidly closed between me and the rest of the world. I was done with people. I was so, so done with people.

Seymour raised his head when I barreled into the room, and seeing it was me, stood and flowed down the bed like water to chirp and purr in my direction. Cats are better than people. Cats are always better than people.

"I bet if cats were the dominant life form on this planet, we wouldn't be getting ready to invade," I said dully, stroking his head. Seymour narrowed his eyes and purred louder. There was a truth I didn't fully understand and didn't want to think about too hard buried in my words, tucked into the corners and contradictions. I flung myself onto the bed, pressing my face into the pillow, and tried to relax as Seymour settled against my side, a warm, comforting weight.

Here is the truth: there are times when I've wondered whether I was, in fact, insane. Whether there might be a pill out there strong enough to make me human, to realign my divergent neurochemistry onto something more ordinary. There's nothing wrong with seeking help when it's needed. It's just that most of the time, I haven't felt like it was needed.

Yes, insisting I'm an alien has complicated my life. Yes, introducing myself with "and my people are on their way across the gulf of stars to devour and subjugate the human race, but mostly devour" as part of my family background has consistently made things harder for me. Yes, I understand I can't prove any of the things I say. I don't know how I know them. I only know that they're true.

But I can hold a job. I can make friends. I know the people who care about me are good, compassionate, and understanding—and they know that once they've accepted my alien nature, I'll always be cool about whatever it is they need me to accept about them. It's give and take, after all. It matters.

Seymour moved from my side up to the pillow. Face pressed against his side, I took a few deep, slow breaths, and fell asleep.

2.

"Stasia?" My name was accompanied by the sound of fingers drumming on my door, like the staccato step of a spider wearing tap shoes. "You awake in there?"

"Mmm?" There was cat hair in my mouth. I spat it out as I rolled over and squinted at the clock. Almost eight. Either my after-work nap had run long, or I was about to be late for work the next—

No. Saturday. If it was morning, it was Saturday. Which meant it wasn't morning, since nothing short of a major cosplay competition gets Mandy out of bed before noon on the weekend.

"That didn't sound like a yes, but it didn't sound like a no, either. Can I come in?"

"Depends." I sat up, rubbing at my face with one hand. The checklist of my dreams was still swimming in the back of my mind—trees, screaming, the flower with the dragonfly-wing petals. They had been vibrating this time, tapping together like some kind of vegetable Morse code, almost comprehensible, if I could just *hold on* and force myself to listen . . .

The images were already fading. Whatever they'd had to tell me was going to need to wait until bedtime.

"Depends on what?"

"On whether Roxanna is with you."

Mandy scoffed before she opened the door and stepped into my room, slipping through as lithely as Seymour weaving his way along the fireplace mantle. Not the worst comparison. Like my cat, she was small, quick, and disinclined to listen when people told her not to do something she wanted to do. Unlike my cat, she had some vague understanding of boundaries—enough, at least, to knock when there was a chance I wouldn't have clothes on.

Her own clothes were more characteristic of "normal Mandy" than her work clothes: a fluffy pin-up girl skirt over an actual petticoat, covered in horror-movie-style Venus flytraps, some with severed human limbs in their mouths. I blinked. She beamed.

"Lucas told me what Roxanna had said, right before he took her out for dinner," she said. "I figured this would be a good dress to have on when she got back." Her smile was a knife, prepared to wound, refusing to be slid back into its sheath.

A warm wave of affection swept over me. I did not rush across the room to hug Mandy, but I thought about it very loudly. "You are the best."

"I know." She preened, fluffing her skirt before patting the perfect waves of her hair. "Just keep reminding yourself that she has many excellent qualities, even if we can't see them, because if she didn't, we would have to kill her, and that would make Lucas sad."

"He'd get over it."

"Yes, but he might also get new housemates, and I don't want to move this close to Comic-Con." Mandy brightened. "Do you want to come help me finish one of my costumes? I have a *lot* of rhinestones to attach."

"Is this a sincere request, or a 'Hey, Stasia, let me distract you for a while' request?"

Mandy shrugged. "A bit of both. I don't *need* the help, exactly—I planned my time much better this year than I did last year—but it would make things go faster, and you'd feel like you'd accomplished something."

"As opposed to . . . ?"

"As opposed to sitting in here sulking until you're sure everyone else is asleep. Come on. Bedazzle things with me." Mandy's smile was less pointed this time, but no less laser-focused. "I refuse to let Roxanna spoil your weekend."

At last, I understood. "She asked you when you're going to get a boyfriend again, didn't she?"

Mandy's grim nod was all the answer I needed.

People who don't understand our dynamic tend to look at our housing situation—two unmarried women and one unmarried man—and assume either we're all having sex with each other, or one day Lucas will push his luck with one of us and we'll wind up on the news for murdering him. People are kind of awful that way. Roxanna is a special kind of awful, because she looks at our situation and, without wanting to move in and give up her perfectly curated lizard habitat, just assumes that whenever one of us is single, we're about to be making a play for Lucas.

Mandy wasn't single when she moved in. Mandy was happily involved with a mountain of a man named Robert, who walked through the world with the exaggerated gentleness of someone who had become very large very young, and knew on a bone-deep level that everyone around him was breakable. He rode a motorcycle and regularly showed up at the house dressed in black leather, looking like something out of a *Mad Max* film. He also had two ginger cats he loved more than life itself, and did cosplay with Mandy at conventions, and she had just raised the question of whether he could move in with her to Lucas when his sister had called to tell us that Robert had been in an accident. A semi had lost control on the bridge. There had been nowhere for him to go.

According to the hospital, he hadn't suffered. That was probably supposed to make us feel better. It did, for me, a little. I don't think it helped Mandy at all. Only time was going to do that. Unfortunately, it had happened long enough ago that Roxanna seemed to think the statute of limitations on mourning had expired, and now every other visit, she was offering to introduce Mandy to someone—anyone—who wasn't Lucas.

Mandy looked at me and sighed.

"You're cute," said Mandy. "You need to learn how to brush your hair more than twice a week, and I would kill to take you shopping for some better clothes, but you're cute. Why doesn't she ask *you* about your love life, and leave me the hell alone?"

"She thinks I'm crazy," I said, and grimaced. "You know, I don't mind when you call me crazy, because you're sort of . . . stating a fact, not using it as a reason I'm not good enough to do something I want to do. Roxanna uses it like a brick to hit me with."

"I call you crazy because you think you're allowed to eat my cinnamon toast," said Mandy easily. "You're not crazy. Your people will be here any day, and they're going to eat us all. I only ask that you let me watch when they chow down on Roxanna."

"It's a deal," I said, through a smile, and followed her down the hall toward the stairs that would take us to the basement craft room.

Nobody improves an evening like Mandy.

Nobody expects me to be happy about hot-gluing eight hundred sequins to a mantis-shrimp ball gown like Mandy, either. She busied herself with stitching on the larger pieces, occasionally pausing to hand me another packet of small, shimmering "scales" and point to the patch of fabric that didn't look enough like an explosion at the bling factory. She didn't talk much, and neither did I. We were both content to be doing something and, better, to be doing it together.

Lucas had been Mandy's friend first. They met in college, where they were both in the same anime society. Weird costumes and flashy cartoons are their points of commonality, and have always been enough to bond them into a tightly functional unit. Before Roxanna, he would have been down here with us, gluing sequins and probably throwing chunks of sculpting foam at Mandy's head. I had come later, when the three of us had started frequenting the same comic book shop.

Three nerds in a house. Two human, one alien plant invader. One "oh, she's kidding about the plant thing," one "it's not hurting anyone either way," and me, who sometimes couldn't make up my own mind about whether I was kidding, or whether I was supposed to be doing something to get the world ready for the invasion.

Mandy tossed me another packet of sequins. Right: I was supposed to be doing something. I was supposed to be gluing these down.

I got back to work.

3.

By the time we stopped for bed, I was properly exhausted. Better yet, Lucas and Roxanna were already in bed, having returned from dinner and retreated into his bedroom without bothering to say good night to us. That was fine by me. I brushed my teeth, collected my cat, and slipped into my own room, Seymour purring in my arms.

I was asleep almost as soon as my head hit the pillow. That should have been a sign that things were about to get ugly. Most nights, sleep comes slowly for me, assuming sleep comes at all.

Instead, I closed my eyes on my dark bedroom and opened them on a forest that I had seen hundreds of times since I was three. Not the forest behind my grandparents' house, comfortable and coniferous and still growing not that far from the house. Mandy and I could drive there in a few hours. This forest . . .

This was a forest made for dreams, or nightmares. Made for a world where the balance of oxygen in the air was different, where things felt less constrained to growing low and close to their own roots. Trees towered around me like California redwoods, some with trunks larger than an office building. Their bark was purple mottled with streaks of red and yellow, and it had a vital quality to it that the trees I knew when I was awake lacked. I pressed my hand against a trunk, the bark rough against my palm, and felt the heartbeat echoing through the tree, a thick, heavy pulse that shook my teeth in their sockets.

When I pulled my hand away, I left a layer of skin behind. This was a dream: there was no pain, only a calm satisfaction at the idea that I was finally to be divested of my human guise.

Evolution has tried on so many gowns, casting them aside the moment they become less effective than something else in her closet. It would be foolish arrogance to assume every world would follow the *Star Trek* mode and settle on something with two legs, two arms, eyes to watch the world, hands to reach out and change it. The octopus, the crow, they're both Earth creatures, and they don't look much like humans. Why would alien plant people?

Whatever I had been before my fall to Earth left me in the body of Anastasia Miller, it wasn't what I would have been if I'd fallen anywhere else, or what I would have been if I had stayed at home. If I had a home. This forest . . . it felt like home, the way my dream forests always did, but it didn't feel like a place I could visit. As always, I looked up, trying to see the sky, and found nothing but more trees, stretching upward and upward, reaching toward forever.

Vines circled the trunks and draped themselves over the branches, festooning them in festival array. Their flowers were the purple-black of bruises, blooming wide to show their bloody pink centers. I didn't know what kind of pollinators might come to those flowers, and I wasn't sure I wanted to.

Higher up, about where Earth trees would have been forming a crown, the branches grew thicker and denser, creating a platform on which smaller trees—these black-trunked and yellow-leafed—took root. It was a beautiful symbiosis, and it continued everywhere I looked.

The air was like honey. I took a deep breath, letting it fill my dream-lungs, and began to walk.

Over the years, the various therapists who've tried to help with my "I think I'm from another planet" problem have remarked that it's amazing how my dream-forest remains the same. It doesn't. It's just that I've never been able to articulate the ways it changes. Over the years, I've seen one of the vast foundation trees fall, seen it covered in knee-high flowers that smelled like rotting meat, which broke it down into mulch before withering away, their purpose in this strange ecosystem served. I've seen smaller trees grow, faster than terrestrial trees but still slowly, swelling upward over the course of years.

If this landscape never changed, I would have had an easier time writing it off as some strange fiction, a way for my mind to code the trauma that changed me from ordinary girl to alien. Instead, it grew with me, following its own rhythms and patterns, over which I had little influence.

I kept walking, touching the occasional trunk, until the ground began to dip under my feet, leading me to a shallow bowl. There, concealed by the trees and roots around them, I found a garden's worth of flowers with dragonfly wings for petals and nests of vines at the base of their stems, taking the place of leaves. The petals vibrated at my approach, almost as if the flowers were saying hello.

Of course they were saying hello.

I stepped carefully over vines as I made my way to the center of the garden, and the vines responded by twitching out of the way, clearing a path. When I reached the center, I sat down, checking to be sure I wasn't going to crush any seedlings before I stretched out and let the vines slither over me.

They closed around my body in a dense cocoon, squeezing until the weight of them blocked out everything but the honeyed scent of the air and the light slanting through the branches. I had never been able to catch so much as a glimpse of the sun, but I had never seen this place in darkness, either.

// here // whispered the flowers around me.

"Here," I replied sleepily. They hadn't always spoken English, these alien plants in this alien place, like I hadn't always spoken English. We had known another language once, the plants and I, but it had faded from my mind the longer I spent in Stasia's skin, until English was all I had left to use. "Home."

// here, home // agreed the flowers. Then, in a softer tone, if flowers can be said to have a tone, they said, *// soon. //*

"Soon?" I asked.

// soon. close. ready? // Their last word had an echo to it, the sound of a dozen different languages layered on top of one another. I had heard that echo before, a reassuring implication that I wasn't alone in this forest when I slept—and more, that I was not alone in my alien condition when I woke. I had never been able to find another person who shared my convictions about the upcoming invasion. I'd met other "aliens," sure, but none of them had the same framework of beliefs and details that I did.

Maybe it's silly, but when I heard the voices whisper through the forest of flowers, it was easy to think each of them might belong to another scout, working alone and without clear instructions in hostile, alien terrain.

That's the thing about being from outer space. I'm an alien to the people around me. It's easy to forget that this also makes them alien to me.

// ready? // asked the flowers again, more urgently this time.

"Yes," I said, and closed my eyes.

The air thrummed with the affirmative, answers coming from all parts of the forest. The scent of honey was thick and heavy in the air, so sweet it was like breathing candy. I relaxed further, slipping toward sleep while I was already dreaming. The vines were wrapped everywhere around me, a maternal embrace so complete, so familiar, that it pulled the stress from my body, leaving me relaxed for the first time since I had left for work. It was going to be all right. Everything was going to be all right.

The forest sang around me, wordless songs of conquest and hunger and the stars, and I slept in its embrace, aware that I was dreaming, equally aware that the dream was finally, blissfully coming to an end.

4.

When I woke up, the sun was shining through the clouds, and the scent of honey was gone. Still, I couldn't shake the feeling that a step had been taken—a step that had been in progress since long before I was taken, long before I was returned.

Ready, whispered the voice of the forest, and I was. Oh, yes. I was.

3

SEATTLE, WASHINGTON: JULY 16, 2031
TWENTY-TWO DAYS PRE-INVASION

1.

Work, again: the slow grind against a stone made of people who hated me for being different and good at my job. Another talk with my supervisor about the way people touched my things, ending with the not-so-subtle suggestion that maybe it was time I clean all the personal items out of my desk. It felt like failure. It felt like giving ground. It also felt like the only way to win. Sometimes retreat is your only way to take the resources your enemy wants away.

A few of my co-workers looked over and snickered when they saw me packing my toys. I guess they saw the failure on my part, and the corresponding victory on their own, as clearly as I did. At least until the message from HR hit our inboxes, stating that since we had shown we couldn't be respectful of one another's things, we could no longer keep any personal items in our cubes. This included family photos and office supplies brought from home. Boxes would be distributed by the end of the day.

The snickers stopped then. So did the smug looks, replaced by glares. I wanted to tell them this wasn't my fault, that if they had left me alone—if they had shown me the simple courtesy I was expected to show them—we would all be able to keep our nice things where we wanted them, and no one would be able to take them away. I didn't say a word. Anything I said would only have made things worse, by proving I was smug about getting my way.

This wasn't my way. This sort of passive, sneaky backstabbing wasn't my way. I had always been open about what I was and what I wanted, and I had at least tried to make friends. I had *tried*.

The end of the work day is always nice, but I don't think I'd ever been so glad to see the clock tick over. I grabbed my bag and my box of personal effects and hoofed it for the door, hoping to avoid confrontation with any of my co-workers. That was the last thing I needed to make my day truly terrible.

Home. Yes. Home, and Seymour, and a big bowl of buttered popcorn while I put some terrible movie on the TV and stopped dwelling on how much I was coming to hate the human race. Moments like this, I truly hoped I was right about my origins, because the invasion couldn't come fast enough for me.

A few people were already at the bus stop when I walked up. They were all from different teams or different offices, and so there was no active unfriendliness in the air, just the tired distance of people who really didn't want to talk to a stranger. I appreciated that. Tomorrow, and the yelling at me for ruining their desks, would come soon enough. I put my headphones on and tuned my iPod to one of my best "hate the world a little less" mixes, trying to let the music soothe my soul.

Bullies are bullies, no matter how old they are, and they always find a way to blame the bullied for the consequences of their own actions. I was weird. That was reason enough for everything to be my fault, and it always would be. It always will be.

Humans are awful.

A few more people arrived at the stop. They struck up a lively conversation, and soon, almost everyone was chatting with a surprising degree of animation for a Monday afternoon. I considered removing my headphones long enough to find out what was going on. No one looked actively distressed. It was probably some development on the latest season of *America's Got Talent,* which had been running since I was a child, and nothing I needed to worry about. I needed the peace and quiet more than I needed to know why they were so excited.

Decisions like that that had long since solidified my reputation as antisocial. I wasn't going to change it any time soon.

The bus pulled up. We all got on, and I sat quietly as everyone chattered and waved their hands. This degree of excitement was unusual, and again, I considered finding out—but the song on my iPod was a good one, and I had been dealing with people for so many hours. I just wanted to get home. If this was such a big deal, there would be something about it online.

People got on the bus. People got off the bus. Some of the new people joined the ongoing conversation, waving their hands enough that I started to suspect this was something bigger than reality television. The more crowded and enthusiastic the conversation became, the less I felt like taking off my headphones. Joining a discussion with six strangers was one thing; joining a discussion with twenty was probably better avoided.

By the time we reached the park and ride where I was meeting Lucas, I was exhausted from the effort of not paying attention to what was happening around me. I hopped off the bus and trotted to the car, relieved to see Lucas waiting for me.

He started to talk as soon as I had my door open, his mouth moving fast as he gestured with one hand. I shook my head and pointed to my headphones.

"Just a second," I said. "I can't hear you."

He knew that. I always got into the car with my music playing, like hearing even a few seconds of unfiltered street noise could hurt me. I slammed the door, fastened my seatbelt, and hooked the buds out of my ears, stuffing them into my pocket.

"All right," I said. "I can hear you now. What's up?"

Lucas stared at me, wide-eyed and apparently stunned. "Stasia," he said. "Have you had those things on since you left work?"

"Yeah. Why?"

"So you don't know. You actually don't know."

I frowned. "Don't know what?" It couldn't have been a terrorist attack or a quarantine or any of the other big, scary things they liked to warn us about on the news. There would have been some sort of announcement, not just people talking on the bus, and they would have been scared, not excited. There was no way I'd missed anything that important.

"Holy shit." Lucas slumped in his seat, raking his hair out of his eyes. It made him look disheveled and younger than he was. It was rare enough to see Lucas off-balance that I didn't say anything, just blinked and waited for the world to start making sense again.

"Okay," he said, after a long moment. "Here's what I'm going to do. I'm going to start this car, and we're going to drive home, where I will show you what I'm talking about. And then we can have a reasonable conversation, without me staring at you like . . . I don't know, like some kind of asshole who stares."

"Right," I said, bemused.

Lucas put the car in drive. He didn't turn on the radio. That, alone, was a solid signal that something was going on. He's like me, in that he lives for his music. A silent moment is a moment wasted. Well, we were wasting a lot of moments now, letting them trickle through our fingers and into uncomfortable stillness. I didn't know how to deal with this sort of silence. I spindled a fold of my T-shirt between my fingers, and waited for it to end.

My therapist says silence scares me. She says it's old scar tissue from what happened when I was three, that my captors probably kept me locked somewhere until they decided what they were going to do with me. I do okay with music, and I do okay with voices, but the absence of both isn't something I handle well.

Luckily, Lucas didn't need to stop for gas or anything else on the way home, which made the ride as short as possible. I sat up and blinked when the driveway came into view. Mandy's car was already there, waiting for us.

"The hell—?"

"Like I said, I don't want to be staring at you like some kind of asshole," said Lucas, and pulled into his side of the driveway. He paused to give me an unreadable look before getting out and heading for the door. I stayed where I was for a long moment, staring after him, trying to get my nascent panic and flowering confusion under control. Something was happening. Something *big*. I just had no idea what it was.

Slowly, I undid my belt, got out of the car, and followed him to the open door.

The television was on inside, paused by the remote in Mandy's hand, while Mandy herself was seated on the couch and twisted all the way around to watch me come in. Lucas was standing off to one side, looking suddenly and profoundly uncomfortable.

I squirmed. "What?" I asked. "Am I being evicted?" Drawn by the sound of my voice, Seymour trotted down the hall and twisted around my ankles, chirping and trilling for my attention. For once, it didn't make me feel any better. My mind was racing, thinking about how much harder it would be to find an apartment that allowed pets—and how I could never leave Seymour behind. Sometimes I thought he was the only good thing about the world, and without him, it would be easy to forget anything about this planet was worth preserving.

Wait. No. That was a bad thought, the kind my therapist called "intrusive," although apparently most people have intrusive thoughts about self-harm and breaking things, not about eliminating all life on Earth. Or maybe the people who have extinction-level invasive thoughts just don't like to admit it. Maybe they're all smarter than I am and know how to keep their mouths shut.

"Does she know?" asked Mandy, attention going to Lucas.

Lucas shook his head.

"Okay. I thought—Okay. We're going to do this. Stasia, come sit down."

I went. I sat. Seymour leapt onto my lap, turning around once before curling into a tight knot of black and white fur. I began to stroke him automatically, letting the familiar motion soothe me.

"I don't know what I did, but I'm really sorry," I said. My voice sounded high and panicky, like I was on the verge of bursting into tears. I probably was. "Please don't make me move again. I don't want to move."

Mandy's eyes widened. She was still in her work clothes, which just added to the surrealistic quality of the moment. Seeing Mandy on the couch, wearing a dress that looked like it belonged on an elementary school teacher instead of something covered in jellyfish or sugar skulls or the word "fuck" printed over and over again in a cheerful cartoon print was . . . jarring. It was *wrong.*

"We're not kicking you out," she said, almost offended. She slanted a glance at Lucas, who winced and took an involuntary step back. Not unwise. "I thought Lucas was going to bring you up to speed in the car."

"I didn't want to do it twice," he protested.

"You mean you chickened out and left it for me," she said sweetly, and turned back to me. She handed me the remote. "I pulled up the report you need to see and paused it for you. Just press Play."

I looked at her blankly. She gave me an encouraging nod. I turned to the television. I pressed Play.

Sometimes I wonder how we survived when televisions were only televisions and not a way to watch Netflix and YouTube and a hundred other streaming services, some more specialized than others. Mandy had paused on the CNN science news stream, which was one of the only sub-streams not inclined to dissolve into wild speculation about the sex lives of celebrities when there was nothing better to talk about.

The talking head of the moment—a redheaded woman with a solemn, lineless face, like she was being CGI-refined in real time—looked at the camera and said, in a pleasantly modulated voice, "We have received confirmation from NASA, the ISS, and other related parties, and can now report with near certainty that the signal you are about to hear is extraterrestrial in origin. Again, this was recorded at seven thirty-five p.m., Eastern Standard Time, by Dr. Anthony Vornholt of the Portland Observatory."

Her composure flickered. Only for a moment. Long enough for me to see the raw animal fear behind her eyes, hot and bright and terrified.

"It is my duty to inform you that we are no longer alone in the galaxy. Our neighbors have finally found us."

The picture cut out, replaced by a black screen with a white rectangle in the middle, framing a single line of text which identified the sound's original location and the astronomer who recorded it. I barely noticed. I was too busy listening to something that should have been static but was the most beautiful thing I'd ever heard, something I had never heard outside my dreams. It was the sound of branches rubbing together in alien air, the song of dragonfly petals trembling in a forest the size of a continent. It went on and on, chiming, climbing, moving through musical formations that were alien to anything Earth had ever borne. I knew that if I listened hard enough, long enough, I would understand it. I leaned forward, completely focused on the sound—

Then it stopped.

I jerked upright, startled. The television was off. Mandy had taken the remote out of my hand while I was transfixed. She was looking at me, mouth a thin line, that same animal fear showing behind her eyes.

"Anastasia," she said. "What was that?"

"It was beautiful," I said. I felt suddenly, utterly serene. I hadn't been wrong. All that time, all those years, I hadn't been wrong. It had taken decades for them to come for me, but now that they were here, things were going to change.

I wasn't crazy. I wasn't a liar. I wasn't a human being. I was what I'd always claimed to be, and my people were coming to take me home, and maybe I should have been upset to realize I wasn't what I seemed to be, but I never asked to look human. I never asked to lie through the shape of my bones, when my voice only ever told the truth.

"But what *was* that?" she pressed.

I frowned, trying to figure out what she wanted me to say. "It was . . . it was 'hello,'" I said finally. "It was the last warning."

"What do you mean, the last warning?" asked Lucas.

I shrugged. "They're coming. I told you they were, remember? They're coming, and they wanted you to know how close they are." They wanted *me* to know.

After all this time, I was finally going home.

2.

There was a long pause. Both my housemates stared at me, Lucas in disbelief, Mandy with a strange sort of acceptance, like she'd always known this moment would come, yet had managed to almost convince herself it was a joke, a cosmic impossibility.

In my lap, Seymour purred. His world, at least, was unchanged.

"What?" I asked, as the silence became too much to bear.

"You're joking, right?" asked Lucas. "When you say you're a—I can't believe I'm saying this with my actual mouth, out loud, where people can hear—when you say you're a space invader, you're joking. Because we've always let it slide. People have weirder nervous habits than claiming to be from another planet, and it's not like you were hurting anyone. But now we need to know."

This time, the silence was mine to meter out as I saw fit. I held it, letting it linger, trying to figure out how to respond—how I was *supposed* to respond. Usually, questions have a right answer. In customer service, questions *always* have a right answer. There's right and there's wrong, and it's difficult to mix them up.

People don't work that way. With people, something can be the right answer once and the wrong answer every other time, forever. With people, the right answer *changes*.

Some things should be constant. I took a breath, frowned, and asked, "What do you need to know? If I was telling the truth?"

"Yes," said Lucas.

He said it so quickly, and with so much certainty, that I couldn't stop myself from shooting a wounded glance in his direction. "You think I'm a liar?"

"The first time I met you, you showed me a picture of your cat and told me you were a plant from outer space," said Lucas. "Remember? I thought it was cute. I thought you were kidding."

"You asked me if I photosynthesized," I said.

"Right," he said. "You fed me some line about mimicry and hiding among the local population and not being a biologist or a botanist and so not really understanding how you function, just that you do."

"It wasn't a line." I knew it wasn't a line. I had always known. Since I was a child, I'd known some things were true and needed to be understood, even if I'd been missing some of the words and concepts I needed to properly explain them.

"That's the thing," said Mandy. "I went to college with this guy who swore he was a vampire. He even used to buy cow's blood from this independent butcher. He drank the stuff like it was coffee—cream and sugar and lots of ostentatious sighs of pleasure. And then, one day, he wasn't a vampire anymore. He was a business major instead. I guess somebody told him being Dracula doesn't get you a seat on the board of a Fortune 500 company."

"I don't understand," I said.

"You're *consistent*," said Mandy. "I've watched people walk away from you for being the weirdo who says she's an alien. It doesn't change your story. It doesn't make you stop or double down. You have blonde hair, you have blue eyes, you came from outer space because you're scouting for an invasion, you like oatmeal more than is healthy for an adult of any species. So I guess what we're asking is not . . . it's not whether you've been lying to us. It's whether you've been telling the truth."

I couldn't quite see the difference, but the way they were watching me made it hard to doubt that *they* saw a difference, somehow. Somewhere in that nest of words, the contradiction had resolved itself enough for them to feel like they deserved an answer. I took a breath.

"Yes," I said. "I've been telling the truth. I am the vanguard of an invading species of alien plant people."

"You keep saying 'invading,'" said Lucas. "Is there any chance that's shorthand for 'coming in peace'?"

"How do you know?" asked Mandy. "You look human. You do human things. You used the last of my tampons last month."

"I just know," I said, addressing the second question first. It was frustrating. I buried my fingers in Seymour's fur, taking comfort from his tactile reality. "I walked into the woods when I was a little girl, and when I came back out, I was an alien."

"What, like an *Invasion of the Body Snatchers* thing?" asked Mandy.

That sounded right. It sounded . . . true, in a way I'd never been able to quite put a finger on. "Sort of," I said. "The book got a lot of things right. It got a lot of things wrong, too." It never mentioned the flowers with wings for petals, the way their centers would yield under fingers, sticking and clinging. It never mentioned their lures, or their place in the life cycle of the organisms they served. Maybe most importantly, it claimed "pod people" could only live for five years before they withered away.

That part of the story scared the crap out of me when I first read it, back in high school. I'd spent the better part of a year waiting to wither and die, before my boyfriend at the time had pointed out that five years from the point of replacement would have had me dead when I was eight, not sixteen.

I'd rewarded him for calming my fears by having sex with him for the first time, further distancing myself from the sexless, short-lived pods of Finney's novel. But the image had still haunted me, and kept haunting, and probably always would.

"This is ridiculous," said Lucas. "We're not having this conversation."

"You're the one who asked me to log off early because we needed to talk about whether our housemate was an alien," said Mandy calmly. "Roxanna will be here soon, won't she? Don't you want this resolved before your girlfriend shows up and makes things even more complicated?"

"Roxanna doesn't make things more complicated," said Lucas.

"Roxanna asked me if I'd considered the possibility that I might have schizophrenia," I said.

Lucas paused. "What?"

"Last year. She said she'd been talking to you about the whole 'alien plant person' thing, and you'd told her I seemed to really believe it but it wasn't hurting anything, and she was 'concerned.'" It was difficult to explain how terrible her "concern" had made me feel, the way it had dropped my stomach toward my feet and turned the whole world gray and sticky.

When you get kidnapped and come back claiming to be an alien, lots of therapists want to talk to you. Lots of people want to do lots of tests, all aimed at being the thing that magically cures the abducted girl. I guess they thought there was a book in me, or a couple of books, if somebody got really lucky. So I'd seen doctors, and I'd listened to diagnoses, and I'd watched my mother and my grandparents beat themselves against the locked doors of the mental health community, trying to prove there wasn't anything about me that needed fixing.

It wasn't until after my grandmother died that I'd learned part of the reason behind her standoffishness. Her mother and older sister had been schizophrenic, and in both cases, they'd been institutionalized because no one knew how to help them live their best lives. For her, having me come out of the woods claiming something she knew couldn't be true had to have been like looking backward through time, staring into the moment where everything had changed, and not for the better.

But I didn't have schizophrenia, and I wasn't a pathological liar, and I wasn't any of the things Roxanna liked to ask about, always smiling sweetly, like her love of lizards and Lucas made up for the invasive, offensive things she said about my mental health. I was just someone who knew the truth. It was no better or worse than the people who knew God was real or the Earth was flat or whatever.

Well. Maybe it was better than the people who knew the Earth was flat.

Lucas scowled. "There's nothing wrong with you."

"Alec has schizophrenia," said Mandy mildly. "He does okay."

Lucas paused again. The poor guy's view of reality was taking a beating today. "What?"

"He's medicated to keep him from hearing things, and he can't drink without worrying about drug interactions, but he's schizophrenic, and he's been schizophrenic since before you met him." Mandy flashed Lucas a dazzling smile. "Hi. It's not the bigotry party hour in here. It's 'figure out whether Stasia has been telling the truth, and if yes, figure out how we're going to protect her' o'clock. Thanks for joining us. I'm your host, Mandy Reyes, and the aliens have made contact for what is either the first or second time."

"Not just the second," I said. They turned to look at me. I shrugged, resisting the urge to squirm. These were my housemates. These were my *friends*. They understood me better than any other humans in the world, except maybe Graham, and he was off in Florida, counting alligators in the Everglades and not thinking about the people he'd left behind.

Would someone tell him about the signal? Somebody had to. There was no way anyone connected to the scientific community wasn't going to hear about this. He'd come home when he heard. He *would* come home when he heard. He *had* to come back to me when he heard. Because this was only the beginning. I knew it, all the way down to my bones.

My bones. My God, my bones. Would someone report me to the authorities? It wasn't like I'd ever been quiet about my origins, but I'd never really been worried about getting arrested for . . . for . . . for illegal immigration before. It didn't make sense to me how humans could think of each other as against the law, especially given how often land has changed hands across the countries: no human life is illegal. I, on the other hand, came from very far away, and I definitely hadn't paused at the border to pick up a passport. Could I be detained?

Could the proper authorities tell I wasn't human? My doctors had never noticed, but I've never been really sick, either. No MRIs, no invasive scans of my head or gut. I could be carrying a whole alien ecosystem in the space beneath my skin, and the doctors who'd given me flu shots and gynecological exams had just missed it, because they hadn't needed to rip me apart in the course of looking.

"Stasia?" said Mandy gently. "What do you mean, 'not just the second'?"

"Oh. Um." I rubbed the side of my face. My skin felt like skin, human skin. Was it going to change, or was I always going to be an alien in human skin, feeling wrong no matter how I looked at things? "You mentioned *Invasion of the Body Snatchers*. Most of it isn't right, or it's half-right, like some of the facts were missing. When we fell here—"

"Fell?" asked Mandy. "You didn't land?"

"This is ridiculous," said Lucas. "What are we even doing? I should go get Roxanna."

"You do that," said Mandy pleasantly. "We won't be here when you get back."

He looked stung. "Why not?"

"Because we have two choices right now: we can hunker down for the aliens to arrive, knowing nothing, or we can take our friend, who's never lied to us about anything else, seriously." She looked back to me. "Stasia has always been incredibly upfront about all this. Maybe it's time for us to start listening. Maybe if we do, we'll be okay, no matter how this plays out."

"When we *fell* here," I said, more slowly, "we didn't pick where we landed, and I think it took longer for some seeds to find a safe place to germinate. I don't really know the mechanism. I sort of know what it wasn't, but it's more instinct and . . . sense of how this goes than actual fact."

"She has a feeling she's an alien, and now we're going to use her to try to benefit from the invasion," said Lucas. "Am I the only one who sees the issue with this?"

"What is your problem, Lucas?" demanded Mandy.

"Aliens aren't real," he said.

"We just made contact."

"No." He shook his head, hard. "We just intercepted a hoax. Or this Vornholt guy is trying to manufacture a hoax. You'll see. This will play out for a while, soak up some news cycles, and then get unmasked as the pile of shit it is. In the meantime, you want to pump Stasia for information about her little fantasy world, and you don't want to think about the way it's going to change things. Because it will. It will change *everything.*" He gave me a look, half-pleading, half-sympathetic. "Once we make her tell us how her game works, it won't work anymore. Everything she does will be proof of her humanity, and we'll have to think hard about how seriously she takes this, and whether we owe it to her to help her find, well, help."

I put Seymour on the floor and stood. I didn't think before I moved, but once I was moving, it seemed like the only possible response to the situation. Mandy grimaced.

"Stasia, don't go," she said.

"I don't think you need me here for this conversation," I said. "It feels like you're talking about me, not to me, and I don't have time for this. Not if the armada is coming."

"That's the problem," said Lucas. He sounded frustrated—but under the frustration, there was fear. "The armada *isn't* coming. The armada *can't* be coming."

"Why not?"

"Because we're *humans*!" He stopped, looking startled by his own vehemence. Then he straightened, cleared his throat, and continued more quietly, "Because you've been telling us this whole time that you came from outer space to conquer the planet, and we laughed at you, and oh my God I can't believe I'm saying this, this is ridiculous, but you realize if you've been telling the truth—which you haven't been, because you *can't* have been—that makes me, and Mandy, and Graham, and Roxanna, and anyone else you've had a conversation with in your lifetime, complicit in aiding the invaders. We're traitors to our species and our planet if we knew what you were and never told anyone."

"No one would have believed you."

"Just like we didn't believe you."

"You mean *you* didn't believe her," said Mandy. We turned to look at her. She shrugged. "Believe everything that isn't actively trying to eat your face. That way, when it shows up and *does* try to eat your face, you'll at least know what it is. I always believed you, Stasia. I just didn't think it was important."

"Me being an alien wasn't important?"

Mandy shrugged. "People called my grandparents 'aliens,' but they were American citizens before they died. You've been there when someone asked me where I was *really* from, and got pissed off when I kept repeating, 'Pasadena.' If you're from outer space, why should I care? I just want you to take me to your place for Christmas. I'd like to see the Milky Way from the outside."

"You're both insane," said Lucas.

"Way to judge," said Mandy.

I shook my head. "I can't change . . . anything. Lucas, I'm sorry this is making you uncomfortable, but I never lied to you. I always told you exactly what I am, and I always told you the invasion was coming. What you did with that information is on you. It's not on me."

It couldn't be on me. Over the course of my lifetime, I'd told hundreds of people—maybe even thousands—what I represented. I'd never been able to explain how one lone, human-appearing girl was supposed to jump-start an invasion, but I'd known telling them was the right thing to do, that I had to tell them, that I had to *keep* telling them, even when I knew they wouldn't believe me. It was a compulsion that had defined my life. That *still* defined my life. If someone asked, or even looked like they might listen, they needed to know what I was.

"Oh my God." Lucas rubbed his face with his hand. "Mandy, talk to her. Stasia, whether I believe you or not, you need to think long and hard about saying this to anyone else."

"Why?" I asked.

"Because for at least the two days it takes to discredit that transmission, people are going to be looking for someone to blame. They're going to be scared, and they're going to be credulous, and they might take you seriously."

I frowned. "So?"

"So do you really want your kneecaps broken by someone who thinks the patriotic thing to do is to strike against the invasion before it gets fully underway? I don't want to visit you in the hospital. You need to be careful." Lucas looked at me solemnly. There was no levity in his face: for better or for worse, he meant every word he was saying. "Even if this is all a joke you don't know how to stop telling, you need to be careful. Otherwise, you're going to be dead."

He turned on his heel then, heading for the door. Mandy stood.

"Lucas—" she began.

"Stay home. Watch a movie. Keep each other safe. I'm going out." With that, he stalked to the door, wrenched it open, and slammed it behind him. Mandy and I watched through the window as he stormed down the front walk to the driveway, disappearing from view.

A few seconds later, we heard the car door slam and the snarl of the engine turning over. Lucas peeled out, and we were alone. Silence reigned.

Finally, Mandy looked at me and asked, "What do you need?"

I needed the invasion to come faster. I needed it to change course and go find another planet to plunder. I needed to know I was right about myself. I needed proof that I'd been delusional all along, and the planet where I lived wasn't about to be in danger. I needed so many big, complicated, contradictory things that I felt like I couldn't breathe, like all those needs were sticking in my throat and cutting off my air.

There was only one good solution for that. "I need to talk to Graham," I said. Hearing the words aloud made it possible for me to relax, just a little, allowing the truth of them to sink into my skin.

Mandy nodded. "All right," she said. "I'll be in the craft room if you need me. All those sequins still aren't going to glue themselves." She turned to head for the stairs.

In only a few seconds, I was alone. No: not quite alone. Seymour twined around my ankles, making the weird hiccupping chirp sound he always made when I seemed unhappy. I laughed a little, bending to scoop him into my arms.

"Come on, weird cat," I said. "Let's go call your daddy."

He purred all the way to my room.

3.

Zoom was all fucked up. After the third time my call dropped without connecting, I started to wonder whether it might have something to do with the alien transmission. Not in the sense of "the aliens are screwing with the internet"—the aliens weren't close enough for that, and I didn't think they knew enough about Earth communications to be jerks on that kind of micro level—but in the sense of "everyone on the planet is talking about this, and that probably means the network is overloaded."

I leaned back in my chair and glared at the screen. Glaring has never been known to fix network connectivity issues, but there's always a first time. We'd never received signals from an extraterrestrial source before, either.

The structure of the thought hit me a split second after the thought itself. I forgot to glare, suddenly sunk in an existential dilemma even more frustrating than my Zoom issues. Were "we" receiving our first extraterrestrial signal? Did I have any right to include myself in that group, given how much of my life had been spent willfully denying inclusion? Or had "they" received their first extraterrestrial signal, while I'd received proof that I was no longer going to be alone in a world filled with complex, confusing mammals?

The screen beeped. The plain white square was replaced by the interior of a high-tech tent, with scientific equipment around the edges of the frame and a man's sweet, earnest face at the center. His cheeks were covered in reddish stubble, signaling that Graham had once again decided that being in the field was the perfect excuse to stop shaving. There were no visible bandages. That was a nice change.

"Stasia," he said, sagging in relief. "I was hoping you'd call."

"Why not call me?" I asked.

"Because I didn't know whether you'd be at your computer, or whether you'd be in any condition to talk."

I lifted my eyebrows. "You're the one in the swamp. I didn't know whether you'd be at your computer, either."

"Of course I am," he said. "I told my team lead I needed to be here in case my girlfriend, the alien, decided to call and tell me to come home."

"Seymour misses you." I held up the cat as a demonstration. Seymour dangled in my hands, a dead weight, not acknowledging my claim. "And yes, I miss you, too. But I'm not going to tell you to come home before you're done. You're doing good work."

"I'm doing grunt work," he said. "It's not the same thing, even though I appreciate your faith in me."

"It looks good on a résumé and it keeps you working in your field, which means you don't have to look elsewhere for your scaled delights, and I don't have to move someplace with more snakes."

Graham smiled, fond and concerned. "That's my girl," he said.

"Always," I said, and smiled back.

Graham and I met in college, when we'd taken the same English elective to round out our course load. He'd been planning to become a herpetologist; I'd been planning to become a computer scientist. We'd both been derailed by the world, but we'd held on to the core of our disciplines, and we'd held on to each other. The make-outs were nice. The sex was nice, too. The friendship, though, the understanding and affection . . . those were better.

After school, I'd decided eighty-hour weeks and nervous breakdowns weren't for me and gone into customer service instead, while Graham had gone to work in the research division of a large software company. His team did general science, with the goal of finding ways to apply that science to new technological breakthroughs for his employers. As long as they were willing to let him keep spending all his free time on his beloved snakes, that was fine with him.

The only bad thing he'd ever done to me was Roxanna. She wasn't a coworker, but she was a colleague, and he'd been the one who urged her to go to Burning Man, just to try it out. Without him, Lucas might have found a girlfriend I was less inclined to drown in the nearest body of standing water.

Oh, well. Nobody's perfect.

"How are you holding up?" he asked. "Is it . . . you know?"

"I'm okay." I shrugged. "A little shaken, I guess? I'm having to ask myself a lot of questions. I don't know that I'm going to like all the answers I get. But I'm okay."

Graham looked at me oddly. "You didn't answer my second question."

"I need you to come home."

It was the sort of bald, needy declaration that rarely arose between us. Graham blinked, looking nonplussed. Then he nodded.

"Okay," he said. "I guess you answered it after all. Is tomorrow soon enough?"

"It should be," I said. "Is it going to be a problem?"

His laugh was unsteady. "Honestly, no. A few of my teammates have asked about you. They wanted me to find out whether you recognized the signal."

Graham has never questioned whether or not I'm what I claim to be. If Mandy chose to believe me because it didn't hurt anything for her to do so, Graham chose to believe me because he didn't think I'd lie to him. That meant he'd known what he was doing the first time he'd invited me to one of his company get-togethers, and hadn't been bothered in the slightest when I had introduced myself to all of them as the vanguard of an invasion. They were computer people, and scientists, and that meant that for the most part, they were exceptionally tolerant of strangeness.

I think some of them actually hoped for proof of my extraterrestrial nature, since it would give them a leg up on the competition. No better way to win the software wars than to be the first to press into the rest of the galaxy.

"Oh," I said, and laughed unsteadily.

Graham went still. He leaned closer. "Stasia," he said, "*did* you recognize the signal?"

I didn't trust my voice. I bit my lip and nodded, trusting his knowledge of my expressions to make my meaning clear.

Graham's eyes widened. "Wow," he said. "So this is . . . You think it's real? It's not some sort of hoax?"

"I don't know this Dr. Vornholt," I said.

"No one knows him," said Graham. "I've been calling in favors all morning, and nobody has any idea who he is."

"Then how—"

"Did he get access to the equipment he'd need to pick up this signal? No idea. I think we may be dealing with someone publishing under a fake name."

"That feels like a vote in favor of 'hoax.'" I frowned. "But I've heard that signal before. I . . . I *understood* it. How could I understand it if it was a hoax?"

For a moment, Graham didn't say anything, and I knew we were both thinking the same thing. I could understand it if there was nothing to understand, if the part of my mind which insisted I was an alien was feeding me false data. My understanding of the signal was both the lady and the tiger, because either it proved, absolutely, that I was truly alien, or it proved—with the same certainty—that I had never been an alien at all.

"We know the signal was intercepted by the Portland Observatory," said Graham. "We could go there and ask to speak with Dr. Vornholt."

"I thought you said you couldn't find him."

"I can't. No one can. Which makes me think the 'fake name' theory is probably the right one." Graham smiled, half-encouraging and half-strained, and the absence of artificial cheer was probably the best part of his expression. "What do you say? Want to go to Stephen King country and see if we can find the person who talks to aliens?"

I didn't have to think. "Yes," I said. "I have some vacation time. I'll make this work. Just . . . come home, okay?"

Graham's smile slowly dissolved into a cautious frown. "You got a bad feeling?"

"I want you to stay near me until this is over. Whatever it is."

Whatever it was, it was going to get worse before it got better . . . and "better" was still very much in the eye of the beholder.

"Come home," I repeated.

Graham hesitated before he nodded.

"All right," he said. "I'll be right there."

4

SEATTLE, WASHINGTON: JULY 19, 2031
NINETEEN DAYS PRE-INVASION

1.

The airport arrivals gate was surprisingly empty. According to Mandy and her hawkish passion for the news, air travel had dropped almost thirty percent since the alien signal was intercepted. People had already started canceling nonessential travel, saying they'd changed their plans, when they'd really stopped wanting to leave the ground.

The alien signal had been ripped apart and put back together by every research institute and think tank in the world, with at least half openly releasing their findings to the public, and some members of the remaining half finding ways to quietly leak their own findings. So far, no one had managed to discredit the thing. If anything, they were proving it more and more conclusively, finding tiny artifacts that spoke to an utterly inhuman method of constructing and compressing the signal.

People were still hoping the alien visitors would be coming in peace, but they were keeping their feet on the ground until they knew one way or another. Fear is a powerful motivator when it comes to that sort of thing.

Passengers began trickling through the gate. I bounced up onto my toes, earning a sour look from the woman next to me, and waved wildly at a short, disheveled man in khakis. Graham paused, face blank, before slowly grinning and trotting toward me. Not running—running in an airport is a good way to attract the attention of the TSA, and no one enjoys that—but moving fast, wasting no time.

He wrapped his arms around my waist and lifted me off the ground. I squeaked. Then he was kissing me, whiskers rough against my skin, and for a moment I focused on that to the exclusion of anything else. Graham was here. I was here. The world was changing, but it had not yet changed enough to make a moment like this one impossible, no matter how improbable it might one day seem.

The kiss ended. Graham grinned, close enough that I could see the wrinkles at the corners of his eyes. I reached out and pressed the tip of one finger against the web of lines.

"When did we get so *old*?" I asked.

He laughed and put me down. "That's what you ask? Not 'How was your flight' or 'Did you want to grab something to eat before we go back through security,' but 'When did we get so old'? Are you having some kind of existential crisis on me here?"

"I just missed you," I said. He removed one arm from my waist, letting me pull my suitcase with my free hand while I used the other to guide him toward the baggage claim. "And this was your idea."

"Yes, when I thought I could get a connecting flight," he said, doing his best to sound pitiful. "I didn't expect to need to change airlines. I'm doing airport security twice in one day. You should feel sorry for me."

"I always feel sorry for you," I said. "You are a sad, sad example of a human being."

"I know." He kissed my temple. "I don't know what I did to deserve your tolerance, but I'm thankful every day that I can manage to keep it up."

I snorted. We kept walking.

The baggage carousel was another demonstration of just how much people were curtailing their flight plans. Only about half the normal allotment of bags came tumbling down the belt, and many of those were overstuffed beyond all logical limits, like their owners were planning to stay awhile. Graham squeezed my fingers reassuringly until his own battered brown suitcase appeared. Then he let me go, retrieved it, and dragged it to the nearest trash can, where he began stripping off the identifying tags that might send it right back to Seattle if he checked it as-is.

"There were no issues getting away from the survey?" I asked, for what felt like the eightieth time. It was probably closer to the eighteenth: it was too many, no matter how I sliced it.

I was nervous. We were going to Maine, one step closer to finding out whether my entire life had been one long lie, and I was nervous.

"None," Graham assured me patiently. He didn't sound bothered. Then again, he'd had plenty of practice calming me down when I decided to get worked up about something.

We met in the same class, but we got to know each other because we had a friend in common—Carlos, who had long since gone off to wherever it is college friends go when you're not in college anymore; having a life without needing to structure it around class schedules and the need to win another round of Trivial Pursuit: The Tequila Edition. Carlos had been infamous for his mixers, which were somewhere between a *Star Trek* convention and a bacchanal.

Graham, who had been going by another name then, had been seated at my table for a game of Truth or Dare. We'd both been asked to reveal one truth about ourselves that people frequently doubted.

"I'm an alien," I'd said, and people had cheered, because why the hell not? We were in college, we were open-minded scientists in training, and if I wanted to come from space, I could damn well come from space.

"I'm a man," Graham had said, and people had laughed, because he was still on his parents' insurance, and they hadn't been paying for his hormone replacement therapy yet, and he hadn't wanted to cut off his hair until he was really starting his transition. So they'd looked at him, these geniuses in waiting, these future architects of the world, and they'd seen a woman with identity issues instead of the man he was, and they laughed.

But they hadn't laughed at me, because me claiming to be an alien who looked like their idea of a woman was more reasonable to them than Graham claiming to be a man who looked like their idea of a woman. They knew what the world was supposed to be shaped like. Somehow I, with my utter rejection of humanity, fit the mold better than Graham did for rejecting what they wanted him to be.

He'd been upset. I'd been enraged. I hadn't been shy about letting them know, either, ripping them up one side and down the other for being disrespectful assholes who didn't deserve to be allowed to have nice things or make good discoveries or survive the inevitable invasion of their world. Graham had been quiet at first, cheeks red and hands shaking, but by the time I'd finished yelling, he'd been grinning, relaxed, and even amused as he watched the show.

We'd walked out of that party together, and made out sloppy and happily drunk behind my dorm before going our separate ways, promising to try this again when we were sober. We had, and then we'd tried again to be sure we'd enjoyed it, and by the time we'd gotten around to try number three, we'd been pretty comfortable with the whole idea. We didn't start dating right away—that had taken another year and a half, until Graham had started HRT and felt comfortable enough in his own skin to feel up to a full-time girlfriend—but we'd been together, one way or another, ever since.

The line at the airline check-in counter was short enough that I was relaxed when we started toward security, now free of our suitcases. We each had a carry-on bag, while I also had a purse stuffed with snacks, anti-nausea medication, and external batteries. Planes are supposedly equipped with outlets these days, but they're broken about half the time, and even when they're not, there's always the risk of running into a seatmate who needs to take up more than their share of the plugs for "just a moment," which always turns into the entire flight.

We came around the corner. The security line came into view. I stopped dead, astonished by the scope of it.

"It wasn't like this in Florida," said Graham, sounding as bemused as I felt.

It seemed impossible for the line to be this long, snaking past three visible checkpoints and extending down the length of the terminal, unless it hadn't moved since the airport opened. There weren't enough people flying to have created this sort of logjam. Even the TSA PreCheck line, normally a haven for businessmen and frequent travelers, was long enough to reach the end of the temporary corral constructed from rope lines and moveable barriers.

There were police everywhere I looked. Some were armed. Others were being towed along by serious-looking canines, the dogs with their noses pressed to the airport floor, the handlers with dour expressions on their faces.

"Something's wrong," I said.

"It's all right," said Graham. He slipped his hand back into mine, squeezing my fingers. I flashed him a grateful smile. He smiled back, looking only slightly strained, as we made for the PreCheck line. It was a frivolous expenditure on our part, and I don't care for what it represents—Mandy calls the whole system yet another punishment for the poor, and she's not wrong—but Graham signed up the second it became an option, choosing to pay a fee and submit to a background check rather than continue the humiliating, sometimes dangerous practice of going through normal security lines while trans.

PreCheck meant metal detectors and civility rather than body scans and hostility. PreCheck meant less of a chance of a pat-down, or of his male agent asking loudly whether he wouldn't prefer a woman. In short, PreCheck was a way to pay for dignity, and Graham had been . . . not happy, exactly, to do it, but relieved when his Known Traveler Number came through.

When I fly, I'm almost always flying *with* Graham, or on my way to meet him and fly somewhere else. Signing up for the service, borderline predatory as it is, only made sense. And normally, it meant we could cut our airport arrivals a little closer, since there was never as much of a line. Not so, today.

One of the canine units cruised by, ears swiveling toward the slightest sound. Graham tightened his grip on my hand. We kept walking.

"Excuse me."

The voice was loud, assertive, and authoritarian: it was the voice of someone who didn't expect to be ignored. Graham and looked behind us. The agent attached to the canine unit was eyeing us. So was the canine unit. It looked as suspicious as I think it's possible for a dog to look, muzzle up, eyes alert, ears slicked back against its head.

"Yes, officer?" I said, letting go of Graham to turn.

"I need you to come with me."

It took everything I had not to turn to Graham in terror. I'd been hoping for some confirmation of whether these were my people, finally coming to collect me after leaving me adrift in a sea of humans for thirty years. This wasn't how I'd wanted to receive it.

"Is there a problem, officer?" asked Graham, mirroring my turn. We couldn't hold hands anymore, thanks to our carry-ons, but I still felt better knowing that he was with me, that he would *be* with me no matter what.

"Routine security screening," said the officer. "This young lady has been randomly selected. You can continue."

"Is it okay if I don't?" Graham leaned forward and whispered, almost conspiratorially, "That line is *incredibly* long, and I know my girlfriend will pass whatever screening you're planning to perform with flying colors. If I can come with her, maybe we can still catch our plane."

"We both have PreCheck," I added, possibly nonsensically.

The officer frowned before nodding and saying, "We're allowed to screen as many passengers as we feel necessary to preserve the safety of this airport. Come with me, please."

It felt like the whole line turned to stare at us as we followed the security officer, and the still-serious dog, away. I squared my shoulders and kept my chin up, reminding myself that I would never see any of these people again. None of them mattered. None of them were ever going to have the opportunity to matter.

I just had to get to Maine.

2.

The officer showed us to a small, square room equipped with its own miniature X-ray belt. The door swung shut behind us with an ominous "click." Graham and I exchanged a look.

"I would check to see if it just locked itself, but I don't think I need to, and I'm pretty sure we're on camera," he said. "If the sound 'accidentally' cut out, it would look like I was trying to escape."

"So let's not do that," I agreed. The TSA has improved since its inception, but they're still a government agency, and they have more power to disappear people than I like to think about. If we pissed them off or drew too much attention to ourselves, missing our flight would be the least of our worries.

This was what happened after a single confirmed alien signal was reported to the public. What would happen when the ships arrived? When the invasion began? There was no coming in peace, not when people were so eager to give in to fear. There was coming in aggression, or there was staying a safe distance away, abandoning me and the others like me to whatever this planet had in store for traitors.

A door on the far side of the room swung open. Three more guards stepped through. One of them had another canine unit, holding tight to its harness as it strained to reach me. Unlike the first canine unit, which had been a standard German shepherd, assistant to police and security forces everywhere, this one was a bloodhound, face framed by droopy ears and droopier skin, eyes sad among concealing folds. There was nothing sad about its nose, which twitched as it tested the air. It kept its focus on me.

The handler wasn't moving fast enough for the dog. "Baroooo!" announced the bloodhound, voice too large for this small space. "Baroooooooo!"

"I didn't think they were supposed to bark when they were working," I said, swallowing the urge to take a step back, to put some distance between myself and the eager beast.

I've never been much of a dog person. They don't care for me, and I don't care for them, and as long as we give each other a wide berth, everything's fine. Something about the way I smell upsets them. That was probably what was happening now, why the bloodhound looked ready to pull its handler clean off his feet in order to get to me.

The guard in the middle held up her tablet, swiped her finger across the screen, and asked, "Are you Anastasia Miller and Graham Fordham?"

"Yes," I said.

"Yes," said Graham. Neither of us offered any more information. That was never a good idea when dealing with law enforcement of any kind.

"I see here that your final destination is Portland, Maine. Is this correct?" The question was mild, but when she looked up to study our faces, her eyes were sharp. "What is your business in Maine?"

"We're visiting the observatory that captured the alien signal," said Graham. "I'm a scientist, I work in novel fields, and we'd like to see if we can get access to the raw data feed."

"I see," said the guard. "Is there a reason this data feed can't be provided to you here, in Seattle?"

"Data changes when it's compressed or re-expanded. There may be no fidelity loss within the signal, but it's possible there's something I can't find unless I study the original." Graham smiled, trying to look easy in his own skin, like this sort of thing didn't bother him in the slightest. "It's like an art historian wanting to go to France to see the Mona Lisa. Yes, she's been scanned and photographed more than any other painting in the world, but there are things that can only be discovered by sitting down with the lady and really getting to know her."

"I see," said the guard. She tapped her tablet surface. "Miss Miller? Why are you accompanying Mr. Fordham? I don't see anything here about your having a background in data analysis. Or art history." There was a cruel lilt to her last two words, like she was mocking not just the analogy but Graham himself.

So much for the pretense that we needed to carry our IDs for easy review while in the airport. We'd shown them at the check-in desk, and that had been enough for the airport security systems to know who we were. Security cameras, complete with facial recognition and gait analysis, had been following us ever since. The TSA knew exactly who we were, and wouldn't be losing track of us until we exited the airport at our final destination . . . if even then. It would be easy to yield to paranoia, picturing a world where we were tracked all the time, no matter what we were doing.

Maybe we were witnessing the latest steps toward exactly that. Privacy has been dying since I was a child, and the alien signal—the potential for invasion—could be the excuse the government needed to clamp down hard and never let go.

"You know who I am," I said, not making any effort to keep the weariness out of my tone. "You know why I'm going."

"Anastasia Miller, age thirty-five, master's degree in computer science, currently employed as a second-tier customer service technician for a local internet provider—really?" For the first time, the guard looked faintly bemused. "Why bother with an advanced degree if you were going to take two steps past entry level and stop?"

"I put down roots," I said. My mother had asked me the same question, on one of the rare occasions when my mother had asked me a question at all. We had fallen out of the habit of questioning each other, somewhere between my disappearance and my insistence that I was my own person and that person was not a human being.

"I see." The guard lowered her tablet. "What is your interest in the alien signal?"

I could feel Graham watching me. Not hoping I would keep my mouth shut—he'd never asked me to lie about my convictions, even as he'd asked me to please tell him if I ever decided I wanted to be human again, to be helped through whatever made me abandon my humanity as a bad dream—but waiting to hear what I was going to say, and how much trouble I was going to get us into.

Smiling my biggest, sweetest smile, I said, "Well, I'm from Mars, see, and I wanted to listen to the signal without any Earth tech in the way, so I could figure out if it was our neighbors, the Jovians, trying to make first contact before we could."

The guard frowned. "The Jovians would be . . . ?"

"Oh, they're from Jupiter. They're sort of big jellyfish with tendrils a mile long and *terrible* breath." I fanned the air exaggeratedly. "You don't want to make first contact with *them*. They're big jerks."

"Is there a problem?" asked Graham. "I didn't think flying while alien was against the law. Since up until a week ago, most people thought aliens didn't exist."

"Anastasia Miller, age thirty-five," said the guard again, more disgusted this time. "According to our files, you have been claiming to be extraterrestrial in origin since you were three years old. That's rather unusual for a child, don't you think?"

"Not really," I said. "Children don't distinguish fantasy from reality the way adults do. I've known children who said they were monsters, that they were ghosts wearing new skins, that they were going to devour everyone they loved—and those are the well-adjusted ones. For a child to say 'I'm an alien' is perfectly normal."

"What about for an adult?"

"I can't speak for everyone," I said, with a shrug. "In my case, I'm pretty stubborn. The more people told me I couldn't be an alien, the more I insisted, and eventually it just stuck." Eventually, it had been picked up by the tabloids and the gossip blogs looking to follow up on the mystery of the disappearing, reappearing child. Various alien-encounter groups had invited me to appear before them as a guest, starting literally on the day I'd turned eighteen and been able to legally insist on receiving my own mail.

I wasn't sure whether my visibility made me a better scout or a worse one. It definitely made me worse at infiltration, since there had never been a hope in hell that I'd be able to stay hidden. But I kept smiling politely at the guards, while the bloodhound continued to strain toward me, nose quivering, bloodshot eyes locked on my body.

"Barooo," it said again, sounding as annoyed as was possible for a dog. It had found what it wanted, and it wasn't being allowed to catch it, or being told what a good hound it was for doing the spotting.

I was okay with that, since what it wanted was me, and I didn't know why, or what it would do if it got me. My hands were tingling, a clear response to stress. Was this how I found out for sure I wasn't human? In an airport security room, with a trained dog trying to—

Wait. "What does that dog *do?*" I asked, suddenly frowning. "Is it an alien-sniffing dog? Do you have an alien-sniffing dog? That doesn't make sense. Nobody even knows what the aliens would look like. How would we know what the aliens *smell* like? I think this is a stunt. I think you're trying to . . . I don't know what you're trying to do, but you're trying to do it to us, right now." I stopped smiling and started glaring.

"Take him out of here," snapped the guard. The bloodhound's handler wrestled the dog back under control before dragging him back out the door. The third guard, the one with neither tablet nor dog, remained where he was, standing at the soft slouch that seems to serve the TSA as attention.

The guard with the tablet returned her gaze to me and Graham. "Were you aware that there are, presently, fifteen thousand American citizens who claim to come from another planet?"

"No," I admitted. Given the size of the US population, the number seemed refreshingly low, like it could also be the number of ambidextrous natural redheads with heterochromia and lactose intolerance. If I were the government, I wouldn't have been worried about the resident extraterrestrials at all. I would have been worried about the ones now coming in my direction.

"Further, were you aware that one-third of those individuals regularly utilize air travel services?"

"Everyone takes a plane to get where they need to go, when where they need to go is far away," I said.

The guard's eyes narrowed. "Not everyone claims to be extraterrestrial in origin."

"Wait," said Graham. "Are you saying this is all . . . what, the TSA equivalent of an improv show? You use a trained dog to make us think you can pick up something strange about us, and then you try to get us to admit to doing something wrong? We're about to do something wrong. We're about to miss our flight."

The guard's smile was arctic. "I'm not sure I see where that's my problem, sir. I'm just a public servant, trying to do my job."

"I would say this was a little farfetched, if it weren't happening to me and my girlfriend right now in real time."

"Life is frequently a little farfetched," said the guard. She looked at me. "Mars, huh? How come that isn't in your file?"

"I'm shy." Shy, and capable of lying. I didn't know the name of my home planet, if I could even be said to *have* a home planet: people don't usually say they're from wherever their ancestors lived, they say they're from where they were born. Well, by that standard, I was as American as anyone. I was born, I died, and I was born again, all in the forests of Washington State. Maybe my genetic material was from outer space, but everything that made me Stasia Miller was from Earth. I wasn't human. That didn't mean I didn't belong here.

The contradiction was painful if I thought about it too much. There were probably people who would be happy to tell me how wrong I was, how delusional it was to assume the place where I was raised was the place where I belonged. They were probably the same people who insisted that naming football teams after racial slurs was "honoring" the people they'd killed and imprisoned in order to take the land the stadium was built on. The question of who's being colonized and who's doing the colonizing has always been a societal one. Individuals can stand to either side of the divide.

Graham looked flatly at the guard. I did my best to do the same, standing my ground and not letting my discomfort show. She tapped her tablet a few more times, not making eye contact with either of us. Maybe she thought that whatever red flags were on our files were catching.

Given that Graham had never claimed to be from another planet, maybe they were.

"If you will put your possessions on the belt, I'll have one of my agents escort you to your plane," said the guard brusquely. "Boarding is about to begin. We'll get you on with the priority group."

"Thank you," said Graham.

"Are we going to get this when we fly home, too?" I asked.

The guard finally looked up, finally met my eyes. She looked haunted, like something had removed all the light from inside of her, leaving her empty and afraid.

"You're going to get this every time you fly for the rest of your life," she said. "We're not alone anymore. Until we can know for sure that you're one of *us*, and not one of *them*, you're going to get this. Because we don't know what they look like. We don't know where they come from. And we don't know what they want." Her smile was abrupt and startling in its ferocity.

"Have a nice flight," she said, and turned and left the room, leaving us alone with the third guard, who moved to start the X-ray belt. Graham and I exchanged a look before we put our bags down. We wanted to object. We wanted to argue. We needed to fly.

The plane wasn't going to wait for us, and after this—after all of this—I didn't want to count on being able to catch a later flight. The invasion might not even have time to start. More and more, I was starting to feel like humanity was going to tear itself apart without our help.

3.

The drink service was finished, and most of the plane had settled down to read or nap or drink their tiny glasses of overpriced scotch. The seat-back entertainment centers were on all around us. About half of them were playing movies, recent blockbuster fare edited for content to make them safe for peeping tots who might be seated in the next row over. The other half . . .

"All these people are watching the news," I said quietly, bending my head so that I was talking only to Graham and not to the people around us. The ongoing roar of the airplane's engines made privacy easier to find, even as I couldn't shake the conviction that we were still being watched. "Did something happen?"

"I don't know," he said, voice pitched equally low. "Do you want me to turn it on?"

It wasn't going to be safe to be on an airplane once our ships arrived: I knew that, with that quiet conviction that was always with me, the conviction from which all the facts and feelings about my species of origin arose. When we took the skies, we weren't going to share them anymore, and we weren't going to be checking passenger lists for our implanted scouts. My own people would strike me down as easily as they would slaughter every human in this floating metal box, and they wouldn't grieve for me after it was done, because a few deaths were the cost of doing business on a galactic scale.

More, maybe, because if I was foolish enough to get on a plane when the signal got louder and the dreams got stronger and the itching under my skin got harder to endure, I would be too removed from my roots to deserve a shot at surviving the invasion. I didn't know what shape the slapping-down would take, any more than I knew what the ships would look like when they arrived, but I knew that the time for this sort of travel was drawing to a close. It was one of the reasons I'd insisted we go right away, rather than giving Graham time to settle in and rest after his most recent trip.

The other reasons were more selfish: I was scared. The invasion was coming, and my people were coming with it, my wonderful, terrible people, the root of everything I was, the reason I was on this planet. They had sent me here with only the most rudimentary awareness of my nature, and now, finally, they were going to be where I could ask them questions. I felt like a child being promised access to the real Santa Claus, or a religious official getting the opportunity to talk to God. Was my lack of specific knowledge a flaw in my training or a side effect of my having taken the form of a human so young, with a mind too unformed to retain fine details? Or was this all by design?

What good would it do for an invasion to begin with untrained, unprepared scouts stumbling through enemy territory, announcing themselves at every opportunity? I didn't understand. That, more than anything else I had ever encountered, had me doing what should have been unthinkable, and questioning myself. What if I was wrong? What if I had *been* wrong for my entire life? What if I wasn't an alien, just a kidnapped little girl who had been so traumatized by whatever had happened to her that she had shut it all out, refusing to let it color her daily existence?

I might not be an alien at all. Just one more human being in denial, meat for the mill that was now sailing, implacable and slow, through the vastness of space.

"No," I said, and put my head down against his shoulder. "Leave it off, or put your headphones in if you want to watch. I don't want to know."

"You're going to find out sooner or later."

"I know. That's why I don't want to know here or now. I can wait until it matters, and let it happen then. Right now . . . it can't change anything. The FAA hasn't grounded the planes or demanded we turn back. There aren't any ships in the sky. Humanity is still in charge here. For now."

I couldn't see Graham's face, but I felt him shift in his seat, twisting to look down at me. The plane was a little more than half full—an artifact of the undersold flights taking off from airports everywhere, I was sure, although that endless, twisting security line might have had something to do with it. Half of our fellow passengers might still be back in Seattle, trapped in the Byzantine web of supposed safety, unable to move either forward or back until the TSA decided they weren't a threat.

"You're really worried," he said. "What are you afraid of?"

"Nothing." I closed my eyes. "Everything. What people are going to do when the aliens get here. What the aliens are going to do when they get here."

He stroked my hair. "You've been here for years. You haven't done anything that bad."

"I jaywalk sometimes." I wanted to tell him about the way people viewed crowds: how as long as less than seventeen percent of the members of a group were female, the men wouldn't be bothered by them, but as soon as they hit eighteen percent—or, heaven help us, more than that—they became a problem. How people thought of a crowd that was one-third women as female-dominated, how a group that was one-third Black was thought of as anti-white, and so on, and so on. Everyone in the world is the product of their local culture, the good parts and the bad parts at the same time, and we can't get away from it.

The culture I grew up with said being an alien invader was a bad thing, and my choices were going to be turning my back on the people who made me or betraying the human race. That was a little worse than jaywalking. That was a little more difficult to see as simple.

Graham let me be an alien because I was an alien when we met, and because, as he'd said, I had never done anything to hurt anyone. I didn't even squash spiders. I didn't *like* very many people, but my misanthropy was the harmless kind, too gentle and reserved to actually cause a problem. I could hate the world as much as I wanted. I was never going to set the thing on fire.

That was going to change soon. I could feel it in my bones, in the strange hum of my blood, which seemed to be getting louder day by day. I left my head on his shoulder, and I left my eyes closed. I knew, without being able to articulate the question, that the time for moments like this was coming to an end. Soon enough, everything was going to change. Whether it changed for the better—whether it was possible for it to change for the better—was anybody's guess. I didn't think so, though. I was pretty sure that, as far as the people of Earth were concerned, things were about to get much, much worse.

4.

The forest again: always the forest. There was a time when I could dream of other things, of shoes and ships and ceiling wax, of cabbages and kings . . . but that time was in the past, covered by a mist of pollen that smelled like honey, sweet enough to lure in almost everything. It was a little shocking to open my eyes and find myself standing there: I hadn't been sure I could reach the forest when I was on an airplane, hurtling through the sky at such great speeds that even the clouds couldn't keep up.

It was hard to tell whether this was a vote in favor of the forest being real, or a piece of proof that it was all a figment of my imagination, a construct I had put together to protect myself from whatever it was out there that I imagined was a threat to me. It was also hard to care. I was walking in the shadow of the trees. I was safe.

The nagging itch at the crook of my left arm distracted me from the study of the rippling colors in the bark around me. I scratched at it idly as I walked, looking for the shallow bowl of flowers. They could tell me what to do. The flowers never left the forest, and they always knew what to do.

"H-hello?"

I whipped around, startled, and found myself facing a man around my age. His skin was darker than mine, brown a few shades deeper than his eyes, and his hair was black and straight, flopping down over his forehead. There was a bandage taped to his right cheek, shockingly, almost obscenely white. He stared at me. I returned the favor.

"You can't be here," he said.

"I was going to tell you the same thing," I countered. I took a step back, still scratching the interior of my left elbow. "This is my forest."

In the distance, a sound like dragonfly wings rattling together, and the thick, oddly spiced scent of honey. The man cocked his head, clearly listening to the sound. I frowned, wary to the last.

"It's not yours," he said finally. "It's not mine, either. It's *theirs*."

There was a wealth of information packed into that word, possessiveness and familiarity and fear and loathing and yes, hope. Hope that soon, all of this would start making sense, and we wouldn't be babes in the woods anymore, wandering endlessly, never knowing where any of this was going to end. The forest would end it all.

I looked at him more carefully. He was a stranger. He could have been any man on the street, dressed in his windbreaker and blue jeans. He could have been my brother, differences in complexion and bone structure aside. Something about him screamed "family" to me, screamed it all the way down my spine, like electricity seeking a grounding wire.

From the way he was looking at me, he was feeling something similar. Then his gaze shifted, going to the crook of my elbow, and his eyes widened, more like an owl's than a person's.

"You're like me," he breathed.

Confused, I looked down. My constant scratching had broken through the skin, tearing it until I should have bled. There was no blood. Instead, a hairline cluster of green, fibrous vines showed through, curled at the ends, like the wires on a scrubbing brush. I stared at them. They didn't disappear. Cautiously, I reached down and tugged on the longest one.

The pain was immediate and electric, racing through a series of connections that felt like a spider web underneath my skin. I let go of the tendril, and the pain receded.

"You can't pluck them," said the stranger. "If you try, it hurts. Don't worry, though. They'll get less tender with time."

I turned my attention from the tendril to him. "What do you mean?"

"Look," he said. Reaching up, he began to carefully peel away the bandage, talking as he did. "My name's Jeff. I knew I wasn't the only one, but you're all so far away, you were always just voices in the vines. I never thought I'd get to meet one of you. Not before the invasion started. Where do you live?"

"Washington," I said, lips numb. There were hints of darker green behind the bandage, like whatever he was about to show me wasn't . . . human. Like the essential humanity we had been hiding behind for so long was finally getting ready to fall away and reveal our true forms, whatever those might be.

I wasn't ready. I might never be ready. I had always been an alien, but I had been a human at the same time, able to walk through the world without drawing attention to myself.

"State or DC?"

"State." I didn't look away. I couldn't look away. This wasn't the time to start running: not if I ever wanted to stop again. "We're on our way to Maine."

"We?" He paused in the process of peeling down the bandage. "Is there another of us with you? Will they be joining us?"

He sounded so hopeful, so *lonely*, that I wanted to lie. Instead, I shook my head and said, "He's human. He wants to hear the signal in its raw form. To talk to the scientist who intercepted it. We're trying to figure out . . ." I stopped, letting the words taper off.

The stranger smirked. "Trying to figure out whether it's real, huh? Well, don't worry. You'll know soon enough."

He yanked the bandage away.

I sat upright with a gasp, opening my eyes on the cabin of the plane, and on Graham looking at me with open concern.

"Bad dream?" he asked.

I grabbed the inside of my elbow with the opposite hand, feeling the unbroken, still-human skin there, and sagged in relief.

"Bad dream," I agreed.

Under my hand, my elbow began to itch again.

5

PORTLAND, MAINE: JULY 20, 2031
EIGHTEEN DAYS PRE-INVASION

1.

We landed after local midnight, collecting our bags from the carousel and following the signs to the taxi station. A man who looked as weary as I felt was there to help us load our suitcases into the trunk of his black town car. Graham rattled off the address of our hotel as we slid into the backseat. The driver nodded, and that was it: we were free from the orbit of the airport, pulling away without interference from the security guards we had seen stationed at unnervingly regular intervals throughout the terminal.

Portland looked like any other city in the dark. We drove past homes and businesses, most with their lights turned low or entirely off, letting the night sky shine through. And what a sky it was. It was like climbing up Mt. Rainier, far from the city light pollution, and looking out across the endless sea of stars. I barely managed to fight the urge to roll down the window and stick my head out of the car, like a dog overjoyed by the idea of going for a ride. I wanted to see those stars. I wanted to see where the signal, *my* signal, was coming from.

I wanted a distraction from the itch that still burrowed in the crook of my left elbow, roiling and stinging and catching my attention every few seconds, whether I wanted it to or not. It hurt. Not constantly, but often enough that I could never quite forget that it was there, or allow it to fade away.

The face of the man in the forest . . . I couldn't quite remember what I'd seen, but I knew it wasn't anything that could ever pass for human, not once he took the bandage away. Jeff. His name was Jeff. It was a silly name for an alien invader, simple and ordinary and *human*.

I snorted soft amusement, earning myself a curious, sleepy glance from Graham. Was "Anastasia" any better? We had picked up our names when we picked up our forms, and this part of the planet didn't really like it when people refused the names their parents had given them. It had taken Graham almost two years to get his parents to stop calling him by his birth name, and his change had come with a physical transformation. Mine hadn't.

Not yet. If Jeff was anything to go by, or if the itch at my elbow signified what I'd dreamt, it was coming.

"You okay?" asked Graham.

I turned to offer him the warmest smile I could muster. It wasn't as easy as I wanted it to be. I was tired, and scared, and I itched. "Just woolgathering," I said. "We're going to the observatory in the morning, right?"

"As soon as we're ready to face the world." Graham grimaced. "I couldn't get us an appointment with Dr. Vornholt, since he doesn't seem to exist. But if we show up, we may be able to track him down."

And once we had tracked him down, he would be able to play the signal for us, without filtering or distortion. That was our goal: to hear the aliens loud and clear and unencumbered, to find out whether this was a hoax or a uniquely distorted episode of *The Brady Bunch* somehow bouncing back to us off of a distant satellite. That was what Graham wanted, anyway. I didn't need to hear the clean signal to know that it was real. I knew that. I needed to know what it *meant*—and how close the people who'd sent it were. Because it felt like they were almost here. Hearing the signal without distortions would give me a clearer idea of what to expect. I knew it.

This—the strange, not entirely voluntary game I'd been playing since I was three years old—was finally coming to an end, and when it got there, I was going to find out where my loyalties really were. I was going to find out what was under my own skin. Again, my memory shied away from whatever it was I had seen when Jeff had revealed himself to me. I wasn't ready for it yet. Maybe I was never going to be ready.

"This is one hell of a way to run an invasion," I muttered.

Graham shifted next to me, his shoulder brushing against mine. "What was that?" he asked.

"Nothing," I said, and I meant it. There was nothing I wanted to say, because I didn't know how to say it. Not with the driver right there, capable of listening to every word we said. Not when my own thoughts were in so much disarray. I needed to get more sleep than I'd been able to manage on the plane. I needed to go back to the forest and make it all the way to the sweet, subtle embrace of the dragonfly flowers.

I could ask them what I'd seen on Jeff's face, what was growing under my own skin, and maybe they would answer me. Maybe they would understand the importance of telling me what was going on. I couldn't do my part for the invasion—whatever that part was supposed to be—if I was busy being scared out of my mind.

Graham's hand settled on my knee. "Hey," he said. "Look at me."

I looked at him.

He was a wraith in the pale glow through the car windows, a figure of smoke and shadows. The short, bristling hairs on his cheeks glowed almost silver where the light hit them, standing out from his skin in a way they never did when the sun was up. He smiled at me, the expression sketched more in motion than in visible skin.

"It's going to be okay," he said. "We're going to figure this out together, and everything's going to be fine."

I didn't believe him. I smiled back anyway. Sometimes that's the only thing you can do: just look at the future racing toward you, and smile, and hope it doesn't hurt when it arrives.

2.

Steam billowed around me as I showered, filling the bathroom with a hot cloud of vanilla-scented moisture. I turned my face into the spray, letting it wash over me, wiping the last of my long night's sleep away. The itching in my elbow retreated in the face of the hot water, wrapping itself tight around my bones. It would be back. I could feel it lurking, waiting for the opportunity to rise and try again.

I had slept soundly once we were finally in our own room, where it was safe to strip and collapse into the mattress, feeling the plastic anti-bedbug liner crinkle under my body as I buried my face in the pillow. The aches in my back and hip from a night of sprawling perfectly still, Graham pressed against me like a personal space heater, were proof of that.

But the dreams had never come. No alien forest for me, perfect trees beneath an unseeable sky; no comforting embrace of impossible flowers with their rippling, rattling petals. If I'd dreamed at all, I didn't remember it, and as the shower blasted away the last of the night's cobwebs, I had to wonder why not. The forest wasn't *always* there, but when I needed it . . .

When I needed it, it came. It had come on the plane, and—

"Stasia?" Graham sounded groggy. I had claimed first shower, and we'd agreed to take turns, not wanting to get distracted with biological needs when we had so much to get done today. "Honey, your phone's blowing up. Are you *sure* you told work that you were going to be gone for a few days?"

"What?" I turned the water off, having long since rinsed the last of the shampoo out of my hair, and pulled the shower curtain aside. Graham was standing there in his boxer shorts, the scars that ran beneath his pectoral muscles flushing red in the heat.

"Your phone," he said. "It's on the bed. Someone's been texting you for the last ten minutes."

It wasn't even nine in the morning yet. That made it not quite six in Washington: if either Lucas or Mandy was texting me, the house was probably on fire. Mom wouldn't text, she'd call, and the odds were good that she wouldn't do either. That left a remarkably short list of people who had my number and had some reason to contact me. Not good.

"Huh," I said, and stepped out of the shower.

Graham grinned as he watched me grab my towel and roughly dry off. "See, if this were a different kind of trip, this is where I'd say I was lying to get you out into the open."

"If this were a different kind of trip, you would have been in the shower with me." I kissed his cheek, wrinkled my nose, and added, "Shave," before leaving the bathroom. His laughter chased me out.

My phone was on the bed, as he had told me it would be, and it was buzzing near-constantly as it lit up with incoming messages. I sat down, frowning at the number on the screen. It wasn't one I knew. I swiped my thumb across the glass, and felt my stomach plummet toward my feet, even as my lungs seemed to forget what they were supposed to do with the air they already held. Taking in more was unthinkable.

I know you're there, read the latest text.

Above it: *come on don't be like this do you know how hard it is to find us?????*

Above that: *Anastasia Miller. You're the only one I've found who made national news when you sprouted. Did you have to go and snatch a toddler? Well done. If the whole invasion is like you, we're screwed.*

Quickly, with shaking hands, I swiped my thumbs in the patterns the screen would recognize as words, asking, *Who is this?*

The reply came only a few seconds later, so fast that it almost seemed like it must have been keyed in before I could even ask.

You know who this is.

Then: *We met in the forest.*

Then: *I work w/computers. Finding your number was easy.*

Then: *You should have hid better.*

Slowly, I let my phone drop to my lap and stared at the wall, my mouth working although no sound came out. Jeff. Jeff, from the forest; Jeff, with the bandage on his cheek and the alien impossibility beneath it.

Jeff, who I'd never met when I was awake: who might as well have existed only in my dreams, until he somehow found my phone number and decided to exist when I was awake, too. Jeff, who walked under the same trees I did, who looked upward and strained to see the same elusive sky.

If Graham hadn't been the one to pull me out of the shower, I might have thought Jeff's texts were an illusion, something I'd invented to alleviate my concerns about going to the observatory. But they weren't. They were real, and Jeff was real, and this was it: the proof I'd been seeking for so long. I didn't need to hear the signal to know the aliens were real. I could simply point to the man who walked, impossibly, in my dreams, and say, "See? If he's real, I'm real, and if I'm real, you need to listen to me."

Not that it would prove anything to people who didn't want it to. Jeff could be someone I'd met online, or a fellow liar, or any one of a dozen things, none of which said "alien" to the average skeptic.

My phone buzzed again. I looked down.

You there?

He wasn't going to stop. If I was being honest, I couldn't blame him. I'd been trying to find proof of what I was for most of my life, and I had to assume he'd been doing the same, fighting to find his footing in a world that didn't want to allow for children to be snatched away and replaced by their own alien counterparts. We were the changelings of the science fiction age, and that made us both terrifying and untrue. Jeff had to be as frustrated as I was by the way he'd been forced to conceal himself, trapped in a world full of humans who never wanted to believe him.

Can't talk now, I typed hurriedly. *Going to observatory.*

To hear the signal?

Y.

Talk later???

Two words, and a lifetime of isolation, of longing, of the need to find someone who would understand. I didn't hesitate. I typed *Yes* and pressed Send before I could change my mind, then dropped the phone to the bed and stood, heading for my suitcase. It was time to get dressed. Graham never took long in the shower, and I didn't want to be the reason we were late.

I was dressed and pinning my hair into a tight, low-maintenance bun that wouldn't look rumpled as it dried when Graham emerged, back in his boxers, toweling his hair with one hand. He had taken the time to shave. The crisp, acerbic smell of aftershave followed him into the room, woody and somehow green, like he'd rubbed an entire herb garden on his cheeks. He raised his eyebrows as he looked at me.

"Who was that?"

"A friend from high school who saw I was in his time zone from Mandy's social media. She's about as discreet as a tank." The lie came smooth, easy, and embarrassing. Lying to Graham was the last thing I wanted to do. But Graham was human and Jeff was not, and while I wasn't ready to shift my loyalties that completely—I loved Graham, loved the reality of him, the smell of his skin when I woke up in the middle of the night, the feel of his stubble against my lips; I barely knew Jeff as anything more than a faintly terrifying figure in my dreams—I knew I needed to keep them apart. Just for now. Just long enough to learn more about what was about to happen.

"Oh, neat." Graham moved toward his own suitcase. "We going to get together before we head home?"

The casual way he said "we" made my heart clench in my chest, reminding me of my own traitorous thoughts. Once the invasion was here, there wasn't going to be a "we" anymore, not in the sense he meant it. There would be "us" and there would be "them," and the lines would be drawn on species, not on emotion.

Somehow, my smile still came when I called for it, curving my lips upward in apparent agreement. "If things work out," I said. "Wear the green shirt. It makes you look more like a professor and less like a grave robber."

"I'm not a professor."

"You're not a grave robber either, and we still get followed by security every time we're in a cemetery."

Graham laughed and kept laughing the whole time he was getting dressed, stealing little glances at me and chuckling to himself. I finished pinning my hair, still smiling, and hoped he couldn't see how frightened I was.

One of the nice things about not liking people very much: I've had plenty of practice at deflection. Make someone laugh and they'll stop wondering what it is you're really thinking about, what it is you're really doing. It works as well with the few people who I actually care about as it does with the rest of the world. Maybe better, even. People know when someone doesn't like them, and they're wary. They look for hidden double meanings. Sometimes they even find them.

It's easier to hate people when you like them, and on that paradox is the whole of human experience constructed.

"How do I look?"

I turned, considering Graham frankly. The green shirt did in fact give him a professorial air, at least when compared to the things he usually wore. His tie was brown, matching his jacket. He was wearing jeans, but that was all right: most of the scientists I know seem to consider jeans a uniform unto themselves, at least when they're outside the lab. It would have been a problem if I'd tried to pull the same thing—women don't get nearly as much leeway in this world as men, at least not where clothing is concerned—but on him, it worked. I smiled. If he noticed the expression was strained around the edges, he didn't say anything, and for that, I loved him more than ever.

"Great," I said.

"So do you." He pulled out his phone, tapping an app to summon our car, and nodded at the screen before putting it away. "Our ride will be here in five minutes."

I nodded. "Then let's move."

The hotel was old enough to be rustic and new enough to be modern, a combination that seemed to fit Portland as a whole, at least based on the narrow slice of it I'd seen so far. Everything was in good repair, clean enough to shine, and yet looked like it belonged in this world of endless trees. It was a lot like Washington, only older. The city's bones were closer to the surface.

We walked through the quiet, well-lit lobby, past businessmen getting ready to head out to whatever meeting had been deemed important enough to drag them away from their homes, past small family groups, the parents looking frayed while the sleepy children read or played with toys as if the world weren't in the process of changing forever. Graham leaned toward me.

"This place should be twice this full during the summer, and a lot of the guests would be staycationers," he murmured. "It's not just travel that's down."

I didn't bother asking how he knew that. His work takes him all over the country, since it's not like reptiles have the courtesy to all live in the same place for ease of study. Everyplace we've ever gone, Graham has had some little piece of local knowledge that makes it clear he's been there before. It's comforting, in a strange sort of way. I can't get lost when I have someone to show me the way. There's no replacement for familiarity.

Something about that thought snagged in my mind like a fishhook, tugging and tugging and refusing to be dislodged. I worried at it as I followed Graham out of the hotel and into the crisp morning air. It was early enough that the humidity hadn't fully descended to wrap the city in a warm, wet blanket yet, but it was coming: oh, yes, it was coming. And when it got here, we were all going to pay for doubting its power.

Our driver was a pleasantly smiling woman in overalls and earmuffs, which seemed idiosyncratic for the season, to say the absolute least, but was none of my business. We slid into the backseat, and Graham confirmed the address of our destination. I leaned against the window, staring at the buildings around us as they scrolled by, dense at first, then giving way to residential streets speckled with trees, and finally becoming nothing but forest.

Familiarity. It was something to do with familiarity. That was the key to everything. That was . . . that was . . .

We turned up a winding road that could have done with some serious repaving. I squeaked as I was jostled away from the window by the bouncing of our tires.

"Sorry," said the driver, in a cheerfully unrepentant tone. "We haven't been able to get this road repaved in years. Budget cuts and private land and you know how it is, right?"

"Right," said Graham, with a laugh, and the two of them began talking rapidly about the difficulty in getting fair distribution of civic and federal funds. I tuned them out, returning my attention to the window.

The trees were so different than the ones in Washington. I was used to oceans of evergreens, a living sea defined by needles and cones and the smell of sap. In contrast, these trees were tall, skeletal things, their bark white, or brown, or even gray, peeling and pitted and altogether strange, but familiar at the same time. All trees were the same trees, in the deeper pulse of root and wood and slow, constant growth. All trees carried the weight of the world.

There are trees everywhere in the universe, but mammals only show up on one planet in four, I thought, and made the conscious decision not to question myself. Answers were starting to bubble up from the topsoil of my heart, and I'd be happier if they came at their own pace. I was absolutely certain of *that*.

Graham and our driver were talking about the observatory now. She was chattering on about the architectural significance of the building, the fights that had been undertaken on a scientific and a civic level to make sure everything was constructed just *so* to maximize their efficiency and flexibility. There were little touches that would be invisible to the uninformed outsider: the planetarium off the cafeteria, too small for school groups but large enough to awe investors who were considering funding the study of the stars; the herb garden out back, which kept the kitchen smelling sweet and the astronomers and astrophysicists smiling. Most of them lived on-site during their shifts, preferring a small dorm and a thin mattress over the risk of missing something.

It sounded perfect. It sounded idyllic, even. Which probably meant there was something she wasn't telling us—and why shouldn't there be? I sat up straighter, looking narrow-eyed at the back of our driver's head. She was an independent cabbie, the sort of person who could be hired via app from a smartphone. Why did she know so much about the observatory, when it wasn't a major tourist destination and didn't hold that much appeal to anyone who wasn't like Graham, hardwired to see science as the answer to every question the world had to offer?

I frowned. Something about this wasn't right.

The road wound up the side of a sloping hill, until we broke out of the trees and into a wide, clear area. A vast concrete-and-chrome building dominated the clearing, topped with several retractable domes. About half the parking spots were filled. Our driver pulled up in front of the doors.

"Here you are, safe and sound," she said.

"Thanks," said Graham. He pulled out his phone and tapped the screen, transmitting the fare and tip—a fairly healthy one, probably inspired by their conversation.

I got out of the car. I walked to the curb. And I waited.

Graham got out a moment later, stepping onto the curb next to me. He followed my gaze to the car, which was idling, presumably while our driver prepared for her next call. "Something wrong?" he asked.

"I'm not sure," I said. "Go on inside. I'll be there in a second."

"I'll go let them know we're here to talk to Dr. Vornholt," he said, and kissed my cheek before heading for the doors.

I took a few steps backward, making it look like I was planning to follow him. And again, I waited. Waited while the car pulled away from the front of the observatory. Waited while it drove, not toward the driveway down to the main road, but behind the building, out of sight. It stopped there, unable to get out without passing me. I frowned, and considered following.

Graham was waiting. I'd ask him to use a different car service to get us home. Turning, I walked into the lobby, into the cool rush of sterile, treated air, kept steady at a temperature several degrees cooler than the outside.

"It gets hot as hell here in Maine," said a friendly voice. Graham and I looked toward it. A tall, beefy man in a white coat over a vintage *Steven Universe* T-shirt was bearing down on us, a wide smile on his round face. His hair was styled in short dreadlocks and pulled back in a ponytail that should have looked silly, yet somehow just looked practical, like all men ought to consider wearing their hair that way.

His smile helped. His teeth were remarkably white, and his skin was dark enough that the contrast drew and trapped the eye, making it hard to look away. I thought he was one of the most attractive men I'd ever seen, which made it a little confusing that he was hiding himself away at a small observatory in the middle of Maine and not starring in some half-baked network drama Tuesday nights at nine.

He seemed to catch my confusion, because the smile softened around the edges as he said, "I can see you've traveled a long way, and you're not reporters, which is nice. They've mostly tapered off by this point. There's nothing new for the news cycles here, and they didn't like the way we kept asking them for donations. To whom am I speaking?"

"Dr. Graham Fordham," said Graham, extending his hand with a bright smile of his own. The stranger clasped it, and the two of them formed a brief, perfect image out of a recruiting poster. Become a scientist, spend all your time surrounded by beautiful men as you unlock the secrets of the universe. Dental plan clearly included.

"Dr. David Tillman," said the stranger, smiling again as he pulled his hand away. He looked toward me, expecting another title, another doctor or professor, another scientist. Why else would we be here, if we weren't with the press, and weren't with the government?

"Anastasia Miller," I said. I stuck my hand out and he took it, staring at me as he carefully, almost timidly, gave it a shake.

"Miller," he repeated, in a tremulous voice.

"Yes."

"The abductee."

"You know, we've been dating for a decade, and I've never seen this many people recognize you," said Graham, voice pitched high, like he was trying to lighten the mood. He looked between us, measuring the situation, deciding whether or not he needed to intervene. "Are you about to start showing up in the tabloids?"

"I think you mean 'again,'" said Dr. Tillman, removing his hand from mine. He made the gesture graceful, even elegant, and not as rushed as he clearly wanted it to be. A professional, then, and a good man: good enough to care about the feelings of a potentially dangerous stranger.

He looked at me, and his gaze was measuring, taking in and breaking down every inch of me, rendering me component and complete. "Miss Miller was in the papers quite a bit when I was in school. Seems she's from another planet, and she's here to provide lucky numbers and diet tips."

My cheeks reddened. "It turns out you can't sue the gossip magazines for making stuff up, as long as what they make up is ridiculous enough," I said. "I never said I knew how to help people lose weight or . . . or get in touch with their cosmic spirit guides or anything like that. I never *would*. Aliens don't need to commit acts of cultural appropriation."

Dr. Tillman blinked. Then he laughed. "I suppose that's true," he said. "Still doesn't explain what you're doing here, Miss Miller. Did I miss the part where your alien friends told you to come to Maine?"

"Maybe," I said.

"I called ahead," said Graham. "I spoke to your administrator. I told her we wanted to hear the alien signal without distortion or modification by the local equipment, and she said it wouldn't be a problem."

"We'd also like to meet Dr. Vornholt," I added. "We've been trying to track him down. It hasn't worked very well."

"Ah." David hesitated. He wasn't a very good liar: maybe astronomers didn't need to be. Maybe a life spent staring up at the stars could be essentially honest, as long as you weren't the one in charge of securing funding for the new telescope or to put a new roof on the observatory. Academia would have eaten this man alive if he'd stayed closer to the universities. Instead, he had sought isolation, and been able to stay a lousy liar long enough for us to meet up with him.

There was a certain beautiful inevitability to the whole thing. I just wished I could understand what it was going to be.

My elbow itched. I put a hand over it, and I didn't scratch.

"Is that a problem?" pressed Graham.

"Nah," said a voice behind us.

We turned. There, wearing a slightly stained white coat over her coveralls, was our driver, earmuffs still clamped firmly over her ears. Her hair was a frizzy corona of white-blonde strands, standing out in all directions like it was doing its best impression of a halo. She had her hands shoved into her pockets and was rocking back onto her heels, looking as if she didn't have a care in the world.

I met her eyes for the first time, and flinched. I *knew* her. I'd never seen her before, but I *knew* her, the same way I knew my own reflection. Something about her made the air electric, made the hairs on the back of my neck stand on end in instinctive warning. I wanted to grab Graham and run.

I stayed right where I was.

"I mean, yeah, if you really wanted to meet Anthony Fabris," said the driver. Tilting her head, she continued philosophically, "Meeting fictional characters has always been difficult without the aid of psychotropic substances."

"Toni," hissed David.

"It's cool," she said, and fixed her eyes on me. "I knew one of them would show up to see the data. I mean, it was inevitable, fictional characters or no. I sort of expected it to be one of the closer ones, or maybe one of the Canadians. Like Rick Patton from Toronto. Did you know he still does his little internet advice show? 'Plant Person Pointers,' it's called. Guy is gonzo for alliteration."

Something about her unwavering gaze made me want to squirm, and made the itch inside my elbow even stronger. I pressed my palm down against it, hard, trying to compress the sensation away. "I don't know what you're talking about," I said, trying to stop looking at her. My eyes refused to focus on anything else.

"No one ever does," said the woman—Toni—with a shrug. Her eyes were that terrible shade of blue that seems almost white as it moves toward the pupil, like it swallowed so much light that there was no possible way she could have seen with any clarity.

"I'm sorry," said Graham. "I don't think I caught your name."

"Antonia Fabris," said the woman. She smiled, sudden and gregarious, and was the chatty driver who'd carried us here from our hotel once more. "I caught the signal out of space, because I've been listening for it for a long, long time. And now I've caught you. I assume you're here because you wanted to get a look at the raw data and convince yourselves it had been fiddled with and there isn't really an alien armada on the way? Anyway, you should follow me."

She turned then, walking briskly across the lobby and down a narrow hallway on the other side. David cleared his throat nervously.

"I, uh. I'd go with her if you want her to remember to show you the data, and not get distracted by hunting for an article she saw somewhere five years ago that will let her prove there's life on Procyon Three," he said. At our blank looks, he shrugged. "Toni sort of sets her own agenda."

"I'm starting to get that," said Graham slowly.

"We need to go after her," I said.

He looked at me. I shook my head.

"Something about her . . . She knows what the signal really is," I said. "She's the answer."

Graham nodded, and took my hand, and we walked, with David close behind us, down the scientific rabbit hole to a stranger's Wonderland.

6

PORTLAND, MAINE: JULY 20, 2031
EIGHTEEN DAYS PRE-INVASION

1.

David shouldered past us to take the lead, guiding us through an increasingly twisted maze of hallways that seemed to go on far longer than could be explained by the size of the observatory. After our third sharp left, he looked over his shoulder and said, "It's bigger on the inside."

"See, that's funny when they do it on *Doctor Who,* but when we've just crossed the country to talk to a scientist who you're now saying doesn't exist, following a taxi driver to an unidentified location, it becomes creepy," said Graham. He was still holding tightly to my hand. "This building is not bigger on the inside. The laws of physics say no."

"True, but the laws of green architecture and fitting into the landscape say we have a lot more tunnels and underground labs than people would expect when they approach from the outside," said David.

"Isn't being underground sort of, I don't know, contrary? When you're supposed to be studying the sky?"

"Astrophysics doesn't require an open window," said David. "We like open windows, or we'd be geologists, but we can work pretty well in the dark."

Graham squeezed my hand and said nothing.

I bit my lip. "Why did, um, Antonia lie about her name? Was it an accident?" That couldn't be right. Whatever this was, it felt more like intentional deception than an accident.

"I'll let her tell you." David stopped at a half-open door, looking at the both of us gravely. He was still a bad liar. Nothing was going to change that. But seeing the expression on his face made me amend my first impression of him. He was a bad liar and a good friend. There were much worse things in this world.

Much worse.

"I'm going to sit in, if you don't mind," he said, tone clearly telegraphing how little he cared whether or not we minded. He was going to sit in no matter what we said. "Toni can get manic with strangers, and it's best if I'm there to mediate."

"Meaning . . . ?" said Graham.

"Meaning her daddy bought this observatory for her so she'd be happy and out of the way, and even if she weren't one of my best friends—which she is—I'd be defending her for the sake of maintaining our funding."

I expected Graham to argue, if only for form's sake. Instead, he grinned and said, "We have a guy in the Everglades whose grandparents gave him the funds to continue his research for a hundred and fifty years when they died. He counts alligators all day. Sometimes the people he works with have to fish him *out* of the alligators. I have never seen a man happier to get up and go to work every morning, and the people on his project don't have to worry their grant will run out at the end of the year. I get where you're coming from."

"Good," said David.

It *did* make sense, in a terrible way. More and more, science comes in two flavors: crowdsourced and privatized. Things that can be distributed over ten thousand hands get done on a shoestring, and things that are lucky enough to land a patron—or better yet, a rich kid with a genuine passion for the project and relatives who want to make them happy—get done with all the bells and whistles. It's everything in between, the dull and difficult and less-than-profitable, that suffers.

David pushed the door the rest of the way open, declaring loudly, "We're here, Toni."

"Took you long enough." Toni was sitting cross-legged in a desk chair with a laptop on her knees, leaning over it to type on a larger console. In case that wasn't enough computing power, she had six more machines in easy view, and might well have a dozen more that were integrated into other systems or concealed by the towers of cardboard boxes.

One wall was dominated by black-and-white pictures and brightly colored cards covered in clearly handwritten notes. Pieces of string connected cards to pictures—sometimes multiple pictures for the same card—and pictures to each other, although none of the pictures had more than a single connection. I swallowed a gasp and pressed my knuckles against my lips as I spotted a familiar face among the gallery: my own.

I was one of three pictures with a piece of string connecting me to the card labeled WEST COAST. Of those three, I was the only one with a string also connecting me to WASHINGTON STATE.

I was also the only one of the three not connected to the card which read, simply, DECEASED. A startling number of pictures were connected to that card. An equally startling number of those pictures were of children, ranging from five or six years old up to their early teens.

"Sixty-three percent."

I turned.

Toni was looking at me with sympathy. Her hands were still moving. She was apparently more than capable of typing blind—that, or she was just keysmashing to have something to do. I would have believed either.

“Excuse me?” I said.

“Sixty-three percent of verified invaders did not survive to reach adulthood. About half died of allergic reactions or autoimmune conditions. As far as I know, none had the sort of autopsy that would have told us exactly why their DNA didn’t encode correctly—Wait.” She turned to David, frowning. “Do plants have DNA? Or are they something weird, like RNA or whatever?”

“Plants have DNA,” said David, in a tone that clearly stated that he had encountered this question before, multiple times. “They have chromosomes, too.”

“Huh.” Toni shook her head. “Okay, that’s weird. Why do plants need chromosomes? Do *you* know, Peony?” Her eyes were suddenly, unnervingly back on me. Again, there was that shock of recognition: I *knew* her. I just didn’t know how.

“Um,” I said. “No? I’m not a botanist.”

Toni blinked. “You’re not? Why the fuck not? You *should* be. I would be, if I hadn’t managed to get away. You stupid, Hyacinth?”

“Uh, my name is Anastasia,” I said. “‘Stasia’ is fine.”

“Oh, like ‘stamen.’”

“No, like a nickname for Anastasia,” I said, and glanced at Graham. He looked as confused as I felt. “I don’t have a plant name.”

“But you are one,” said Toni. “A plant. You didn’t run, run as fast as you can, and so the thing from space gobbled up the little gingerbread girl. I assume you’re here about my signal?”

“I—” I began.

Graham squeezed my fingers hard enough to break my train of thought. I glanced at him. He was shaking his hand, not vigorously, but just enough for me to see. I stopped talking.

"Yes," he said. "We called before coming. I really want to see the source data."

"Are you an astronomer, or an astrophysicist, or anything with 'astro' in the name?" She managed to make the question sound mild, but there were teeth in it. I could see them in the shadows around her smile.

"No," said Graham.

"So you are . . . ?"

"A herpetologist."

"A herpetologist. I see. Do you normally figure out where the lizards are by listening to celestial signals? Because if that's so, I may have missed my calling. I'm great with celestial signals, and I never know where the lizards are."

"No," said Graham. "I usually figure out where the lizards are by finding the places the lizards *aren't*, and then following the lizards I know about back to the rest."

Toni raised an eyebrow. "Okay, so maybe you do understand what I do. But the signals still aren't going to make more sense to you in their raw form, unless you'd been hoping I'd make you copies to take back to someone who actually speaks the language of the stars."

"Really, I was hoping you'd play them for us." Graham seemed possessed of an almost-supernatural calm, like he had been playing games of verbal tag with this woman for years.

In a way, he had. Graham had always been happier to fight with words than with fists, and unlike me, he really wanted people to like him. Part of that was in the code-switching he did so easily, jumping without hesitation from one set of linguistic metaphors to the next. It made him an effective communicator and the life of the party, and I loved him for it, even as it could draw things out until I wanted to scream.

"Why?" asked Toni. She jerked her chin toward me. "Hoping she'll be able to translate it for you, tell you it says 'we come in peace' and then you can go home feeling good about yourself, like the invasion isn't on its way? Because I'm pretty sure that even if she says that's what it says, that isn't what it says at all. Nobody who takes this much time to infiltrate is coming in peace. Even if they're lousy at infiltration."

"I wouldn't lie," I said, before Graham could volley the ball back into her court. "If it doesn't say they're coming in peace, I won't pretend it does."

"Oh, no? Have you gone native? Is this going to be like *Avatar* in reverse?"

Graham blinked, looking between Toni and me. Finally, he settled on Toni. "Are you saying you actually believe Stasia is an alien?"

"Oh, no," said Toni, making her eyes wide and guileless. "Gosh, golly, not at all. I maintain a cliché conspiracy wall for all *sorts* of things I don't believe. Come back next month and you can see my wall explaining how *The Blob* was originally a documentary and that's where all the high-fructose corn syrup in your breakfast cereal comes from."

"Pretty sure the Blob was an alien too, Toni," said David.

She snorted, as if that didn't make any difference. Which maybe it didn't. This was all ridiculous.

"Can we stop this and just hear the signal already?" I asked.

"Not until I believe you'll tell the truth about what it says," said Toni, folding her arms. At least that meant she wasn't typing anymore. She glared at me, and there was a shattered menace in the expression that I hadn't been expecting. "I'm not here to help you."

"So why did you release the signal, anyway?" I pointed to David. "He says your parents fund this place, which means you keep your job even if you don't release a signal from space—or maybe even if you do, when what you put out there is basically an announcement of invasion. You could have kept it. Picked it apart. Not helped the aliens you seem to believe are already here."

"Seem to believe? *Seem* to believe? Hey, David, wanna see a neat trick?" She didn't wait for his response before smiling at me, sticky-sweet, and asking, "Are you from this planet?"

"No, I'm the vanguard of an invading species of alien plant-people," I said, before clapping my hand over my mouth. Through my fingers, I mumbled, "I didn't mean to say that." I wanted this woman to help us, and she seemed, if not outright hostile toward the aliens, at least to have some ulterior motive I couldn't quite make out.

"But you did, because you always do. All of you do. It's a compulsion. I think it's part of the conversion process: they make you look like a human, they even make you *think* like a human, but they also make sure you'll give yourself away if given the slightest opportunity to do so. Like, ordering fries at McDonald's, would you like an alien invasion with that. It's a bullshit tic and you all have it and it's amazing."

I frowned. Graham frowned. Graham recovered first.

"How many people with this compulsion have you met?" he asked.

"People? None. Alien invaders wearing skin suits? Fifteen. Sixteen if you count the one who was in the coma when I got there." Toni was serene. "No way to confirm that one was an invader without a full autopsy, and her parents didn't see the need for one, since she'd just eaten something that didn't agree with her. People are so short-sighted sometimes."

"You really *do* believe Stasia is an alien," he said.

"Well, yes," said Toni. "Don't you? You came here with her."

"Of course I do." Graham glanced at me, and then back to her. "I love her. You believe the people you love. Believing she's from outer space doesn't hurt me. Choosing not to believe her would hurt *her*, and part of loving her is never hurting her when I have any way to avoid it."

"Why do you believe me?" I asked.

Toni looked at me coldly, and rolled up her sleeves.

Exposed, the skin of her arms was paler than the skin on her hands and face, as if it had never seen the sun. Even so, I could see the thin web of scars that covered her from fingertip to bicep, extending up to where her shirt still covered her shoulders. It was like someone had used a tattoo gun filled with white ink to draw a grid, freehand, on her body. The lines weren't straight. They curled and twisted from point to point, creating an unpredictable mesh that would have been virtually impossible to escape.

"I could strip, but this should give you the idea," said Toni, and her voice was ice and ashes.

"I don't—" I looked away from her skin, focusing on her eyes, and was momentarily struck silent by the hatred in her face. She looked like she would have happily set me on fire, just to see how long it would take for me to burn.

Was this how everyone was going to look at me, once they realized that I'd been telling the truth all along? Mandy and Graham believed me, but they believed me mostly because it didn't *hurt* them. The invasion was going to hurt people. I knew that, as surely as I knew that it was coming—and that I needed to hear that signal.

"What happened to you?" I whispered, finally finding my voice.

Toni's smile was like a razor.

"I tried to pick a flower," she said.

My mouth went dry.

2.

"My father owns a summer home on one of the little islands off the coast," she said, eyes on me. I might as well have been the only other person in the room. Someone from the wall was finally here to listen to her story—and no matter how many times she'd told it, I got the feeling that until someone like me heard it, none of those tellings would really count. Not to her. “We used to go every year, until I had my accident.”

I said nothing. Neither did Graham. David, who had clearly heard this all before, remained beside her, setting one heavy hand on her shoulder, like he could keep her from floating away if he held on tightly enough.

“I was eight. I used to *live* in the woods. I was planning to go to work for the National Forestry Service. Daddy used to joke that he’d wind up buying me half of the Appalachian Mountains for a birthday present, and I always said it would be a great gift, because I wanted to keep them safe and protected. I’d been hiking around our summer home since I was six. They kept a close eye on me the first summer, and not such a close eye the second summer, and by the third summer they trusted me enough to let me go wherever I wanted, as long as I made it home by sundown.”

Toni’s stare was fierce and unforgiving. “They didn’t have to worry about kidnappers, because we were in the middle of nowhere and you couldn’t get to the island without a boat, and no one came out there unless they had good reason. They didn’t have to worry about paparazzi, because we’ve always been the boring kind of rich, the stock market and investments and getting normal jobs anyway, so you’ll know the value of a dollar kind of rich. Not the sort of rich that has a reality show and a clothing line and attracts a lot of attention.”

“You have an observatory,” said David.

Toni spared him a quick smile. “Not interesting enough, and most people don’t know I’m here. I’m Daddy’s little secret now. The girl who went into the woods and hurt herself so badly she lost her mind—which I didn’t do.” She returned her glare to me. “I’m not insane. Everything I say is true. It’s just a truth most people don’t want to see, because it’s not comfortable, or convenient, or easy.”

“No one said you were insane,” said Graham conciliatorily. “This is all just a little hard for us to swallow.”

"To be fair, I do have PTSD, for reasons she"—Toni jabbed a finger at me—"would totally understand, if she were human. Did she ever tell you how she got here? How a plant person could look exactly like a normal, ordinary human?"

Graham looked uncomfortable. Toni smirked.

"Didn't think so," she said. "See, it's not a nice process. It's not some sort of alien-telepathy thing where they drop a baby on a childless couple and suddenly, bam, they're accepted—and it's not a Midwich Cuckoos thing, either."

"Midwich Cuckoos?" Graham asked blankly.

"*Village of the Damned*," I said.

"Of course you read the classics," said Toni. "How can you throw an alien invasion if you don't understand how the fictional ones failed?"

I said nothing. I just scowled at her.

"Back to my story, if you don't mind," she said. "I was eight: I went into the woods, hoping I would find something interesting: I found it. Or rather, I smelled it. It was like . . . fruit punch and popcorn at the movies and my mother's sugar cookies, all blended together. It shouldn't have smelled *good*, not with that mix, but it did. It smelled so good that I wanted it more than anything else in the world."

She stared at me as she spoke, until it felt like her gaze had physical weight. I squirmed. She smiled, slow and predatory.

"Oh, no," she said. "You get to listen. I've had to live with this for my *entire* adult life, and so now *you* get to *listen*. You're the first one to stand still long enough to hear it. Aren't you lucky?"

"Only if you're going to let us hear the signal when you're done," I said, voice shaking.

"Of course I am," she said, with a shrug. "I was always going to. They're coming. I want to know why. You owe me that much."

I was starting to be direly afraid I did—that we, my distant, unknowable people, did. Because those scars on her arms matched the pattern of light caresses that sometimes ran along my own, when I nestled into the patch of alien flowers in my impossible midnight forest.

"I followed the scent," said Toni. "I found a flower that didn't look like any other flower I'd ever seen. It had dragonfly wings for petals. It *moved*. It knew I was there, and it wanted me to come closer. The scent got stronger. My feet kept moving. I knew it was a bad idea. I didn't want to get any closer to a flower that could actually *see* me, and I kept walking anyway, because I didn't have a choice anymore. It was the worst thing that had ever happened to me. I mean, it only got to be the worst thing for a few minutes, but that was long enough."

She looked at me, and I looked at her, and she continued, in an almost singsong voice, "Smelling that flower took away everything I had. If the whole invasion is like that, we're doomed. Mammals depend too much on scent to handle an invasion of evil perfume."

I didn't say anything.

"So I walked to the flower, and when I got close enough, it grabbed me." For a moment, she looked . . . affronted, like a plant grabbing a person was offensive on some deep, unendurable level. Like it was something that should never have been allowed to happen. "It had these long vines, all tucked around the base of it, where they wouldn't be as noticeable, and it *grabbed* me."

That was how the pod-delivery blossoms worked, if you didn't touch the flower quickly enough. I remembered, very dimly, my encounter with one—or the original Anastasia's encounter, to be more precise, since I had still been a seed sleeping in the heart of a flower. I had come later. "How did you get away?" I asked.

"I screamed," she said. "I don't think I was supposed to. I think the plant was supposed to stop me from doing it. But it didn't get the vines around my neck fast enough, and I screamed like I was being murdered, which I guess I was. My father was close to hear me. He came running, and he cut me free. Not fast enough." She held up her arms again. This time, with the full story behind them, the scars were less familiar than they were sinister, terrible reminders of what had happened to a little girl in the Washington woods, the little girl whose life I had stolen.

It didn't matter that I'd been a seed at the time, unable to decide for myself who my host was going to be, and it didn't matter if I had lived her life as fiercely and honestly as I knew how. It didn't matter if I was an alien who thought like a human, thanks to nurture triumphing over nature in almost every way that mattered. She was still dead. Anastasia Miller was still dead, and she was always going to be. I was a replacement, but I was no substitute for the woman the real thing might have become.

"When he pulled the vines off me, they ripped off half my skin," said Toni serenely. "I had to be airlifted off the island. It was touch-and-go for over a week. I can't stand being surrounded by trees anymore. I didn't eat vegetables for years. Had to get my vitamins from PediaSure and pills. And then there was the part where I needed therapy because hello, post-traumatic stress disorder, while my father was in total denial about what he'd seen, so he didn't even want to look at me anymore. I lost my future. I lost my father. I lost everything because a pretty flower in the woods tried to eat me up like a cookie. So see, I believe you, because I almost *was* you. I almost died and came back a traitor. Aliens are real. No one wants to hear it, because what the hell are we supposed to do about this sort of situation? But they're real, and they're coming, and they're already here. You're already here."

"Yes," I said softly.

"Do you remember how much it hurt?"

"No," I said. Graham was staring at me, cheeks pale and eyes bulging. He'd always done his best to believe me, but there was choosing belief, and then there was being forced to confront it.

Not that this proved anything. He could convince himself I was incorporating Toni's delusions into my own, if he wanted to: that her scars were self-inflicted or the result of some childhood ailment, and I was playing along because if she'd seen the flower in the forest, she was proof of everything I'd ever tried to explain. I didn't expect him to turn me into a liar for his own peace of mind, but then, I'd never expected him to believe me in the first place. Humans were always going to be a mystery, in some ways, no matter how close I came to being one.

The itch in my elbow was closer to a throb now, like something was worming its way through muscle and bone. I clasped a hand over it, looking steadily at Toni.

"I don't really remember much of the time right before Anastasia was converted," I said. "Part of that is because the mind doesn't consciously retain much that happens before the age of five or so. Even humans are a little chaotic when they're infants and toddlers. Add in an alien intelligence trying to file and categorize all those memories, and it shouldn't really be a surprise when some things get lost."

"But you know it had to hurt her."

"Yes." Even if I didn't remember the pain, I remembered the *process,* remembered it with a clarity shared by few of my childhood memories. I remembered it as an intimate, wonderful thing, the flower that was my twin using all its resources to construct a new home for me to live in, the precious second seed that needed to be planted in the best possible soil. I remembered the caress of root-threads as they coaxed me out of the shell that had been my salvation, moving me into the next phase of my existence.

I didn't remember the taste of Anastasia's blood, but I remembered the feeling of something wonderful nurturing me, swelling within me, until I was so tight and full I burst my shell, and the next stage of my life could begin.

"Did you have a choice?"

That was an easy question, finally. "No," I said. Then, in case that wasn't enough, "I don't think the flower did either. We were both doing what we were made to do. It was made to take care of me until it could find somebody for me to replace, and I wasn't even a sprout yet. That happened after we caught Anastasia." The real process was much bigger and more complicated than that, enough so that even after a whole lifetime of considering it, I didn't fully understand. Why hadn't my flower grabbed a deer or an escaped dog or any of the other large mammals that roved the forest? How had it known to go after a human? Really, why wasn't "I" a moose right now?

What made people different enough to make them good targets?

"Okay," said Toni. She yanked her sleeves back down and turned to her computer, beginning to type again.

"Okay?" I asked blankly.

"None of this is okay," muttered Graham.

I shot him an alarmed look. He refused to meet my eyes. I felt the blood rise to my cheeks, burning hot and bitter in my veins, and kept my hand clamped over my itching elbow.

"Nope," said Toni, with surprising cheer. "None of this is okay *at all*. This is all basically the opposite of okay. But it's what we have to deal with, and if we're going to stop an alien invasion from taking out our planet, we need to start working."

"There's no invasion, Toni," said David. He sounded weary, and the look he gave me wasn't kind in the slightest. I couldn't decide whether he believed her and hated me for being an alien, or whether he was humoring her and wanted to shake me for encouraging her delusions. Either way, he didn't like me anymore, if he ever had.

"They're coming," said Toni serenely. "They're almost here, or they wouldn't be calling ahead to tell their little spies to start getting things ready."

"That's why you released the signal," I said. "You knew people like ... people like me would hear it, but that wasn't as important as making sure the *government* heard it."

"Heard it, and couldn't pretend they hadn't," said Toni. "If I'd sent it through proper channels, instead of releasing it to the press, they could have said, 'Gosh and golly, little astronomer, that was awfully nice of you to record that piece of deep-space chatter, now go away and let the big kids deal with it.' Which they wouldn't have done."

"If you mention Area 51, we're leaving," said Graham.

"No, you're not," said Toni. "If you were going to leave because I sounded like a conspiracy theorist, you would have walked out like, twenty minutes ago. You're just threatening to walk out because you don't like that I made your girlfriend sound like a monster which, PS, she totally is. Just because Felicia decides to fight against the rest of the Darkstalkers, that doesn't make her any less of a bad guy."

I glanced at Graham, baffled. He shook his head, looking as confused as I felt, and the icy shell that had been forming around my heart seemed to crack and fall away a little. We could still share confusion. We could still share each other.

He didn't think I was a monster. Even if he was being forced to think about what his beliefs really meant, that didn't mean he thought I was a monster.

"Government might have known about aliens before this, might not," continued Toni easily. "I mean, the shape of the invasion sort of implies there are other species out there—or there were, once, before they got devoured alive by the plant people. You don't go zero to this sort of hunting strategy. So maybe there's been contact before, from civilizations that aren't even there anymore, because they've been eaten. Or maybe we've been in constant contact for decades, and that's where frozen yogurt and memory foam really come from. None of that matters."

"So what does matter?" Graham asked.

Silence, I thought. What mattered was that if the government had been in touch with all those people, they'd never told any of the rest of us about it. They'd never sent out a warning about flowers with wings for petals, or the unexpected scent of every good thing in the middle of the forest. They had never been willing to tell, to share what they knew, choosing the status quo over preserving lives and changing the world.

Toni glanced at me and smirked, reading my thoughts in my face. "None of you can lie for shit, you know that? Every one of you I've ever met has been an open book. It *must* be part of the process, because I'm an awesome liar when I need to be. What matters, dude who dates plants, is that even if the government has known about aliens for years, we haven't. We've been allowed to bumble along in the dark, with no idea what is or isn't out there. So maybe I'm not giving them the benefit of the doubt and this is going to be as much of a surprise for them as it is for the rest of the world, or maybe they've been hiding shit. It's cool either way. My signal's out in the world, and people can hear it anytime they want, and even if no one knows what it says, they know it's from space. They know that we're not alone."

"That isn't going to stop the invasion." My voice: my words. Graham shot me another stricken look. I kept my eyes steadfastly forward, refusing to look at him. If he was starting to hate me, I didn't want to see that shining in his eyes.

"No, but it may help us get ready," said Toni. "Humans are pretty badass when we need to be. We survive all sorts of shit that should kill us. If we're prepared when you fucking space weeds come to take our world, maybe we'll stand a chance."

I didn't say anything. Toni swung between resignation and defiance like an out-of-control pendulum, and I wasn't sure how to deal with it. If she had been one of my customers, I would have asked her to calm down before I was forced to terminate the call. Sadly, that didn't work in face-to-face interactions.

"So I just need them to believe me," she said, and hit a quick series of keys. "If that means kicking off an international panic because everyone is expecting the aliens to swoop out of the sky at any moment, I'm cool with it. I've been living with the idea for most of my life, and I'm still standing. So come on, Marigold. Tell me what this says."

She hit another key, and the signal out of space filled the room in static pop and strange harmonics, like a whalesong stolen out of the sky. It was white noise at first, fizzes and hums and other, deeper notes, none made by any intentional mind.

Then the signal began.

It rose and it fell and I closed my eyes, letting it wash over me and carry me away, because I *knew* this sound, I *knew* this song. It was the signal from the news and it wasn't at the same time. That signal had been flattened down and equalized to sound more dramatic, trimming away the fat—the pauses, the hisses, the hesitations that were the message taking form. This was what I had been supposed to hear all along. This was what the forest had been trying to whisper to me when I went there during the night.

The sound cut off abruptly. I flinched, unable to keep from reacting to the sudden hole where the world was supposed to be. I opened my eyes, and they were all staring at me, Toni and David and yes, even Graham, who had never looked at me with quite so much confusion in his eyes.

"Well?" demanded Toni. "What does it say?"

"Stasia?" said Graham. "Is it real?"

They were conflicting questions. They were the same question. I swallowed, reaching up with both hands to push my hair back from my face, and said, "It's real. It's ours. I mean, it's from our fleet."

Graham's laugh was tight and bitter. "I guess that's a good thing. We don't have two invasions heading for us at the same time. Hoorah for that."

Somehow, I didn't think he meant what he was saying. I raked my hands through my hair again, trying to let the motion steady me, and said, "They're coming. They're . . . I think they're really close now. It won't be much longer before they get here."

"You're not answering my question, Tulip," said Toni. "What does it *say*?"

I looked at her. "I can't tell you."

Her eyes narrowed. "That wasn't the deal."

Right. "Okay, first, we didn't have a *deal* so much as you talked a lot and assumed because I wasn't making you stop, I was agreeing with everything you said. I'm sorry you nearly got eaten by one of our conversion flowers when you were a kid." That was mostly true. I *was* sorry, because it seemed to have messed her up pretty seriously. But there would still have been an Antonia Fabris in the world if she had been consumed, and maybe that one would have been happier. It was difficult to say. "I didn't do it. I sprouted on the other side of the country, and I'm not sorry to be what I am."

"I bet your parents would say otherwise."

That stung. I squared my shoulders, and said, "That doesn't matter, because they're not here. I'm here, and I say I never agreed to anything. I'd tell you anyway, because it's only fair, except I *can't*. The message is . . . It doesn't translate to this language. I'm not sure it translates to any language on this planet."

"How do plants even have a language?" she spat.

"I don't know," I said, with absolute sincerity. "There's a lot I don't know. I've been waiting for the ships to arrive for my whole life, because maybe they know the things I don't. I hope they do, at least. But I know what it *says*. I just don't know how to put it into Earth words."

"Try," said David, and his voice was cold: for the first time, he sounded like he might actually believe what Toni was saying.

"Um." I raked my hands through my hair again. "Okay. They're saying they're some distance away—I can't tell you how far, the distance *literally* doesn't translate into anything I can say in English—but they're coming, and they're so proud of us for surviving, they know we've been waiting for them to come and get us, and they're going to be here soon. Very soon. Less than one full sprouting season."

"How long is a sprouting season?" asked Graham.

"I don't *know*." I glared at him, making no effort to conceal my frustration. If anyone was going to understand how much this bothered me, it should have been him. "The words they're using, they're just . . . I can understand them, sort of, but it's like knowing what the cat means when it starts meowing. You don't really share a language. You share some basic ideas of what it is to be alive, but that's where it falls apart. That's how it is with me and this signal. I think that's how it's going to be for all of us and the signal. We'll recognize it, because it was meant for us, but we're not going to be able to translate it the way you translate the Swedish instructions on your IKEA furniture."

"How can you even understand that much if you don't speak the language?" asked Toni.

"I don't know," I said. "But they're coming. If that's what you wanted to confirm, it's confirmed. They're coming."

"Can we have a copy of the raw data?" asked Graham.

Toni turned to stare at him. "You come here, you don't tell me anything I didn't already know, and now you want me to share my findings with you? With *her*?" She jabbed a finger at me. "She's the enemy. Even if you can't see that now, you're going to see it pretty soon, when her people get here and you have to pick a side."

"You seem pretty confident that I'm going to pick humanity."

"We all will. Even those of us who don't have much reason to like people are going to choose humanity, because the alternative is extinction. You, Rose." She focused on me again, and I successfully fought the urge to take a step backward. "Do you know where you're going to take your stand? Because I'm betting it's not with the species you introduced yourself to with a murder. That little girl you killed, she's dead. You can walk around with her face and her name and her family and pretend you're doing all the things she would have done, but you know it's not true just as well as I do. You're a liar and a thief, and you're not going to choose the monkeys over the trees. It's going to cost you everything, and you're going to side with your own species anyway, because that's what people do. We side with our own."

"Graham is one of your own, and he's the one asking for a copy," I said.

Toni drew back, looking surprised. Then she laughed. "I guess that's true," she said. "So sure. I'll run one off for him—for you too. Maybe you'll figure out what you want to know. But you haven't finished paying for it yet."

"No?" I asked.

"No." She narrowed her eyes. "I said I wanted to know why. You said you'd tell me. You owe me that much."

I didn't owe her anything. She was just a woman with a telescope and a satellite array, which she happened to have pointed at the sky at the right time. I could walk away with my conscience clear, and never look back. But she had made the choice to share the signal with the world, which was why we were here, listening to it, having some small degree of warning that whatever mission had seen me planted on this planet was finally drawing to an end. So no, I didn't owe her, but maybe I pitied her a little. Maybe pitying her was enough.

"They're coming because that's what we do. We come, and we harvest, and we go. Maybe someday we come back, but it takes a long, long time."

"Why?" asked David. He was the one who supposedly didn't believe in any of this, but there was a certain fascination in his expression all the same.

"Because it takes a long, long time for another harvest to be ready," I said.

I saw the horror on his face. I saw the confusion, and the denial, and the hope that maybe he was right and I was wrong: this was all a lie.

"I'll be outside," I said, and turned, and walked away.

3.

Some bird I didn't recognize was whistling and croaking in the trees across from the observatory. It sounded like a kind of owl. I walked toward it, head tilted back, trying to spot it against the foliage. Any bird that loud would have a certain amount of camouflage to help it out.

The parking lot fell away one step at a time, until I was standing in the shelter of the trees, surrounded by brown bark and leafy green, safely embraced by the growing world. I closed my eyes, thoughts of the owl forgotten as I breathed in deep, filling my lungs with the scent of the forest.

Lungs. There was an interesting question. Would my people even have lungs, or would they photosynthesize? Would *I* photosynthesize? The strange harmonics of the signal still echoed in my ears, making everything seem twisted and strange. I was the result of an alien seed blending with a terrestrial girl named Anastasia Miller. I had never delved too deeply into the question of my own biology, not because I wasn't curious, but because there was no safe way to know. Hand myself over to a scientist and spend the rest of the time before the invasion held captive in a lab, waiting to be scraped across a thousand slides, studied in a million petri dishes. Enlist a friend and start a conspiracy. No. None of those things were for me. Better to live as an alien in a human world, knowing what was true without having any proof of it. But now . . .

The signal was here. People knew the invasion was coming, and whether or not we came in peace—"the harvest" didn't sound like coming in peace—the humans weren't going to see it that way. They would look at the vanguard, at people like me and Jeff and all those other faces on Toni's wall, and they would see nothing but an armada of dead human children being worn as masks by alien intelligences. It wouldn't matter that when we had done our replication, we'd been mindless seeds, acting on instinct alone, feeding on the meat our flowers provided for us. It wouldn't matter that sometimes human infants killed their mothers in the process of being born, making us no different, really.

We were a loss of identity and a loss of life and an infiltration that had been going on for decades. They would feel the need to destroy us, if only for their own peace of mind. And that was if we were coming with open hands, as friends who just didn't have the same ideas about the sanctity of the individual, who thought wearing familiar faces would make us seem like we were already part of the same team.

I didn't think, I couldn't think, that we were coming in peace. No one crosses that much distance, or sends scouts that far in advance with no way to contact the fleet and says, "No, don't come; this place isn't safe for us" if they're coming in peace.

The wind whispered through the trees around me, the familiar, terrestrial trees, and I hesitated. Maybe we *did* have a way to talk to . . .

home, or whatever I was supposed to call the nursery where I had been cultivated. What was the forest if not some vast communication device, one tailored to keep us connected to one another despite the incredible distance between?

Maybe we'd been talking to them all along.

I wandered deeper into the wood, trying not to think about Toni, who would never wander freely into the woods again. For her, just staying at the observatory, surrounded as it was by trees, had to be a trial. She did it anyway. There was something very foolish, and very human, about that.

A rock turned under my foot. I kicked it away, pausing as I heard it skid over leaves and fall over a previously unseen drop. More cautious now, I inched forward and peered down. The land cut away, revealing a long expanse of open space that ended when it reached the road.

Three white cars were winding their way along that stretch of gray concrete. This far above them, I couldn't see any markings on their sides . . . but I could see the lights on top. They were turned off now. They could start flashing with the flick of a switch.

The cars, and their lights, were heading for the observatory.

I pulled my phone out of my pocket, nearly dropping it in the loam as I fumbled to bring up the main screen. Once there, I swiped on Graham's number and brought the phone to my ear, counting anxiously down from ten until—

"Hello? Stasia? Where are you?"

"In the woods across the parking lot," I said hurriedly. "Graham, you have to get out of there."

"I'm in the lobby. Looking for you."

"The police are coming!"

There was a split second of frozen silence. Then Graham snapped, "Turn your crowd beacon on and stay exactly where you are." He hung up.

I lowered my phone, gaping at it in horror before bringing up my app list and activating the crowd beacon. It had been designed for public places like amusement parks and shopping malls. When it was on, anyone who had your specific key could use it to find you. Since it wasn't on by default, like some of the kid trackers, it wasn't so much an invasion of privacy as it was a way to keep the party from being split. Better yet, the security locks on a crowd beacon were proprietary and couldn't be used by law enforcement—despite several lawsuits that had tried to change that. If the police turned on a wide-band signal detector, they'd be able to follow my phone into the woods, but without a warrant or an unethical computer technician, they wouldn't know it was *mine*, just that it was there.

And despite that, I carefully set my phone on a nearby stump, covering it with a handful of fallen leaves, before retreating behind a thick-trunked tree. Better safe than sorry. Better out of sight than presenting a clear target.

Hunching down slightly to make myself seem even smaller, I waited.

Seconds slid by, blossoming into minutes, until I began to fear we'd been too late: whatever instinct had told me the police didn't mean Graham any good had come too late, and he had been taken, arrested and carried off to tell them everything he knew about the alien signal. It didn't matter if what he knew was best categorized as "not much": he was a scientist, he'd traveled across the country to listen to the raw data, he was a threat. People were scared. They were looking for something to point at and say, "That, right there, is the enemy." Graham would work well enough.

Humans love having an easy bad guy. Plant people from outer space, that's hard. Someone who was conspiring with them somehow, but was otherwise entirely human and comprehensible? Now that was a bad guy to believe in.

Someone was walking through the woods. More than one someone, if I could believe what I heard. I drew farther back behind my tree, trying to be as unobtrusive as possible.

Graham walked into view, heading unerringly for my phone. David and Toni were close behind him, Toni hanging limply off David's arm. Her eyes were closed. She looked like she was about to be sick. Fleeing into the forest like this must have been virtually impossible for her. She'd done it anyway. My instincts about the police must have been correct.

Pulling my phone from beneath the layer of leaves, Graham straightened and looked around himself in a slow circle, scanning the trees—first at ground level, then higher up, like he thought I might have decided to hide by fleeing straight up.

"The police aren't with us, Stasia," he said quietly. "It's safe. Come out."

I stepped out from behind the tree, not missing the way he sagged in sudden relief at the sight of me. "What happened?" I asked.

"I don't know," he said. "When I told them you'd seen police cars coming, they insisted on coming with me. We barely made it into the trees before they pulled up outside."

"That's not so bad," I said. "Maybe I was overreacting."

"They shot the receptionist," said David flatly.

There didn't seem to be any appropriate reply to that. I just stared as he shook his head, still holding Toni up.

"Not with a bullet," he said. "I'm not sure a Taser is any better, but at least she's not dead. She'll be able to sue the pants off of them."

"Assuming they don't disappear her to some secret prison in the middle of nowhere," said Toni. She jabbed a finger at me. "This is all *your* fault."

"How the hell is—?"

"You're the one who had to tell the world you were an alien! You flying to see me right after the signal went public must have thrown up a million red flags. Even people who didn't want to believe this was really happening would have questions about that. You needed to stay *down*."

I frowned. "You're the one who said disclosure was a compulsion for us."

"Yeah, and if you've lived with a compulsion for your entire life, you learn how to deal with it. You learn how to make it not so damn bad." Toni cast a frightened look back over her shoulder. "If they come looking for us, they're going to find us. Who knows what happens then? I'm too young and brilliant to go to prison. I need to stay wild and free and join the Earth resistance against the invasion."

"I'm a little more concerned about what happens when we try to fly home," said Graham grimly. "If they've put us on a no-fly or tagged us for the TSA to detain, we're never going to make it back to the West Coast."

"Yes, that's far worse than getting shot," said David.

"It might *include* getting shot," said Graham.

"I have an idea." I looked at my phone, and then back at the others. "But you may not like it very much."

"What is it?" asked Graham.

I told them.

4.

Working our way down the back side of the mountain took the better part of an hour. David had to carry Toni almost the entire way. She'd be fine for a few steps, and then she'd brush up against a tree, and suddenly her legs wouldn't work right. It was all unreasoning terror, and I felt a little bad about it. After all, it had been one of our conversion flowers that had done this to her.

Then again, if it had worked, if she had been digested and remade as my sister, would I have felt bad about that? Or would I have been overjoyed to meet someone like myself, someone who remembered what it was to follow the scent of heaven through a dark forest and come out the other side, transformed into something better than they'd been before?

The thought of Graham meeting a conversion flower, coming out vegetable and perfect, flitted across my mind and disappeared, leaving my cheeks hot and my skin uncomfortably tight. That, too, was a conundrum of a sort. If we were plants at heart, why did I have these damned mammalian biological responses?

Graham caught up with me, catching my elbow and pulling me closer as he whispered, "Are you sure about this?"

"Nope," I said. There was no point in lying to him. We were committed to our course. More, I had already lied to him once today, and that was my limit. "I don't have a better idea, though. Do you?" No car, no resources, no one to come and rescue us.

No one except Jeff, who was close enough to come get us from the base of the hill, and who had been able to track me down in the dream of a forest, where humans had no business going. He might not be the perfect answer, but he was the answer we had.

Graham shook his head, looking even more frustrated. "I wish you'd told me about this guy sooner."

"Why? So you could have explained why he wasn't who he was saying he was, even though it didn't make sense for him to be anyone else?" I paused. "I hope you followed that."

"I wish I hadn't." Graham glanced over his shoulder at David and Toni before looking back to me and saying, "I have always believed you when you told me where you came from. *Always*."

"Yes, you have. But I feel like that was a lot easier to do before things started getting complicated."

"Honey, things have been complicated since our first date. Remember?"

I smiled despite myself. It had been Halloween. Graham had dressed up as Steve Irwin, binding his breasts until he could barely breathe, while I had dressed as Audrey from the musical *Little Shop of Horrors,* poking fun at what I knew the other students thought of me and putting my own breasts on convenient display at the same time. I'd been trying to get Graham to like me. He had . . . but he'd also been too enthusiastic about his binding, and he'd passed out from lack of air in the middle of our embrace. I'd wound up supporting him, screaming about how I'd killed my boyfriend, until someone called campus medical. Not exactly the sort of first date that makes the world believe in romance.

"I remember," I said, and sighed. "I'm sorry. This is complicated for me, too."

"Yeah." He was quiet for a moment before he asked, "Stasia? You'd tell me if there was a way to make this less dangerous, wouldn't you?"

He was still being so careful not to question the invasion. I couldn't decide whether that was because he truly believed me, or whether it was because he had long since decided it was better not to argue with me about whether or not I came from outer space. In the end, it didn't matter. The invasion was coming, whether he believed in it or not. Whether *anyone* believed in it or not. The invasion didn't care whether people believed it. It was a fact, as implacable as gravity or the speed of light, and it was going to happen no matter what anybody had to say on the matter.

"I would," I said, and I meant it. If I had known exactly what form the invasion was going to take, the shape of any places that might escape their notice, I would have drawn him a map. I loved him. I wanted him to be safe.

That, too, was a part of cultural literacy: having the connections within a community to care about the people it contained. Again, something about the thought gnawed at me, like there was something in the shape of the concept that would tell me everything I still needed to know. The inside of my elbow itched for the first time since I'd stepped into the trees. I scratched it idly, and felt skin tear beneath my nails. Felt the strange, almost-lumpy shape of the flesh beneath.

The edge of the forest caught us like a knife's edge, so abrupt it was almost unbelievable. One moment we were walking through the trees, and the next we were stepping onto a muddy embankment, with only a few feet separating us and the road. A white van was parked there, a radio station's logo and call sign on the side. The distinguishing markings were more than half-covered with mud, making them more of a puzzle than anything else. Was that a *5*, or the letter *S*, or something else? Was that a falcon or the curve of a very strange wolf's flank?

The van door opened.

Jeff stepped out.

I gaped, briefly unable to find the words to say anything. He was *here*. He was *real*. I'd known he existed since his first text, but somehow I hadn't quite made the leap that would translate that into the material world where Graham and I could meet him.

He was taller than either of us, although not as tall as David, with light brown skin, black hair, and dark brown eyes. His Chinese heritage showed in the shape of his face and the cast of his features, while his blue jeans and gray sweatshirt were as nondescript as his van. No one who saw him would think twice about what he was doing there, or think to report him to the police for anything less than witnessing him actually committing a crime.

There was a white bandage taped over his right cheek.

He looked at the four of us, scanning each of our faces before his eyes settled on me and a grin spread across his face. "Stasia," he said, and his voice was longing and relief and yes, affection, so bone-deep and pure that it made me want to sink into the ground. I didn't even know this man, and he was looking at me like I was the solution to every question he had never quite known how to ask. "You came."

"We could say the same for you," said Graham, angling his body slightly so that it was between me and this relative stranger, this man of my literal dreams. "Thanks for coming to get us. We could have been in real trouble back there."

"You still could be," said Jeff, his smile fading, replaced by a coolly calculating expression. "Did anyone see you go into the woods?"

"No," said Graham.

"Are you sure?"

"The man's sure," said David. "We'd have noticed if a bunch of armed police were following us through the forest."

"And you didn't mention my name while you were inside the facility?"

"No." This time it was Toni who spoke. She gave him a level look. "You're not on my wall of crazy, either."

Jeff blinked, visibly confused. "What?"

"I'll tell you in the van," I said. "Can we get out of here? I don't know how long we have before the cops come back down the road."

"Your wish is my command, literally," he said, and opened the front passenger door for me. There was only one seat up there with him. Refusing to take it seemed unwise. I still glanced back at Graham, waiting for him to say something before I got in.

He nodded.

I got in. The others climbed into the back; Jeff started the engine, and we were away.

7

PORTLAND, MAINE: JULY 20, 2031
EIGHTEEN DAYS PRE-INVASION

1.

Jeff was silent until we reached the bottom of the hill and merged onto the local highway. It was a two-lane road, with a number instead of a name, and there was enough traffic that we would no longer stand out as a lone vehicle where it had no business being.

Once we were safely rolling along, passing houses and rickety gas stations, he glanced at me sidelong and said, in a low voice, "I wasn't sure you were really real."

"You texted me."

"I could have been texting . . . anybody. You could have been literally anybody. But you're you. You're the girl from the forest, and you're real and here and in my van." His cheeks turned red, the skin around the bandage showing its color patchily, like something was interfering with the blood flow. "I've never met anyone like us before."

"Like us?"

"You know . . . us." He glanced at the rearview mirror. The van was partitioned inside, with the passengers sharing bench seats that put them too far from the driver for reasonable conversation. I got the feeling that wasn't an accident. He didn't want them involved in this moment.

He didn't want them anywhere *near* him—or near me. Given a choice, he wouldn't have let them in the car. He would have just left them in the woods and driven away.

I thought of Toni's wall of pictures, of the labels reading DECEASED and the calm way she'd talked about the mortality rate among people like the two of us, and I couldn't blame him. I might want to, but I couldn't do it.

"Oh," I said softly. Then: "Neither have I. Before I saw you in the forest, I wasn't even sure there were others."

Jeff scoffed. "Of course there are others. That's how plants work. They drop a million seeds and hope one or two will sprout."

"Not a million," I said, unable to stifle the slow twisting feeling in my stomach. Not a million, no, but the logic was sound. What was the point in an invasion that started with only one spy?

Even before I'd seen Jeff—even before I'd seen Toni's wall—I should have known there would be dozens of us, hundreds, maybe even thousands, scattered all around the world. Because kids die. Not many kids, not even most kids, but still, kids die. They run into traffic or they eat the wrong thing or they catch COVID or the wrong strain of flu. An invasion that could lose whatever advantage we represented because of a bad hamburger was no invasion at all. It was a farce masquerading as a threat, and there was no point to it.

"Not a million," Jeff agreed. "Still. Lots of us, and I never managed to meet a single one before you flew close enough to my house for me to pick you up. You're real. You're real, and that means I'm real, and that means I'm not . . ." He touched the bandage on his cheek, eyes troubled.

"It means I'm not broken," he said finally.

"No," I said softly, and looked out the window at the wooded roadside rolling endlessly by. The trees seemed to go on forever. Maine was a lot like Washington, at least in that way.

There was a scuffle behind us before Toni jammed her head between the seats, looking first at Jeff, then at me. Jeff yelped, grabbing at the wheel as he fought not to lose control. Toni rolled her eyes.

"Don't be a big baby," she said. "If you're all like this, the humans are going to win no problem, and then you're going to look pretty damn silly. Right before we lock you in some secret government lab and experiment on you for twenty years."

Jeff stared at her. That seemed somewhat unsafe, given that we were still driving; I reached over and pushed his head gently back toward the road.

"Toni, please don't antagonize the driver," I said wearily. "Jeff, this is Antonia Fabris, the astronomer who intercepted the signal from the fleet. She probably knows more about what it can tell us regarding the position and timing of the invasion than anyone else in the world."

"Also I was nearly assimilated by one of your fucked-up pod flowers and I hate you," said Toni.

"There's also that," I agreed.

Jeff scowled, keeping his eyes on the road. "Then what is she doing in the van?" he demanded. "If she was a failed conversion, there's no way she's on our side."

"I don't think any sensible human is going to be on your side, Seymour," said Toni blithely. "I mean, there is a distinct lack of coming in peace in your overall game plan. But see, the human race is not on my side either, because they think there's something wrong with me, on account I've been playing the role of the heroic football quarterback in a nineteen-fifties monster movie for most of my life."

"*What?*" squawked Jeff.

"Sadly, I understood that," I said. "She means no one believes her when she says the aliens are coming."

"Bingo," said Toni. "And see, if this *were* a classic creature feature, I'd have a beautiful cheerleader girlfriend to protect and I'd figure out how to defeat you and then you'd go away forever while we made out chastely in front of the chagrined adults. Alas, that is not to be. No one is ever going to believe me, not until you're here, and if you're half the invaders I hope you are, you're not going to be easy to stop once that happens."

"You just said you hated us."

"I do," said Toni blithely. "Thing is, I hate everyone else even more than I hate you. You're not my own kind. You're under no obligation whatsoever to be kind to me or take care of me, and they were, or should have been, until they decided I was too damaged to be useful. This isn't the Victorian era. An asylum wasn't an option, on account of how at some point we figured out that locking people up and throwing away the key doesn't work. So they got me an observatory in the middle of nowhere instead, and as long as I keep taking my meds, the checks keep coming, and that should probably be enough, except that it's not. I hate them for throwing me away. All your people will do is kill me. Somehow, that seems like the better deal."

"You still released the signal," I said.

Toni shrugged. "Can't be the hero of the horror movie if you don't at least *try* to alert the authorities. And then run like fuck when they come to make you disappear for the crime of being inconvenient. Where are we going, anyway?"

"Back to the mothership, where we can take you apart to figure out what makes you tick," deadpanned Jeff.

Toni laughed. "Yeah, okay. I'll believe it when I see it." She withdrew, presumably going back to her seat. To be honest, I didn't care, as long as she wasn't cramming herself between us and muttering about monsters.

Were we monsters? I didn't know. I didn't think of myself as a monster. But Mom, who had never forgotten the day I came out of the woods and told her the aliens had taken her real baby away, might have had something different to say about the issue. A lot of people might have had something different to say.

I couldn't stop thinking about the pictures on Toni's wall, all those children and teenagers with pieces of string connecting them to the word 'deceased.' We'd been killing people since we got here. I rubbed the inside of my elbow with the heel of my hand, trying to soothe away the last lingering echoes of the itch.

Jeff glanced at me, looking knowingly at my hand. "Itches, doesn't it?" he asked.

I still couldn't remember what was underneath that bandage. Only that it was bad, somehow; only that it wasn't human, or hadn't been, when recast through the forest's lens. "It does," I admitted.

"I think it's the signal. I think when we hear it, it speeds some things up that were pretty slow before. It's not going to hurt you. This is what's supposed to happen."

"How do you know?"

"Because a flower ate me, and then I couldn't stop telling people I was an alien invader," he said matter-of-factly. "Clearly, that sort of compulsion is a 'supposed-to' thing, or it wouldn't have been there. I was supposed to warn everyone I spoke to that the invasion was coming, and I was supposed to do it while I looked just like the kid next door. While I *was* the kid next door. Now there's a signal from space, and I recognize it, I know it like I wrote it, and it's making me itch and doing strange things to my body. So that must be a 'supposed-to,' like the compulsion. It doesn't make sense otherwise."

"Not unless the invaders are totally incompetent." I made the statement lightly.

There was nothing light in the look Jeff leveled on me. "I don't think they are. Do you?"

"No," I admitted, and we drove on in silence, me rubbing the inside of my elbow, the green world rolling by around us.

2.

It took a little over thirty minutes to reach Jeff's "safe house": a rickety-looking old colonial home standing in the center of a clearing, surrounded on all sides by trees. There was a detached barn slightly off to one side and behind the main structure. Moss grew green on its roof, and the door stood ajar, allowing me to catch a tempting glimpse of some mysterious machine. Signs were posted along the drive, indicating that we were crossing onto private property, and trespassers would be prosecuted.

"Home sweet home," said Jeff, parking in front of the house and turning off the engine. Sitting up a little straighter, he called into the back, "We're here. Don't touch anything until I've turned off the security system, and do *not* try to walk across the field."

"Gopher holes?" I asked.

"Sure, if by 'gopher holes' you mean 'land mines,'" he said, and opened the door, sliding out of the van.

I hurried to do the same, careful to keep my feet on the paved drive as I ran around the front of the van to catch up with Jeff. "Land mines?" I demanded. "What the hell do you mean, *land mines*?"

"I mean explosive devices primed to explode if someone steps on them," he said. "Sometimes it rains raccoon in the middle of the night, which is messy, but I know nobody's going to break in."

"What the *hell*?"

"You just said that," he said, and glanced meaningfully over his shoulder at the others as they climbed out of the van. "Maybe you should go fill your friends in, before they decide to go for a walk off the beaten path and get themselves a one-way ticket to kingdom come." Then he strolled toward the porch, leaving me to decide which way to turn.

Graham's voice drifted around the van, slightly raised in the way I'd come to recognize as uncertainty. He got boisterous when he didn't know what else to do. A boisterous Graham was a Graham inclined to do big, bold things that made him look confident—like walking into a stranger's field to poke around for snakes.

I spun on my heel and ran toward the voices. Sure enough, there was Graham, moving toward the edge of the driveway, clearly intending to go on an unchaperoned field trip. I put on an extra burst of speed, grabbing his arm before he could step into the grass. Graham turned to blink at me, surprised.

"Land mines," I said.

His surprise melted away, replaced first by shock, and then by horror. "*Land* mines?" he echoed, at a much higher volume. "Stasia, what the hell?"

"That's what I said when he told me about them." I glanced over my shoulder at the house. Jeff was on the porch. He'd produced a tablet, and was typing something out—presumably the code to deactivate the security systems. There must have been more than one. There was no other reason for things to have taken this long.

I looked back to Graham. He was still staring at me. At least he wasn't trying to pull his arm away. "He's not a friend. He's just someone who could get us out of there."

"That's not what you said this morning."

I resisted the urge to look away. "I lied this morning."

"I figured that out." The horror slipped out of his eyes, leaving something even more distressing behind: disappointment. "I just can't figure out exactly why. How do you know this guy?"

The forest. The dreams that weren't dreams, that were some kind of . . . what? Neural network generated by people like me who were trying to live among the humans, all while knowing we would never really belong with them? It was as good an answer as any, and it wasn't a good answer at all.

"I don't know how to explain," I said, and watched the storm clouds roll in on Graham's face like a warning of trouble to come. "Graham . . ."

"Just give me a minute, okay?"

"Okay," I said, and backed off.

In our last year of college, when Graham had finally been able to convince his insurance company to let him start testosterone, he'd lost his temper more than a few times. Not because he wanted to: because his body, after years of dealing with mostly estrogen, didn't know how to handle the new hormones. They made him angry. They made him impulsive, and rash, and occasionally jealous in a way that frightened me. We'd nearly broken up over his temper, because it scared me and he didn't know how to control it and no matter how much I loved him, no matter how much I wanted to stand by him, I couldn't live with the fear that one day he'd punch me instead of the wall.

Instead of breaking up, we had gone to counseling together, offered through our school's Queer Alliance. They'd taught us about the way some people reacted to hormones, and given us the tools we needed to cope. We had even signed a contract, agreeing that the day either of us struck the other would be the day we separated. Graham had held to it. So had I. And part of holding to it was knowing when to open space between us, to let the anger drain.

Toni and David looked at me, her with interest, him with resignation, like he'd always known his association with her would end in a field full of land mines somewhere in the middle of nowhere, where his body would never be found.

"Lovers' spat?" asked Toni.

"We're allowed," I said.

"See, I think when the fate of the human race hangs in the balance and the police are coming to arrest innocent astronomers for the crime of listening to the music of the spheres, relationship drama should maybe go on a hiatus in favor of not winding up dead," said Toni. "But what do I know? I'm just the human lady."

"Graham is human," I protested.

"But he knows you're not. That makes him a traitor at best, and a sympathizer at worst."

"Toni," said David.

"No." She shook her head. "People who side with the invaders get to enjoy the full spectrum of shame and disappointment as the aliens ride in and destroy everything humanity has ever worked for. There's no 'Oh, he's a nice guy, it's not his fault his girlfriend is a face-eater.' He's a nice guy. His girlfriend—you—is a face-eater. He gets to live with that."

"I've never eaten a face," I said.

"Wait for it," she replied.

I sighed, rubbing the crook of my elbow. I wanted to peel off my sweater and see what it looked like. I was afraid to find out. "Just don't go into the field, okay? I think Jeff might be your soulmate. He's super paranoid, and there are land mines in the grass."

"Huh," said Toni, with grudging respect. "A man after my own heart."

"He's a plant," I said. "Don't get too attached." Then I turned and walked toward the porch.

Jeff was tucking his tablet back into his bag when I walked up, having apparently finished the lengthy process of unlocking the door. He flashed me a tight-lipped smile. "You told them about the land mines?"

"I don't think they're too happy with you."

"That's fine. I don't concern myself overly with the happiness of apes. It never ends well for anyone—not me, and not them." Jeff pulled an ordinary key out of his pocket, sliding it into the deadbolt. "You hungry?"

My stomach rumbled. It had been a long time since breakfast. "I could eat."

"I'll make us some scrambled eggs. Come on." With that, he pushed the door open, and led me into the house.

I'm not sure what I had been expecting. Something desolate and creepy: the kind of place that belonged in a dark, creepy forest, surrounded by land mines and trees. Instead, the foyer was decorated in a clean, minimalist style that could have been stolen from the most recent Hollywood blockbuster. Simple black-and-white photos of forested areas hung on the walls, evenly spaced, so that each of them had to be considered on its own merits. The floor and walls were hardwood, and while they were stained and sealed, nothing was painted.

"It's all eco-friendly," said Jeff, looking over his shoulder at me. "I'm off the power grid entirely, thanks to the solar panels on the roof, and I get my water from a natural aquifer. I'm connected to the municipal gas lines and I get my internet from the cable company like everybody else, but that's it for me and dependence on the local grid. If I had to, I could stay out here for six months at a stretch without needing to pay a bill or see an inspector. It's a pretty sweet gig."

"Where are your parents?"

His shrug was fluid. "Ultimatum when I turned sixteen: stop telling everyone I was an alien, or find someplace else to live. You know how *that* story ends."

"Yeah. I do." No one can be ordered out of a compulsion; that's not how compulsions work. If it were, there would be a lot fewer compulsive people in the world. So his parents had told him to stop or get out, and he'd gotten out. I would have done the same thing in his situation. I sort of had: my mother never quite said I needed to change my song or leave her home, but she'd implied it. She'd whispered it when she didn't think I was listening, trying to convince my grandparents this was "tough love." Like the way to make me normal was to forbid me to be strange.

Luckily for me, my grandparents had been having none of that bullshit, and as long as they'd been alive, I'd had a room in their house. Once they'd passed away, I had taken the last of my stuff from their attic and bid my childhood home a sad farewell. Mom would probably have allowed me to live there for at least a little while, but some fights aren't worth having. Some fights just need to be walked away from.

"Anyway, it's not like I was going to be able to save them when the invasion came, so it's probably for the best that they made it clear where their allegiances were." Jeff looked at me levelly. "Don't you think it's best if we don't struggle to save people who have already been lost?"

I thought about Graham and the others, standing outside, trying to compose themselves after fleeing from the police. I thought about the look on Graham's face when I'd said the words "land mines."

"I don't think anyone is already lost," I said softly.

Jeff didn't say anything. He just looked at me.

The house was warm and quiet, and most of all, *safe*. It felt like nothing bad could ever happen here, like I could lock the door and sit down on the couch with a cup of hot tea and wait out the apocalypse.

"I wanted to . . . I mean, I don't know . . . I mean . . ." I stopped, rubbing the inside of my elbow again before I said, in a small voice, "I don't know what's under that bandage, but I wish you'd show me."

"Maybe I cut myself shaving."

"That isn't what it was in the forest last night."

The corner of Jeff's mouth twitched. "There you go. You're admitting it."

"Admitting what?"

"That we"—he moved a finger back and forth between us, pointing to each of us in turn—"are connected. We're the same. We're on the right side of this invasion."

I frowned. I wasn't ready to commit to our side being the "right" side—not yet. Not until I knew what we were coming here to do. I didn't think we were coming in peace, but I had been wrong before, and I could hope. I could hope there was a way this ended well for everyone, for me and for Graham and even for people like my mother or Jeff's parents. The humans had been here first. They deserved to keep their world.

Or did they? The whisper was sweet, insinuating itself into my thoughts as smoothly as a worm slides into the soil. The humans had done nothing to keep their planet safe. They hadn't put up orbital defense stations, hadn't learned to protect themselves from asteroids—hadn't even listened when the scouts of another world's army started loudly announcing themselves. We had never been subtle. But we *had* been laughed at.

"It's all right," said Jeff. He reached for the bandage, beginning to peel back the tape. "You don't have to know what you want yet. You're still figuring yourself out, and that's cool. That just means you're going to be real sure when you finally believe. You're going to be a juggernaut."

"How are you sure already?" I asked. "You know as much as I do."

"Like I said, I'm in computers. I like to understand things. I started digging a long time ago, looking for the holes that fit us. I found a lot more than most people. More than a human could ever have pieced together, that's for damn sure. Did you know we're not alone? I mean, literally. There have been earlier waves, although they were never quite as dense as ours. I think there might be people like us in their eighties, still wandering along, waiting for an invasion they don't believe is ever coming. Can you imagine? Getting old waiting to be needed, and then turning around and realizing there's a line of people behind you young and strong enough to do what needs to be done? It's got to be breaking their hearts."

He pulled the last of the tape off the edge of the bandage and rolled it down, revealing the skin beneath. My breath caught in my throat and my heart stopped in my chest, leaving an aching stillness inside me. It didn't hurt, exactly. It didn't even feel all that uncomfortable. It was like a system had gone offline, something unnecessary but convenient, and the rest of me was adjusting to its absence.

The skin on Jeff's cheek had been ripped cleanly away, leaving thin, jagged edges to outline the wound. They were translucent in places, like they were being slowly worn away.

The wound itself was not a wound, not exactly: it was a patch of skin as green as maple leaves in the spring. Thin lines ran through it, sketched in darker green, like the veins on those same leaves. I made a soft sound of protest and dismay. Jeff smiled, a little ruefully.

"I heard the signal," he said. "The next day, I was fixing a solar panel on the roof when I slipped and scraped my cheek. Pretty standard . . . except this time, the scrape didn't heal. Instead, the skin started to die and peel off, and this was what was underneath."

"Was that *always* there?" My voice barely crested above a whisper. I couldn't take my eyes off that torn place, that green place.

My future.

"It can't have been," he said. "I grew up a normal kid, you know? The 'I am from space' stuff didn't even bother people until I was like, nine. I skinned my knees. I saw the dentist. I got sick, I got better, I did the stuff kids are supposed to do. If I'd been green inside, somebody would have noticed. Didn't you ever go to the hospital?"

Mutely, I nodded. Pneumonia when I was eight; a broken ankle when I was eleven. X-rays and antibiotics and human systems functioning and breaking down in human ways. None of this smooth greenness. None of this impossibility.

"I think it started growing when the signal played. Like we had to hear it for it to take hold of us." Jeff glanced at the door as he taped his bandage back into place, checking that we were still alone before he nodded toward my elbow. "It still itches?"

It took me a moment to remember that he'd seen me scratching at it in the forest, where I had looked under his bandage for the first time. Only it hadn't been smooth green skin there, had it? It had been something *else*, something even less human. Something that could never have been concealed under a simple sheet of taped-down gauze. I couldn't quite remember what I'd seen—it slipped away whenever I grabbed for it, like my subconscious understood that I wasn't prepared for the truth—and yet I knew it had been impossible.

"Yeah," I said softly.

"Is he going to stand with you when the skin tears?"

I flinched. I couldn't help it. Jeff smirked, and somehow that was the last straw. I took a step toward him, hands balled into fists, fury in my eyes. To my immense satisfaction, he took a step back.

"Graham is none of your concern," I snapped. "Be as smug as you like. Be as confident in our victory as you want, but be assured, I *will* protect what's mine, and I *will* see them through to the end of this invasion. Do not touch them. Do you understand me?"

"I didn't threaten your people."

"You were going to. It goes from 'They're useless' to 'They're dangerous' to 'Get rid of them.' You think I don't understand how this sort of thing works? I come from the same vine you do. I am grateful you got us out of there. I would like to know someone who is like me and understands what's about to happen. But if you lay one finger on anyone I have claimed as my own, we're done. Do you understand?"

"Heh," he said, taking another step back. "Has anyone ever told you you're scary as hell when you want to be?"

"Lots of people. I'm in customer service."

The sound of the door opening pulled us both from the conversation. We turned. The others had worked up the courage to walk along the pavement, where the land mines weren't, and were stepping inside. As they did, they looked around with a familiar wide-eyed curiosity. Toni and David hung back, apparently studying the material used to construct the walls. Graham moved away from them, hurrying over to me.

"Hey," he said.

"Hey," I replied. "Feeling better?"

"Not really, but I'm feeling less irrational, and I'll take it." He turned to Jeff. "I didn't thank you for bringing us to your home. It was extremely decent of you. So thank you. Now what the fuck do you think you're playing at, putting live land mines in your yard?"

"How are you so sure they're live?" asked Jeff. "I didn't hear anything explode."

"I'm taking your word for it," Graham said. "If I can believe my girlfriend is a plant from space, I can believe you're enough of an asshole to set land mines. Which are totally illegal, by the way. You could go to prison for a long, long time."

"Since I just saved you from getting your ass disappeared to an unmarked government facility for the foreseeable future, how about we call it even?" Jeff folded his arms. "I have land mines because I am the vanguard of an invading species of alien plants, and I didn't feel like getting dissected in the middle of the night. The land mines are illegal. They also keep people from dropping by uninvited and taking me away."

"Now that's a kind of alien abduction we don't hear about all the time," said Toni blithely, strolling over to join us. She looked Jeff up and down. "I don't know you."

"Okay," said Jeff.

"You don't understand. I know all of you in this area. I have pictures. I know where the bodies are buried. How come I don't know you?"

"My flower bloomed on Oahu, if that helps." Jeff shrugged. "I moved here to be isolated."

Toni's smile was brilliant. "Of course it bloomed on Oahu. That makes total sense. Volcanic ash must have been amazing for the growth cycle, and anyway, I knew you couldn't be local."

"I'm local now," said Jeff. "What the hell do you mean, you know where the bodies are buried?"

"Metaphorically speaking," said Toni. "I know how many of you come from around here. I even know where most of you are. I lost track of three kids when their parents moved them across the country before they were eighteen. My PIs found two of them, but the third is still a mystery. I think he's somewhere in Utah, if he's still alive. That's always the big question."

"What are you talking about?" Jeff looked at me. "What is she talking about?"

"Toni met one of the seeding flowers when she was a kid," I said. "It tried to absorb her. It didn't succeed."

"I was too tough to eat," said Toni, smiling sweetly. "Now you vegetable motherfuckers get to deal with your worst fear: a scientist who knows where the weed killer is."

"And we got her out of the observatory because why, exactly?" asked Jeff.

"Because she's the one who recorded and released the signal," I said. "She can help us learn more about it."

"Or she can lie to us about its composition and make sure we're not properly prepared to do what comes next," snapped Jeff.

"Do you know what that is?" The question came from an unexpected source: Graham. We turned slowly toward him, my heart sinking as I realized I had all but forgotten he was there in my focus on Jeff and Toni's debate. He was my boyfriend and I loved him. I was ready to defend him from the coming invasion, no matter what that defense entailed . . . and I had already forgotten he was there.

Jeff frowned. "What do you mean?"

"Do you know what comes next?" Graham moved closer to me, putting a hand on my shoulder, making it impossible to forget him again. I leaned into it, feeling grateful and sick to my stomach at the same time. Everything was shifting so fast.

My elbow still itched. The memory of green tugged at the edges of my awareness, refusing to be ignored, and I was afraid.

"No." Jeff shook his head, frustration clear in his expression. "I don't have a damn clue what comes next. I didn't even know the invasion was coming until I heard that signal."

"Maybe I faked it," said Toni tauntingly.

"You didn't fake it," I said, before I could think better. Everyone turned to look at me. I didn't squirm. I stood a little straighter, lifting my chin, and said, "I don't know what it says, but I understand it. There's no way you could have done that good a job faking something you've never heard before. It's real. They're coming."

"And the police have taken the observatory," said David bleakly. "What do we do now?"

"You come back to Washington with us." I looked at Graham, and smiled, just a little, when I saw him nod. Returning my attention to the others, I said, "There's room. Between his place and mine, there's room. We can work on this together."

"Why should I leave?" asked Jeff. "Why shouldn't you stay here?"

"Because cultural literacy is part of why we bloomed here," I said, and was gratified by the way his eyes widened, ever so slightly. "See? You feel it too. You've isolated yourself. Maybe that's what you had to do in order to survive, but it isn't going to make you as useful as you could be. As they're going to *want* you to be."

"And David and I?" asked Toni. "I've already told you I'm not going to be your ally. We'll work against you."

"That's fine," I said. "Keep your friends close and your enemies closer, that's how it goes, right? We don't have an observatory for you. We don't have the police on our doorstep either—not yet, anyway—and since I'm a homegrown crank, we'll probably have some time. You can analyze the signal. You can try to find a way to stop us. One of us will have to succeed before the other, but that's what it takes to be the hero of that horror movie, right?"

"I think it's more of a creature feature, but you make a good point," said Toni, with a glance at David. "I can make a few calls. Get the things we need delivered to the airport without involving the local authorities."

"Won't they just, I don't know, arrest us *at* the airport?" asked David. "The TSA could disappear us forever without thinking about it twice."

"But they won't," said Toni. "They like to have cause. They like to be able to say, 'This is why we did this thing, and if you're not careful, we'll do it to you.'"

I thought about my own fears on the flight here, and said nothing. David was right. If the TSA decided to get involved, there was nothing we could do. But we couldn't stay here, and it wasn't like the trains were any safer, not since the powers of the TSA had been expanded to cover them as well as air travel. Taking the train just made it more likely that we'd disappear somewhere in the middle of the country, vanishing into a private government facility that might never let us out again. At least if we were on a plane, they'd have fewer options to snatch us.

Toni might like that. Then again, she might not. She had come close enough to assimilation that there was a chance the people who decided to organize against the invasion—assuming they did so in time—would decide she was on our side and not humanity's.

Sides. It all came down to drawing sides.

I slipped my hand into Graham's, holding tight, holding fast despite everything that was ahead of us. If I drew a side, I was going to make sure my friends were standing on it with me. That mattered more than planet, more than species, more than *anything.*

"So," I said, and my voice was strong and steady. I was proud that it belonged to me. That was the voice of a woman who could survive an alien invasion, and see her people safely to the other side. "Do you have a guest room?"

3.

Jeff had three guest rooms, part and parcel of his ridiculously oversized house. I wasn't sure why someone with such an attraction to solitude would want to have that many extra beds, but I also wasn't going to argue with it. Not when it gave us a place to spend the night.

Toni and David were bedding down together, in the room closest to the front door, as if needing to run a little less to reach the door if Jeff and I decided to move on to human experimentation in the night was the solution to all their problems. I still wasn't sure what their relationship was—friends, lovers, or simply very close colleagues—but it didn't really matter, because Graham and I were, for the first time since leaving our hotel, finally alone.

Jeff had produced toothbrushes and toothpaste from a stockpile that looked like something from a survivalist compound, only grunting when I'd asked him why he had so many. He seemed like a very lonely man. Maybe that was explanation enough for why he'd tracked me down after meeting me in the forest: he was alone, and he wanted to find his own kind. The urge had to have an urgency for him that didn't exist for me.

Not yet, anyway.

I sat on the edge of the futon that was going to be our home for the night, my sweater still on and my hand clamped over the bend of my elbow, like I could somehow force the world to take it back—to take it all back, all the way to the moment when Anastasia Miller had wandered into the woods and met the pretty flower that would steal her life. It wasn't that I didn't want to exist. It was just that I wanted this all to have been easier. I wanted to have been one thing from birth until now, with no question of where my loyalties were going to go.

Graham stepped out of his trousers, leaving himself clad in nothing but his boxer shorts, and turned, looking slightly nonplussed to find me still fully clothed. "Stasia? Is everything all right?"

No. Nothing was all right. It was possible nothing was going to be all right ever again: that we had passed the last moment of normalcy sometime in the past few weeks, and now it was gone forever. Biting my lip, I shook my head.

Graham frowned. He walked over and sat beside me, reaching for my hand. His frown deepened when it remained clamped over the bend of my elbow, unyielding. "Hey. What is it? Can I help? I'm sorry it's not safe to go back to the hotel. But we'll be able to change our clothes before the flight."

The idea that this might be about something as pedestrian as clean underwear was almost enough to make me start laughing. The only reason I was able to resist was that I knew if I started, I wouldn't be able to stop. I'd laugh and laugh as the world fell down around us, and I wouldn't be able to save anyone. Not even Graham.

Not even myself.

"I need to show you something," I said, voice carefully level, "and I need you to promise me you won't freak out about it. Can you do that?"

"Don't be silly."

"Can you do that?" My voice was ice eating away at a sapling's roots, harsh and cold and unforgiving. Graham froze, leaning back to look at me with wide, startled eyes.

His beard was coming in the patchy way it always did, making his cheeks look like they'd been half-plucked by some rogue beautician. He was a little flushed, making the scars on his chest stand out white against the red, and he had never been so handsome, and I had never loved him more. This could be the moment when I lost him. Because I had always believed him when he told me he was a man, and we had always pretended his belief in me was the same thing, but it wasn't, was it? It wasn't the same thing at all. Gender was a social construct and a part of the soul, and humans had always been capable of getting it wrong. I, though . . .

I was something alien and new, and while we had built a relationship on believing each other, our secrets weren't the same at all.

"Okay," he said, in a hushed voice. "I won't freak out."

It was an impossible promise. It still made me feel better, enough that I could whisper, "Close your eyes."

He closed his eyes. I peeled off my sweater, dropping it on the floor before allowing myself to look down at the bend of my elbow, at the place that had started itching in an impossible forest.

The skin was torn. The edges were red and raw, and probably should have hurt me, all things considered. There was no blood, but there was a small amount of cloudy fluid, like sap leaking from the torn leaf of a bush. Where the skin had been, where the skin had ripped away, there was . . .

There was . . .

It was still skin. I touched it gingerly with the tip of one finger, and I felt the contact exactly like I expected I would. There were even tiny hairs there, filaments that probably served some biological purpose, mammalian or not. It was a small tear. If not for the color, it would have looked human.

I was a deeper shade of green than Jeff was, less tropical and more Pacific Northwest. I was the color of pine needles, of evergreens, of places where the snow was never quite strong enough to conquer the trees. I touched the patch of alien skin again. It was mine. It was me. I had always been telling the truth. I had never, despite the cries of parents and classmates, been crazy.

"You can open your eyes now," I said softly, pulling my hand away and extending my arm, giving Graham the clearest view possible. This was his moment. If he wanted to run, if he wanted to turn against me, this was his moment.

He opened his eyes and looked at my arm. For a long time, he didn't say anything, and neither did I. Finally, he took a breath.

"Is that makeup?" he asked. "Is this a joke?"

"No."

"Is it a bruise? A really . . . a really strange bruise?"

"No."

"Can I touch it?"

Graham had touched every inch of my body during our time together, had scoured my skin with fingers and tongue. If I had ever turned green before this, he would have known before I did, teasing the taste of chlorophyll from my flesh. Maybe that was why I nodded acquiescence and held my arm out toward him, allowing him to reach for me.

His fingertips were gentle as they brushed against my tender new skin, and the tiny hairs that might not be hairs at all stood on end at the sensation. He paused before running a single finger over my skin a second time, focusing on the hairs. They bent under the pressure, springing back up when it was taken away.

"It's real," he said softly. He looked up, meeting my eyes, and only the fact that he didn't flinch away kept me from crying. "You were telling the truth. This whole time, you were telling the truth."

"Yes," I said.

"The invasion is coming."

"Yes."

"Can we stop it?"

"No."

"Can we survive it?"

"I don't know," I said, and the tears finally came, rolling down my cheeks in slow lines. Graham put his arms around me, and held me, and if he noticed that my tears were thicker than they should have been, he didn't say a word.

Neither of us did, as all around us, the night—one of the last nights of a free and human world—went on.

8

TUCSON, ARIZONA: JULY 21, 2031
SEVENTEEN DAYS PRE-INVASION

1.

"Ladies and gentlemen, this is your captain speaking. Some of you may have noticed that we're a little off-course. We have been diverted to Tucson due to an equipment problem. We'll have this taken care of and get you back in the air as quickly as possible. My apologies for the inconvenience."

Our plane, filled with weary travelers, emitted a collective mumbling groan. Some people had been asleep until the loudspeaker's announcement. Others were trying to focus on their tablets, their books, anything to keep them from remembering where they really were, and being jerked back into the harsh reality of air travel was not comforting to them.

Toni, nestled against David's side in the row across from ours, continued her open-mouthed snoring, even as David blinked blearily at the speakers. "What the hell?" he mumbled, just loud enough for me to hear. "That doesn't make sense."

"What about it?" I asked.

"If we're making a landing for a technical issue, it shouldn't be in Tucson. That's entirely in the wrong direction."

"Maybe there's a flying unicorn outside, and the pilot's changing course to keep it from being sucked into the engine. Now shut up so I can get some goddamn *sleep*," muttered Jeff, not opening his eyes.

I had been sandwiched between him and Graham since we boarded. I wasn't sure exactly how Toni had been able to seat us all together and get an open middle seat on her side of the plane, but I was willing to bet her credit cards and family fortune had a lot to do with it. Why fly first class when you can just as easily annoy your alien acquaintances in coach?

Graham didn't say anything. His eyes were open and alert, and he was eyeing the speakers with the wariness of a man who knew nothing good could come of a mid-flight announcement dripping with that much tension.

"Folks, I apologize, but it seems we've developed a small problem with one of our fuel couplings, and will be making an unscheduled landing in Tucson," continued the captain. "It's nothing to be alarmed about, and you'll be compensated for your time with a drink on us as soon as we're back in the air. We expect to be on the ground for thirty minutes tops while our engineering team does a quick but thorough repair, and then it's back in the air and on to Seattle."

The murmurs of irritation had been replaced by murmurs of alarm. Graham's hand clamped down on mine, suddenly squeezing hard enough to hurt. I glanced at him. He was still staring at the speaker, face white.

"What?" I asked, keeping my voice as low as I could. Jeff could hear me—he was leaning close to make sure of it—but I was reasonably sure we wouldn't be overheard by anyone else. That was one of my favorite things about air travel, the way flying in a giant white-noise machine provided a sliver of privacy in what was really a very public place.

"That's not how airplanes work," Graham murmured.

"How would you know?" asked Jeff. "I thought you were a snake scientist."

"I am," said Graham. "That means I know a lot of people with private planes, who use those private planes to fly me to the middle of nowhere to look at rare or difficult to locate snakes. No one is that calm about a problem with the fuel. Not even a commercial air pilot, and part of their pay is based on their ability not to panic passengers. Did you hear his voice? No waver. No fear. Irritation and confusion, but that was not the voice of a man who's afraid his engine is about to run out of gas. He's setting down for another reason."

"Why?" asked Jeff.

"Why do you think?" I couldn't keep the bitterness out of my voice. "Because of us. It's the same damn problem as the trains. We just got here faster."

"And more publicly," said Graham. "When they come to take us off the plane, don't resist—resistance only gets you hurt—but be loud. Demand to know why they're doing this. Yell about your rights, about the fact that you're an American citizen. Get people filming the incident. That's not going to save us right away, maybe not ever, but at least the people who care about us will be aware that we're gone."

I didn't say anything. I sank back in my seat and closed my eyes, feeling the plane tilt around me as it entered its initial descent, and wondering how the hell we'd ended up here.

Our trip from Jeff's house to the hotel had been easy enough: despite our fears, there were no officers waiting on the road to start a car chase, or stationed in the hotel parking lot to arrest us. No one had said a word as we'd walked across the lobby in our little group of five, headed up to our rooms, and collected our things. Going back had been a calculated risk, part bravado and part necessity. We didn't want to be scared away from our luggage—and more, we needed to know how deep the hot water really was. In the absence of an arrest, we'd assumed we were in the clear.

Getting into the airport had been just as easy. Graham had called for a ride while Jeff hid his van in the woods behind the hotel, where it might be found tomorrow and it might be found never, but either way, it wouldn't be in the parking lot attracting attention. Confirmation numbers in hand, we'd sailed through security, answering the intrusive questions from the TSA and smiling, smiling, smiling until our faces hurt. Smiling like we weren't terrified, like there wasn't a patch of dark green skin on my arm, hidden under the sleeve of my sweater, but *there*, marking me finally and immutably as what I had always claimed to be.

I was an alien. I was not of this world. And one way or another, I was going to have to reconcile that with a lifetime lived among these people, who had been my friends and my family and my home. For the moment, however, I couldn't focus on that. I needed to focus on *getting* home, back to Lucas and Mandy and Seymour, who was only a cat and couldn't understand any of this.

Jeff had gotten it worse than I had with the TSA. I looked white, even if I was a vegetable, and I was better at smiling like nothing was wrong, while he was a surly Asian-American man with a bandage on his cheek. There had been a moment where I'd been sure the TSA agent was about to ask him for a doctor's note clearing him to fly, but then Toni had blown him a kiss and called him "darling" in a voice like treacle, and suddenly we'd been in the clear. It was almost offensive, seeing the power of the white woman at work. We might have to live with misogyny and the patriarchy and all that fun bullshit, but because we'd been placed on such a high pedestal of purity and innocence, our approval could take a dangerous fellow and turn him into a nice guy.

It was another form of oppression. How else could people say that women only wanted to reform bad boys, if they didn't set us up to do it all the fucking time? But in that moment, even as I prickled, I was grateful. Without Toni's intervention, we might not have been able to get Jeff onto the plane.

That didn't seem like such a good thing anymore. We were descending steadily, moving toward an uncertain and unfriendly future. Toni was still snoring away. That might be for the best. There was a chance, however small, that she could escape notice if she didn't seem to be too unsettled.

Assuming David didn't blow it for the both of them. He was looking increasingly agitated. As I watched, he moved to shake her shoulder. I caught his eye and shook my head, motioning for him to leave her alone. There was a pause as he realized what I meant, and he settled in his seat, waiting for the inevitable.

I sort of envied Toni. Neither Graham nor I had gotten much sleep. We hadn't been talking or having sex or anything fun like that; we'd just been lying side by side, listening to the night pass by around us, neither of us sure how to start the conversation we needed to be having. He was dealing with the fact that I wasn't human. That couldn't have been easy. I was dealing with the same thing, but also with the fact that on some level, he'd never really believed I was what I said I was. I had never doubted him when he told me about himself, and he hadn't believed me. Not entirely.

It wasn't the same thing. It wasn't even in the neighborhood of being the same thing. It *felt* like the same thing, and it ached like the same thing, and that made it close enough to hurt.

The plane kept descending, the discontented murmurs of our fellow passengers growing ever more pronounced. Graham gripped my hand, anchoring me in the moment.

"It'll be okay," he said. "I'm sure whatever this is, it's just a misunderstanding. We'll be able to clear it all up and get on our way."

"Sure," I said. I wasn't sure, but if this was helping him, I wasn't going to argue.

The sky outside the window disappeared, replaced first by a thick layer of clouds, and then by the rapidly looming Arizona desert. The airport was a gray concrete smear across the landscape, penned in by mountains and surrounded by the glittering glass of the city. I'd never been to Arizona before. As a Washington girl, I don't like that kind of heat, and as a vegetable in human disguise, I don't like that degree of dryness. It had never seemed like a good place for me.

How right I'd been.

"Flight attendants, please take your seats for landing," said the captain. The helpful men and women who'd been keeping us happy and calm since takeoff disappeared, and the plane angled even more aggressively downward, slicing off the last few meters of sky—the last few meters of safety—in its bid for the ground. Graham squeezed my hand. I closed my eyes.

Because I hadn't slept last night, I hadn't been able to return to the forest. Maybe that was a good thing. Jeff and I had both started experiencing physical changes, but his had followed the signal, while mine had followed our meeting in the forest. Maybe staying out of it was the key to staying as human as possible, for as long as possible. Not forever—I already knew that was beyond me—but for a while. Long enough to figure out what came next.

It was a foolish quest. The forest came for me when I slept; it always had. I could no more order it to stay away than I could decide "Well, this was fun, but I don't want to be an alien invader anymore, I want to be a human girl again for the first time, so can we get on that?" But it was something to focus on apart from the fact that we were probably all . . . about to . . .

I opened my eyes and dug my phone out of my pocket, pressing the button to turn it back on. Graham turned to blink at me.

"We're supposed to keep those off until—"

"I am aware," I snapped, shaking the little device as if that would speed the boot-up process in some intangible but essential way. The plane was dropping lower and lower. The flight attendants were seated—good, they couldn't make me put the phone away—but that meant we didn't have much time. "Why the hell do phones take so long to start?"

"Because they're tiny computers," said Jeff. "You're holding more processing power than NASA had when they put John Glenn into orbit."

The urge to turn and glare at him was strong, and it might have been relaxing, under other circumstances. Glaring at people who stay stupid, pedantic shit is practically one of my hobbies. At the moment, I had more important things to worry about.

The screen lit up, the phone's logo flashing for a second before it was replaced by my lock screen: a picture of my cat on Graham's chest. Graham was barely visible behind the mound of black-and-white fur, and they both had their eyes closed. It was one of my favorite moments ever, and I normally loved that I got to look at it every day. This time, I swept it aside with a swipe of my thumb, bringing up a text window.

We were too high to have service. That would stop soon. Selecting Mandy's number, I began composing my message.

Mandy. About to be detained by law enforcement in Arizona. Tell Luke. If not home by end of week, tell EVERYONE. We have done nothing wrong. We are being held against our will.

Maybe it wasn't true that we'd done nothing wrong. I started my time on this planet by devouring and replacing a little girl, after all. But I'd been a different creature when I'd done that, and I'd sprouted on American soil. Didn't that make me a citizen? I still had rights. I still deserved better than to disappear into a lab somewhere while the invasion crept ever-closer and no one took care of the people I needed to protect.

I pressed Send, trusting the network to deliver my message as soon as we landed. Then I hesitated, and started again.

I know this is all v/scary, and probably pretty confusing. I will explain everything when we make it home. I will keep you safe. Please feed my cat, and can you go to Graham's to feed his mean lizard? Not even an iguana deserves to starve to death. I love you more than you will ever know.

Again I hit Send, this time lowering my phone. I leaned until my head was resting against Graham's shoulder, and closed my eyes. It was out of our hands at this point. Out of *my* hands.

It was time to let gravity take us.

2.

The flight attendants reappeared as soon as the plane touched down, walking the aisles to make sure no one had been bounced from their seat or decided to get up and go for their carry-on. If they noticed the phone still held in a death grip in my right hand, they didn't say anything about it. It was impossible to say whether that was compassion or a lack of comprehension. The pilot had sounded confused and annoyed. There was an excellent chance the crew didn't know who had forced this stop.

Or maybe it wasn't us. Maybe it really was some sort of fuel problem, and we were going to be just fine. I would happily apologize to Mandy for frightening her, if that was the case. I would get down on my knees and swear to being the worst housemate in the history of time. If they let us walk away from this . . .

"Folks, I'm going to have to ask you all to stay seated for the duration of our stop," said the captain over the loudspeaker, his voice wavering. "We're about to dock at our temporary gate, and we're going to have a quick visit from local law enforcement."

A murmur broke out around us, people looking at each other and then at their fellow passengers, trying to figure out who could have attracted the attention of the police. Jeff, with his bandaged face and his scowl, attracted more stares than Graham and I did, but nothing lingering enough to mean he'd been recognized.

"What the *fuck?*"

Toni's voice was like an icepick. I flinched. On some level, I'd been hoping she'd stay asleep until the plane was back in the air. Maybe they would have left her as they pulled us off, assuming a slumbering astronomer was a waste of resources. Probably not, but as I was running out of pretty lies to tell myself, I'd been hopeful. I'd been so damn hopeful.

David shushed her, murmuring something I couldn't hear above the ongoing rumble of the engines. Toni leaned back, giving him a stunned look which transformed into a scowl as she leaned forward and focused on the three of us.

"This is *your* fault," she spat. Several other passengers turned to stare.

"You're the one who released that damn signal," said Jeff.

"I wouldn't have needed to release it if you hadn't decided to invade my fucking planet in the first place," she countered. Her voice climbed with every word, until it felt as if the entire plane had turned to stare. I shrank back against Graham, less out of fear, and more in an attempt to get all those eyes off of me. I didn't want to look at them. I didn't want *them* to look at *me*. I wasn't their business. I wasn't their concern.

Cultural literacy again, I thought, half-nonsensically. *I only know how to feel shame because I've spent so much time among these mammalian monkeys. It's not* fair.

I should have been striding onto their soil, ready to take it for my own, to spread the seed of my own garden across the universe, colonialism writ large and finally coming home to roost. Instead, I was quailing away from them, like one of the weakest of their kind, and I hated—

I stopped, embarrassment fading in the face of cold realization. Somewhere in the middle of all that, it had gone from "us" to "them." There had always been an element of that, but now . . . now it was complete. I looked at the faces around me, and found no fellow-feeling, no urge to keep them or their planet safe.

If my loyalty to the species that had raised me was that fragile, Earth was doomed.

"Toni, calm down," muttered David.

"No," she said. "I will *not* calm down. *None* of us should be calming down." She looked at me again, and winked. Broadly and blatantly winked.

Slowly, I began to realize what she was doing. "Jeff's right," I said loudly. "You're the one who released that signal, and now we're sitting ducks, waiting for the feds to sweep in and make us all disappear forever. What the hell, man?"

"Both of you, shut up," snapped Graham. "We need to stay calm."

We didn't look like any popular ideas about terrorists, and we were yelling at each other about aliens, labeling ourselves comfortably as kooks—at least for now. When the authorities hauled us off this plane, everything we'd said was going to loom a lot larger in the minds of the people who'd been seated around us. Suddenly, going home and looking up that supposed message from space was going to be a lot more appealing. It would spread. Even if we vanished for a while, the signal would spread.

And I *wanted* it to spread. I wanted everyone in the world to hear it. That, too, was important to me, although I couldn't have explained exactly why. I wanted to know that when the sky went dark with ships from another world, it wouldn't be a surprise. Everyone would have been warned. Everyone would *know*.

Next to me, casually, Jeff unbuckled his belt. He looked at me and nodded. I swallowed hard and nodded back.

Never hesitating, never moving with any real urgency, Jeff slid out of his seat and started toward the back of the plane. No one moved to stop him. No one said *anything.* Not as he walked; not as he reached the bathroom; not as he slipped inside. We looked too normal, and the things we seemed to be concerned about were too strange. Taken together, it was reasonable for Jeff to be moving away from our little nexus of weirdness.

People didn't believe in the invasion yet. That was going to change. Until then, we could use their unwillingness to accept what they'd been told was coming, at least long enough to give Jeff a fighting chance.

I had no idea what he could do to evade capture on an airplane, which seemed like the very definition of a closed system. Luckily, that wasn't my problem anymore.

Unluckily, my problem had just walked in through the front door.

There were five of them, three in what looked like the uniform of the local police, the other two wearing black suits that could have come straight out of a Will Smith movie. We all stopped arguing to watch them warily. Maybe they weren't here for us. Maybe we were going to be fine.

They walked down the aisle, two of them passing us by, while the other three stopped to look directly at us. My heart sank. We weren't going to be fine.

"If you would come with us, please," said the woman at the front of their small formation. She had skin a few shades darker than Jeff's, with straight black hair pulled into a tight braid. She would have been beautiful, if she hadn't been looking at me like I was some exciting new species of insect for her to dissect at her leisure.

"May we ask what this is about?" Graham couldn't push himself in front of me, but he could sit up straighter and puff out his chest, all the hallmarks of the human male getting ready to defend his mate.

"You are being detained for questioning," said the woman. "Please, don't make this more difficult than it has to be. We're prepared to use any necessary force."

The unspoken threat was clear: if we made them use force in an enclosed space, people were going to get hurt, and it was going to be our fault, legally speaking. All we had to do was go quietly and no one would need to be any more inconvenienced than they already were.

"Why are you detaining us?" asked Graham loudly. "Is it because we listened to that signal from space? Are you here because aliens are real?"

The woman looked at him flatly. "Do you really feel the need to make a scene?"

One of the men grabbed me by the shoulders, hauling me to my feet. I squeaked as his fingers dug into my flesh, the sound a combination of pain and fright. He was hurting me. Maybe more importantly, he was putting the kind of pressure on my skin that could bruise—or tear. I had never been so aware of how fragile bodies can be.

If I was going to try to hide the damaged spot on my elbow long enough for us to get out of there, I needed to avoid additional injuries. That, more than anything, made me freeze rather than fighting against the hands of the man who held me.

On the other side of the aisle, goon number two was having considerably more trouble getting David to his feet. David was the larger of the pair of them, and while he wasn't shouting like Graham, he wasn't coming quietly, either. He seemed to have planted his feet in such a way that they had become inseparably bonded to the floor of the plane, creating a wall of flesh and scientist that would not be swayed. Toni . . .

Toni was crawling over the back of the seat in front of her, ignoring the protestations of the man sitting there. Well, that was one way to get around the problem. Graham was still loudly objecting to this treatment, and I was trying not to yank myself away from the man who held me. Yanking was another thing that could tear skin.

Was I going to spend the rest of my life feeling this fragile? I sincerely hoped not.

Toni made it over the back of the seat. The man shouted as she landed on him. The woman from the government snapped her fingers, and the two men who'd stayed with her moved to recover Toni before she could make it out of the aisle.

"Fascists!" shouted Toni. "Government goons! My father will hear about this!"

"Your father has already been notified of your un-American activities," said the woman. She sounded almost bored, like this sort of thing happened every day. "If you would please calm yourselves, we can finish this unfortunate encounter with a modicum of dignity."

David punched one of the officers in the nose. The man shouted. The woman sighed.

"Or perhaps we can make things worse. How unexpected." She didn't sound like it was unexpected. As she pulled the Taser out of her pocket, her expression betrayed nothing more than mild irritation, like she'd been hoping she could resolve this without doing anything that was going to wind up on social media. I could see phones out all around us, and many of them were in the hands of teenagers. That was a good thing. Even if the adults got their phones confiscated, the teens would be smart enough, and swift enough, to squirrel away at least a few in backpacks and seatback pockets. This would get out. Unless they wanted to detain the entire plane, this would get out.

"Please," I gasped. "Please, what did we do? I just want to go home! I just—"

The Taser fired. Two electrical lines grounded themselves in my body, and the world became suffused with jittering power. It didn't hurt, exactly, but it robbed me of intentional movement, leaving me jerking uncontrollably in the hands of the man who held me. I was dimly grateful he hadn't dropped me when the lightning came, and even more dimly concerned that I was going to hurt myself worse before the surge stopped.

There was one way to handle that. I closed my eyes.

I went away.

3.

When I opened my eyes again, I was alone in a small room with gunmetal gray walls. My clothes were gone, replaced by pale green hospital scrubs. The inside of my mouth tasted like wheatgrass and blood, like I'd been chewing on my own tongue and trying to rinse the taste away at a trendy juice bar. I blinked at the ceiling a few times, feeling the thin cot beneath me shift with my renewed motion.

Alone. Clothes. Room.

Wait.

Cautiously, in case I could buy myself a few minutes by seeming to still be asleep, I reached around and felt my left arm. There was a bandage there, taped flush against my skin. It wasn't the one I'd put on before leaving Jeff's house. I closed my eyes, too slowly to stop the first hot tears from escaping and trickling down the sides of my face. They knew. These people, whoever they were, whatever government agency they worked for, they knew.

It was almost too bad they hadn't decided to ground our plane in New Mexico. At least then Toni could have been held at Area 51. It would have done her conspiracy-loving heart good to become part of one of the biggest, stupidest conspiracy theories in the world.

There was a click. The world outside my eyelids brightened as the lights came on. I didn't open my eyes.

"Miss Miller, if you would please acknowledge us, this could all go considerably faster." The voice belonged to the woman from the plane. I kept my eyes shut.

She sighed. "I don't know what sort of situation you believe yourself to have fallen into, but I assure you this is serious, and you can go a long way toward keeping yourself and your companions safe by choosing to cooperate. This is a matter of national security." She paused, chuckling grimly before she said, "Or perhaps I should say this is a matter of global security. Do you think that might be more accurate, Miss Miller?"

I didn't move.

"Perhaps you're under the mistaken assumption that you can somehow, shall we say, wait me out. That if you're patient, I will go away. You're entirely wrong about that. I have all the time in the world to get you talking."

That wasn't true. If she knew what I was, and if she knew what the signal was, she knew the invasion was coming. Her time was limited. She might not know *how* limited, but she knew it was running out. She couldn't toy with me forever.

"Your companions are human, Miss Miller. Of course, you knew that. The little one has been talking nonstop. She seems to feel like we've lent her validity by taking her from the plane, that we have to listen to her and involve her in our decision-making. All because she pointed a satellite dish at the wrong sector of the sky." The disgust in the woman's voice was palpable. "She did no one any favors with that little trick. She's brought us to the verge of a national panic, and for what? She knows nothing about their ships, about their armaments. She shouted 'fire' in a crowded theater, and now she wants us to reward her for it."

The urge to defend Toni tickled the edges of my mind. That was definitely something I'd picked up from humanity: the quick assimilation of people into the category I considered "mine." I wouldn't save her over Graham, or Mandy, or even Lucas's obnoxious girlfriend, but I would still take her side over this stranger, who had pulled me off my plane and prevented me from getting home.

The woman sighed. "Miss Miller, all I'm asking here is for you to be reasonable. I've been reasonable. You're unrestrained. You're covered. You have freedom of motion within the confines of your cell. I'm sure you're saying to yourself that you're an American citizen; you have rights. But I ask you, is a dog an American citizen? Is a redwood tree? Yes, they can be protected, but they can't hold citizenship. That privilege, I'm afraid, is reserved for the *human*."

Her voice dipped on the last word, turning venomous and cold and making it clear exactly how carefully she had been speaking before that moment. The hairs on the back of my neck rose.

I'd considered what it would mean to choose humanity over my own kind, or to choose my own kind over the people who'd raised me. I had never considered whether it was possible that the nature of my "birth" could mean that I had no rights.

"That one bothered you, didn't it?" The warm, harried bureaucrat was back. "Had you not realized your origins would make you ineligible for birthright citizenship? Oh, dear. I'm *so* sorry to have caused you distress. Perhaps you could open your eyes, and we could engage in this conversation in a civilized manner."

"Where are my friends?" My eyes stayed closed. That much, at least, I could do.

It didn't seem to bother my captor. She sounded positively delighted as she said, "You're awake! Oh, this *is* excellent. Are you ready to discuss the situation with me, or are you going to continue to be obstinate?"

"How can I be obstinate when I'm unconscious?"

"Our scientists have been waiting for you to wake up for several hours."

The thought that they'd waited to take whatever samples they thought were necessary until I woke up should have been soothing. Instead, it raised questions of pain-tolerance tests, and other things that would require me to cooperate.

"They can keep waiting," I said. "I do not consent to any medical testing."

"Miss Miller, you are here in the presence of three American citizens. All of them are human. We are *very* acquainted with damaging the human body without leaving permanent marks. What do you think would happen to your friends if we lowered the temperature in their cells? Or if we withheld their medications? Technically, refusing to provide access to antipsychotics and artificial hormones is legal. It's not even torture. It's simply a termination of unnecessary medical treatment."

I didn't know whether it was Toni or David on the antipsychotics, and honestly, I didn't care. It would be torture either way, no matter what the law had to say about it. I opened my eyes, sitting up and looking around the gunmetal gray room. There were no windows. There wasn't even a mirror, which I could believably have taken for two-way. There were just the walls, smooth and metallic and unrelenting.

"There," said the woman. Her voice came from nowhere and everywhere at the same time. "Wasn't that easy? If you cooperate, we don't harm your friends. We don't *want* to hurt them, you understand. Unlike you, they're American citizens, and people saw them taken into custody. If we harm them, we'll have to deal with the consequences, and we would really rather not."

"So let us go," I said.

"I'm afraid I can't do that. Are you from outer space, Miss Miller?"

"I am the vanguard of an invading race of alien plant people," I said automatically. I clapped my hand over my mouth as soon as the last word was out, but it was too late: the damage was done.

"You all say that," said the woman. "Every single one of you that we've been able to locate, worldwide, has said that exact sentence in whatever local language they were raised to. We've located members of your species on every continent capable of supporting human life. We've found you in places we would never have considered to be of tactical or military significance, and you all say the same thing. Why?"

"I don't know." Honesty seemed like the best approach, in part because it was all I had. "I can't stop myself when someone asks the question. Sometimes even when they don't ask the question. It just comes out."

"Interesting, isn't it? That your species would go to all the trouble of sending you here, equipping you to blend in with the locals—with us—and then make it impossible for you to endure any degree of scrutiny without revealing yourself. Don't you think there's something contradictory about the whole situation?"

This wasn't a question I was compelled to answer, and so I didn't. My silence felt like defiance, and defiance felt good.

The woman sighed. "Don't you feel any loyalty for the nation—for the *planet*—that raised you? That gave you everything you needed to succeed? These aliens dropped you here like you didn't matter. They programmed you to reveal yourself to the most casual questioning. You don't have any weapons. You don't have any defenses apart from a camouflage that's already started to fail. Why would you choose them over us?"

"Well, for a start, they didn't pull me off a plane in front of a hundred witnesses and lock me in a cell with no windows so they could lecture me about how I'm not a citizen," I said. "Where are my friends?"

"The little one is selling you out as fast as her mouth allows."

"You already told me you're not going to listen to her. Where are my friends?"

"You have a very one-track mind."

"So far, you've threatened me indirectly, and threatened to withhold Graham's hormones," I snapped. "My one-track mind is focused on their safety." And, on some level, on the idea that if I could keep her talking, she couldn't do anything else. She would have to stay here, talking to me, until she convinced me to reveal . . . whatever it was she thought I was going to reveal. Some grand invasion scheme. Some details about my species. *Something.*

There were details about my species contained in this room, details not even I knew about. All they had to do was take their argument that I was not a citizen to its logical conclusion, and cut me open. They could probably learn more about the coming invasion from the structure of my lungs and the tensile strength of my bones than they could from talking to me, no matter how endlessly they chose to do so.

I couldn't stop that from happening. All I could do was continue buying time, and hope that someone—Graham, or Mandy, or the strangers from the plane—would come up with a way to get us out of here.

"What if I guaranteed their safety—what if I was willing to sign a contract promising they would not, under any circumstances, be harmed while in our custody—in exchange for your cooperation?" The woman's voice dropped half an octave, becoming cajoling, almost conspiratorial. "They don't know anything, apart from 'you exist,' and honestly, everyone is about to know that. We could even release them, if it meant you would allow us to perform the necessary tests."

"You're going to do those anyway."

"Yes." There was no shame or hesitation in her declaration: she had a job to do, and she was going to do it, regardless of my feelings on the matter. "But your cooperation would make things substantially easier. Anyone can vivisect an unwilling subject. Studying a willing one is much more profitable."

"Who *are* you?"

"I'm the person in charge of your case."

"Are you CIA? FBI? From some other agency that handles contact with alien races?"

Her laughter was low, and surprisingly sincere. "Believe it or not, your kind are the first actual aliens we've encountered. Oh, we've been watching the sky for decades, but either life is scarcer in the stars than anyone guessed, or your people are very, very good at what you do. That's all right. We're very, very good at what we do as well."

I said nothing, but slid my right hand over the bandage covering the inside of my left elbow, pressing down, like I could somehow will the human skin to grow back.

This woman's organization couldn't be as good as they thought they were, or they would have captured Jeff as well. There was a chance they had—I couldn't exactly ask without giving away the fact that someone had managed to escape—but I didn't think so. She was trying too hard to keep me talking, and she wasn't threatening to hurt him if I didn't cooperate, or telling me he was cooperating and hence I was the extraneous one. I was their only alien. They didn't need me to work with them. They still wanted it, badly enough to put on this little routine.

"You'll let them go," I said flatly. "All three of them. You'll give them their things, and provide them with their medication, and let them go."

"Will we, now."

"They're citizens. You can't disappear them the way you can disappear me." Honestly, I doubted her ability to disappear me without consequences. I might not be a citizen in the eyes of the government, but everyone who knew me—my housemates, my friends, my family—believed I was a real person. They believed I *mattered*. Unless the government wanted to announce I was an extraterrestrial, they were stuck.

"There's a word that invalidates your entire argument."

"What's that?"

"Terrorist." There was no disguising the pleasure in her voice. It was enough to make the hairs on the back of my neck stand on end as she continued, "People believe what they're told loudly enough. I don't have to say you're an alien. All I need to do is leak the story that a domestic terrorist is being detained for questioning and I can make you disappear so completely that no one will ever figure out where you went. You don't hold as many chips as you think you do."

"If you want me to cooperate—"

"If I want you to cooperate, I'll haul your little girlfriend in here and make you explain to her why you're keeping her away from her medication. You'll do whatever I say after that."

It had been so long since I'd heard someone misgender Graham that for a moment, I thought she was talking about Toni. The moment passed. Rage replaced confusion. I was on my feet before I had the chance to think better of it, hands balled into fists, turning as I shouted, so that I would be facing my captor at least once.

"Listen here, you . . . you . . . you whatever the *fuck* you are, you may be the human here, but that doesn't grant you a scrap of humanity," I snarled, making no effort to pretend I was playing nice. The time for playing nice was over. "If you hurt them, I swear to you, I will make you pay for it. I will get out of here, and I will find you, and I will make you sorry that you ever touched a hair on any of our heads. Do you hear me?"

"I hear you." There was a click behind me. I whirled, and watched in wide-eyed dismay as a section of the wall slid open, revealing a hallway on the other side. The woman from the plane was standing there, a smile on her face and another Taser in her hands. She was alone, and for one dizzy moment, I considered rushing her, knocking her back and making a break for it.

"Uh-uh," she said, shaking her head. Her smile turned predatory. "I know what you're thinking, and I promise you, it wouldn't work out the way you expect. You'd be captured and restrained before you found yourself anywhere near an exit—and once you had been, there'd be no more question of whether you were going to play nicely. Your friends would absolutely become extraneous to needs at that point, and your own feelings on the matter of what was or was not to be done with you would be irrelevant. Do you understand me?"

"I understand that this is bullshit," I spat. "You're wasting my time."

The woman's eyes widened marginally.

Understanding swept through me, chasing away the remains of my rage. "You're *wasting* my *time*," I breathed. "You're trying to keep me busy, to keep me too distracted to notice something. What don't you want me to notice?"

"Nothing," she said.

"There's something," I countered. "You're here. You're close enough for me to reach out and grab."

The woman took a half-step backward, further from the still open door. I frowned.

"What don't you want me to realize?"

"If you move, I will shoot you," she said, lifting her Taser.

"Okay. You do that." I turned and walked back to the cot, where I sat down, folded my arms, and waited.

"What are you doing?"

"I'm not moving." With the door open, the room seemed less

oppressive. I could stay here for a while. I might need to stay here forever. The idea wasn't appealing, but it wasn't the end of the world. If I needed to get used to being a houseplant, I could do it.

At least until the invasion came. When our ships darkened this planet's skies, then things were going to change, and quickly. There was no way to say that without making my own situation worse, and so I said nothing at all.

"You need to talk to me."

"No, I don't." I looked over my shoulder at her. "You've threatened my friends. You've threatened me, through them, and with your casual little comment about your 'scientists' waiting for me to wake up. You haven't introduced yourself. You haven't even told me which agency currently has us detained. You've done literally *nothing* to make me feel like I need to talk to you, and a hell of a lot to make me think the silent treatment may actually be more than you deserve. So give me one good reason to have a conversation that consists of something more than me telling you to go fuck yourself."

"They're coming."

I said nothing.

"That signal your friend—Dr. Fabris—decided to release wasn't the first one we'd intercepted. It wasn't even the tenth. They've been getting more frequent over the last few years, but we'd been able to keep them from making the news before this. It helps that people still think anything that includes 'and it came from space' is a lie." The woman lowered her Taser. "We'd been hoping to keep suppressing them until we figured out how to approach your species. Unfortunately, Dr. Fabris has made that impossible."

"So you abducted us from a plane."

"Miss Miller, I don't think you understand how important this is to national security."

"I don't think you understand how much I don't like being abducted from a plane," I countered. "I want to go home. I want to see my cat. Is that a thing you can help me with?"

"Miss Miller, you will be lucky if you ever see the outside of this facility again."

My hand went to the bandage on my inner elbow. "Because of what I am."

"Yes." She nodded once. "Because you're not a human being. You have no right to walk freely on the soil of this world, and we want you to cooperate. We want you to help us prepare."

"Why me? Why not one of the others?"

"I'll be blunt: you were a target of opportunity. The others have stayed close to home. They've surrounded themselves with people who would miss them. You put yourself into a position where we could take you and most of the people who might object at the same time."

"You could have said 'please.'"

"Could we? Could we have just strolled up to you and said 'Hello, we're from the government, we know you're a representative of an alien species which may or may not intend to harm us, can we convince you to tell us all your secrets'? Because you'll forgive me for being dubious if I say that sounds more than reasonably unlikely."

"You could have tried," I said stubbornly.

She sighed. "We have no way of knowing precisely when your ride will be here—but rest assured, we know it's coming. They're on their way."

"You still could have tried."

"Is there anything we could do to make you cooperate? As you say, we have you. To a certain degree, we can do as we like. But we would prefer you answer our questions willingly."

Something about this whole situation didn't smell right. Either I'd been taken captive by amateur hour—which didn't match up with the way they'd been able to ground our plane before it reached Seattle—or they were trying, very hard, to pretend that I had. And whichever it was, I needed to get everyone else out of here. It wasn't altruism; it was the mathematics of escape.

Once I was the only person here, I could focus on me. Once I knew Graham and the others were safe, I wouldn't need to worry about getting them away, or about them being used as levers against me.

"I want my companions released," I said flatly. "If the footage from the plane has made the news, I want some sort of public statement that they were detained in error. I want proof I'm your only 'guest.' Do that, and I'll tell you whatever you want to know."

"You have no rights, no standing, and no way out," she said. "Are you sure this is a deal you want to make?"

Again, something was off, and again, I couldn't afford to care. "Yes," I said firmly.

She smiled.

SPROUT

...and looking across space with instruments, and intelligences such as we have scarcely dreamed of, they see, at its nearest distance only 35,000,000 of miles sunward of them, a morning star of hope, our own warmer planet, green with vegetation and grey with water, with a cloudy atmosphere eloquent of fertility, with glimpses through its drifting cloud wisps of broad stretches of populous country and narrow, navy-crowded seas...

—H.G. WELLS,
THE WAR OF THE WORLDS

The only things we reap are the things we sow. I was sown. Is it time for the reaping to begin?

—STASIA MILLER

When counting and accounting for the venomous creatures of a region, many people will tell you that you should be looking for the creatures themselves. Look for holes, look for burrows, look for fallen logs suitable for use as nesting sites. This is not bad advice: if followed, it will lead you inevitably to locating the snakes you're trying to find.

But if you want to find them faster, any good field herpetologist will tell you to ignore the holes, to skip the flat rocks and fallen trees. Instead, they'll say you should be looking for the signs of rodent activity. By following the prey, you can always locate the predator—and save yourself a great deal of time in the process.

Remember, however, if you follow this advice, that the

absence of one half of this equation does not equal the absence of the other. Sometimes, it simply guarantees that you're about to find a very hungry rattlesnake.

—FROM THE INTRODUCTION TO *A LAYMAN'S SURVEY OF THE VENOMOUS SNAKES OF NORTH AMERICA*, BY DR. GRAHAM FORDHAM, ORIGINALLY PUBLISHED 2031.

It has been a delight having Anastasia in my class this year. She has a nimble mind and a creative flair that will no doubt serve her well in her future endeavors. I am writing, not to criticize your daughter's intelligence, but to offer my concerns about its focus.

Anastasia continues to insist, when prompted, that she is a representative of an alien species. It is an unfortunate truth that children can be cruel: her peers delight in triggering this idiosyncratic response, going out of their way to ask her what planet she's from and whether she will be going back there at the end of the school year. It would be in her best interests to channel this creative energy in a new direction.

If I may be frank, Ms. Miller, while it is against school policy to blame students for their own bullying, Anastasia does not make things easy on herself. I am sincerely concerned about her well-being if she does not find a way to move past this fantasy, and quickly.

Thank you for your time.

—LETTER HOME FROM MR. ROY HAGAR, TENTH GRADE TEACHER. SENT NOVEMBER, 2012.

9

TUCSON, ARIZONA: JULY 27, 2031
ELEVEN DAYS PRE-INVASION

1.

The forest unfolded in a beautiful array of impossible greens and browns, their colors familiar and yet new, like they were coming into prismatic focus. I stood. The air was cleaner than it had ever been, and the taste of it was faintly acidic, like it was eating away the skin at the back of my throat. The sensation wasn't painful—almost the opposite, a quiet cleansing that would make everything better, if I just allowed it to happen.

"There you are."

I whirled.

Jeff was standing on a low rise some ten feet behind me, one hand resting on the trunk of an alien tree, a weary expression on what remained of his face. The bandage was gone. So was most of the skin. In their place, he had a twisting mass of vines and roots, some thin as filaments, others thick as garter snakes. They were in constant motion, twining around each other in complicated knots that unlooped themselves as quickly as they had formed.

Breath catching in my throat, I looked down at my left arm.

The skin was gone from the elbow to the tips of my fingers, replaced by a mass of vines thicker than the ones on Jeff's face, darker in shade and covered with thorns like a blackberry creeper. I raised my arm to the level of my eyes, drinking it in. There were small white flowers with petals like a butterfly's wings hidden at the center, visible only in glimpses between the moving vines. The thorns smelled sharp and astringent, and I knew they were tipped in some sort of complicated poison, something that would stop hearts with a touch.

"Is this . . . ?" I whispered, and stopped, unable to finish the question.

"Once," said Jeff. I looked up. He was watching me with sympathy in his still-too-human eyes. "A lot of worlds ago. You and me, we'll never have this in the real world. Only here."

"Why?" I couldn't keep the relief out of my voice; I didn't even really try. After a lifetime lived in a human skin, the thought of becoming whatever Jeff was turning into—whatever *I* was turning into—didn't appeal.

"We adapt. World after world, we adapt. Are you all right?" He took a step toward me, his still-human hands reaching out for mine. I took them, fingers on one side and vines like tendrils on the other. "I've been so worried."

"You got away."

"They knew there were four of us. They didn't know there were five. Thankfully." He cocked his head. "You weren't sure?"

"No. I couldn't be. They haven't let me see anyone, and it wasn't like I could ask 'Hey, do you have another plant person in your holding cells?'" I had only the word of my keepers that they'd released Graham and the others. Maybe they were still captive somewhere in this sprawling compound, unwitting hostages against my good behavior. I hoped not. I didn't trust the people holding me, but I wanted to believe they were trying to do the right thing for their own species. I was the only alien here. Let the humans go.

As if he'd read my thoughts, Jeff said, "Your boyfriend and the others are fine. They've been going on every conspiracy-theory podcast you can think of to talk about how the government is holding you. Listening to them try to say it without outright calling you an alien invader is sort of fun, in a weird kind of way. They don't want to turn their audience against you."

I blinked. "Even Toni?"

"Your weird little astronomer friend? No. She's going on a *different* set of podcasts, telling anyone who'll listen that you're coming to devour us all and we shouldn't let the government hide you. Funny thing is, since all those podcasts have different audiences, they're working up a pretty good head of steam. Half the listeners want to save you and the other half want you tried for treason, but they're paying attention."

"Huh." It was hard to say whether or not that was a good thing. At least they were free. "How . . . What took you so long to find me? Where *are* you?"

"I'm not going to tell you that." Jeff's face took on a grim cast. I realized I could understand the slow twine of his tendrils, even though they were like nothing I had ever seen before. Apparently, the part of me that remembered the stars remembered what we'd looked like among them, too. "If you knew, they could try to make you tell them. Are they torturing you?"

"Not yet." It was coming; I knew it was coming. The shape of their false flag was becoming clearer with every test they set before me. Quiz after quiz, maze after maze, even video games and books of puzzles. They were trying to figure out how smart I was, to find the places where my intelligence deviated from their ideas of the human norm. They knew if they dug deeply enough, they'd find something that could be used to distinguish the way *I* thought from the way the humans around me thought. After all, if I had one compulsion that betrayed my nature, why wouldn't I have more?

So far, none of their tests had found anything more than an increasingly annoyed subject—me. Which would have been fine, if they hadn't been murmuring in the corners of the room when they thought I was busy focusing on my math worksheets or word problems. This wasn't working. They weren't getting the results they wanted. They were going to move on to something more invasive than workbooks and the occasional blood test, and they were going to do it soon.

"Good." Jeff shook his head. "I'm trying to figure out how to get you out of there. Officially, you're not being held. Officially—"

"Did you know we're not citizens?"

For the first time, he looked surprised. "What?"

"Our seeds may have sprouted here, but a bear's not a citizen, and that means we're not either. Citizenship is for humans." I smiled bitterly. "If we want to insist we're not members of their species, they're going to stop treating us like we are."

"That makes . . . sense, I suppose," said Jeff. He frowned. "But they're not torturing you."

"No." Now it was my turn to frown. "Why are you focusing so much on torture? What aren't you telling me?"

"I'm fifteen miles away. I'm not going to tell you which direction. This is the first time I've been able to find you in the forest."

"So?"

"So I've been here for three days." This time, his expression was pure anguish. "I couldn't get into the forest until I moved out more than ten miles. It's taken boosting the signal to—"

"You're not alone." I stared at him. "You found more of us."

"Yes."

It was a small admission. It changed everything. Suddenly, my boring days and lack of torture seemed less amateur hour, and more like a way to lower my defenses. "Are any of them scientists?"

"A few," he admitted. "One is—"

"*Don't* tell me," I snapped. He fell silent, a surprised expression on his half-vegetable face. I shook my head. "Ask them whether there's any way someone who isn't one of us could know about the forest. Ask if we give out a . . . a signal, or something people could track."

Jeff's surprise faded into wariness. "Why?"

"Because I think they've figured out a way to block that connection, at least over short distances," I said. "I haven't been able to reach the forest, and you haven't been able to reach me. That's not *normal*. When I'm upset, when I'm alone, I come to the forest." Until I had recovered my connection, I hadn't even realized it was lost. There was something chilling about that. We were so close to human, thanks to upbringing and outward appearance. It would have been so easy to let go of the things that distinguished us and melt into the quiet comfort of belonging to this world, of fitting in.

It would have been easy, that was, before Toni had decided to boost our fleet's signal around the globe. I untwined the vines of my transformed hand from Jeff's fingers, trying not to see the sorrow that bloomed in his eyes in response to my withdrawal, and held it up for him to see.

"The green hasn't spread outside of here," I said. "It's still just a patch on the inside of my elbow."

"Maybe it's beneath the surface."

"They're taking blood samples and X-rays daily. I should probably be worried about the radiation. But it hasn't spread. They find meat, meat, meat, and suddenly, this little patch of vegetable." They had taken scrapings and biopsies and samples, enough so that the bend of my elbow looked like a warzone and ached every time I bent my arm.

If my vegetable skin scarred like my meat skin, it was never going to be the same.

I sort of hoped it would. I wanted to remember this forever. I wanted to *know* why I could no longer trust the bulk of humanity. I wasn't theirs and they weren't mine. Maybe we never really had been.

"So what do you think that means?"

"I think . . . the signal primed us to start changing, and the forest spreads and speeds the change." I put my pseudo-human hand over the base of the vines, feeling them twist and twine beneath my fingers. There was strength in those creepers. The kind of strength that could put a plant on a level with the animals around it. The kind of strength that could, if properly marshalled, conquer a world.

Jeff nodded. It was getting easier and easier to read the expression in his vegetative face. "That matches up with what the rest of us have been experiencing. I'm glad you're all right. I'll check on you as much as I can. We're trying to find a way to get you out of this."

"Good," I said. "Please keep an eye on my people. Don't let them get hurt."

Jeff's smile was quick and wry. "This is a war, Stasia," he said. "Everyone's going to get hurt."

I nodded and closed my eyes, letting my chin dip toward my chest. When I opened them again, I was looking at the ceiling of my room. The lights were set at a constant dim almost-twilight, making it easy for me to see what I was doing as I sat up and rolled back my sleeve, rotating my arm. I wasn't worried about the hidden cameras around me picking up the motion. There were no secrets here. Better for me to know as soon as possible.

The skin around the edges of the green patch on my arm was peeling and thin, like the papery coating on an onion. I plucked gingerly at one of the edges, tugging until it came loose and tore away in a long, lifeless strip.

The flesh beneath was dark green and healthy, smelling of sap and loam, like the forest had somehow followed me back to my cell. I lowered my nose and breathed in deep, taking every particle of that perfect, utterly alien smell into my lungs. I almost thought I could feel this new air moving through me, making little changes as it went, getting me ready, getting things *prepared*.

Everything was changing now. It was too late to turn back. Maybe it always had been.

Propping my shoulders against the cell wall, I closed my eyes and waited for the morning.

2.

As expected, the scientists were in a tizzy over the sudden expansion of the green patch on my arm. They made me peel away several more strips of papery skin, making me wish I'd spent more time picking at myself in the middle of the night. At least then I could have breathed in the scent of my own body in peace, instead of watching every scrap I removed whisked away for further analysis while people in white coats pressed in to study and record every little thing they could.

When the last of the skin was peeled away, the patch had grown from the size of a quarter to a long streak extending all the way down my forearm, stretching almost to the base of my wrist. A strip of raw, red flesh off to the left clearly demonstrated the demarcation. That wasn't my fault: one of the scientists had insisted more skin could be removed, and had sliced away a piece that was still pretending to be human.

It wouldn't have been so bad if she'd just been *sorry* about it. Instead, she had said something delighted about having a sample of the transitional zone, tucked the bleeding piece of me into a petri dish, and run off, presumably to pick it apart at her leisure. Everything about me was something to put under a microscope.

With a click-clacking of heels against the industrial linoleum floor, my original captor, the still-nameless agent of whatever alphabet agency I currently belonged to, made her return. I raised my head and watched her approach, my eyes narrowed in consideration. This place was too sterile, too featureless and simple, to have been built by accident: real government agencies don't look like they're part of Barbie's Dream Interrogation Complex. This place had been designed. Designed for *me*, or for whichever lucky member of my species had happened to become vulnerable first.

I had been here for days without being able to access the forest or communicate with my own kind. The forest *had* to be more than a network for those of here on Earth. I hadn't even known that it could be used as a network until I'd stumbled over Jeff. So who benefitted from my being able to go there? Who, if not the fleet, slowly approaching, needing to *know* things about the world it was about to take? Cultural literacy. Those were the words that kept haunting me. Something about them held the answer, and as soon as I knew exactly what it was . . .

I would still be locked in a featureless room, watching people who refused to give me their names as they came and went around me. No weapons, no way of initiating communication with the outside world, no way out.

"Sleep well, Miss Miller?" purred the nameless agent. There was a bright, smug note in her tone, like she already knew what my answer would be.

Then again, maybe she did. The green patch on my arm was an announcement of its own kind. I tried to pull my arm against my body, instinctively shielding it from her, and stopped as the scientist who had been trying to take my blood pressure jerked my elbow back into position. It hurt. I bit the inside of my cheek, and did my best not to let it show.

"There was a glitch in the wireless field surrounding the complex last night," said the agent. "It was nothing serious—we were never concerned about losing physical containment—but for a short period, we were unable to maintain a closed circuit."

"I don't understand what you think this has to do with me," I said. "I was asleep. It's not like there's anything else for me to do in here."

"Of course." She gave the green patch on my arm another meaningful look. "Did you have pleasant dreams?"

"Oh, sure. I dreamt you'd known about us for long enough to build an entire facility just to keep us in, one where we couldn't possibly learn anything we'd be able to use against you—not that we'd be looking, since I'm pretty sure few, if any, of us are trained spies—but you could learn about us at your leisure. I dreamt you know how to keep us from communicating with one another." I looked at her levelly, fighting the urge to yank my arm away again. "This needs to end."

"If you wanted this to end, you shouldn't have invaded our planet." The levity drained from her face. "Thus far, we've been more than pleasant to you. We've practically turned your incarceration into a vacation getaway."

"Most vacations don't require me to give this much blood," I snapped.

"They might, if they knew what you were." She took another step forward, looking around at my swarm of scientists. "Give us the room."

They stopped, some looking shocked, while others simply looked resigned. None of them argued with her. They just gathered their equipment and left the room, pouring out around us, until it was only the two of us left, me and the agent without a name. She folded her hands behind her back, looking down her nose at me. I crossed my arms, hiding the green patch from her view. I felt better knowing that she couldn't see it. Even if nothing could make her forget that it was there, she couldn't see it.

Jeff didn't have that option. I felt a pang of relief that my skin had started ripping in a place I could cover so easily, and smothered that feeling quickly in a veil of guilt. Jeff hadn't chosen to have his face start melting into green. Neither of us had ever had a choice, in any of this.

"You went somewhere last night," said the agent, once the last of the scientists was gone. "Where?"

"I didn't go anywhere. I was right here all night. I'm a plant invader, not a ghost."

"Your arm tells me otherwise."

"What's your name?"

"That information is classified."

"Well, so is any information relating to where I may or may not have gone last night." I leaned back, looking at her coolly. "I don't have to tell you anything."

"Do you honestly think we can't make you tell us anything we want to know? We had a deal. We let your friends go, and in exchange, you answer our questions. Do you want to face the consequences of going back on your word?" The corner of her mouth twitched in what might have been the beginning of a smile. "I promise you, you're not the only one who would regret that."

"I've answered all your questions up until this moment. You haven't answered a single one of mine."

"That wasn't our agreement."

"Maybe not, but how am I supposed to know what you need to know if I don't have any information?" I glared at her. "I didn't know there *was* a wireless field around this place. Why the hell is there a wireless field?"

"Because you invaders seem to know what's coming before it gets there," she said calmly. "We don't know how you're sharing information. We would very much *like* to know. You're going to help with that."

"No, I'm really not."

"Again, you promised—"

"I'm not, because I don't *know* anything." I allowed myself to smirk. Trying to school my emotions was just going to make me look like I was hiding something. And I *was* hiding something: I was hiding the fact that Jeff was nearby and gathering an army to recover me. As long as she didn't catch on to that, I was in good shape. "Until you told me, I had no idea a wireless field could interfere with anything. I sleep, I dream, sometimes I wake up knowing stuff I didn't know when I went to bed the night before. I thought it worked that way for everybody. Aren't dreams supposed to organize things you learned the day before?"

"It doesn't work that way for humans," she said, through gritted teeth. "What else have you been hiding?"

I sighed, frustrated. "I'm not hiding anything. I wasn't hiding *that*. I didn't know; that's not the same as hiding something. Unless you have a complete, totally accurate map to the way humans are supposed to work, I can't tell you where I deviate from it, because *I don't know*. I've been what I am for my entire life."

"That's not true." Her face lit up, and for a moment, she looked like nothing more than some grand predator preparing to pounce. "Anastasia Miller, age three. *Human*. Disappeared in the woods behind her grandparents' residence for several hours. Returned claiming to be from another planet. You killed that little girl. You stole her life. You took her place. You know you're not human."

"Yes," I agreed. "I've always known I wasn't human. I told everyone who would listen. I told people I knew would want to hurt me for being a weirdo. I never lied. I never concealed anything. And look where it got me. You still won't admit this place is a . . . a Habitrail for aliens. All I'm missing is an exercise wheel."

If the agent was disappointed that I wasn't more upset, she didn't show it. Instead, she shook her head, and said, "You don't understand how good you have things right now. You don't see how lucky you are. We'd be within our rights to take you apart."

"Okay," I said. "I mean, you're mostly going to find human bits, at least if what your scientists say is anything to go by—they sort of assume that since I'm not one of them, I'm stupid, and they let a lot slip. Nothing useful unless I want to fully understand my own currently hybrid biology, but hey. Everything's got to go somewhere."

"You need to cooperate."

"I am cooperating. You need to tell me what you think I'm supposed to be doing that I'm not. I can't be a good little test subject with no information."

"All you're supposed to do is answer our questions and tell us what we want to know."

"I can't do that if I don't know what you want to know." I couldn't miss the fact that she'd made those things different clauses. She wanted me to answer the questions I was asked, and volunteer the information I wasn't asked for. There was one big problem with that: I was telling the truth when I said that I didn't know what was remarkable. I was concealing the existence of the forest, yes, but until she'd interfered with my connection to it, I hadn't realized it was something that could be blocked off.

They knew more about me than I did. That was chilling. Even more chilling was the fact that I still didn't know who *they* were. I could talk back and roll my eyes all I wanted, acting like a bratty teen who didn't want to clean her room, but that wouldn't answer my questions, and it wouldn't really slow them down. It was a nothing more than a show of powerless defiance. On some level, I wished I could quit it, go along with their requests and be a model prisoner . . . but that, too, wouldn't change anything. All it would do was undermine the last coping mechanism I had.

I wasn't that ready to give up.

"You need to get better at predicting what we need."

"You need to tell me who you *are*."

To my surprise, she smiled. "You really aren't prepared for what you came here to do, are you?" she asked. "You should have figured it out by now."

"Since the Men in Black aren't real, I think I'm doing okay."

"You're not. Sadly, you're not going to have a chance to recover from your own errors." Her smile thinned, tightened, became the triumphant snarl of a predator. "Now that we know how to accelerate the changes, we may be leaving the field down a bit more frequently. We need something to show our superiors, if we're going to get permission to move on to the next stage. You should be getting down on your knees and thanking me for letting your little 'boyfriend' leave. Do you really think he'll want to touch you after the last of your skin peels away, and he can see you for want you actually are?"

I spat at her. It was a foolish, childish thing to do. It was the only thing I could think of.

She was still laughing as she walked out of the room. The door shut behind her, and I was alone. Sort of.

The problem with solitude in a place like this was that it wasn't real. It was an illusion, designed to make me feel like I had privacy. I didn't. I *couldn't*. They were monitoring everything about me, from the amount I ate to the number of times I asked to be taken to the bathroom.

Closing my eyes, I leaned back in my seat and waited for the scientists to return. They had more tests to run—they always had more tests to run—and if my nameless captor was planning to leave the wireless field down again tonight, if she wanted to see the evidence of my nature continue to spread, they were going to want a complete picture of what I looked like right now. I was less human than I had been the day before, and I was more human than I was ever going to be again.

The thought should have distressed me. At the very least, it should have had me worried about the way the people I cared about were going to respond the next time they saw me. Would Lucas still be happy to rent me a room when he could no longer pretend that I was an ordinary woman with a weird fondness for claiming to be an alien? Would Mandy still want to be my friend?

Would Graham still love me?

Those were big questions. Important questions. Not as important as the question of who was actually holding me here. Of the alphabet agencies, the TSA and CDC seemed to be the least likely—the one because I would never have made it onto the plane in the first place, and the other because I wasn't an infection. I wasn't contagious. I was just from someplace else.

The FBI and CIA seemed similarly unlikely, if only because this was all too byzantine. I was looking for an organization with a lot of time on its hands, one that could have spent decades monitoring alien activity on Earth without stepping in. The CIA would have rounded us all up years ago if they had actually believed we were what we claimed to be. The FBI might not have arrested us, but they would have made their presence known. I would have seen them long since, if only from a distance.

That left two big candidates, one likely, one a little more out there. If this was the NSA, a lot of the coy, surreal, cat-with-mouse behavior would make a lot more sense. The NSA had plenty to keep themselves busy, but they had always struck me as the alphabet agency with more of a desire to grow up and become an evil empire. Setting James Bond-esque alien traps would only appeal to them.

If it was NASA, I was in trouble.

NASA had a genuine interest in space, and in the things that came from space, whether friendly or not. NASA had the telescopes and the probes and the monitoring equipment. Most of all, NASA had the constantly dropping budget, the picture of an agency in unwilling freefall, and they needed a win. Strange as the facility was, I could easily tilt my head and see its oddities as cost-cutting measures. Buy your plans from the lowest bidder and hey! No windows. Poor ventilation. Rooms in the middle of nowhere, with no logical air flow.

It made sense, and I didn't want it to, because if this was NASA, I was more than just screwed: I was well and truly fucked.

The door opened. I opened my eyes, trying to look impassive as the scientists poured back in with their scalpels and sample kits and endless, insensible questions. Half of them weren't for me, even though I was the one they asked: they were for the biosphere that formed me, the atmosphere that was supposed to fill my lungs. They were for the roots I left behind when I pulled myself from the vine, and since I was the only one available to ask, they were asked of me, one after the other, as if repetition might somehow unlock the truth.

Two familiar faces passed me, as nameless as the agent who controlled my fate. Behind them, wrapped in a tight white coat, her hair pulled into a messy bun, was someone whose familiarity was less of a trial and more of a slap across the face. I sat up straighter, fighting to school my expression of surprise and dismay into resignation.

Mandy met my eyes for a moment, then looked away. She didn't nod. She didn't do anything to betray the fact that she knew me. She simply followed the others to the table, where they began setting up their equipment, talking loudly about how inconvenient these interruptions were. One of them suggested I be sedated when not actively taking tests, since it wasn't like I was telling them anything useful. Another said they couldn't wait until my bone marrow began to mutate, since then they'd be able to really understand the interaction between the mammalian and vegetable cells in my body.

Through it all, Mandy moved, carrying things for other people, making adjustments when called upon to do so. She never said a word, and apart from that first glance, she didn't look at me.

One of the other scientists—a tall, gray-haired man who seemed to take my lack of communication as a personal affront, as if I were targeting him specifically, and not being balky with everyone—approached me, a phlebotomy kit in his hand. "Arm," he said, not bothering with anything as trivial as a greeting. "I need blood from the margin of your mutating cells."

"Does it really count as mutation when it's a natural transition?" asked another scientist. "I really think we should be referring to this process as 'metamorphosis.'"

The scientist who wanted my blood snorted in disdain, while several others started arguing over which term was more appropriate. I wasn't the only one going stir-crazy in here. Only Mandy hung back from the discussion-slash-argument, looking like she had no idea what she was supposed to do with her hands now that the equipment was all lain out. She was a cosplayer and this was a role, but all the fake scientists she'd played over the years weren't going to be enough to give her actual training.

I stuck out my arm, willing Mandy to find something else to do, willing her to keep refusing to look at me. If she just didn't look at me . . .

She looked at me.

The scientist was tying a plastic loop around my arm, just above the elbow, to make my veins easier to find. The dark green patch of skin was impossible to miss, and only grew more visible as it suffused with blood. It began to brighten, going from pine to emerald green, and I fought the urge to close my eyes. The scientists might notice if I did that. I usually watched when they took my blood, refusing to give them the satisfaction of making me look away. I had so little control left over what happened to me. There was no way I was ceding what remained.

In that moment, I would have given up all the control I had and then some, if it meant Mandy wasn't looking at the green patch on my arm. Then the needle slid into my flesh, the vial beginning to fill, and I had something new to distract me.

The blood was red, mammalian and bright . . . at least at first. After the vial had filled roughly a quarter of the way, the red began showing streaks of brackish gray-green. The scientist made a wordless sound of amazement, and his peers flocked to watch as I continued bleeding. First the red gave way completely, and then vivid green overwhelmed the gray. Finally, just as the vial reached capacity, the green faded as well, replaced by clear amber, like pine sap.

Sap. I was bleeding sap.

"Don't just *stand* there, you stupid thing, give me another vial!" snapped the scientist, holding his hand out to Mandy. She broke out of her frozen shock with a gulping noise, fumbling to grab what he was asking for.

Luckily for her—maybe luckily for both of us—the scientists pressing in around me were too distracted by the scientific miracle of the year to notice that their new assistant was incompetent. Several set up cries for blood samples of their own, and one began demanding a bone marrow sample with such vehemence that I was briefly afraid she might grab a scalpel and try to take it for herself.

Mandy handed over the replacement vials and stepped back, out of the fray, finally allowing our eyes to meet. I blinked slowly, but didn't look away. I'd been locking eyes with the scientists since I got here, daring them to see me as a human being. Mandy was no different. If I wanted her to go unnoticed, Mandy *had* to be no different.

Run, I thought fiercely. *Get out of here and never look back.* The others were gone, hopefully safe somewhere the people running this facility would never touch them again—not without causing a public-relations disaster that the world, leery of invasion and unwilling to admit to the existence of aliens, wasn't ready to face. They could stay free, if they were careful.

But Mandy, for whatever reason, was *here.* She had walked right into the jaws of the enemy, and if someone figured out who she was, she wasn't going to be walking out. All issues of national security and classified facilities aside, she was something they hadn't had since they'd released Graham and the others: she was leverage on two legs. They could make me agree to anything, make me tell them anything, if they threatened her.

Would they hurt her? Honestly, I didn't know. They'd been working hard since the day they'd taken me to make sure they didn't—and wouldn't—think of me as human. I was a person, sure. I could answer questions and solve logic problems and be a pain in their collective asses. But I wasn't human, and that meant hurting me wasn't wrong. Hurting me was *protecting* humanity. Of such loopholes are a horrifying number of atrocities born.

Mandy though, Mandy was human, and while the people now doing their best to exsanguinate me might be willing to torture an alien invader, they'd done nothing to indicate they'd do the same to their own kind. They'd threatened, sure, but I wasn't sure I could—or should—believe them. They were trying to save the world by taking me apart. They probably thought of themselves as noble, heroes of the coming triumph of mankind over the vegetables from space.

Go, I thought.

Mandy didn't go. Mandy wasn't one of us, wasn't connected to the forest where we could share information without speaking—and the forest wasn't true telepathy anyway. Jeff and I hadn't shown any signs of reading one another's minds when we were together. Whatever connected us, it wasn't nearly that useful.

Instead, Mandy took a tray laden with vials of my blood—because what else was I going to call it—and asked, in her clear, careful "I am performing here" voice, "Where should I put this?"

"I'll go with you," said the first scientist, a greedy, proprietary note in his voice. He'd been the one to draw the first sample; he was the one who got the vial where my blood transitioned from human normal into something that should never have come out of a body that looked like mine.

"How much blood have we taken today?" asked one of the others, reaching for her notes.

"Too much." The voice belonged to the nameless agent. Everyone in the room turned toward the door, even Mandy, who was picking up her cues from the crowd.

Please be careful, I thought. *I'm not worth this.*

It was almost funny. I was anticipating the moment when the skies would go black with ships, a whole alien armada swooping in from the depths of space to do . . . what, I still wasn't entirely sure. Whoever had dropped me here hadn't seen fit to give me a lot of details about the invasion, or maybe I'd been on this planet long enough to forget them the way I'd forgotten so much about my childhood as Anastasia Miller. I knew the invasion was real. I knew whatever my people intended for this planet wasn't going to be much fun for the locals. People—human people, people like Mandy—were going to die. But I could still worry about the humans who were my friends. I could still want to know that they would be protected from their own kind, if not from mine.

Hypocrisy isn't a purely human trait. I think it comes from the natural contradictions inherent in being a sapient creature in a world where it's impossible to survive without causing harm to *something*. Herbivores eat plants. On a world like Earth, where the plants don't talk or have opinions, that may seem like the least harm possible, but on a world like the one where my people evolved? A world I've never seen and never will, where I would have looked like the thing I was becoming in the forest? The plants there would have had a few opinions on the ethics of veganism.

Mandy was human, no question. Mandy was *meat*, hot flesh and red blood and everything else that came with humanity. But she was also *mine*, and things that belonged to me deserved to be protected.

The agent stepped into the room. There was something almost dainty in the way she walked, like she was crossing some invisible line between the past and the future. Her eyes were on the tray of my blood, partitioned into individual vials for easier examination. By the last few, there were no traces of red or green remaining. It glimmered golden and clear, like maple syrup, like the honey at the heart of the world.

"Well," she said. "This *is* a new development, isn't it, Miss Miller? It seems your camouflage may be beginning to fail you."

"It's not camouflage if it's not intentional," said one of the scientists. The agent turned a mild gaze on her. She reddened but continued, "It's mimicry. Camouflage involves an intentional act of blending into one's environment."

"Fascinating," said the agent. She turned to the scientist who initiated the blood draw. "I'll want copies of all your reports. We need to understand the biological makeup of these things if we're going to develop a proper weed killer before they get here."

"We could be coming in peace," I snapped, unable to stop myself from stealing a glance at Mandy. She was watching the agent, apparently no longer aware of my presence.

We weren't coming in peace. I knew that down to my bones, or to whatever might be replacing them one sliver at a time as my vegetable heart began to bloom. But *she* didn't know that. No one born to this planet knew that for sure, and if there was one thing I truly believed to be an inborn trait of the human race, it was their willingness to hope for the best.

Sadly for me, that particular trait was frequently wedded with a desire to plan for the worst. "Are you?" asked the agent. "I wasn't aware friendly visits often began with murdering and replacing the children of one's neighbors. Suddenly the history of this planet starts to make a great deal more sense. It doesn't matter one way or the other, Miss Miller. You're here. People are going to find out you're here—the ones who don't know already—and when they do, we're going to have a weapon in hand that can be used to keep you from destroying us. If you come in peace, those weapons will never need to be used. If you don't, we'll be ready."

"And when I tell them?" I snapped. "When my people get here and I go, 'Oh, hey, the monkeys have something that can kill you all, maybe we need to change our minds about peace and jump straight to outright war'? What's going to happen then?"

"My mother was a gardener," said the agent.

I blinked. Personal information normally flowed from me to her, not the other way around. "Okay," I said.

"Every year, she'd plant a few hundred seeds, and every year, half of them would fail to sprout. It was like something in the soil didn't get along with them. That, or nature understood that not every seed was a good one, and wouldn't let the bad ones grow." Her smile was quick and feral. "Do you think your people will notice a few missing spies? Or will they just write you off as seeds that didn't sprout, and go about their business? If they come in peace, well. Every one of you represents a dead one of *us*. They'll probably look the other way out of pure politeness."

"And if they don't?"

"If they don't, they didn't come in peace to begin with, and if they didn't come in peace, all we'd do by taking you apart before they get here is get a jump start on the enemy." She looked around at the scientists. "You've got your blood. Go run your tests. I'll tell you when she's available again."

They surged toward the door, taking Mandy with them. I was starting to feel shaky from blood loss; the room was swimming in and out of focus, like a camera with a bad lens.

"Can I have some juice or something?" I asked.

The agent smiled again. There was no kindness there.

"Juice is for the dominant species," she said, and closed the door, leaving me alone.

3.

Blood loss is a tricky thing. It sneaks up on you, especially when it's managed with tubes and needles and civilized trappings, rather than with stab wounds or lacerations. I tried to stand. The room spun around me. I sat back down and considered my options.

The bed was inviting all out of proportion to its thin mattress and scratchy blanket. I'd never bothered making it, taking the occasional comments from the scientists or my hosts as an opportunity to point out that they were the ones insisting on coming into my "bedroom" to jab me with needles and make me take invasive personality tests. If they didn't like to be reminded that I lived here—against my will—they could find another lab rat.

Of course, the bed was also almost six feet away, and even if I managed to stand, I wasn't sure I could walk. Normally, that kind of blood donation would have been followed with cookies and orange juice, healing sugar sharp on the tongue like forgiveness, like restoration.

There wasn't going to be any of that here. Only a silent room, and the sound of my heart beating sluggish and unsteady in my ears. There was a squishiness under the familiar beat, like even it wasn't sure what to do with the current situation.

I closed my eyes. I only meant to blink, but as the darkness deepened and the unsteady thudding of my heart grew louder, I realized I was on the verge of losing consciousness.

Fine. Maybe sleep would make the healing process seem faster, or at least less disorienting. I stopped clinging to consciousness, letting myself tumble down the rabbit hole that was opening inside my skull. If I fell out of the chair from dizziness, at least I wouldn't be likely to feel it.

Down, down, down I tumbled, until the dizzying sensation of the world spinning around me faded, replaced by the nothingness of slumber. It seemed silly to keep my eyes closed when I was asleep, and so I opened them, relaxing at the familiar, reassuring sight of the forest around me.

"Stasia?" The voice was female, and unfamiliar, with the sweet hint of a Newfoundland accent making my name into something altogether new. I turned. She stood in the shade of the alien trees, far enough back that it was difficult to tell where she stopped and the foliage around her began. Her hair—a writhing mass of vines thinner and finer than the ones comprising my hand—helped with that impression. I couldn't tell whether she was green or not. The hair made it a moot question. She was ours.

"Hi,'" I said. "I don't believe we've met."

"I'm Tahlia. Jeff has us sleeping in shifts, in case you come back." Her accent made her amusement a broad, unmistakable thing. "He'll be sorry to have missed you."

"I don't know how long I'll stay."

"They've taken down the field that was keeping us out. Unless they slap it back up again, I'd wager you can stay as long as you like."

"It's not that," I said. "I'm not asleep, I'm unconscious."

She stepped forward, and I saw that her hair sprouted not only from her scalp, but the sides of her neck and the slopes of her shoulders. She was a tree walking, in the process of coming into bloom, and the scowl on her pale green face was a terrible thing to behold.

"Unconscious?" she repeated, amusement giving way to anger. "What have they done to you?"

"Took too much blood, too fast," I said. "I'm not bleeding red anymore, by the way."

"What color?"

"Gold."

"Sap, then." She smiled, expression doing nothing to chase the anger from her eyes. "Congratulations."

"Do you know . . ." I hesitated, fumbling over the words, which felt heavy and almost foreign on my tongue. Finally, I continued, "Do you know what that means? To stop bleeding?"

"It means you're closer to flowering." She took another step forward, coming out of the shadows.

The vines of her hair were fruiting, clusters of purple berries with an iridescent sheen, like a beetle's back, clinging to their length in groups of three and four. There were flowers there as well, tiny things with ladybug wings that shivered in the air. She was the daughter of a people who had evolved very far away from the world where I'd been raised, and she was beautiful, and she scared me all the way to the soles of my feet.

She still had two hands, with ten fingers and smooth palms, but her feet were gone, replaced by slithering root balls that seemed to anchor her with every step she took. Those roots retracted just as fast; there was no stutter in her step.

Tahlia saw me staring and smiled again, wryly this time. "It's a hard transition, no?" She nodded toward the vines of my left arm. "I bet that wasn't the easiest thing to wake up and see."

"Is it really waking up when we have to go to sleep to get there?"

Tahlia shrugged. "You tell me."

"It's not what I expected. Jeff tells me we won't ever look like this when we're awake."

"No. We're like watermelons grown in square molds. What's inside looks like any other of their species, but the rind isn't going to reshape itself just because the mold is taken away. We'll always seem like miscolored humans to the people of this planet, and to each other. Maybe that's a good thing." She shrugged again, setting the vines of her hair rippling. "This isn't our first house call. We've had a lot of forms, and we've kept them all, because we owe that much to the fields that feed us."

"How do you know that?" I couldn't keep the frustration out of my voice. "I don't know what's going on half the time, I don't even know which alphabet organization is holding me captive, and you—"

"It's NASA."

I stopped.

"They don't have any real terrestrial authority, but we've sort of muddied the waters, what with being a threat from another planet." She ran her fingers idly through her hair, which twined and tangled around them, pulling them deeper into its mass. The petals chimed. It was a surprisingly pleasant sound. "I think they pulled it off by claiming this was probably a hoax, but since they have yet to discover life on Mars or anything like that, they had the time to kill. Now it's not a hoax anymore, and they still have ownership."

"We have to get me out of here. NASA doesn't have anything left to lose, and now that I'm getting obviously alien, I'm going to become the goose that lays the golden eggs. I can be their funding for a decade."

"Or until the armada gets here, but yes," Tahlia agreed. "As to how I know this, we have a senator."

I blinked. "Come again?"

"The honorable Senator Franklin Davis of Denver, Colorado, had an encounter with an interesting flower in the woods when he was five years old. He's got one of the best special-effects makeup artists in the world—also one of ours—working around the clock to keep him appearing human on camera for as long as possible. He's been feeding information to his copse, and they've been feeding it out to the rest of us. Our broadcast range isn't what it could be—yet. Once the ships get here, we won't need to play relay anymore."

"The forest gets . . . stronger?"

"The more of us there are, the better we'll be." She pulled her hand out of her hair, holding a few dozen of those glistening berries. She held them out to me. "Your friend. Did she make it in?"

"You mean Mandy? You know about her?" I fought the urge to slap her berry-filled hand away. "What the hell do you think you're doing, sending her in there?"

"Getting you out," she replied calmly. "We couldn't send one of us. Since taking you, they've been able to figure out how to spot us. It's all about the level of oxygen we emit through our skins. Set up the right kind of scanners and we'll set off alarms just by walking past them. The airports all have those now, by the way, and the train stations will be next. They're going to narrow our options one avenue of transit at a time, until they have us pinned down, and then they're going to collect us."

"They'd have to know where to *find* us."

"And that's why we sent your friend." Her eyes—which were entirely green, I realized, just different shades, from a green so pale it was almost white to a green so dark it could have passed for black—narrowed slightly. "They've found the range of electromagnetic signals we use to generate this forest. It's a talent we developed on our homeworld, before we knew how to uproot ourselves. Right now, they can block it by blocking a vast swath of frequencies. The longer they have you, the more closely they'll be able to narrow in on where we are."

"Until eventually, they know exactly what frequency we're on," I said, with slow horror. "Will they . . . Do you think they'll be able to listen in?"

"We don't know," she said. "We have a French physicist who thinks it's possible. They've learned to do so many clever things, these meatlings, and there's no way of saying they *can't* figure out how to access the forest. If they make this space unsafe, we won't be able to communicate with the armada. Our usefulness will be at an end."

"What *is* our usefulness?"

"Don't you know?"

"I . . . Sometimes I think I do, and then it slips away, like it isn't anything." I shook my head. "It's something to do with cultural literacy."

Tahlia shook her head. "That's as far as most of us have gotten. I don't know why knowing the release order of the original *Star Wars* films, or being able to sing all the lyrics to *Mary Poppins* in Hebrew, would help with an alien invasion, but the concept of cultural literacy keeps coming up. It matters somehow. I just wish we knew why."

"We're getting off the subject, and I don't know how long I can stay here." I'd never passed out from blood loss before. I might wake up at any moment, disoriented and alone. "Why did you send Mandy in? How did you even know about her?"

"Your boyfriend located Jeff after he returned home. He's a clever one, for a human. Good at communicating without being caught. Keep him as long as you can; you'll miss him when he's gone." She didn't sound like she believed that. If anything, she sounded like his presence was a necessary evil, a way of consorting cleanly with the planet's dominant species. "They found out where you were being held, and, when they learned—through us—of the air samplers, decided it was time to free you. Mandy is human. She triggers none of the human failsafes. I don't think they've considered that we might have human allies who will continue helping with our goals as our own humanity drops away."

The pit of my stomach twisted painfully, like everything I'd eaten in the last year was going to make an unplanned reappearance. "We don't know that she will."

"Who, your Mandy?" Tahlia waved a hand dismissively. "She's already seen me, and my own blooming is quite pronounced."

"You're not her roommate." She had never stolen Tahlia's towels or asked if she had a spare tampon. She had never slept in a house where Tahlia waited, blooming in progress, alien and strange. All those experiences were reserved for me, the girl who had never claimed to be human, and who was now, at last, being proven not to be a liar.

"She says she understands the risk, and that it's worth it. Human or no, you remain her friend. I suggest you treasure that. Friendship is about to become a much-rarer commodity."

I wanted to ask what she meant by that. Did plant people not believe in making friends? Why would we have a great communal non-space where we could gather if we didn't crave each other's company? Jeff certainly hadn't reacted like he didn't want to have friends—but Jeff, like the rest of us, had been raised human, and there were certain things humanity, however borrowed, made inescapable.

There wasn't time. "What's Mandy going to do?"

"She's going to get you out of there. When the time comes, be prepared to run." Tahlia smiled, wryly. "If you can. I think you're going to wake up about now."

"What do you—"

The forest lurched like it had been grabbed by some vast, unseen hand and shaken briskly. I yelped as I stepped backward, trying to maintain my footing. It was no use. I fell, tumbling downward until my cheek slammed into something that felt more like linoleum than loam, and I opened eyes that every fiber in my being screamed were already wide open.

I was back in my cell, which had somehow rolled onto its side, making everything distorted and strange. I blinked slowly, trying to still the pounding in my head, and realized the room hadn't changed: I, however, had fallen out of my chair. That was just great. A solid knock against the floor was exactly what I needed to make me feel better.

Oh, wait, no. That wasn't true at all. I tried to sit up, and groaned as my head began throbbing so hard my eyes refused to focus. Slumping back to the floor, I considered my admittedly limited options.

I could stay where I was. That was the easiest, safest short-term option. Sure, I was missing a daunting amount of blood, and with my luck I had probably given myself a concussion, but at least I couldn't fall down again. My current exsanguinated state probably wasn't going to get any better. I was the only alien these people had. How were they going to give me a transfusion?

I could crawl to the bed. That was tempting, but fraught. The room had never seemed so large, and the pounding in my head was severe enough that I wasn't sure I could move without vomiting. Then I'd be crawling through a puddle of my own sick—although throwing up might summon the scientists, who would doubtless love such a valuable biological sample. If only I had faith that they'd help me to the bed. Which they wouldn't. They'd stand around making notes on my progress until they decided it was time to draw more blood, and I'd have no way to stop them.

Passing out again wasn't so much tempting as it was inevitable: I was on the floor, I was dizzy and in pain, and the forest waited on the other side of unconsciousness. I wasn't sure yet what I thought of Tahlia, but she was only the second of my own kind that I'd ever met, and talking to her seemed like a good use of time that I couldn't use any other way. I needed to start making new friends if I was about to start losing old ones.

Friends like Mandy.

Mandy was here, and Mandy was defenseless, and yeah, she was smart and quick on her feet and she looked the part, but she didn't have any training, and whatever ID she was using to infiltrate the facility couldn't possibly stand up to serious scrutiny. If one of the scientists ran her credentials for some reason, they'd catch on to her deception. They'd catch *her*, and then NASA would have a hostage against my good behavior.

Would I let them take me apart in order to save Mandy? Yeah. I was pretty sure I would. I didn't like people—had never liked people—but individuals who stuck around long enough for me to start giving a damn were rare enough that I wanted to protect the ones I had. Lucas and Graham were going to need her once they figured out I was never getting out of here.

Graham. My eyes, which had somehow drifted shut again, snapped open. Graham had tracked down Jeff; Graham had suggested they use Mandy to infiltrate the facility where I was being kept. Graham was *here*. Maybe not physically, but close enough that any ramifications Mandy faced were likely to spill over onto him as well.

"Can't . . . No." I mumbled, and pushed myself up onto my elbows. My head spun. My veins felt like they'd been hollowed out and filled with sand, shifting through my body, weakening and wearing me away. Even the green patch on my arm hurt, a sharp, stabbing pain that only got worse when I straightened my arms and pushed myself onto my palms. I risked a glance at it, expecting to see the green gone sallow, or cracking with dehydration.

Instead, I saw green lines, like lightning strikes or veins, radiating out from the edges of the patch, lancing through the still-human skin around it. I made a low moaning noise. I was in distress: my body was reacting the only way it knew how. By changing. My blood had still been red when they'd started taking it away. Had these people syphoned off some irreplaceable percentage of my humanity, forcing me to embrace the reality of my roots faster than I should have?

Chillingly, the thought was accompanied by a question: if they could force the change, how long before they would start cutting off strips of my skin to see whether they could observe the blossoming from peach to green?

I had to get out of here. I had to get out of here, and I had to get Mandy out of here, while there was still a chance I could pass for human. The chair I'd fallen out of was on its side, but that actually made it slightly better for my purposes. I gripped the edge of it, pushing it down against the floor as I pushed myself up. My head throbbed. The room spun. And just like that, I was standing.

My feet felt like they were rooted to the floor. I glanced down, almost afraid to find they had done exactly that: grown roots and anchored themselves fast, becoming immoveable. They were still just feet, human-seeming, with bare toes pressed flat against the linoleum. If there was a green tint around the edges of my toenails, I could ignore it for now. I needed to get out of here.

The door was even farther away than the bed had seemed when I was in the chair. What's more, I knew it was locked, and even if I'd known how to pick a lock, I didn't have anything to pick a lock *with*. This was hopeless. I was helpless.

I took a step toward the door. It felt like falling, like I was pitching forward until my leg reconnected with the floor and caught me. I stopped for a moment, taking a deep breath and bracing myself to do it again. And again. And again. After four steps, I was exhausted, my head hurt even worse than it had before, but I was almost to the door. One more step. One more chance to fall.

I didn't fall. My hands struck the door, palms out and open to catch me, and I stopped, simply blinking at the wood in front of me. I was here. I had no idea what to do next.

"Oh, what the hell," I muttered, and tried the knob.

It turned without resistance. I took a stumbling step back, not letting go, and the door came with me, swinging smoothly on its hinges. On the other side was a plain white hall, unornamented, and occupied only by a slim, black-haired woman in nursing scrubs.

Mandy stared at me for a moment, the lockpicks she'd used to make this miracle possible still held in front of her. Slowly, she lowered them, blinking. I blinked back.

"Uh," I said. "Hi. Have you been feeding my cat?"

"Your cat is an *asshole*," she said, voice shaking. Shoving the lockpicks into her pocket, she lunged forward and pulled me into an embrace. I smelled the sweet apple shampoo she always carried with her on trips, and the hot, anxious animal smell of her sweat.

Wait. Sweat? She was wearing deodorant—I could smell that, too, more clearly than anything except for the shampoo. How could I smell her sweating?

And why did it smell so *good*?

"He wouldn't eat for like, a week, and he peed in Lucas's shoes," she said, pushing me out to arm's length and looking me frankly up and down. "I think he's going to leave hairballs in your bed every night for the rest of your life. What the hell do you think you're doing, getting arrested by NASA instead of coming home?"

Arrested by . . . My eyes widened, and I tried to pull away from her. "What are you doing here? You can't *be* here, it's not safe."

"Why, because the people who think shooting another satellite into orbit is super fancy might come to check on me? Please." Mandy rolled her eyes. "They don't even have cameras on this hallway."

"They have cameras on my room."

"Which are currently showing a nice loop of you passed out on the floor, drooling. Nice touch, by the way."

"It wasn't a nice touch. I passed out from blood loss."

"Still makes you look like you're going to be out for hours, which is what we need right now. Not that we're going to have hours. We're not even going to have fifteen minutes, if you keep standing around like this. Come on." She grabbed my arm and began tugging me down the hall.

Maybe it was the confusion and maybe it was the blood loss, but I let her take me, leading me past several identical, unmarked doors until she reached one that had been propped open with a brick.

"Through here," she said, hip-checking the door open to reveal a gloomy stairwell. It extended both up and down from where we were standing: this facility was larger than I had originally assumed. That was a sobering thought. If I had somehow managed to make it out on my own, I could have been wandering in here for days.

"I don't think I can do stairs right now, Mandy," I said, bracing myself against the wall with my left hand. This had the awkward side effect of exposing the green streak running along the inside of my elbow. I thought about pulling it back. I didn't. I needed the balance, and more, Mandy needed to see what she was trying to save.

I wanted her to stay my friend. I wanted her to love me the way she always had, the simple, unornamented love of close friends. And I wanted her to run as far and as fast as she could, because it wasn't safe to be around me. Not anymore; not now that the invasion was on its way.

"That's fine," she said. "I checked the testing roster. You've got another hour before anyone is scheduled to check on you. These people . . ." She shook her head. "They don't deserve to own a turtle, much less have custody of a *person*. They should have stuck with spaceships. At least those are harder to kill by accident."

I laughed. I couldn't stop myself. "They haven't killed me."

"Not for lack of trying. You're . . . I can't believe I'm saying this, but you're a *plant*, Stasia. A green, growing, oxygen-producing plant. You need sunlight and fresh water and not to have people sucking your blood out like a bunch of giant asshole mosquitos." Mandy made a sour face. "I don't have a fucking clue how your biology works, and I still know keeping you in a windowless room and feeding you cafeteria meals isn't a good way to keep you healthy."

Slowly, I blinked at her. "I didn't think about sunlight." Did I need sunlight? Did I photosynthesize? "I live in Seattle. The sun doesn't shine half the year."

"But plants still grow. A cloud cover doesn't mean there's no sun, just that the sun isn't getting through as well as it would in, say, a desert." She fished her phone out of her pocket, checking the screen, and pulled the stairwell door more tightly closed. "The lights are going to go out in a second. Stay quiet, and don't panic. This is all part of the plan."

"There's a plan? Was anybody going to tell me that there was a plan?"

She smiled quickly. "There's a plan."

The lights went out.

The stairwell was plunged into immediate, absolute darkness. There was a rustle as Mandy stepped closer, clapping her hand over my mouth just before the wail of an alarm split the silence. It was loud enough to make my head, which had never stopped throbbing, hurt even worse; I moaned before I could think better of the sound, and was suddenly glad for Mandy's muffling palm. I shrank back against the wall like I could somehow physically move away from the alarm. It didn't help. I couldn't think of anything else to do. If I moved, I would either collapse or fall down the stairs. Either way, I was going to be in an even-worse position than I was already.

The door opened.

Dim, watery light spilled into the stairwell. Mandy shoved herself closer to the wall, hauling me with her, and the door blocked us from the view of whoever was there.

"Clear," snapped a voice. My nameless agent friend. "Keep moving."

The door slammed shut. Mandy didn't move. Five seconds later, the door slid more slowly open, and someone stepped into the stairwell. I closed my eyes against the dark, waiting for the bullet, waiting for the blow, and smelled chicory and moss, a sharp, vegetable combination that reminded me of sleeping forests and green places.

I opened my eyes.

"Rampion," said a soft voice.

"Fiddleferns," Mandy replied.

The door closed again, this time with the newcomer on our side. Still soft, the voice asked, "Is she awake?"

"I am," I said. "Who is this?"

"Not important."

I swallowed a flood of irritation. It damn well *was* important. If I was being asked to trust somebody, I wanted to know who they were. This spy bullshit was a waste of time, and it was going to get us all killed.

It had also gotten me out of the room where I'd been held for the last however long, and gotten me closer to freedom than I'd ever expected to be again. I glanced uneasily in Mandy's direction, even though she couldn't see me any more than I could see her, and asked, "So what *is* important?"

"Getting out of here." There was a click as our guest turned on their flashlight. The beam was aimed at the floor, but there was enough backlight for me to recognize—

"Lucas! What are you *doing* here?"

"The usual. Saving your ass. Trying not to get thrown into a dark hole by NASA." He grimaced. "That last one is a little more important than usual at the moment. Can we move? We should move."

"You're the one with the flashlight," said Mandy. "You lead."

Lucas nodded, angling the beam onto the steps, and we began to move, leaving the roar of the alarm and the sound of running feet behind.

10

TUCSON, ARIZONA: JULY 28, 2031
TEN DAYS PRE-INVASION

1.

NASA's alien-containment facility had definitely been designed by the lowest bidder. We continued down the stairs for what felt like a year, until we reached an imposing door. It was banded with metal and had a bulky keypad next to it, the sort of thing that belonged in a 1980s movie about nuclear bunkers and the Cold War.

Lucas pushed the door with his foot. He didn't even touch the knob. It swung open easily. I stared, first at it and then at him.

"They never got around to installing locks in the sub-basement," he said flatly. "I guess they figured a bunch of guards drawn from a non-military clerical pool and a team of scientists who thought aggression was something to safely observe from a distance would never let a prisoner get this deep."

It was the first time he'd spoken since we'd started our descent. I swallowed, and said, "You don't sound like you approve."

"It's bad design," he said. "Never construct a prison you can't actually use for its intended purpose."

"Lucas—" I reached for his arm.

"No." He shrugged off my hand, turning his face away so that I couldn't see his expression. "Let's get out of here. I don't want to do this right now."

"I've got you," said Mandy, sliding her arm around my back, so that her hand was in my right armpit and my left arm was slung around her shoulders. It was the sort of hold that people use for someone with a sprained ankle, and it provided a surprising amount of support. I leaned in to her gratefully, trying not to dwell on Lucas's reaction.

It wasn't working. He wasn't looking at me. He'd been willing to come here, to help break me out—that meant he couldn't hate me for telling him the truth, right? We'd known each other for years. We were *friends*. And I had never lied to him, not once.

But maybe that didn't matter. Graham's family hadn't sought out his company in years. They still believed he was lying, that one day he was going to wake up and announce he was tired of pretending to be something he wasn't and go back to being their good little girl. He had never lied to them about anything that mattered. Maybe he'd lied about who ate the last cookie when he was a kid or why he'd been twenty minutes late for curfew, but those weren't *real*. They mattered in the moment, not in the grand sweep of a lifetime. Those weren't lies that got held against him.

The truth, though . . . the truth was something they couldn't seem to forgive. Maybe Lucas was going to be the same way with my truth. It had been fine as long as he'd been able to pretend it wasn't real, that I was lying for my own amusement, and now that it was real . . .

I tightened my grip on Mandy's shoulder, letting her pull me down the long, dark tunnel toward freedom, and tried to think about a future where I wasn't this dizzy, where my friends didn't need me to be a liar if they were going to love me.

I don't know how long we walked. I think I passed out at one point, still walking but no longer aware. The air rang with the distant sound of rattling petals, a sound that faded into footsteps on concrete and then back out again. The smell of alien greenery washed over me, only to be replaced by wet stone and Mandy's shampoo. It was like moving through a nightmare, unwaking, unable to free myself.

Then a rectangle opened in the wall of the world, and light spilled in. *Real* light, not bright, but vital and alive. Mandy hoisted me a little higher, and we walked together into the moon-washed strip of pasture outside the concealed back entrance to the facility where I'd been held. I blinked repeatedly, trying to get my eyes to adjust.

Gradually, a landscape appeared. We were standing in a divot carved out of a larger hillside, ringed on all sides by dense trees. The ground was covered in patchy grass, the sort of thing you'd see after a bunch of cows had been through. I spotted the first cow patty a moment later.

"Private grazing land," said Lucas, confirming my suspicions. "There's not a lot of it out here, but there are farmers almost anywhere you go. No good mining rights, so they sublet a large percentage of their underground to the government."

And no one would look for a secret NASA facility under a bunch of hungry cows. "Smart," I said, and closed my eyes again, breathing in the scent of a green, living world. Even the distant smell of cow seemed pleasant after the sterile confines of the NASA holding cell.

"We need to keep moving," said Mandy. "They're unprepared, not stupid. Someone's going to check the fire exits, if they haven't started already."

"This way," said Lucas.

We walked across the cow pasture as fast as my condition allowed. I opened my eyes occasionally, watching the world flicker by, and I let myself be led. No matter how Lucas felt about me now, I trusted him. I trusted Mandy. And if they were leading me to my death, at least I would die outside, in the company of moonlight and trees.

The ground changed underfoot. I stumbled, looking down, and realized we had crossed onto a gravel road. Deep ruts ran down either side of it, marking the places where trucks had passed. I groaned. Mandy flashed me a quick, encouraging smile.

"Almost there, pumpkin," she said. "Hold on, and soon we'll have the best medical care we can give you."

"How?" asked Lucas. "We don't have a botanist on staff."

Mandy glared. We kept walking.

The road was harder to walk on than the fields. The gravel turned under my feet, and the smoothness of most of the surface made the dips a more unpleasant surprise. Still, we stuck to it, following it around a shallow bend into the shadow of the nearby trees. There, parked off to one side with the doors standing open, was a black van with tinted windows. And standing by the bumper was—

"Graham!" I tried to pull away from Mandy, intending to run to him.

Grip firm but calm, she tugged me back. "No," she said. "If you trip and scrape all the skin off your face, we're going to need to buy a *lot* of foundation. No one has the budget for that. I'll get you there."

She kept walking, carrying me along with her. Graham stepped away from the van, and she let go, letting me literally fall into his arms.

Like Mandy, he smelled of soap and shampoo and sweat. I'd never noticed how strongly mammalian he smelled before. I inhaled, and flinched as my mouth started watering.

"Hey, baby," he said, and kissed the top of my head. "Let's get you out of here."

He swept me off the ground into a bridal carry, cradling my head against his shoulder. I let my eyes drift closed, and this time, when the world slipped away, I didn't try to hold on to it. I was safe. Whatever else I might be, I was safe.

The last thing I was aware of was Graham hoisting us both into the van and the engine coming on, setting the metal vibrating around us. Then I knew nothing at all, and I was glad of it.

2.

"—not human." Lucas's voice was pitched low, possibly in the hope that I wouldn't be awake enough to hear him. Poor guy. If he'd talked a little faster, I probably wouldn't have been. Everything still felt fuzzy, like it had been wrapped in too much cotton. "We shouldn't be doing this."

"You did it." Mandy sounded crisply annoyed. It was familiar enough to be soothing. She always sounded like the queen of efficiency when she was mad. "You get to be an enemy of the state just like the rest of us."

"Only because I was going to be arrested for being her housemate anyway," he snapped.

"Liar." Now Mandy sounded sad. I felt a hand stroke my forehead. I assumed it was hers. "You came because you love her; again, just like the rest of us. You can have cold feet if you want. It won't change anything that happened."

"Have you *looked* at her arm?" Lucas demanded. "She looks like a—"

"Don't." Graham's admonition was soft. "You don't get to say those things."

The world wasn't vibrating anymore. The van had stopped moving. Were we even still in the van? Slowly, I forced my eyes open and found myself looking at exposed wood beams below a ceiling covered in white flocked stucco. It looked like something that had escaped from the late seventies by the skin of its teeth, old and unchanged and refusing to be judged. I blinked.

Graham's face appeared above mine, a strained smile on his lips. "Hey, you," he said. "How are you feeling?"

"I . . ." I stopped. How *was* I feeling? Still dizzy, but not as bad as I had been. It was like waking from a bad cold to find that my fever had broken in the night. "I don't know."

"I'll go tell Jeff she's awake," said Mandy, rising from her seat next to me and walking quickly away.

"Where's Lucas?" I whispered.

"Here," said Lucas, from somewhere off to my left. "You're awake."

"Yes."

"How long have you been awake?"

I wanted to close my eyes. I couldn't. If I did, I wouldn't be able to see Graham anymore, and I'd been so sure I'd never see him again that I couldn't bring myself to do it. "Long enough," I said. "I'm sorry you had to break the law for an alien."

Graham scowled. "Don't apologize. You stayed there to save me."

"Not just . . . Where are Toni and David? Are they here?"

"Yeah." He smiled. "I think they're trying to stop the invasion by infiltrating your ranks. It's sort of cute, in a deeply delusional way."

"Toni slipped me a twenty and asked me to buy her some weed killer the last time I went to the store," said Mandy. "I'm really not sure what she thinks that's going to accomplish."

"NASA is trying to do the same thing, only they're making their weed killer from my blood." I thought about sitting up. It seemed like a bad idea. It also seemed like the sort of thing that was only going to get harder if I let myself keep putting it off. In the end, I sat up, and groaned. "I feel awful."

"Same amount of awful, or less awful?" asked Graham.

"Less awful," I admitted.

"That's my fault," said Jeff. I turned. He was stepping into the room, with Mandy close behind him. I stared.

The bandage was gone, exposing the smooth expanse of green skin covering the entire left side of Jeff's face. His eye was still there, but the sclera had turned a pale jade, and his iris was a bright neon lime. Even a streak of his hair had turned green, so dark that it could almost blend into the black around it.

He smiled and asked, "Not quite what you were expecting?"

"What happened?"

"Time." He shrugged. "Once the process starts, it doesn't stop. It can be put temporarily on hold by outside forces—your blooming doesn't appear to have progressed as much as it should have, probably because they were shielding you from us—but it doesn't go away, and it doesn't go back. Humanity was only ever a husk for us."

I bit my lip and didn't say anything. Graham's hand settled over mine, a warm weight that clasped and held fast.

"What . . ." My throat was dry. I swallowed and tried again. "What do you mean, it's your fault I feel less awful?"

He held up his right arm. There was a cotton ball taped there, surrounded by radiating lines of green. The sight made me want to look at my own arm, to see how much of the skin had lifted up and peeled away. I didn't. Knowledge was something else that couldn't be taken back. I wanted to put it off for as long as I possibly could.

"We don't appear to have blood types—sap types—the way humans do. Your blood mimics type A when it's red, so I couldn't have given you a blood transfusion, but once we filtered the remaining blood out of my sap, I was able to donate nearly a full pint. Tahlia will be doing the same, when she wakes up. That should get you almost back to normal."

"Tell her about the 'almost,'" said Graham softly.

Jeff scowled. "I'm not sure she's awake enough for that."

"She deserves to know."

I looked back and forth between the two of them as I tried to determine exactly what it was that they were trying to hide—or not hide—from me. "Tell me what?" I finally asked, gaze settling on Jeff. "What did you do?"

"It's not what I've done, it's what I'm about to do." He held up his other hand, showing me a cooler. "We've been networking while you were in custody. It was helpful, actually, having you under lock and key. Not because we didn't miss you—we did—but because it meant we had proof the humans were starting to see us as a real threat."

"Tahlia mentioned something about passing information along."

"She found me through a pair of intermediates. She's a forestry worker, you know, with a botany degree. Currently on indefinite leave from her job due to an undisclosed medical problem."

Lucas scoffed. "Undisclosed, my ass. She's *green*."

"Which is normal and natural for her," said Jeff implacably. "She's been researching our biology for years. She may have been the first of us to know for sure that we weren't kidding when we told people we were aliens. Having the ability to run invasive medical tests on herself helped. If we'd all had access to fully equipped labs, we might have figured certain things out years ago."

I didn't say anything. He was talking around something. The green skin of his right cheek had a darker tint to it that matched the human-looking flush on his right. Whatever this was, it didn't make him comfortable: not yet.

"Photosynthesis was never going to be enough for plants with your size and energy needs," said Graham. Jeff almost looked relieved to have the reins of the conversation taken away from him. "Trees can do it, but they have extremely slow metabolisms, and they depend on very specific soil and water conditions. You . . . you've been a plant this whole time, and yet you move as fast as a mammal. You burn hot and have a very high energy requirement. There was no way you could do that and not need something . . . well, *else*."

"We think—Tahlia thinks, and I agree—the human shells we've been growing inside have been sustaining us this entire time. We constructed a crude machine from the people we used as our imprints, and that machine was enough to keep us healthy until the blooming began."

I blinked slowly. "Like the yolk in a chicken's egg?"

"Very much like," Jeff agreed. "It was a self-replicating system, until it took too much damage. My system is in the process of shutting down. Yours has failed."

My stomach clenched painfully. "What does that mean? Am I going to die?"

"No, sweetie." Graham kissed my temple. "Keep listening."

"Fortunately for us, Tahlia disabled her own support system several weeks ago, to see what would happen. The blooming accelerates after the supports are gone, giving way to a process she calls 'flowering.' Because of that accelerated process, it's not possible to bring the supports back. There's no room for them."

I scowled. "This is a lot of prologue. I'd like the text, please."

"Your body needs blood to live. You don't make blood anymore." Jeff walked over and set the cooler next to me. "We're carnivorous plants. Hooray for us. I suppose all those *Little Shop of Horrors* jokes Toni was making weren't too far off after all."

I stared at him.

"Stasia named her cat 'Seymour,'" commented Mandy. "Think she knew on some level?"

"She knew she wasn't a vegan, and she knew she liked her meat rare," said Graham. They both had a teasing, jocular note in their voices, like they'd known how difficult this was going to be for me, and wanted to make sure I came through it as easily as possible.

"We eat *people?*" I squeaked.

"What did you think you were invading our planet for? The weather?" Lucas finally moved toward me, a scowl on his face and his hands balled into fists. I couldn't think of the last time I'd seen him that angry. "You're coming here to *eat* us. To steal our world and *eat* us. How do you think that makes us feel?"

"I never lied to you."

"You didn't say 'Hi, my people are on their way to *eat* you,' either."

"Ignore Lucas, he's in a bad mood because Roxanna told everyone he'd been harboring an alien in his house, and that makes him a sympathizer." Mandy looked coolly at Lucas as she spoke. "Then she dumped him. In the middle of a dinner party. It was incredibly embarrassing, and if I were him, I'd probably still be locked in my room. But he's not, because his friend was in trouble, and he needed to help. He's not as much of a dick as he seems, even if he is pissed off."

"I didn't know we were coming here to eat you," I said. I stroked the cooler unconsciously. It wasn't hard to guess what had to be inside, not with all this talk of blood. "I'm sorry. It wasn't my idea."

"Do you think that makes it better?" he asked.

"I don't know. I don't know a lot of things. I don't even know what day of the week it is, or where the invasion is, or when it's going to happen." Part of me—a large part of me—hoped it would happen soon. I could no longer pass for human without a long-sleeved shirt, and a glance at Jeff's green face was enough to tell me even that wouldn't be enough for much longer. My time as a member of this planet's dominant species was slipping away, replaced by new identity as an invader.

"It doesn't."

"I . . . I never lied to you."

"I know." Lucas ran his hand through his hair, looking down at the floor. "And that's why I'm here, really. You're my friend, Stasia. My annoying friend who likes shitty music and never remembers to unload the dishwasher. I'm having a little trouble reconciling it with you also being . . . that." He waved a hand vaguely at the streak of green on my arm, indicating and denying it at the same time. "I'm trying."

"He has to, since we can't allow him to leave," said Jeff. "Open the cooler."

I opened the cooler.

Inside were several bags of red liquid that my brain initially insisted on reading as fruit punch. I picked one up. It was cool to the touch, and squelched oddly in my hand.

Blood, I thought. *You're holding a bag of human blood.* Of course it had to be human. If it had been anything else, Mandy wouldn't have been so pale. Lucas would have been willing to look at me.

Only Graham was still looking at me the way he always had, with love and sincere concern, like he believed I was a human being and deserved to be treasured like one. Or . . . maybe he'd never believed I was a human being. Maybe I'd been lucky enough to fall in love with one of the only people in the world who understood what it was to tell the truth about your identity, over and over again, until you found the few people who could believe in you.

Well, I was about to test that belief. The blooming wasn't going to stop, and if it was going to give way to the flowering—whatever that was; if it was a more extreme form of what I was already going through, I couldn't imagine it was pleasant either to experience or to watch. The blooming hadn't hurt so far. It was pins and needles and itching, and the sensation of my humanity—which I'd never asked for but had always been able to count on—dropping away to reveal the invader underneath. Jeff said we would always look vaguely human, the consequence of sprouting and growing to maturity in these forms, but how did he know? Honestly, how *could* he know? He had as much information as any of us: his own experiences and whatever he'd been able to glean from talking to people in the forest. But they knew as much as we did. It was a vicious cycle.

What was coming might hurt or it might not. Might leave me recognizable and might not. Honestly, my real concern was whether it would make me dangerous . . . and whether it would drive away the people who'd been willing to come this far to help me. So I looked at the first bag of blood, and then I looked at Graham, and finally I turned to Jeff.

"If this is what I need, I guess I don't have much of a choice about that," I said. "What do I do?"

Jeff wrinkled his nose, clearly uncomfortable with whatever he was about to say. That actually helped. If Jeff, who was shunting off his humanity as quickly as he could, didn't want to tell me what came next, at least that meant I wasn't going to be the only one who didn't enjoy it. I wasn't going to be suffering alone.

"You drink it," he said. "That's all."

"Wait." I stared at him. "We're going full *Little Shop of Horrors* here? Blood? We're vampire plants from outer space?"

"Actually, H.G. Wells did it long before those science fiction hacks," said a familiar voice. I turned. Toni was strolling into the room, David a living wall behind her, a cat-in-the-cream expression on her face. "Finally embracing your roots, are you, Miss Miller? I guess it was inevitable. You're all going to reveal yourselves as the aliens you are, and we're going to sit back and watch the world turn against you."

"You talk like a supervillain, and yet you're still with us," I said. "That's a little self-contradictory, don't you think?"

"No better place to be than the bosom of the enemy," she said.

"Plus, we can't go back to Maine," said David. "The government shut down the observatory. Mr. Fabris is fighting it as best he can—

less because they've inconvenienced his daughter, and more because they've touched his stuff—but they're claiming national security. If they'd let us into the think tanks working to thwart the alien menace, we'd be there instead, but . . ." He shrugged helplessly. "They think we're collaborators."

"We weren't free for twenty-four hours before I started seeing people following us on the street, and half of them were even real," said Toni, in a dry, matter-of-fact tone. "I have enough trouble leaving the house *without* being followed by government agents looking to do me harm. Can you imagine how quickly I'd lose my shit if I went wandering around in the open? No, thank you. I'll stay here where it's safe, and observe you fuckers learning your own biology. That way, when NASA is ready to play ball and treat me right, I'll know everything there is to know."

"Mmm," said Jeff. His lips were a thin slash across his face, and I got the feeling Toni was going to find leaving more difficult than she assumed.

Leaving . . . "Where *are* we?"

"Drink your breakfast and I'll explain," said Graham. I turned to stare at him. This was blood in my hand, *human* blood, and he was telling me to drink it like . . . what? Like it was nothing, no big deal, his girlfriend had always been a vampire perennial from beyond the stars?

Except I had been. He had always known that. He was just one of the people who'd decided to believe me.

"It's okay, honest," he said, apparently taking my silence for displeasure. "I donated it. Not all at once, but . . . we started figuring out what you were going to need pretty quickly, and then Tahlia joined us and confirmed what Jeff and I already suspected. We've been putting blood aside for you ever since. You need to be healthy if you're going to deal with this bullshit."

"Not sure I'd call an alien invasion 'bullshit,' but sure," said Toni cheerfully.

That was it: the last straw. My head was throbbing, my arm was aching, and I could almost *feel* the dead skin around the puncture wounds in my elbow beginning to detach and peel away, becoming nothing more than medical waste. I hoisted the bag of blood, popped open the seal, and raised it to my lips.

It tasted the way I'd always assumed the air at Disneyland would taste, back when I'd been a kid and the fact that I was an alien invader didn't mean I wasn't allowed to go on vacation. It tasted like ice cream and rainbows and lazy afternoons, like bacon dipped in frosting, like every good thing in the universe. It tasted like stardust, like I was drinking stardust, and before I had time to even register the first swallow, Jeff was there, plucking the emptied husk out of my hand and replacing it with a plump, unopened bag.

"Keep going," he said.

I obeyed without stopping to think about the humans around us, or what they might think of this scene. I had been given permission to glut myself, and that was exactly what I was going to do.

The second bag of blood tasted faintly different—cotton candy instead of funnel cake, early morning instead of late afternoon. I made a wordless, quizzical sound. Jeff, still standing in front of me, nodded enthusiastically.

"That's from another donor," he said. "The first one was from Graham, and this one is from Amanda."

"Mandy," said Mandy sharply.

"Whatever," said Jeff.

I took another long gulp, drinking the essence of the woman who had been my friend and housemate for so many years. She tasted *amazing*. If all humans tasted this good, we were going to have a real problem convincing the invading armada not to eat them. If that was even possible. Would the humans agree to some sort of mass blood drive in exchange for us not swallowing them whole?

"That should be enough for now." This time, when Jeff took the empty pouch from my hand, he didn't replace it. I started to reach for the cooler. He whisked it out of my grasp with a shake of his head.

I glared. "Why did you do that?"

"Because you need to give your system time to adjust," he said. "Your stomach is still largely modeled on the human digestive system. It isn't set up to deal with blood. If you drink too much, it will make you sick, and that will be a waste of a limited resource." He glanced meaningfully at Toni. My blood-filled stomach lurched.

Human blood wouldn't stay a limited resource if we got hungry enough. There were lots of humans around, at least for the moment. Living humans who were willing to donate their blood, on the other hand . . .

We could eat all of those in less time than it took to decide we were going to do it.

"Oh, hell." I dropped my head into my hands. "When did everything get so *complicated?*"

"When you kickstarted this whole adventure by eating a kid," said Toni, almost cheerfully. "If you hadn't done that, things would have stayed real simple."

"If she hadn't done that, she would have eaten someone else," said a new voice—Tahlia's voice, transposed from the forest, where she could have passed for a safe hallucination, into the real and material world. I didn't bother uncovering my face. I knew what she looked like under the skin, in the space where the alien flowers bloomed. No matter what she looked like here, that would be the face that mattered. "Once we germinated, our course was set."

"So you've said," replied Lucas tightly. "I don't see it."

"We're not thinking creatures when we sprout, not as you measure the concept. We grow with the mindless needs of the young. We hunger, and so we eat. We yearn to be more than we are, and so we implant upon something that can carry us to greatness."

"Wait." I lifted my head. "How does that work? We come from another planet? What did we eat there?"

"Something else," said Tahlia, and smiled. "Hello, Stasia. I'm glad to see you well."

I said nothing. Only looked at her, and saw my future.

There was no human skin left on her face, only the smooth green that was spreading over Jeff—that would soon be spreading over me, once it made its way from my arm to my torso. Like him, her eyes were green. Unlike him, her teeth had been replaced, becoming hard, woody squares that looked like polished bone. A streak of her hair had somehow become long, twining vines no bigger around than a thread, covered in small, bright green leaves.

Her smile widened as she saw me looking. "Do you like it?" she asked. "Jeffrey mentioned you were concerned about losing your human form. I assure you, it will stay, and be replicated as closely as the vegetable world allows."

"Because that's not a mockery of humanity or anything," muttered Toni.

"We don't need you all," said Jeff sharply.

Graham took my hand and squeezed it. "You're wrong," he said. "The invasion is coming. Your people look almost as human as we do. And how much do you really know about the aliens, huh? You were born here. You don't remember anything *but* here. Maybe they're not going to be so kind to you. Maybe you were just canaries, meant to show them whether or not they could survive our world."

There was a certain insidious appeal to his words. If we assumed the armada was not going to be on our side, we could join forces with the humans who were inevitably going to form a resistance. We could be the good guys when the dust settled, the new Vegetable-Americans taking our oaths of citizenship and helping to make this country great. Although Tahlia was Canadian, so she might not go for that. And according to Toni's research, there had been seeds all over the world, which meant a lot of countries would need to agree not to punish us for coming from another planet and eating kids before we had the brains to stop ourselves. And—

And people would still taste like summer vacation felt when I was a kid, and I would still know that we were lying to ourselves. The armada didn't send us here because they wanted to betray us. I might not have a clear idea of why they *did* send us—not yet—but I knew it had been for a good reason, and I knew we still belonged to them. The forest, with its reassuring rustling leaves and beds of welcoming flowers, was proof enough of that.

No species that dreamt of a place like that, of a communal peace so strong it endured even over gulfs of space and time, could ever throw its children away. We would be alien to our ancestors when they arrived here, as alien to them as they were certainly going to be to us, but we would all be the same in the forest, and we would all have the space we needed to understand.

"I don't think that's the case," I said, delicately tugging my hand out of Graham's. He looked at me with bewilderment, but he didn't try to hold me when I clearly wanted him to let go. "They wanted us to be here when they arrived. We're not just atmosphere testers."

"If we were, they wouldn't have needed to send seeders," added Tahlia. "They could have planted ordinary trees to test the environment here. For all we know, they did. Maybe there's a strange tree in every forest on this planet, something that shouldn't be there, comfortably growing, proving the soil here is good for us."

"And it's not like you've been chowing down on people this whole time." Everyone stopped what they were doing and turned to stare at Toni. She shrugged, unrepentant. "If the scouts were just supposed to confirm that hey, this place can support life, they would have fallen, sprouted, had no one to teach them how to be whatever the hell you people are, eaten as many humans as they could get their vines on, and then died in a hail of gunfire. Instead, you were designed to sprout, infiltrate, and thrive. Almost every death I've documented among your number has been a consequence of allergic shock."

"Makes sense," said Graham. "Even on this planet, you run into issues with people from one continent not being able to eat fruit from another continent, or developing a nasty intolerance to unfamiliar foods after one or two exposures. Allergies should be a serious concern when you're talking about interstellar differences."

"Cats," I said abruptly. The rest of them turned to look at me. I shrugged, feeling suddenly awkward. "I was . . . We always had a cat when I was a kid. Then I went away to college, and I didn't have a cat anymore, and when I went home for Christmas break, I had an allergic reaction to the cat. I had to reacclimatize after I graduated, before I could adopt Seymour." My eyes widened. I stood, or tried to, anyway; I actually wobbled, nearly falling, before Graham could pull me back into a seated position. "If you're all here, where is Seymour? Who's feeding him?" My furry little asshole could starve to death two feet away from an open bag of cat food. If it wasn't in his dish, it didn't exist.

"Roxanne," said Lucas.

Now it was my turn to stare at him. He squirmed. "I know you don't like her, and she doesn't like you either, but you know she would never let anything hurt him. She'll stand in front of the invasion and demand it back off until he gets his Fancy Feast."

Tahlia started laughing helplessly. I glanced her way. She wiped a tear away from the one eye that still looked halfway human, shaking her head. "Oh, how human we become, and how human we remain," she said. "Will you worry about missing next season's television? Or whether your library books verge on the overdue? We are at the cusp of a transformation. We begin to bloom. And all you care about is a cat."

"Cats matter," I said.

"For once, I agree with the salad bar," said Toni. "Cats matter."

Tahlia shook her head again, harder. "You may be proof that this invasion is doomed. Then again, you may be proof that we've already succeeded. I honestly don't know. But I do know this: welcome home."

She smiled. Hesitantly, I smiled back, and knew the world would never be the same again.

3.

Our safe house was located in Tucson, Arizona, just like the NASA facility where I'd been kept. With NASA locking down travel pathways, moving seemed like a bigger risk than holding still, especially since the relay network of scouts was finally beginning to pull itself together.

Each of us, according to Tahlia, had a "broadcast radius" of approximately three hundred miles, growing exponentially every time another mind was added to the group. With the three of us sharing one physical location, our personal pathway to the forest was almost three thousand miles in diameter. We could talk to our own kind all over North America, and as we made contact with them in the forest, we extended our range even further.

Given thirty of us in the right places, we could cover the entire planet. It was a daunting thought that held its own strange appeal. What would it be like to talk to members of my own species anywhere in the world? And when the invasion started, what would happen then? How far would we reach?

Would we reach the stars?

The safe house was about ten miles outside of the city proper, secured for our use by a staffer of the senator Tahlia mentioned before. Thanks to him, we had all the privacy we could ask for, along with a fence around the entire property and an empty swimming pool which Graham assured me was absolutely full of rattlesnakes during the day, when they came out to sun themselves on the tile.

We also had space enough for each of us to have our own room—and for about eight other people to have their own rooms, too. That made me more than nervous. It looked like we were planning to be here for a while, and to bring others here as well. We were digging in for the long haul . . . or at least until the sky went dark with alien ships, and the world changed forever.

The room I was going to be sharing with Graham was small and featureless. White walls, white curtains, a door connecting to the back yard and the aforementioned empty swimming pool, and a bed large enough to hold us both, plus another couple if we started running out of space.

Graham waited until I was seated on the bed before closing the door and turning to face me, his hands folded behind his back like he was getting ready for a job interview. "So," he said.

"So," I agreed.

"Did they hurt you?" He looked at me, eyes wide and pleading for a no. He'd always been easy to read, and right now, he might as well have been a billboard. "Those NASA bastards, did they hurt you? Did they . . . do anything?"

"They drew a lot of blood and took some skin and tissue samples, but they didn't do anything I can't recover from." I glanced at my increasingly green arm and chuckled bitterly. "My human . . . Fuck, what do I even call it? Skin? Body? Cocoon? Whatever it is, it's not going to recover nearly as well. Will you still love me when I'm an orchid?"

"You were always an orchid." He crossed to sit next to me. "Well. Maybe not an *orchid*. Those are delicate and sort of hard to take care of. I always thought of you as more of a succulent or something in the climbing ivy family. You're tougher than you think you are. Of course I still love you. I'll love you even when you're so green you can wear yellow lipstick as a neutral."

"Mom's going to have a fit." I leaned over, resting my head against his shoulder.

"Can I be there when that happens? I love watching your mother freak out."

"Sure." I closed my eyes, trying to enjoy the closeness of him, rather than focusing on the enticingly spicy scent of his skin, like the best meal I had ever not allowed myself to eat.

I didn't sleep much that night.

11

TUCSON, ARIZONA: JULY 29, 2031
NINE DAYS PRE-INVASION

1.

Graham was up and out of the room when I finally opened my eyes, squinting in the light that cascaded through the window. Fresh clothes had been laid out for me on the chair next to the door. They were new, the tags still on, and all my size. I smiled as I pulled the jeans on, buttoning them snugly around my waist. One major advantage of having a cosplayer for a housemate: I think Mandy usually knew when my sizes changed before I did.

Having clean, fresh, *real* clothes made me feel better than I would have imagined. While I was NASA's "guest," they'd kept me in surgical scrubs, like stripping me of my clothing would make it easier to strip me of my individuality and—consequentially—my identity. They could make me the perfect lab subject if they just refused to give me a bra.

If they'd been trying to make sure I would think better of the invaders than I did of the human race, they'd done a bang-up job. At least my fellow aliens treated me with the dignity I would have expected them to extend to a dog.

Opening the door revealed a long hallway, and the sound of voices drifting back from a central gathering point. I walked toward them, realizing as I did that I couldn't remember entering the forest the previous night. It had never been a nightly occurrence for me, but I'd never been sharing physical space with two of my fellow aliens before. It was going to take a little while for me to figure out what the new normal was.

I stepped out of the hall into the dining room. Graham and Mandy, who had been stealing bites of egg off of one another's plates, stopped what they were doing and smiled at me. Jeff, catching the shift in their attention, looked over and smiled. The others—David and Lucas—kept eating.

"Where are Toni and Tahlia?" I asked, heading for the table. There was an open seat next to Graham. I settled into it, reaching for the platter of toast.

Jeff shook his head. It was a very small motion: if he hadn't been directly in my field of vision, I would have missed it. I stopped, hand extended, and frowned at him.

"I'll get you a smoothie," he said, standing and heading for the back of the room.

"What Captain Grumpy-pants is trying not to say in front of the humans is solid food isn't really good for you," said Mandy. "You can eat it—it won't make you sick or anything—but you'll only get nutritional value from it if you prime your system first."

"Which you do by drinking blood." Lucas stabbed his eggs with more force than strictly necessary. "In case you needed the reminder. Drink blood, digest cereal. Don't drink blood, have fun shitting cornflakes for a week."

"Lucas," said Mandy quietly.

"What?" He looked up. "Don't you like me reminding her that things have changed? That things are still changing? We're prisoners in this house because we agreed to help a friend. A friend we thought was a person. I think she can handle a little honesty."

"I don't need to be reminded that things are changing," I said, looking pointedly at my arm. "And I *am* a person. I never claimed to be human."

"You never did anything that would prove you weren't," he countered. "I work in tech. I talk to people every day who want so badly to be special that they'll swear they see ghosts, or talk to the fairies, or have prophetic dreams. Weirdoes who don't hurt anyone don't get corrected when they're weird. They get tolerated. You were tolerated."

His words, true as I knew them to be, still stung. I looked at him as levelly as I could manage, and said, "Well, maybe it's time to think about who else you may have blown off for no good reason."

"Maybe it is," he agreed, and stabbed his eggs again.

Jeff returned with a tall ceramic mug, setting it gingerly in front of me. "That's all you get for the day, but it should be enough to let you digest human food," he said. "Drink it slowly."

The blood had been heated to body temperature and swirled with something dark. I took a tentative sip. The dark swirl was chocolate, bittersweet and miraculously perfect against the salty backdrop of the blood. I took another, larger sip, trying to savor the taste, trying not to let myself gulp it down.

My stomach grumbled. I put down the mug and resumed my reach for the toast, and this time, no one stopped me.

"Since we're all up now, how about you get around to the top-secret invasion planning?" Toni flashed Jeff her brightest smile. "Tell us your secrets so we can betray you better."

"What's terrifying is that you clearly think that will work," he said flatly.

"Actually, I'm with her," I said. The toast tasted like, well, toast. It wasn't a symphony of flavors like the blood, but it didn't turn to ashes in my mouth, either. I licked my lips, resisting the urge to reach for my mug as I continued. "I sort of need to know what's going on. I'm grateful to you for breaking me out, but I have no idea what's been happening. I'm pretty sure I've been fired from my job by now. I couldn't call in while I was being held captive by NASA."

"Last alphabet org I expected to see getting serious about the invasion, by the way," said Toni. "Sure, it's aliens, and aliens are technically a space thing, but they have no budget. They're at like, cans with string stretched between them levels of funding. People never understood how important space planning was."

"Honestly, that's probably why they were able to focus on the invasion," said Graham. "They don't have much public funding, but there have always been people willing to throw them a little money here and there to look into their pet projects. I wouldn't be surprised to find an entire privately bankrolled alien affairs division."

"Which suddenly has the chance to become relevant," I said. "Did anyone catch the name of the woman who pulled us off the plane? I'd like the chance to thank her personally for how she handled things while I was in her care."

"Agent Donna Brown," said Jeff. "She's been working with their alien-monitoring team for years. They have files on all of us. Even a few Toni didn't know about."

I wanted to ask how they knew that, but it would have been a waste of time and energy. We had multiple trained computer professionals in this room; Jeff alone had been good enough to track me down based on a single encounter in a space that didn't actually exist. If he'd been able to convince Lucas to work with him, or get Mandy on the phones and working the social-engineering angles of the problem, there was nothing they couldn't uncover. And then there was the forest to consider. So many people, with so many different skills, all working toward a common, if fuzzy, goal.

"I have printouts," said Toni. "I've recreated my wall in the pool house, since no one was using it. I can show you if you like."

"Huh." I eyed her. "Are you helping us, or are you plotting against us?"

"I'm planning to betray you at the earliest opportunity, carrying as much information as I can back to my own species," she said. "If I want them to believe me when I say I have what it'll take to take you down, I need to have lots of good data. Only way to get that is to cooperate with you people. I'm not doing it under duress. I'm doing it because those fools refused to listen when I told them there were aliens among us—and now I find out they were listening to someone *else*. Well, I'll show them. I'll show them all."

"And if you help the enemy in the process?" asked Lucas.

Toni shrugged. "If I help the enemy enough, maybe I can claim sanctuary when our vegetable overlords assert their dominion over the planet. I can be flexible. I hate them for what they tried to do to me, but I like my own skin better than I like my high horse. You might want to consider a little flexibility yourself, buddy-boy. You're in this room as much as I am. If the humans think you're a traitor and the houseplants don't want you, you're going to find yourself in an awfully tight spot."

"I can take care of myself," said Lucas sullenly.

"Well, I can't," said Mandy. "I'm not saying I want to side against my own species in the upcoming war, but I don't want to be alone out there, and we were already targets, just for living with Stasia as long as we did. Sorry, Stasia. You know it's true."

"You're right, I do," I said. "I'm sorry. I never meant to endanger you. I guess I didn't think the invasion was really going to get here." I turned to Jeff. "What do we know?"

"More signals have been coming in while you were out of play," he said. "They're getting strong enough that people with ham radios and satellite phones have started picking them up. They come in on just about every band humanity knows how to access, and they're *loud*. I'd guess we have maybe a month before the armada gets close enough that we can pick them up within our broadcast range, and another month after that before they're here."

I frowned. "I thought our range was continental."

"For now," he said. "We've been reaching out. People are relocating, quickly, quietly, before the new security measures go into wide distribution. A surprising number of humans refuse to believe that we're here."

"It doesn't help that NASA, for whatever reason, didn't release any footage of themselves studying you," said Mandy. "If they'd been smart, they would have made you the face of their invasion."

"They were intending to," said a man, walking in a few steps ahead of Tahlia. "Hello, Stasia. It's a pleasure to meet you."

I blinked, running quickly through the list of names that could be his. He was roughly my age, with neatly brushed, side-swept brown hair and a carefully neutral expression, like someone had told him not to move his face too much lest he develop wrinkles. His suit probably cost more than any of us made in a year, even Lucas. If he and Toni's father shopped at the same tailor, I wouldn't have been surprised. Which meant . . .

"Hello, Senator." I waved the hand that held my toast in what I hoped would look more like a polite greeting than a threatening gesture involving food. "I didn't know you were coming here. I thought I was going to meet you in the forest."

"Plans change," he said, walking to the table and settling in one of the open seats. Mandy and Lucas were staring at him: one with hope, the other with fear. Toni and David appeared unflustered. Maybe growing up rich—or in David's case, working with Toni, who was sort of a whole barrel of oiled ferrets in a woman's skin—had inoculated them against this sort of thing. "Agent Brown decided to call a conference in Washington about the alien menace this morning, which seems to be her way of staving off accusations that she mishandled Miss Miller. Which means the cat is well and truly out of the bag. Even if she had managed to limit journalistic access to the event itself, no one was going to keep that quiet."

"National security—" began Lucas.

Senator Davis silenced him with a look. "Please, son," he said. "National security has been a farce for a long time. We're frankly lucky we haven't had the keys to the White House stolen and the whole place posted as a vacation rental. Which someone would attempt to occupy, getting themselves shot by the Secret Service. When we're having a good week, we don't leak nuclear launch codes. National security says, 'Try not to start a war you can avoid.' It doesn't say a damn thing about aliens. Even if it did, we're not the only ones on this planet. Every single country on this big blue marble gets to have an opinion about an alien invasion. Most of them, it turns out, feel negatively."

"What does that have to do with you being here?" I asked.

"I'm getting there," he said. "Agent Brown stood in front of a room full of people and said, 'The aliens exist, the aliens are definitely real, we had one in our custody, we let it get away.' Then she took questions. Most folks wanted to know if we were here to enslave the human race."

"Eat, maybe, but you don't seem like the enslaving type," said Mandy.

Senator Davis laughed. "I like this one," he said. To Mandy, he added, "For an oxygen-sucking primate, you're all right."

"Thank you?" Mandy ventured.

"Think nothing of it." His attention returned to me. "She didn't say anything about our dietary needs. I assume . . . ?"

"They never got around to testing me on human blood," I said.

"Amateurs." He shook his head. "Well, regardless, she's held her little press conference, and she had sufficient proof to rattle a few cages. They'll be putting their oxygen sniffers in all the airports by the end of the month. They'll get plenty of false positives off senior citizens and the unwell, but they may flush out one or two of our scouts if we can't warn them all that the airports are unsafe. Tell me, Stasia, before your blooming began and your condition became apparent to the naked eye, did you reliably believe in your own nature? Or did you, at times, question whether you might have fallen to a very specific and seductive delusion, one which painted you as special, unique, with no need for human mores?"

"I thought those were supposed to be princess fantasies, not space-plant fantasies," I said.

Senator Brown smiled. "To each their own."

"Right. Um. To answer your question, sometimes I sort of doubted myself, but I was so consistent, and if I didn't try to think about it, I *knew* I was telling the truth. I couldn't be anything aside from what I was."

"And why do you think we were planted here so early?"

"Cultural literacy," I said, without hesitation.

"That's the answer every one of us gives," he said. "Do you know what it means?"

This time I did hesitate, trying to find the answer that had been eluding me. Finally, I shook my head. "No. I've been thinking about it, but it doesn't make sense. We've been here so long. Even if the armada was on the other side of the galaxy, there was no reason to send us this far in advance—no reason except for the cultural-literacy thing. But we could have accomplished that in a year. They gave us decades."

"That's another word you all use, you know," said Toni. "You all say 'armada.' Not 'fleet,' or 'ships,' or even 'invasion.' 'Armada.' Doesn't that say something?"

"Yes, it says 'armada,'" said Jeff, raising an eyebrow. The effect was surreal, given his largely green complexion.

Toni snorted. "It's nice to know that stupidity isn't a purely human trait. Even if you assholes eat us all, you'll still have to deal with the limitations of your own intellect. I've listened to you argue about whether you were coming in peace, and here's the final answer: you're not coming in peace. Even if we weren't delicious, you wouldn't be coming in peace."

"You can't know that," protested Mandy. "Cows are delicious, and PETA exists."

"Going to ignore the part where you just compared humanity to cattle, and move on to the more-salient point that PETA exists *because* people abuse animals. I don't like their approach, I don't like the way they treat pets, I don't like basically anything about them, and yet I can't pretend we didn't bring them on ourselves by acting like assholes toward our fellow creatures—who, by the way, at least share an evolutionary origin with humanity, which is more than we can say about our uninvited guests."

The senator raised an eyebrow, looking genuinely amused. "All right, then: how do you know that we don't come in peace?"

"No one brings an armada when they're 'coming in peace,'" Toni said. "They might bring a fleet, or an expedition, or even a detachment, but they don't bring an armada. An armada is what you bring when you're looking to fuck shit up. Your people are coming here to fuck shit up, and I don't expect them to apologize for it."

"Interesting," he said. "So you think our cultural literacy will come with a precise vocabulary? Do you honestly believe every scout on this planet will choose the same words for the same situations?"

"You do," said Toni. "And when it's important, so do I. I've spoken to dozens of you. More than just about anybody else who *isn't* one of you.

You're consistent. You understand that, right? When someone asks if you're an alien invader, you say yes. When you meet someone new, you tell them exactly what you are. How did you learn to suppress that instinct long enough to get elected?"

"I didn't." For the first time, Senator Davis looked uncomfortable. "It was a running joke throughout my campaign. Politicians can't be trusted, so why not elect an alien? It played remarkably well with my constituents, and with some finesse, it didn't do too badly with my peers. I was hoping to learn to suppress the instinct, as you call it, long enough to make a run for the White House, but I'm afraid some things were never meant to be."

"Oh, poor little fern, denied access to somebody else's nuclear weapons." Toni mock-pouted. "I bet that hurt your green alien heart. But yeah, see, where it *matters*, you all seem to have been programmed to spill your guts when given the slightest opportunity. So you tell strangers you've come from your home planet because Mars needs women and Alpha Centauri needs water, and you always call your ride an 'armada.' You're not coming in peace."

"Fascinating," said the senator.

Toni wasn't done. Maybe it would have been better if she had been. "That's the real reason you're here: because that programming doesn't go away when it gets inconvenient, does it? Lots of your political rivals probably know you ran for office on the friendly neighborhood alien platform. They've been waiting for you to come out and say something about the current situation, and as soon as Agent Brown held her little press conference, your clock ran out. Now it's speak or be looked at with suspicion. Maybe a blood test. Maybe one of those nifty oxygen sniffers in your office, where you won't notice until it's too late. No one gets to pretend to be human anymore—and that could be part of why your programming makes you so *eager* to blow what little cover you've got.

This way, when the chips are down, you side with your own kind. Have you found anyone who's decided they'd be better off throwing their lot in with the humans?"

I could feel Graham's gaze on my face, warm and comforting. I wanted to turn toward it. I wanted to tell him I was going to stand with humanity. Humanity had adopted me, taken me in, and raised me as its own. Even if it had done so assuming I belonged, the fact was that all my formative years had been spent among humans. Humanity was what I knew, what I *understood*.

And just like that, I understood everything.

"I need to go outside," I said, standing so abruptly that my chair nearly went over backward.

No one said a word as I walked out of the room. Not even Graham.

2.

The sun was so hot it felt like the light had weight, smothering any trace of coolness or comfort. I walked to the edge of the empty swimming pool and sat, dangling my feet above the basking rattlesnakes. A few shook their tails in a disinterested manner before they returned to their silent sunbathing. Either they were too comfortable to put on a proper threat display, or they were already starting to dismiss us as threats.

Was it because they were rattlesnakes, the baddest of the bad and the kings of this desert? Or was it because they didn't register me as human? I wanted it to be the former. I was direly afraid it was going to be the latter.

Someone's foot scuffed the concrete behind me. I turned my face toward the sun and closed my eyes, refusing to let myself look. If I didn't know, I wasn't deciding who to tell. If I didn't know, I wasn't confirming my loyalties—not yet. Even though really, my loyalties had been decided the moment my unthinking vines had grabbed hold of a little girl whose only crime had been following a delicious scent into the forest where she wasn't supposed to go.

"I know what the cultural literacy is for," I said. "I know why they dropped us here so early."

The person behind me said nothing as they moved to the edge of the pool and sat down. I resisted the urge to reach for their hand. Whoever they were didn't matter as much as the fact that they were there: they were listening.

"Cats don't hate mice. They like to chase them. They like to hunt them. They may even like killing them, although I guess most cats like eating them better than they like the hunt itself. Mice are a means to an end. Want a full belly, catch a mouse. So when a mouse gets away, the cat isn't mad. The cat doesn't care enough to be mad. If you put a cat in a barn *full* of mice, some of the mice will always get away. They wouldn't, if the cat cared more. If the cat knew how to hate."

Silence. If I hadn't been able to hear my unknown companion breathing, I would have thought that I was hallucinating.

"They sent us here to learn how to hate. To learn how to think and hold grudges like a human. The cultural literacy isn't about preserving human history or making sure the universe will remember them. It's about telling us what form the rebellion will take. We can't afford to be cats chasing mice. We can't afford not to care. We have to know how the mice think. We have to . . ." I stopped, catching my breath, thinking of all the people who'd mocked me or made me feel like I was crazy over the years. All the people who'd seen my insistence that I was from space as an excuse to treat me like I was less than they were.

My own people—my species, whatever it was—had done this to me. Had turned me into a freak among the ones who should have been my own kind, and all so I could learn to hate.

I opened my eyes. I turned. Graham didn't flinch away. Instead, he slipped his hand into mine and looked at me sadly, nothing but acceptance in his eyes.

"We have to hate," I whispered.

He held my hand as I leaned over to rest my head against his shoulder, and the Arizona sun beat down on us, and I had no idea what to do.

STEM

. . . I think everyone expected to see a man emerge—possibly something a little unlike us terrestrial men, but in all essentials a man. I know I did. But, looking, I presently saw something stirring within the shadow: greyish billowy movements, one above another, and then two luminous disks—like eyes. Then something resembling a little grey snake, about the thickness of a walking stick, coiled up out of the writhing middle, and wriggled in the air towards me—and then another . . .

—H.G. WELLS,
THE WAR OF THE WORLDS

I won't say I'm sorry for something I never got to decide to do.

—STASIA MILLER

Nobody tells us how much time we get. I wish somebody could. I wish that as soon as we fell in love, a little man with a pocket watch would appear like something out of . . . out of a Lemony Snicket novel and say, "The young lovers did not yet know, although they were soon to learn, that they would only have three years, six months, and two days together before their love would end in tragedy."

It would still have been worth it. We would both have stayed. But I might feel a little less like I was dying.

Robert was the kind of man people say can't possibly exist. He was kind and funny and loud and aggressive when he needed to be and gentle whenever he could be. He loved me. I loved him. If I ever needed proof that the world was good,

I got it when he chose me. If I ever needed proof that the world was cruel, I got it three years, six months, and two days later.

—EULOGY BY AMANDA REYES
FOR ROBERT GILMORE,
DELIVERED 2028.

Go back to your home planet, you freak.

—INSCRIPTION IN THE YEARBOOK
OF ANASTASIA MILLER,
JUNE, 2015.

12

TUCSON, ARIZONA: AUGUST 6, 2031
THE LAST DAY BEFORE THE INVASION

1.

Somehow, they still didn't know where we were.

The news had been filled with stories about aliens. After Agent Brown's press conference got rebroadcast around the world—as Senator Davis had predicted it would be—people had put two and two together: signal from space plus aliens among us equaled invasion on the way, and extraterrestrial fever had gripped the world.

"We don't need to destroy them," Jeff had muttered, after the first riot had been reported on social media. "We need to sedate them so they don't destroy themselves out of sheer . . . I don't even know what this is."

"Proof that they're prey," Tahlia had replied. "Proof that we're right."

Toni, who had been sprawled over the entire couch with a star chart and a highlighter, had sneered without responding.

That had been the house for the past week: lots of judgment, lots of silence, and lots of aimlessness. Senator Davis had moved in full-time, claiming to be able to serve his constituents just as well from Arizona as he could from Washington DC. David and Toni were working constantly on their star charts, convinced that if they could just figure out where the invasion was coming *from*, they could somehow make it go *back*.

After the third day, Graham had started hesitantly helping them. I should probably have been hurt by that, but honestly, it had been more of a relief than anything else. He had something to keep him busy while I was outside of his reach. More and more, all I wanted to do was sleep.

When I slept, everything was okay, because when I slept, I wasn't part of a species coming to take over a world that didn't belong to us. I was in a world that *did* belong to us. I was home.

With every passing night, the forest grew grander, the trees straining for the sky like gravity had been rescinded, the dragonfly-petaled flowers growing lusher and denser in their chiming groves. The sound of crystal petals knocking against each other was a constant now, lulling me to sleep and waking me in triumphant peals. There was a language there, something I couldn't understand and didn't want to, because it wasn't for me. What the flowers said when they were alone was theirs. I didn't need to share it to be grateful for its existence.

// here // they whispered, when I—when any of their bipedal children—drew close enough to converse. *// here, welcome. coming, here. coming, soon. //* Their language, strange and subtle as it was, was getting easier and easier to understand. All it cost was a few sheets of skin, peeling away while we slept, to be found like dried-out husks at the foot of the bed when the morning came.

We were blooming, all of us, faster and faster all the time. Even Tahlia, who insisted her own blooming was over, replaced by flowering—which seemed like basically the same thing to me, and maybe that just meant my own flowering hadn't started yet, or maybe it meant I didn't recognize it. Whatever the nomenclature, the process was definitely accelerating. My own skin was more than half-green, and while there were no mirrors in the forest, I knew I no longer looked even remotely human when I walked there by night. None of us did. As for what we *were* . . .

When I opened my eyes, it faded, replaced by a quiet sort of regret, like somewhere deep down, I was *sad* that I would never be made of twisting vines and trembling fonds. Like my bipedal, almost-human shape was somehow wrong. That was the worst part of all this. The feeling that I was wrong.

Outside our retreat, the whole world was looking for us, and for people like us. Our faces—mine, Graham's, even Senator Davis's—had appeared on the news a few times, circulated and recirculated through social media. Interestingly, Graham was branded as a possible alien, while the senator was labeled a sympathizer and possible traitor to his own kind. The intel these people were working from wasn't perfect. And still they didn't find us.

We were lucky that way. Some folks had vanished from the forest while their bodies were asleep, snatched from their beds while they were defenseless. Surprisingly few of them had been betrayed by their families or loved ones, possibly because, as we went, I was on the more social end. Three whole people—four, if I wanted to count Roxanne—had been primed to notice my disappearance. Most of the people I'd met in the forest hadn't even had that much.

Maybe that, too, was part of the reason we'd been dropped here so far in advance of the armada. If the flowers in the forest were an accurate reflection of the flower that birthed me, it was easier for them to consume children. They were too small to duplicate a fully grown adult; it would have strained the resources of the root system past sustaining. So we all started out as children, seemingly human, inwardly alien, running across this strange new world with children's eagerness to see everything, touch everything, learn everything. That was useful. That made us better at gathering the information the armada needed.

But even the least social children are likely to have people looking out for them and taking care of them, making sure their daily needs were met—making sure their skin wasn't falling off and revealing the green ripeness underneath. The invasion had been timed to give us all time to reach adulthood.

It was funny, in a way. The more I thought about the timing of things, the way it had all been laid out and double-designed, the more obvious it became that some things were universal. I could posit a hundred things about not only my own species but all the other aliens we had met and devoured as we made our relentless way across the cosmos. Life spans had to be roughly equivalent for the majority of sapient races, or else our planting season would have been wrong. Biology had to be similar enough to let us adapt, a few fatal allergic reactions notwithstanding.

We were the weeds of the universe, and if we could grow somewhere, then that place was similar to everyplace else we'd sprouted.

I sat at the kitchen table, sipping a glass of blood mixed with orange juice and scrolling through the news reports on my tablet. Another six aliens had been captured. I recognized three of them from their locations, although their faces were too human to be familiar. In the forest, they were miracles of leaf and vine and flower, not glowering bipeds in handcuffs being shoved into the back of government vans.

Agent Brown was being smart about the arrests: I had to give her that much. Somehow, there was always someone standing by to capture the moment the "alien terrorists" were brought to justice, and somehow, the chaos of bringing them in always resulted in a torn sleeve or a missing jacket—anything to reveal the patches of green on their arms and throats. We came in every shade of the verdigris rainbow, from a green so pale it was almost like ivory to a green so dark it trended into black, and the photographers captured it perfectly, over and over again. See, said those pictures; see how unlike us they are. How strange, how foreign, how alien.

Human hate crimes were down, except for the part where most of the people being attacked because they were from outer space were actually from the apartment complex down the block, the one that had always been viewed as “other.” Whatever the reason, it didn’t matter anymore, because finally, there was something that could be hated without any consequences. We weren’t from around here. We didn’t deserve the benefit of the doubt.

One man, upon seeing the first strips of green on his wife’s back, had set her on fire. They had been married for over a decade. According to the reports, his actions had been fully justified, and while he was likely to go to trial, he was unlikely to face any real consequences. Killing a walking, talking plant from space wasn’t *murder*, after all.

It was probably a good thing we were an armada and not a friendly diplomatic mission. By the time our ships got here, they were going to have so much to avenge.

The sound of someone walking down the hall got my attention. I raised my head and watched Mandy enter the room. The spring in her step was long since gone, replaced by a weary plodding so out of character that it hurt. She should have been home with her things and her coworkers, planning her costumes for the next con and keeping herself distracted from the impending alien invasion. She should have been, for this last little stretch of time, *human*. Instead, she was here, in a house packed with aliens and surrounded by desert, watching the world revile her before they even knew her name.

I felt bad for her. But not too bad. Of the two of us, she was the one who’d had a choice.

“Hey,” she said, when she saw me. “Any news?”

“Plenty,” I replied. “Not anything good, though, and not anything game-changing. They've caught three more of us; they've killed two." I chuckled mirthlessly. "It's funny, you know? None of them can say for sure that we killed the kids we replaced. Maybe we made the replacements at birth. Maybe we're like the Midwich Cuckoos, and there were never any 'real' kids to swap out. But the second humans know we're not, they're happy to start with the murder."

"You drink blood," said Mandy. "You need it to live."

"Yeah, but they don't know that." We knew they didn't because they hadn't been broadcasting it on every news report. As soon as it got out that we were not only aliens, we were *predators*, it was going to be game over. The little rumbles of resistance from the fringe groups were going to stop, and it was going to be all anti-alien, all the time.

We were getting close to that point. All of us who were like Tahlia, flowering instead of blooming, had abandoned solid food entirely, subsisting on nothing but blood and the occasional sunbath. The fact that they *could* drink other kinds of blood didn't mean they wanted to. The logic was straightforward: donations from our small supply of sympathetic humans were free and easily accessible, whereas pig or cow blood required going to the butcher and placing a special order. Harmless enough, done once, but over and over again, for weeks? Someone was going to get suspicious, if they weren't already.

"How much time do you think we have left before the rest of your, you know"—Mandy waved vaguely at me—"before they get here?"

"I don't know," I said. "No one knows. NASA has to be watching for them, right?"

"Sure, but they're not going to tell us the danger is getting worse." Mandy shook her head. "I still don't understand their deal."

"Their deal is, they stayed alive by taking any source of funding they could, and now they're run by the people who've been sure for years that the aliens were coming to eat the world."

Mandy laughed, small and bitter. "So NASA is the only government agency in the control of people who know what they're talking about, is that what you're saying?"

"I guess even a stopped clock is right twice a day." I started to reach for my juice and stopped myself, looking instead at the lines around her eyes, the pallor of her skin. She looked shaky. "How are you holding up?"

This time, her laughter wasn't nearly as small. "Oh, I don't know. My best friend is *really* a killer space fern, not just pretending to be, and now I'm helping protect a group of invaders from my own government while we wait for their armada to get here. Also, none of them actually know why they're here, so maybe they want to be friends and maybe they want to slaughter my entire species, but hey. It's not like I could leave if I wanted to, so I may as well sit back and enjoy the show. Did you know that I've been doing most of the grocery shopping? Half the people out here speak Spanish, so I blend better than Graham or Toni—not that she wouldn't betray you for a shiny cereal-box badge—or David. Or God forbid, one of the green people. Do you know how much foundation makeup I've bought?" Her voice rose on the last question, ending in an almost hysterical peak.

"No," I said cautiously. "I don't. Mandy, is someone making you do something you don't want to do?"

"No." She looked at me, misery written clearly across her face. "Everything I'm doing, I'm doing of my own free will. I can't even pretend you're somehow compelling me, because I know I would do it even if you didn't care. Even if you had another way. I love you and I want you to be safe and happy."

I blinked slowly. "I don't understand."

"Of course you don't, you jerk. You've never been good at friendship." Mandy tried to smile. The expression died before it fully formed. "When I met you, I thought, 'Wow, this is someone who's *excited* about spending her whole life alone.' If Graham hadn't been so happy about having a girlfriend, I probably wouldn't have given you a second look. You were almost violently antisocial. Don't you remember?"

I remembered Mandy coming around with fast food and cans of soda, anime DVDs burned from streaming services and platitudes about how it wasn't really piracy, not when they refused to sell it to her. I remembered her knocking on my dorm-room door for a year, until she didn't have to knock anymore—until I'd given her a key more out of self-defense than anything else—and then somehow, when the next rooming lottery had come up, the two of us had been rooming together while my original roommate raced triumphantly toward her own friends, free of my lurking, gloomy presence at last.

What I couldn't remember was the moment when we had decided to be friends, rather than people who kept crossing paths for some inexplicable reason. Graham and I had met through Carlos, who had been my friend mostly in self-defense: he and I had been partnered in our math labs, and if we hadn't been able to get along, we would both have failed. So Carlos led to Graham, and Graham came as a package deal with Mandy, and Mandy had been dedicated enough to break through my shell of standoffishness and sarcasm.

Mandy looked at my frown and broke out laughing. It was the most sincerely amused sound I'd heard her make in almost a week. "I wish you could see your face right now," she said. "What, do you not like hearing that you're lousy at friendship?"

"I thought I was a pretty good friend," I mumbled.

"Oh, you are. Once somebody convinces you to care, you're an amazing friend. But sweetie, most people—human or not—don't have a social circle they can count on the fingers of one hand. Most people go looking for folks they want to have in their lives."

"I have more friends than that."

"Now you do. Have you noticed you're more tolerant with the green people? I can't decide whether that's because you feel trapped, or because you recognize your own kind."

I opened my mouth. Then I paused to think about what I was going to say, leaned forward, and said, "I don't actually like them very much. Tahlia makes me seem warm and fuzzy, the Senator is super bossy, and Jeff makes me uncomfortable. It's like he thinks we're going to start a whole garden of little plant-babies, just him and me." I was the first female of his own kind that he'd ever seen, and he'd imprinted more than I was comfortable with. It would have been fine if he'd been flirting with Tahlia, or if he'd wanted to be friends, but no. Somehow Graham didn't count, and I was still seen as available.

I was used to men assuming Graham didn't count, once they found out where he'd come from. He'd broken a few noses in the process of defending me from men who thought I needed a "real dicking" before I'd thaw. I hadn't broken any noses, but I'd slapped some faces, and on one occasion, bruised some balls. Self-defense and bigots, I could handle. Someone who thought my boyfriend didn't matter because he was *human* . . . that was new.

If our species turned out not to be sexually dimorphic when not mirroring the human form, Jeff was going to be pissed.

Mandy clapped a hand over her mouth. "Really?" she said, through her fingers.

"Really-really," I confirmed. "I can't decide whether I come from a whole species of jerks, or whether we've all been alone—or mostly alone—for so long that none of us know how to play nicely, but whatever it is, they're all sort of . . . weird."

Mandy lowered her hand, looking like she was about to reply. Instead, she froze, going pale, and said nothing. I stiffened.

"We may be 'weird,' as you say," said Jeff, mildly, "but we're your peers, and we're the ones who will leave this world by your side as we embark on our next great journey." He placed his hands on my shoulders. I caught a flash of green out of the corner of my eye, but didn't turn.

I knew what he looked like.

Before meeting Tahlia, we had both been blossoming at our own speed, losing pieces and patches of our human skins every day. Then she had walked in, and Jeff had risen to the challenge. He'd been drinking as much blood as he could get his hands on, bleeding himself until not a trace of red remained in his veins, and baking himself in the desert sun, forcing his body to photosynthesize. The end result was stunning.

While the rest of us still contended with the visual reminders of our fading humanity—even Tahlia, who had a few patches of her original olive complexion, a few locks of curly brown hair—Jeff had traded it all for clear green skin and fronded leaves that covered his scalp in careful imitation of hair. He smelled like sap and flowers. His feet were always bare, letting his rooted toes "taste" the ground as he walked. If he'd looked a little less human, he would have been miraculous. As it was, he looked just human enough to seem *wrong*. Looking at him for too long hurt my eyes. I couldn't imagine what it was doing to Mandy and the others.

"Nothing human will leave this planet," he said, leaving his hands resting on my shoulders. His voice was the only part of him that hadn't changed. If I didn't look at him, he could have been as human as anyone. "Now's the time to shed your attachment to that which bleeds red, because this is where we leave it all behind."

He was wrong. I wanted to tell him that. I wanted to tell him that as long as he remembered the sunset in Oahu, as long as I could name every *Star Trek* captain in order, as long as Tahlia could make terrible jokes about house hippos, something of humanity would be leaving this planet even if we left the humans themselves behind. That's the thing about cultural literacy: it doesn't go away when it stops being useful.

No matter how far out of childhood I'd grown, I'd never forgotten the theme songs of my favorite cartoons or the taste of Lucky Charms and orange juice, so wrong it became right. Whether we were human or not, we were taking them with us to the stars.

I didn't say a word. Arguing with Jeff was never a good idea. As his metamorphosis progressed, his temper had grown shorter and his hatred for the humans around us—even the ones who were helping us—had grown stronger. There were days when I worried I'd get out of bed and find that he had painted the house red in blood. The only question was whether Toni's cheerful intent to betray us would beat out Lucas's grim determination to survive in determining who he ate first.

"Senator Davis wants you, Stasia," said Jeff, leaning harder on his hands, driving me deeper down into my seat. "Something about the signals your astronomer picked up this morning. He says it may be relevant. If you're finished with your little girl-talk moment, we could go now."

"What if I say I'm not?" I asked.

"Then we would still go now, but I would be unhappy with you," said Jeff. "I would have to remember that you made me look silly in front of the senator, and I might not be on your side the next time there was something important to make a decision about."

"Important how?" asked Mandy, in a small voice.

Jeff took his hands off my shoulders. "Eventually we're going to have to decide which of you we're going to eat," he said calmly. "Five humans and four of us has been a good ratio so far, but as the flowering progresses, we'll need more blood to fully transform. Someone will need to give more than they have been. You know what that means."

"It means you don't hurt my friends." I shoved my chair back and stood, turning so my butt was pressed against the edge of the table and I was between Jeff and Mandy. "They are here because they wanted to *help* me. Helping me does not mean getting eaten by alien plants."

"Not even if that's the only way to help?" Jeff raised one delicate eyebrow. It was made of tiny root-like filaments, strikingly alien, even as it fit perfectly into the lines of his face. "They're meat. You're going to need to come to terms with that sooner or later. These people aren't your kind anymore."

I was horrifyingly aware of Mandy's presence behind me, and of the lingering coppery taste of blood on my tongue. Whose was it? Was it hers? Was it Graham's? Or was it someone else's—voluntary or no? All five of our resident humans gave blood more often than was necessarily safe, even Lucas, who recognized that keeping the plants well fed might be the difference between a little blood and a lot of it. They dealt with dizziness and risked anemia to keep us healthy and functioning. And they knew it wouldn't be long before more of us showed up here, or before more of us became like Jeff, unable to even supplement our diets with solid food.

Jeff looked at me and smirked. "What's wrong?" he asked. "Afraid I'll hurt your little pet?"

"If you touch one hair on her head, I will march into the nearest town, buy all the weed killer they have, and test NASA's theory about how to get rid of us." My voice was steady. I was proud of myself for that. I was also pretty sure I was going to throw up when this was over. Nothing's perfect. "The same goes for all my people. I may not be human anymore, but they are still my friends."

"You were never human."

"Uh, tell her something she *doesn't* know?" Mandy's interjection was enough of a shock that we both turned as she pushed her chair back and walked around the table, stopping next to me. She folded her arms, looking Jeff up and down before making a disgusted face, like she saw nothing in him worth favoring. "That was one of the first things she ever said to me. Hello, nice to meet you, I came from outer space. Probably going to invade your world. Then she ate my potato chips. So see, she's been in my shit since day one. But she's earned it. You haven't."

Jeff scowled. "I could have you bled dry."

"You know, you keep saying that, and you keep not doing it. I can't decide whether it's because you know you *can't*, or because you're scared to try." Mandy leaned a little closer to me, bumping me with her hip. "Stasia'd have your head if you made the attempt. My money's on her."

"I'm more developed than she is."

"You're greener. Whatever, Marvin the Martian. If green is the only thing that matters, Kermit is your lord and master, and he would never drain a girl's blood just because she got tired of listening to a lesser Muppet talk shit." She snorted. "You need us. You need blood and you can't exactly go out on the street to get more, and that means you need *us*. So calm the fuck down."

"Better willing donors than kidnap victims we'd have to monitor around the clock," I said. "Mandy and the others have been giving you what you need to have. She's right. Calm down."

"They won't be useful much longer," said Jeff. His eyes went back to me, narrow and furious. "The senator wants you."

"Great," I said. "Let's go." I took Mandy's hand, holding it tightly. Jeff continued to glare, but he didn't say anything about my bringing the human with me. He just turned and walked out of the room, leaving it up to us to follow.

2.

Senator Davis was sitting at a round table on the back patio, the sun beating down on him without obstruction. He had his increasingly green face tilted upward, a smile on his lips, like he had been thinking of nothing but this moment since getting out of bed. I stopped at the patio's edge, trying to blink my surprise away.

The senator was no freer to move outside the house than the rest of us—the sudden appearance of an elected official wanted as a "person of interest" in the question of an alien invasion would have raised a few too many eyebrows—but he'd been keeping up his cosmetic regimen, covering his face every morning with carefully blended foundations and powders in case of a conference call. Officially, he was traveling on personal business, and while he had been refusing to report to DC to answer questions about the "alien menace," he'd been taking video calls from his staff and his constituents. Right now, however . . .

His skin was a mellow green, shot through with delicate lines of buttercup yellow and sweet lime. It was a beautiful combination, and startlingly advanced. His hair looked like a wig set against all that green, and I was gripped by the sudden conviction that if I grabbed it and tugged, it would all come away, leaving only vines behind.

"Ah, Miss Miller," said the senator, not opening his eyes. "You were so long, I had started to worry I might need to send out a search party."

"Jeff decided now would be a great time to start threatening Mandy," I said. Jeff shot me a sharp look. I did my best to ignore him. If this was going to happen, it was better to let it happen quickly. "So I'm sorry if we made you wait, but he needed to understand why that wasn't okay."

Senator Davis cracked open one eye, giving me an amused look. "Our people are on their way. Once they get here, all that is of Earth will be devoured, and we'll make of this world a garden to grow us good food for the work ahead. Why should it matter if he threatens your friends, when we have a whole universe ahead of us?"

"It matters to me. They're here because of me. I won't have them harmed."

"Then they won't be harmed." The senator closed his eye, giving an airy wave of his hand. "Jeffrey, don't threaten her pets. They've got little enough time."

"Wait." Mandy took a step forward, bringing herself even with me. Her hand grasped at the air, and I slid mine into it, letting her cling to my fingers like the lifeline they were. "Why do you keep saying that? What do you mean, we've got little enough time?"

"The astronomer—" he began.

"Toni," I interrupted. "Antonia Fabris. The one who released the signal."

"Yes, and don't think I haven't considered draining her dry as thanks for that egotistical little power play." This time, Senator Davis opened both eyes and sat up. "We shouldn't have been forced to scramble for cover because a human scientist decided to release her findings. That message was never for her."

"Then they should have made sure there was someone here to sign for it," I said.

"They did. They sent us." He leaned farther forward, eyes slowly sweeping across my face, and finally frowned. "Have you been eating?"

By which he meant "Have you been drinking human blood?" I didn't credit his discretion to Mandy's presence. No one went into politics without developing a habit of talking around the subject. "I have," I said. I wasn't ashamed. I still didn't look at Mandy. I didn't want to see the betrayal in her eyes, if there was going to be any . . . and I was almost more afraid to find acceptance there. I no longer knew how to feel, and so I decided to go with what had served me well in the past: anger. "Now a question for you. Didn't you have a wife back in Washington?"

"I did, and I do." His smile was quick, practiced, and gone almost before I could blink. "Julia understands her current role. She has been keeping our house, speaking sorrowfully to the press when necessary, and avoiding radio transmissions. She sleeps as little as possible. I promise you, she'll be among the last to shed their human guise. She makes this sacrifice for all our sakes, to make it easier for us to move on to the next stage."

The penny dropped. My eyes widened. "You married one of us."

"Not an easy thing to arrange, with how widespread we were in the beginning. It took me years to find her, and years more to have her groomed into a perfect politician's wife. Officially, she's my childhood sweetheart: we met at summer camp, and we're very happy together. The records are perfect, and support our story, although she's worried about those dreadful things people are saying about me in the press." He made an exaggerated face of concern. "To be honest, we were originally planning to reverse our positions. She would listen to the signal and connect through the forest, and I would tell people she was ailing while I continued to go about my business, undetected. Unfortunately, Agent Brown thought we needed to understand what we were going to be facing, and played that damned signal for the whole Senate before I could get out of the room. My conversion was triggered, and the plan changed. Julia can't wait to meet you all."

"She will soon." The voice was Toni's. We turned.

Toni and David were walking across the patio, Tahlia at their side. The Newfoundland plant woman looked faintly amused, like babysitting two humans was the thing she'd been hoping to spend her morning doing.

Two . . . I did a quick, unnecessary count. Graham and Lucas were the only ones missing. I glanced at Jeff. He didn't seem to be smirking as much as he would have been if he had eaten my boyfriend. I switched my focus to Toni.

"What do you mean?"

She looked at me gravely. For once, there was no levity in her expression. There was no triumph, either. She looked exhausted, like she'd been checking and rechecking her own work for hours, only to come up with the same results every single time.

"The signal changed," she said. "At approximately five o'clock this morning, local time, it grew faster, with an altered timbre and a higher data rate. I would play it for you, but listening to it directly has proven painful, as it accelerates the rate of change."

"What are you saying? Are you saying they're coming faster?"

"No," said the senator. "Miss Fabris is saying they're already here."

3.

I don't remember deciding to run. I just remember yanking on Mandy's hand and spinning on my heel to race toward the house, where Graham and Lucas were waiting. Where they *had* to be waiting.

If the armada was here, everything was about to change. Part of me wanted to rejoice in the knowledge that the invasion was finally about to begin: after thirty years of living on this mudball that never wanted or welcomed me, I was going to have the opportunity to go home, to go someplace where the things that made me a lousy human might make me a wonderful alien. My exile, whatever I had or hadn't done to earn it, was coming to an end.

The greater part of me wanted to get my friends—the human people, few as they were, I actually cared about—as far away from here as possible, because once the armada truly darkened Earth's skies, whatever fragile truce had kept them safe thus far was going to be over. Earth had billions of humans. *Billions.* They were about to become Big Macs for the invasion, endlessly devourable and disposable.

To her credit, Mandy didn't ask why we were running. She just pulled up alongside me and asked, "What about Toni and David?"

"Toni's the only one who's here because she *wants* to be, not because she was trying to save someone," I replied. "They can take care of themselves."

A shadow crossed Mandy's eyes, but she nodded and kept running. This was about to be a war. No matter what side we were on, sacrifices were going to have to be made.

The house was almost shockingly cool after the patio. I dropped Mandy's hand as I charged across the living room. The door to the room I shared with Graham was still ajar; he wasn't there. That left Lucas's room at the end of the hall, which we had all been avoiding out of courtesy since our time in Arizona had begun. He'd made no bones about how unhappy he was to be there, surrounded by aliens, or how much he resented needing to pay for his safety with blood. If it hadn't been for the discreet bars on all the windows, he would probably have made a break for it long since, and been punished accordingly.

Lucas and Graham were sitting on the bed when I shoved the door open. They turned, eyes wide, to behold the spectacle of me and Mandy filling the doorway, winded and frantic.

"Now," I gasped, between great gulps of air. "We go *now*."

Graham, to his credit, didn't argue. He just stood, crossing quickly to join us.

Lucas was more difficult. "Go?" he asked, not rising. "Go where? I'm done following you, Stasia. I think I've already done enough."

"We're getting out of here, you ass," snapped Mandy. She stepped forward, grabbing Lucas by the wrist and hauling him to his feet. "Or did you want to wind up buried in the backyard? Because we'll leave you if that's what you want."

Lucas paled. "Don't leave me."

"Great. Come on."

Graham's hand clutched in mine, I turned and ran back down the hall. The house seemed suddenly too big, filled with an echoing silence that would have been terrifying if there hadn't been so many more concrete things to be afraid of. Where were the others? Where were the aliens who shared this house with us, where were the human collaborators willing to throw their own species under the bus for the sake of being proven right among the ashes? It couldn't be this easy.

It was. The door was unlocked; the car keys were hanging on their hooks next to the mail slots. I grabbed the keys to the van they'd used to bring me here from the NASA stronghold. I wasn't clear on who owned it—I wasn't clear on who owned anything around here, except that a rental agency owned the house, and the bills were in the senator's name—but whoever it was could use one of the other three cars parked on the property. I was getting my people out.

No one stopped us as we made for the van. I tossed the keys to Graham, who slid into the driver's seat and turned the engine on, relaxing slightly. "We have a full tank," he reported, turning to me . . .

. . . and going still. Slowly, the color drained from his face, leaving him paler than I'd seen him since the time we'd both contracted food poisoning from one of the local greasy spoons. We'd spent the entire weekend curled up in his bed, miserably racing one another to the bathroom, throwing up what felt like a lifetime's worth of lunches we should never have eaten in the first place. According to Lucas, who had come over with a sack of Gatorade and Pepto-Bismol, we had both been lucky to avoid being hospitalized for dehydration if nothing else.

"What?" I asked.

He didn't answer. He just reached out and touched the curve of my jaw, letting his fingers rest against the patch where my skin had dropped away, revealing the green beneath. This time, the stillness was mine, the world narrowing to the touch of his fingers and the sound of my heart thudding in my ears.

"Oh," I whispered.

The world was watching for aliens. The world was *waiting* for aliens, and while there were plenty of people who thought the invasion was a hoax, there were plenty more who wanted the chance to take out one of the invaders. There had been a blip on the news about a science fiction convention getting raided by a militia who thought body paint was proof of extraterrestrial origin. No one had died, but several people had been hospitalized.

Mandy and Lucas were staring at me now, the one in sympathy, the other in shock.

"We could buy some foundation—" Mandy began.

"No." I stepped away from the open van door. It seemed like an impossible barrier all of a sudden, something too big and terrible to ever get past. How could I have thought I could just run away? The invasion was coming, and I was a part of it. Had been a part of it for my entire life, since the day I'd fallen from the sky and taken root among the Washington trees.

I'd always been the kind of person who liked to observe the world unfolding around them, watching people without interacting, letting the circumstances and situation pull me along. It had been better to observe than to act. Well, that was going to change now. I had one great action in me, and it was time for me to take it.

"No," I said again, and slammed the door. "Go. You're all human. You'll all be safe if you're away from here."

"We won't," said Graham. He leaned across the seat, reaching for me through the open window. "They're coming. We know too much. We won't be safe no matter where we go."

"Then at least you'll have a head start." I felt a pang of guilt. This was going to leave only Toni and David to flesh out the menu. Four plant people and two humans was a very different balance than four and five.

But it wasn't going to last for long. That was why it had to change.

"Stasia, please."

"No." I stepped forward, grabbing his hand and kissing it fiercely. It had been days since we'd made love, but in that moment, it felt like I could remember every time he'd ever touched my skin, every brush of his body against mine. It should have been overwhelming. Instead, it felt like coming, however briefly, home. "I love you. I love all of you, in different ways—even you, Lucas, you asshole. Get out of here."

"What if we tell the authorities where to find you?" Lucas demanded.

"Then you tell the authorities," I said. I shrugged. "I don't know that I care anymore. The armada is coming. You don't want to be here when it arrives. Now will you *go*?"

"I'll see you again," Graham promised, pulling his hand out of mine.

I forced myself to smile. "I know," I said, and stood there watching as he threw the truck into gear and drove away, rolling for an impossibly long time down the stretch of road between us and the curve of the nearest mountain. Then the land dipped beneath the tires, and they dropped out of sight, heading for freedom, heading for the future.

Everything seemed suddenly very real to me. The sun baking down on my skin was a furnace, and I knew it was encouraging my vegetable heart to grow and digest what little life was left in my stolen humanity. The air was virtually motionless. What little wind there was seemed entirely devoted to blowing sand against my uncovered ankles. I realized with a start that I wasn't wearing shoes, and more, that my feet didn't hurt. I looked down. The driveway was covered in small stones, like every other piece of smooth ground I'd seen in Arizona. Cautiously, I lifted one foot and twisted it so I could see the bottom.

The skin had sloughed fully away, replaced by a textured expanse of brown that looked almost like bark. I poked it. The feeling transmitted sluggishly, more concept than actual sensation. I closed my eyes and lowered my foot again.

Staying behind had been the right decision. Getting them out of here had been the right decision. The fact that both currently felt so very wrong didn't matter. I'd done the right thing. I had.

Eyes still closed, I turned and walked back to the house.

As I had more than half-expected, the others were waiting for me in the living room. Toni and David were crammed uncomfortably into the loveseat, Jeff looming behind them like a warning. Tahlia was seated on the corner of the couch, while Senator Davis sat in the recliner, utterly relaxed, still smiling.

"Thank you," he said, when I entered. "I was wondering how we'd get them to leave. I knew you wouldn't be happy if they had to die, but they couldn't remain here any longer. Not given the current situation."

"What the hell is that supposed to mean?" I demanded. I had a lifetime of being snotty to people who got in my way. It was time to start putting all that practice to good use. "What is the 'current situation'? We knew the invasion was coming."

"As of five o'clock this afternoon, oxygen detectors have been placed in every train station and bus terminal in the United States." Senator Davis's usually measured tone flickered for a second, revealing the deep irritation beneath. "The measure was pushed through and funded in special session, and kept quiet until it was time to begin implementation. For our 'safety,' of course. Even now, they're beginning to round up the American side of the invasion."

"Who aren't considered human, and hence aren't considered citizens," I said. "We're never going to see them again." Not that we had seen them in the first place, except in the good green place that we sought out in our shared dreams.

"Some of them will survive long enough to be released," said Tahlia. "Some of them will have friends or family, as you did. They'll be able to hide themselves. But yes, many will die for the sake of our cause."

"We don't have a *cause,*" I said. "We have an *invasion,* and we didn't volunteer. We were sent here as seeds. This doesn't have to be our fight."

"I don't think there's ever been an intelligent species which will take the murder of their offspring and the infiltration of their ranks as a peaceful act," said the senator. "Even if we'd wanted to side with the humans—even if they weren't so damn delicious—we wouldn't have been allowed. Not knowing we were the mirrors of their own dead."

Toni, who had flinched a little when the senator called her delicious, sat up straighter and added, "I can promise you that much. I was in therapy for years after my little encounter in the woods, and I remember my father grilling my therapists, trying to get them to figure out whether I'd survived a kidnapping attempt. He might have been willing to shuttle me off to the middle of nowhere as a broken adult, but as a kid? I was *his.* The proof that he was a real, virile man who could get a woman pregnant any time he wanted to. The thought that someone had tried to interfere with that infuriated him."

"Thinking people do not appreciate attacks on their children. We are, by our very nature, by the faces we continue to wear even as their colors peel away, a walking, breathing attack on their children. I fully expect the first charges to be filed against one of our own within the next twenty-four hours." The senator's voice was back to its calmly measured smoothness.

"Charges?" I asked. "For what?"

"Murder. We are each of us a murderer, however unintentional the killing was. It's almost elegant. As seeds and flowers, we're unthinking, unable to tell right from wrong. We seek the largest source of available protein. We consume it. We *become* it. The woods may be crawling with emerald deer and malachite bears . . . but they're still animals. We, on the other hand, became intelligent when we imprinted on our human prey, which means we can be considered murderers."

I stared at him. "You can't be serious."

"I am." He looked at me levelly. "My wife has already been detained, and her parents never liked me. They thought of her as strange, maybe a little unwell, but their own. And then I came along and remade her in my own image, using the lever of our shared origins to convince her to join me. They'll charge her with the death of their daughter as soon as they realize it can be done—and I expect someone is telling them it can right about now. A good, high-profile murder trial does a great deal to make a war look winnable."

Toni leaned over, resting her head against David's arm. "Things are about to get ugly, fast. Thanks for including us in your little 'free the humans' stunt, by the way. I can really feel the love."

My mouth moved silently. None of the words I had available seemed to fit. Seeing that, Toni laughed.

"It's fine," she said. "I know my role in this little drama. I was the resistance and now I'm the collaborator, remember? I sold out my own kind when they refused to listen to me. So now I'm on your side, in as much as I'm on anyone's side. When your ships get here, I'm going to be at the front of the queue to step onboard and find out everything there is to know."

"Then you'll switch sides again and betray us all," said Jeff sourly.

"Yes, but you'll know it's coming, and until you have more humans, you can't afford to kill me." Toni's smile was almost serene. "A flock of chickens is expendable. The only chicken you have is worth the world."

David, sitting next to her and playing the spare chicken in this scenario, said nothing.

I looked around the room, at this little group of people I didn't like and hadn't chosen, and asked the only question left that mattered:

"How long do we have?"

"Not long," said Tahlia. She tilted her head back, like she could somehow see the sky through the ceiling, and smiled. "Not long at all."

13

TUCSON, ARIZONA: AUGUST 7, 2031
INVASION DAY

1.

As it turned out, we had until midnight.

I was asleep, walking through the forest and listening to the chiming, delicate whispers of the flowers surrounding me. The flowerbeds pulsed as they twined over and around the forms they cradled, my fellow invaders sinking deep into the play of roots and stems and breathing in the scent of a distant, alien world. I walked on, not wanting to disturb my peers or draw them into conversation. What would we talk about, anyway? The only thing we had in common was where we'd come from. That wasn't enough to make us friends. The people I was living with were proof enough of *that*.

Besides, we didn't need to talk to be together in the forest. We only needed to *be*. This was harmony, this was home, and conversation would only have complicated it. I wondered whether the people we would have been, if we'd been allowed to sprout here instead of scattered across the Earth, would have even wanted to converse. Maybe quiet and solitude came naturally to us.

But no. That couldn't be right: the flowers grew in great tangled heaps, constantly chiming, constantly in conversation. This forest was a form of communication, sketched between us in nothingness and involuntary thought. We came from a social species. We had to.

Did that make us the aberrations, as children of Earth who had grown up isolated and untrusting? I looked toward the nearest flower-filled hollow, worrying my lower lip between my teeth. The flowers would know. The flowers always knew.

// come // they whispered. I took a step forward.

The forest flickered. Then, with no warning or fanfare, it began to grow.

The changes were subtle at first, only noticeable because they came on so *fast*. The trees, always alien, began swelling, stretching upward as their bark took on complicated, unearthly patterns. Rivers of fungus burst through the wood, bloating and expanding into complicated shelves in a thousand shades of crimson and gold. Some of them began to glow faintly. All around me were startled exclamations and shouts as the other visitors were shocked out of their mossy beds and back to their feet.

The ground rippled, new growth exploding everywhere—mosses and bushes and grasses, patches of flowers where only mud had been a moment before. It was like time had been accelerated, transforming this from a forest that was established but not yet mature into something stately and ancient.

I opened my eyes.

The room was dark, dim light shining through the open window, and the bed was cold, chilled by the absence of Graham's startlingly efficient metabolism. I could have been a hothouse flower as long as I was sleeping with him; he would never have let me freeze.

My longing for his presence was an icepick in my heart. I pushed it aside and stood, padding barefoot out of the room and down the hall. The bark-like soles of my feet snagged and tugged on the rugs, making the trip feel oddly dreamlike. I had a lifetime of memories telling me that walking didn't feel like this.

Tahlia was in the living room when I arrived, standing at the window, eyes searching the empty desert. Lights flickered in the distance, like a mirage cast against the dark. She turned toward the sound of my footsteps, frowning slightly.

"You felt it too," she said.

I nodded. "I did. What . . . what was it?"

"I don't know." She looked back to the window, her frown deepening. "I was in a grove of our fellow flowers, speaking with poets from around the world. They see scents differently in different cultures. Sweet and sour change meanings. We were arguing about the relevance of the scent of lilacs when everything began to shake and grow, and first the forest turned strange, and then it threw us out. I woke here."

Slightly ahead of me. I looked at my arm, green-skinned, concealing veins which ran rich with sap, no longer capable of generating blood. Tahlia had reached that stage before me. If my guess was right . . .

"What the hell was that?" Jeff barged into the room wild-eyed and bare-chested, his hands balled up like he thought he was going to be called upon to fight the world. "I was—"

"In the forest, and now you're not." Tahlia waved a hand, dismissing his distress as so much noise. "Welcome to the program already in progress. Something's happened."

"No," said the senator. Unlike the rest of us, he walked into the room fully clothed and even more fully composed. He joined us at the window, a warm smile on his lips and cool murder in his eyes. "Something's *here*."

The lights in the desert took on new meaning. Tahlia and I both turned to look at them, moving closer together, like that would keep the chill at bay.

As we watched, a bright bolt shot out of the sky and slammed into the earth somewhere between us and the horizon. It was like watching a star fall. We all knew it wasn't a star.

"I'll get my coat," I said, and that was that: we were on the move.

2.

There were no roads from our house into the desert. There might have been other ways, access roads and gravel trails blazed by the local park service, but we didn't know them, and this wasn't the time to go and meet the neighbors. More, we knew everyone in a hundred miles who had seen that light smashing into the earth would be on their way to investigate, hoping to find it before anyone else did. Some of them would be treasure hunters. Others would be government officials.

Maybe some of them would be like us, spies who had made it this close to our little copse and no farther, stopped by whatever barriers the world had left to throw up in front of them. We would all come together now.

Of the four of us, only the senator was wearing shoes. Tahlia walked with smooth confidence, unbothered by the obstacles in her path. I was a little more cautious, wincing when I put my foot down on a particularly sharp stone or uneven patch of ground. Jeff hopped and swore, trying to seem unconcerned, but flinching away from everything he stepped on. I glanced back, once, and saw dark smears on the ground, like he'd been bleeding as he walked. It was difficult to suppress a fierce joy at the sight. He still had blood to spill? Good. Let him spill it.

Of course, if he spilled it all, he was going to need to replace it that much sooner. It was hard not to worry about Toni and David, still back at the house, unaware that absolutely everything was about to change. Maybe. Maybe we were just following a fallen star into the desert, and all of this was going to be for nothing: maybe we were succumbing to a group delusion, convincing ourselves our alien lives weren't going to be wasted sitting in someone's vacation home and waiting for the sky to fall. I didn't think so, though. The air was rich with the smell of ozone and loam, more green than there should have been in this desert, which lived, yes, but more slowly, more simply than our swift vegetable existence allowed.

We walked and the desert unfolded around us, night birds flashing through the towering cacti as they made for safety, tarantulas rustling out of sight and rattlesnakes sounding their staccato warnings. Nothing bit us, or struck at us, or impeded us in any way. The sky was a sea of frozen diamonds overhead, glittering as they led us toward the inevitable. We walked in silence. When Tahlia reached for my hand, I let her take it, as behind us the senator and Jeff walked similarly joined, all of us clinging to each other, to the short shared existence we had etched between us like lines in the sand.

We crested a small ridge, and the smell of ozone grew stronger. That was our last warning before the land dropped away and became a long stretch of sloping hillside, revealing the crater at the bottom of the rise. It looked like nothing so much as a wound punched into the skin of the world.

Jeff yelped in delight and dismay, pulling his hand out of the senator's and running for the edge of the hole. It *was* a hole, deep and dark and impossible to see the bottom of. The scent of the green was drifting out of it like a mist, invisible and everywhere.

"We should stop here," said Tahlia serenely. She matched her deed to her words, digging her toes into the soil. Continuing would have meant losing my grip on her hand. That suddenly seemed like a very bad idea, for reasons I couldn't entirely articulate.

I stopped. She turned to smile at me. Either my eyes had adjusted or there was more light than there should have been, because every line in her face was visible, even the uneven demarcation where flesh tone met jeweled green.

"He should be all right, if he's careful," she said. "I can't say the same for all of them."

Asking wouldn't have done me any good. I turned back to the horizon, squinting into the gloom until I spotted the first dot of light. That was like the key that caused my mind to put everything in order, because once I saw one, I saw a dozen of them, spread out across the hills on the other side of the rise like smaller stars following the leader down to Earth. I gasped before clapping my hand over my mouth, trapping any further sounds inside.

"We weren't the first ones here," said the senator. He sounded disappointed. More, he sounded *cheated*, like he couldn't believe anyone had had the audacity to beat him to the prize.

"We were the first to matter," said Tahlia.

Inside the pit, something stirred.

It wasn't a mechanical motion, or a human one: there was nothing jerky or jointed about the motion. It *slithered*. It was the sound grass makes when ruffled by the wind, all smoothness and natural yield of one moment into the next, so that it becomes impossible to tell where the motion truly began or ended. Jeff moved closer to the edge. I wanted to call him back, but my breath caught in my throat, becoming something thick and choking, impossible to either spit out or swallow.

Tahlia squeezed my hand.

Below us, someone—someone whose voice I didn't know, someone unfamiliar—shouted something, and the specks of light began moving faster, converging on the pit's edge. There was another shout, and I knew Jeff had been spotted. With that many beams of light slashing around, it had only been a matter of time before someone lit up the green shade of his skin and realized they were standing within striking distance of an alien.

The shouts got louder. The specks of light began closing on Jeff. I saw him turn toward us, but only for a moment, only long enough for him to realize that he couldn't make it back to us in time, and even if he did, he couldn't use us to save himself; he could only endanger us all. He looked back to the people, the humans, who were coming toward him, and then he took the only avenue he had left.

He jumped.

Jeff fell soundlessly into the pit, disappearing in an instant. That deep, distant movement repeated itself, a shaking, a slithering. The people with the lights shouted more, distance and dismay turning their voices into wordless noise. Some of them aimed their lights over the edge, trying to see what was below them.

Someone screamed. It didn't sound like Jeff. It didn't sound like anyone I knew, and maybe that was a mercy. Two vines as thick around as my leg rose out of the pit, wavering in the alien air, against that diamond-studded sky. They grabbed the nearest figure from the pit's edge and calmly, deliberately tore it in two. The blood was a black flag against the darkness. Several more someones screamed, dropping their flashlights in favor of pulling their guns. Each bullet was a bright, futile flash summoning another twisting vine out of the shadows to grab and rend and destroy.

// come // whispered the voice of the forest, ripe and ready to burst at the back of my mind. It brought the taste of sweetness with it, like I'd filled my mouth with a blackberry the size of my fist. I took an involuntary step forward, my hand slipping out of Tahlia's. She shot me a startled look.

I didn't say anything. I couldn't. My head was spinning, filled with sounds I didn't know and couldn't name, as foreign and familiar as the fruity sweetness covering my tongue. They twined over and around the voice of the forest, bolstering and concealing it, and I knew them, and I had never heard them before.

// come // was the repeated request, and then, *// we will know you. we will see you. we will bloom with you, bloom in you, be you. come. come. come. //*

I took another step, and after that, another, unable to stop my feet from moving, not sure I wanted to. The voices were everything, filling the world with security and sweetness. The sound of gunfire had almost stopped. The gunmen, such as they were, hadn't been expecting a pit filled with waving tendrils primed to strike and slaughter. They hadn't come prepared for the challenge.

Out of the corner of my eye I saw a few small, shadowed figures running for the other side of the ridge, away from the pit. They'd be back with bigger guns and more forces. Not that it would matter. All a seed truly needs to sprout is time. The more time we had here, the better and the more boisterously we would grow.

// come // whispered the voice, and I came.

My feet seemed to stick to the side of the ridge as I descended, not slowing me down, but adding traction to my steps, like I was walking on Velcro. I knew without looking that the bark-like surface of my soles had split into tiny roots, driving them into the soil each time I put my foot down, ripping them free each time I lifted it. Through them, I could taste the subtle life of the desert, fierce and sturdy and eager to survive. There was so much green here, only waiting for the rain to come and set it free.

// come. //

The others were behind me on the ridge, Tahlia and the senator standing side by side and watching me go. They weren't following. Why weren't they following? Why wasn't the voice of the forest calling them to come as well? It had Jeff. Now it was claiming me. Shouldn't they have been included?

Who was I to speak for the forest? I shook the thought away as the ground leveled out beneath my feet, tilted ridge becoming gravel-covered plain. Blood was pooled in the sand, slowly absorbing into the earth. I stepped on one of the bloody patches, and stopped as the sweetness in my mouth was washed away by the sudden flash of lightning copper flowing through the sole of my foot. If there had been any question about my roots, this answered it: I could taste the dead man with my entire body, drinking him in more intensely, more intimately than I'd ever tasted anything before.

He tasted like sunlight and shame, like forty years of hard labor, waiting for things to get better while they never, ever did. He tasted like anger, bitterness, and xenophobia, and like a strange, fierce joy at the idea of space invaders coming for *his* planet, in *his* time. If there were aliens walking the world, he could kill them without compunction. He could feel like a hero, a protector, and not the failure life constantly told him he was. He tasted like oranges and axle grease, and the sudden shock of his death was a sweet spice, like garlic and red wine. I walked through and over his life, and I was sad when my feet hit simple sand again. The world was nowhere near so delicious.

The pit's edge loomed, sharp and unforgiving. I stopped when I reached it, digging my toes into the soft sand at the drop-off. In the back of my mind, the part of me that still wanted to hold on to humanity—the part of me that loved Graham, that cared about Mandy, that wanted to be a person, and not a pawn in some intergalactic conquest—was screaming. I ignored it.

I stepped off the edge.

3.

The fall was interminable. I felt like Alice plummeting into Wonderland, only to realize that this time, gravity wasn't going to be kind; this time, she was going to fall all the way down. I closed my eyes, and the space behind them was immediately filled with the soothing hum of the flowers from the forest, with the rustle of their dragonfly petals and the chiming of their leaves.

// stop fighting // they whispered. I went limp, allowing my body to relax completely into the moment. A vine whipped out of the deeps and wrapped around my waist, gently, like a lover's hand. Two more followed, wrapping around my legs, and then more, and more, and more, cocooning me like a caterpillar being wrapped in silk, pulling me deep into a biological embrace.

When the first threadlike creepers wormed their way through my skin, I tried to open my eyes, scared of what this could mean. My eyes refused to respond. My everything refused to respond. It was like the creepers had paralyzed me, turning me into an observer in my own existence. Not even an observer: with my eyes closed and the vines wrapping around my head, I couldn't experience anything outside the cocoon.

Maybe that was the point. I was trying to decide how hard to struggle when the vines drew tight, and the voice of the forest whispered, in a querulous tone, *// ours? //*

I couldn't move my lips, couldn't speak, but could think. *My name is Anastasia Miller. I am the vanguard of an invading species of alien plant people.* How many times had I introduced myself that way? Hundreds. Thousands. So many encounters that began with the truth and ended with me being called a freak or a liar or a nutcase; so many attempts to connect, and so many of them had been rejected. I could count on the fingers of both hands how many times I'd been able to turn "hello" into something lasting. Most people were far more eager to reject than to accept.

// ours. // This time there was no question. Instead, a strange satisfaction filled the word, like the forest hadn't been sure until that moment. *// where? //*

Washington State. I thought of my home, of the evergreens and blackberry tangles, of the deep, mossy forests where the streams were full of salmon and the underbrush was full of deer. I had seen a bear there once, when I was out hiking, and it had looked at me silently for almost a minute before it had turned and lumbered away.

I thought of Seattle, concrete and steel and the crush of people, the buzz of the tech industry, the slow decline of the suburban fringe. I thought of the green that was still everywhere, even in the urban centers, breaking through the cracks in the sidewalk and rooting itself in stone.

I thought of my house, my bedroom, my cat and my roommates, the way we fought over nothing and laughed even louder at the same exact things, the way we had each other's backs. Humanity wasn't all bad. It was self-destructive and contradictory and cruel, but it made good things, too.

// ah // whispered the forest. *// thank you. //*

The vines tightened, constricting until I couldn't breathe. Another forced its way past my lips, filling my mouth with the taste of green, and with that same impossible sweetness. I tried to scream. Nothing came out. I was still choking when I lost consciousness, still struggling against a force so much larger than myself that I, like Earth, never had a prayer.

Graham, I'm sorry, I thought, and let go, and fell the rest of the way into nothingness.

14

TUCSON, ARIZONA: AUGUST 7, 2031
INVASION DAY

1.

I opened my eyes on the alien sky I normally saw above the forest. For the first time, it was perfectly clear, unobscured by trunks or branches. I gasped, sitting upright, digging my fingers into the grassy knoll beneath me. They felt strange. I glanced to my left and saw that my hand was a hand again, even though this was the landscape of my dreams, the place where my slow mutation had been more than skin-deep. Disentangling my fingers from the grass, I raised my hand to eye level and studied it carefully. The green shade of my skin was what I had come to expect, but the hand itself was back to a perfectly human norm, shaped and sculpted by Anastasia Miller's DNA.

"This should be less traumatic for you."

My head snapped around as I shoved myself to my feet, stumbling away from the woman standing next to me. She looked like me or, rather, she looked like Anastasia Miller, refined down to the purest expression of what she might have been, had she remained perfectly human. She was tall, slimmer than I was, with an athletic build I had never aspired to maintain. Her hair fell around her face in perfect waves, sleek and cut to flatter her bone structure. Even her makeup was perfect.

She blinked in confusion. "Is it not?" she asked, and her voice was an eerie echo of my own played through a set of speakers, rendered foreign to my ears by its distance. "Most have appreciated seeing the face of their foster species, at least in the beginning."

I eyed her warily. "Who are you?"

"We have names, but not in the way your 'humans' do. Verbal speech has never been our primary means of communication." She sounded apologetic, at least. That was something. "You may call me 'First,' because I have been chosen to carry the honor of being the first to contact this world's harvest. We are so happy to meet you, as we have always been happy to bring our bountiful children home."

My wariness faded into a suspicious frown. "This isn't what you really look like. This isn't what *I* really look like."

"No, this isn't what I really look like. Your own face, however, is the one you will wear for the length of your growth in this or any other world. You are lovely." She smiled. "All of you are lovely. What a strange garden this has been, to make you so! Every garden is different, but it is always a delight to see the first harvest home."

"What do you look like under there?" I waved a hand. "How are you doing this?"

"This place, this . . . 'forest' was the word you used, yes? This forest belongs to us all, but it can be shaped by those with more experience. I have been here for a long time by the standards of one as young as you. I can make the forest sing to match my breath. Without a guiding hand, it will turn itself toward what was lost. You were seeing the self you wear here shift to what will never be, to fit a soil so long lost that it may as well be left forgotten. That is fair, because it is true. It is also unfair, because it can never be again. Better for each harvest to hold to the shapes they bloomed in, here, where time has little hold."

I stared at her, this woman who wore my face and spoke in riddles, trying to see through her pink skin and sweet smile to the alien I knew lurked beneath. It was a word filled with dark connotations: "lurk." Like she meant to do me harm. But then, she might. We were, as everyone had been so eager to point out, killers, murderers, seeds scattered on unfriendly soil and left to germinate in our own way and in our own time. Maybe the ones who'd planted us—as carelessly as they had—had never intended us to be anything but harvest.

Her smile faltered. "There are no secrets here," she said. "Not from your elders. Not from each other, in time. Once you have fully flowered, you will understand. You will step into the song, and you will know how much we love you. How is it you do not already know, when we found you such a good garden to grow in, when we left the shadow of the forest to keep you in comfort? What has this world done to you, to leave you so suspicious of your sister?"

"I'm an only child."

"Oh, my dear, no. No. You have never been that." She spread her arms. The meadow around us began to bloom, great flowers with dragonfly wings in place of petals breaking through the ground. Their perfume filled the air, and it was the scent of blood. Not human, but so close, coppery and rich with nutrients and iron. I breathed it in, and knew these flowers for both my past and my future, as they had always been, as they would always be.

The flower closest to First grew into the height and maturity I was used to seeing in the forest, its heavy head drooping slightly. She placed her hand on the fleshy spot where the stem joined with the flower, and said, "We come from such beautiful, humble beginnings, all of us. Almost any soil can nurture us this far. Then, if the soil is good, the next step is reached."

The flower began growing again. Its stem swelled, becoming almost barrel-like at the base, while the top foot or so remained more slender, only as thick around as my wrist. The petals grew longer, taking on a thousand iridescent colors, so that when they rippled, it was a mesmerizing rainbow, as rich as the sheen of oil on crystalline water. The scent grew stronger as well, and began to smell of so many impossible things, Graham's spaghetti and my grandmother's perfume and Mandy's favorite hairspray and cookies fresh out of the oven. Every good thing the world had ever known was in that smell, and all I wanted was to be closer to it.

No, whispered a deep-buried instinct, and I stayed where I was, watching the flower become glorious and grand. First smiled at me.

"The pollen is no longer needed to attract a mate, for the flower is no longer determined to reproduce. It will transform itself instead, and it spends its resources on attracting the resources to fuel that transformation. The soil is good. Now is when it finds out whether the *world* is good." The vine-like structures around the base of the flower rose delicately off the ground, hovering around knee level. It was easy to picture them striking and seizing their prey, pulling it toward the center of that glorious flower—

—which began to open, not like a mouth, but like a second unfurling, like the petals within the petals were finally grown and mature. What they revealed was nothingness, a maw leading into the center portion of the plant.

First saw me seeing the change, and nodded. The vines pulled tight against the bulb of the body. The flower closed itself, first internally, and then externally, as the dragonfly petals furled tight. It drooped before finally dropping off, leaving the severed stem behind as the barrel swelled and glowed from within, ripening with the strange biological process of duplication.

"This is, sadly, often where we fail," said First. "We find the world is not good, that the soil is sweet but the flesh is sour, and we watch our seedlings wither and die unfed, unable to reproduce themselves. We can and will try again, seeding the world over and over until it decides to grow. And when it grows . . ."

The barrel swelled further before it finally burst, spilling a small version of me—of First—of Anastasia Miller out onto the ground. It stood, wet with the juices of its alien origin, and wiped the sap from its eyes before it smiled and ran away, disappearing into the flowers like the phantom that it was.

"Once our seedlings become mobile, they grow. They absorb the nutrients and possibilities of their new world, and they find the ones who look like them, to tell them of our coming. Some will die during this process, unable to digest the specific slice of world they have consumed, and we will learn from that. Others will sprout later than their siblings, and join them after the bulk of the work has been done. All are welcome, always. We are so joyous when we reach a new garden and find a good harvest waiting for us."

"Is this planet a good harvest?" I asked numbly.

First shook her head. "No," she said. "Less than half of the seeds we sent have sprouted and survived to meet us. The creatures this world evolved for its own pleasure are not gentle. The soil is good but the hands that work it are cruel. How fortunate, that we have found it, and will be better stewards."

Her voice was cool, calm: she sounded like one of my neighbors back in Seattle talking about weeding their garden. My mouth went dry. I swallowed, trying to chase away the sudden dread that filled me.

"What do you mean?"

"When enough seeds have sprouted and reached mobility, when enough of them have reached maturity among their host species, they form the forest between them," said First, ignoring my question. Or maybe not. Maybe she understood that my question had never really needed an answer. "We see it flicker and form, becoming a bright beacon across the gulf of space. 'Come for us,' it cries. 'Come and bring us home.' When we see the forest form, we know the soil is good and the meat is plentiful, and we turn our sights toward our newest destination. That is what has brought us here, to you, to reap what we have sown."

She had to be getting her words from the forest: there was no other way she could be using English idiom and imagery with such ease. Still . . . "I thought you sent us here to obtain cultural literacy, to make it easier to hunt the humans."

Her smile was the sun on a rainy afternoon. "It's always so delightful when our seedlings are able to reach that conclusion on their own. Of course it would be you. I have known so many of your cultivar, and you have always been clever, always been swift to understand what is needed from you. First the seeds test the soil. Then the flowers test the flesh. Then the seedlings test the world. If all of you had died before you could form the forest, we would have grieved you, but we would have known we didn't belong here."

"I don't understand."

"You will." First stepped forward, reaching out to touch my cheek with one familiar, unfamiliar hand. "This is such an *interesting* form. The biology of this world must be fascinating. Is everything here bipedal and symmetrical?"

"Symmetrical, yes, bipedal, no. Some things don't have any legs, some have hundreds."

Her eyes lit up. "What a wealth of things to experience! But this is the dominant life form, yes? We have chosen correctly?"

"Chosen . . . I didn't choose this . . . I *ate a little girl*."

"You gave her a chance to transcend the limits of her origins and become something more," said First. "Everything your first meal would have been in life, you have been, and more."

It was difficult to believe we had each somehow managed to consume an antisocial misanthrope by random chance. It was also tempting to believe her, to let everything she said be the absolute truth. Of course I'd lived Anastasia Miller's life the same way she would have lived it, apart from the whole "alien plant person" thing. I hadn't done anything wrong. I hadn't stolen anything from anyone.

I knew that wasn't true. But oh, it was tempting to pretend.

"These humans, they are the dominant species, yes?" First looked at me expectantly.

I couldn't lie to her. I didn't know why I couldn't. It just didn't seem possible. "Yes," I said. "They number in the billions."

"The *billions*," she said, in a tone of delighted wonder. Her eyes grew heavy-lidded and hungry. "Think of the harvest to come. We will dine for years on the spoils of this garden."

"I still don't understand."

"You will." Her hand cupped my cheek. "You have a question for me."

I had a million questions for her. Right now, however, there only seemed to be one that *mattered*.

"What are we really? When we're not wearing something else's shape?"

"Look."

Slowly, her human mien melted away, first turning green to match my skin, and then shredding completely. Vines slithered out of her hair as it receded, and flowers bloomed where her ears had been. Then she began to grow, swelling and expanding until she was the size of a small hill. Flowers with dragonfly-wing petals sprouted out of her back, turning their faces toward the sun, and I knew without asking that this was how seeds were made: our ancestors grew the flowers from their own bodies, and when they withered, they left their children behind. I had grown from a flower like those ones. These were my kin.

Her eyes, such as they were, were holes filled with gleaming beads of sap. I didn't know how she could see me. I didn't know how she could *think*, with every inch of her made of vegetation and captive loam, chunks of soil held by the roots and creeper vines that ran all through the bulk of her body. I blinked, and realized that my eyes were filled with tears.

"You're so beautiful," I whispered.

She had no mouth. She had no lips. And still, I felt she smiled.

2.

The forest dissolved as the vines that had been covering my face let go, setting me gently on a smooth wooden path that wound off into the distance. The lights were as bright as the noonday sun, and I was surrounded by trees. *Real* trees this time, not the phantoms of the forest. The path was warm beneath my feet, and surrounded by beds of greenery the likes of which I had never seen. I stared, shamelessly drinking it all in.

It was like someone had taken a botanical garden and Disney's Epcot theme park and crammed them together before enclosing them in a geodesic dome made of glittering, translucent material. Everything was green and brown, alive and vital. The trees were a patchwork, clearly originating on a hundred different worlds. As I watched, something that looked like a fruit bat crossed with a toucan soared overhead, only to be snatched out of the air by a vine that whipped out from a tree that resembled nothing so much as a piece of rainbow chewing gum stretched into a corkscrew. The bat-thing didn't have time to squawk before it had been stuffed into a woody maw and consumed.

I blinked slowly, breathing in the mingled pollens of a million different worlds. The air held scents I couldn't identify, thick and rich enough to make my head spin. I was pretty sure the oxygen balance wasn't the one I was used to. I blinked again, trying to figure out whether putting my head between my knees would help the way it was supposed to. Did my body still work that way? Clearly, plants could get dizzy—I was dizzy as hell—but that didn't mean the solutions were the same.

Sitting down seemed rude, since this was clearly a walkway, and moving closer to those alien trees seemed like a very bad idea. What if they thought I was the same as the bat-thing, and tried to swallow me? It would be a stupid way to die after everything I'd been through already.

Something touched my arm. I jumped, whipping around and then staggering as the dizziness intensified.

The something that had touched at me backed up a bit, its dozens of segmented limbs waving in what I automatically translated into apology. It had a face that looked like something from the lemur house: big, round eyes, a small, pursed mouth, and no nose to speak of. Its torso was more like that of a gigantic skink, covered in overlapping scales, and its "arms" were explosions of tentacles, each ending in a barbed hook. Following its body down continued the skink theme, until it reached floor level and became more like the result of an unholy melding of millipede and squid.

And every inch of it was green. The same family of shades and gradations that I saw in my own mirror every morning. There were no commonalities in our shapes; we couldn't have looked more like we came from different planets. At the same time, something deep in my instinctual memory looked at this thing, this impossible thing, and knew we were kin. However much the shapes we wore might vary, it seemed that green was the color of the seeds we'd grown from, and so green was the color we would be forever.

// sorry, I'm so sorry // said the creature. It spoke as the forest spoke: a voice in English, ringing in the space between my ears. I wasn't sure I could call it telepathy, exactly, but I could hear the creature, and I could understand what it was saying, and under the circumstances, that might be enough. *// I didn't mean to startle you. I should have thought. I'm so sorry. //*

"I don't know how to talk like that," I said. "In your head. Can you . . . can you understand me?"

The creature's tentacles waved in a pattern I interpreted as amusement. *// you talk through the air, as we all do. the pollen brings me your words. I understand you, little sister. oh, it is such a joy to meet you. //*

I frowned slowly. "You mean when I talk, you hear it in your head?"

The creature twisted its torso slightly to the side in agreement. *// yes. yes yes yes. you speak, and the pollen translates it into image for me. the world where I was sprouted was not a sound-world, but a sight-world. the Great Root will never let the children of the good harvest become separate from each other. //*

Sorting through that would have taken too long. I looked around me, noting the ongoing absence of anything else I could interpret as a person—it was only trees, and the occasional rustling of something squirrel-sized or smaller. I returned my attention to the creature. "I'm Stasia. What's your name?"

// for you, for now, it is Second // said the creature—said Second. The name wasn't a surprise. *// I am here because you are my sister. it is good for those of the same seeding to help each other, when the gathering-in begins. //*

"How . . . how are you my sister?"

It was impossible not to interpret the twisting of Second's tentacles as a silent smile. One of those tentacles dipped into a gap between the scales, pulling out a seedpod the size of a small avocado. It offered the seed to me. I took it automatically, unsure how to politely refuse.

The seed weighed more than should have been possible, as if it had been sculpted from a piece of solid lead. The surface was ridged, like a walnut shell, or a mammalian brain. It sparkled in the light, filled with a captive brightness that reminded me of the glow from the barrel of the dragonfly flowers. As I tightened my fingers around it, it thrummed softly, warming up to match my body temperature.

// seeds // said Second. *// we are all seeds, in the beginning, and we are all the same. we scatter them across the sky, and where they root, we grow. you and I are sisters, for we sprout from seeds harvested from the same source. //*

"You're female?"

// I am myself. the species which templated me did not have the same genders as the one which templated you, but 'female' will do well enough, and I think you would like to have a sister here, to replace the one you leave behind. // Again, that twisting, silent smile. *// I will guide you to your next destination. are you well? are you not afraid? //*

I hesitated. I wanted to be afraid. I wanted to be scared out of my mind, because it seemed like the human thing to do, and while I had never particularly *wanted* to be a human—had spent my entire life denying humanity even mattered to me—it was the model I had to go on. Anastasia Miller had been a human child, and I was, as Second put it, templated on her. Shouldn't my responses have been human?

But I wasn't afraid. The taste of alien pollens filled my mouth, and the sound of alien thoughts filled my mind, and I was more curious than anything else, Alice finally down the rabbit hole and about to discover all the secrets of Wonderland.

"I think I'm well," I said carefully. "I want to know more. What is this place? Why do all these trees look so different? How is pollen translating for us?"

Second waved her tentacles in amiable acceptance. *// all your questions will be answered. come. your friend is waiting for us, and when we reach him, we will tell you both. //*

My friend . . . she had to mean Jeff. Belatedly, I remembered Tahlia and the senator, both waiting on the bluff for us to come back. "He's not my only friend."

// no. but you are of differing seed lines, and by telling you, we will put the knowledge into the entire forest. we can only do so much while a person is in their seed. the warning and the knowing are the limit. to do more would be to risk losing one of those. // Second began to make her way down the path, the hundreds of tentacle-legs that lined her long body slithering easily against the wood.

Lacking any clear alternatives, I followed. "So we have to explain this all over again, for every one of us on Earth?" I paused. "What are we called, anyway? Is there a name for our species?"

// your templates were very concerned with the naming of things // observed Second. *// we have a name. //*

I waited. She kept walking.

"Well?" I finally asked.

// we have a name, but what you are now cannot say it. what I am now cannot hear it. it lives in the forest, in the shadows of the Great Root, but each new harvest must come up with our own words for what we are. my harvest called ourselves // and she made a complicated motion with her tentacles, one which rippled from the top of her head to the tip of her tail and back again. It was beautiful. It was poetry. It wasn't something I could have recreated in a million years. I didn't have the appendages.

"I don't . . . Wait." We kept moving. More motion was starting to appear, out amongst the trees. I couldn't see any of it clearly, but I had the distinct feeling we had an audience, more of our mutual and divided kind creeping as close as they dared as they tried to steal a glimpse at what our shared species had most recently become. "First showed me something that looked like a walking hill. Is that what we were on our home planet?"

// yes. //

"Why did we leave?"

// patience. all will be made clear in time. //

I didn't like that answer one bit. I had been being patient for thirty years, walking through a world that didn't belong to me and waiting for someone to make it all start making sense. I swallowed my frustration and asked, "Does anyone look like that anymore?"

// seeds planted in untemplated soil will grow according to the old ways. we plant our ships in the same soil, cultivate and crew them, and set them among the stars to continue spreading the harvest from one end of the galaxy to the other. you and I, and all our sisters and brothers and others, we will always wear the faces of the worlds which made us. we are marked and we are memories. we will have our own names for what we are, our own ways to describe the mysteries, and when the last of us dies, we as a people will be poorer for our passage. //

Faces—at least, things my eye insisted on interpreting as faces—peered at us from between the trees. Some were feathered. Others were covered in mossy hair. All of them were green, a hundred different shades of green, matching me, or Tahlia, or the senator, or matching no one at all, belonging to no clade I recognized. I stayed close by Second's side. She was an alien, yes, the most obviously alien thing I had yet to encounter, but she was also my sister, and I found it surprisingly easy to trust her.

Maybe that was something I needed to be concerned about. "Why aren't I afraid of you?" I asked.

// pollen // she said, "sounding" pleased with herself. *// very good. some go a long while before they remember that they should be afraid. you do not fear me because we share the same scent. your mind knows I am the same as you, and*

it forgives me for the difference in our forms. it knows family even when everything else about you does not. //

We had reached a mossy curtain hanging over the path like a shroud. Second reached out with one tentacle, tapping it lightly, and it retracted, revealing what I could only view as, well, a conference room.

It was a small space, especially compared to the cavernous expanse of trees and walkways that we had been strolling through. A circular table dominated the room, and it was only as my eyes adjusted to the dimmer light that I realized it was actually an enormous mushroom. The light was coming from its gills, which glowed a soft and lambent shade of white. The smaller mushrooms growing around it and serving as chairs had the same glow.

Jeff sat on the far side of the mushroom, along with someone who looked like a green kangaroo—its fur matched his skin—and someone else who seemed to be the result of hybridizing a caterpillar with a sparrowhawk. Second bowed elaborately to the group and slither-stepped inside. I followed, and the moss swung shut again behind us, blocking out the scent of the alien forest.

The light coming from the mushroom immediately brightened, increasing to fill the space. The kangaroo turned toward me and cocked its head.

// you are of the new harvest // it said. *// my brother has told me much of you. you are the Stasia, yes? //*

"Um," I said. "Yes. Hi, Jeff."

"Hi," said Jeff. He looked as rattled as I felt. It was something of a relief to realize that he still had to open his mouth to speak with me. Whatever strange form of quasi-telepathy the pollen in here enabled, it hadn't reached us yet.

// I am the Second // said the kangaroo politely. *// it is an honor and a delight to meet you, the Stasia, and bring you home. //*

"This is going to get really confusing if you keep deciding on your names based on who you talked to when," I said, with a glance at my Second. She looked confused, as much as a many-tentacled caterpillar creature could. I pointed to the kangaroo. "If they're the Second because they were the second person to talk to Jeff, and you're Second because you were the second person to talk to me, we're never going to be able to keep you straight."

// ah! // said my Second, with all apparent delight. *// we see. we apologize for any confusion: the last harvest did not believe in personal names, but in the context of the group as a whole. we learn each new world through the harvest it grants us. you have so much to give to our garden. //*

Jeff made a wry face. "This is how it's been for me since I got here. Is this how it's been for you?"

"I don't know." I dropped into one of the open chairs without waiting to be asked. A small puff of spores drifted up from the glowing gills of the mushroom. They smelled like mint and blueberry. "My head is so full of things that it feels like it's going to explode."

// I remember when my harvest was gathered in // said Jeff's Second, in a tone I could only call nostalgic. *// we had been waiting so long, surrounded by those who would never know us as we knew each other, and then from the sky came salvation, family, home. we were so fortunate on that day, and we are so fortunate now, to carry that day across the stars to you. my harvest believes in personal designations. you may call me the Swift, for I have always been quick and sure in defense of our gardens. //*

// I will remain Second // said Second, with an apologetic wave of her tentacles as she slithered into the seat beside me. *// it is a title, not a name, and so it does not discomfort me as a false name would. //*

"When you say 'garden,' what you mean is 'world,' right?" I asked, looking between them. At Second's gesture of agreement, I asked, "How many gardens have you, um, harvested?"

// we of this vessel have harvested from hundreds since it was grown // said Second proudly. *// we have done so very well. you will join us in doing so very well. //*

"The ships are planted, like we were," said Jeff. "They draw the nutrients and necessary minerals from the soil, and when they reach maturity, the technicians use biochemical processes to make them mobile. Every world adds its own ships to the armada. They'll mostly be crewed by people like us, when they come from Earth, because they'll also be the preservation ships for Earth's culture."

I stared at him. "The preservation ships?" Belatedly, it occurred to me that Jeff had been in the pit longer than I had, and his questions weren't likely to be the same as mine. I was in customer service. I didn't *like* people, but that didn't exempt me from learning to understand them. If anything, it meant I had to work harder to have a chance.

// you are not on such a ship now // said Second, sounding concerned that I had failed to miss this very simple idea. *// the ships are too vast to dock, and too precious to risk. meat is weak. it iterates thoughtlessly, breeds without cultivation, does not replace what it destroys. we are strong. we endure. so the Great Root has put it upon us to preserve what the gardens of the universe create, to sample their best fruits and carry them with us forever. this world is large enough to grow at least ten such ships without cracking the firmament. there will be food in plenty until the work is done, and perhaps we will come again someday, to make another harvest, to carry another garden's fruits high and everlasting. //*

// your body is on a scout vessel // said the Swift. *// everything you see is a gift of the pollen, to keep you comfortable and begin to ease you into the reality of what we are, what we will be. we carry your shadows with us on the ship above, for we are of the same seeding, I and the Jeff, yourself and the Second. we are the same, and that means we can communicate when the distance is brief enough. //*

"So we're astral-projecting from an alien scout vessel, onto a great big alien Costco in space?" Laughter rose in my throat. I swallowed it hard. I didn't want to risk offending the Swift, not even if we weren't really in the same place. "Why? Why are we here?"

// it is necessary, when approaching a new garden, to first perform a final test, to see whether the fruit is good. // Second sounded genuinely apologetic, like whatever she was saying was horribly rude and would have been good reason for me to be infuriated. *// sometimes the fruit is . . . not good. sometimes the fruit has been tainted by the soil in which it grew, and we must start again, lest it pose a danger to the greater garden. //*

"She means sometimes when they come to pick up the new kids, the new kids like the people who raised them better than the people who planted them, and they not only don't want to help Mommy and Daddy invade their planets, they actively want to fight off the invasion."

Guilt twisted in my stomach. It was hard to relax, surrounded by telepathic pollen and harboring what suddenly felt like treasonous thoughts about the world where I'd grown up. Humanity as a whole didn't appeal to me all that much, but Graham? Mandy? Even Lucas? Specific humans appealed to me a great deal. I didn't want to see them hurt. "What happens when a harvest . . . resists?"

// it is cut down // said Second sadly. *// the soil is bad, if it grows such poor seeds. so we cut the harvest, and we change the soil. //*

"Meaning they sterilize the planet and leave it to develop life again in its own time," said Jeff. He met my eyes across the table. "Once the armada comes, the question isn't whether they die. It's how quickly, and how."

// we have such high hopes for this harvest // said the Swift. *// the air is good. the soil is good. the seeds have sprouted strong and well. you will bring such wonders to our people, and we will travel the universe with you beside us, and you*

will never know want, or hunger, or need. you will only know the goodness and grace of coming home. //

// we are so glad we will not have to kill you and plant again // said Second happily.

I looked at the Swift, and then I looked at Second—my sister, grown from the same seed, in soil so alien that I couldn't even imagine it—and I said nothing. For what felt like the first time in my life, I couldn't think of anything to say.

3.

The tendrils set me and Jeff side by side on the rim of the pit before untangling themselves and retracting back toward the unseen bulk of the scout ship. Despite having been held inside it for some unknown length of time, I still had no idea what it looked like—or what the larger ships of the armada looked like, for that matter. We had dreamt ourselves inside them, dreamt ourselves surrounded by our own species. That didn't mean we'd been dreaming the truth. We had no control over the pollen, or over whatever mechanism had allowed Second and the Swift to connect us to the gestalt, which seemed like a greater, more refined version of our forest. They could have shown us anything.

Deep down, though, I knew it was truer than it was false. They had no reason to lie to us, especially not now, when their ships were close enough to slingshot scouts across the void. The invasion was underway. We, their information-gathering children, had been nothing more than the advance scouts, and now that they were here, we weren't essential anymore. They didn't need to buy our loyalty with lies. Not when they were about to block out the stars.

The tendril that had been covering my mouth and nose withdrew, taking the taste of alien pollen with it. The strange berry flavor still lingered on the back of my tongue. I tried to step forward, away from the pit, and wobbled as my legs refused to fully obey my commands. I began to fall. Jeff grabbed for me, only to collapse in turn, unable to keep his balance any better than I could.

This is it, I thought. *We're going to fall back into the pit, and this time, nothing's going to catch us. This is it.*

Someone grabbed my arm before I could hit the ground. I raised my eyes to the familiar face of Tahlia, beaming at me, as radiant as a woman who had just seen evidence of the divine. I glanced to the side. The senator was holding Jeff, smiling just as broadly. I had never seen either of them look so happy. It was unnerving.

"We need to move away from the pit," I said.

"Why?" The senator's expression turned mulish. He cast another glance at the depths, covetous this time, before turning to me. "What did you see that you don't want to share?"

"Gravity," I said. "Falling sucks. And I think you're going to see plenty in a minute."

As if in answer, the ground under our feet gave a lurch, small rocks and bits of gravel beginning to shake and dance. The sand was still soft with spilled blood; it slid, threatening to take us with it down into the depths. I pulled against Tahlia's hands, and was relieved when she came with me, moving away from the edge.

The Swift and Second—and even First, strange and terrifying as she had been—had been kind. They had answered our questions, mine about what we were and how we'd gotten here, Jeff's about how the ships worked and how our people could cross the gulf of space. They had been excited for the harvest, and about the potential of this planet. But us?

They hadn't been excited about *us* as individuals. We were sprouts from the same seeds, and while they might delight in the idea of new brothers and sisters, they weren't here for us. We were a bonus. If we fell into the hole and died, they weren't going to mourn longer than it took to find someone else to act as their guides to this bright new garden.

I wasn't sure how I felt about that. I'd always assumed when my people came for me, they would come for *me*—after all, what was the point of being a spacefaring race solely for the sake of divesting planets of their resources? There were cheaper, easier ways to synthesize almost everything a world could need. Clearly, the spies mattered. But there were so many more of us than I'd ever expected, and we didn't matter individually. They could afford to lose a few. They'd still be able to win their war.

The ground continued to shake as Tahlia and I moved away from the edge of the pit. Jeff swore softly under his breath and followed, hauling the senator along with him. Even having started moving as quickly as we had, we were barely clear when the pit's edge crumbled, falling down into the crater. My foot hit a rock and twisted, sending me toppling, taking Tahlia down with me.

I rolled onto my back, watching in awe as the scout ship pulled free. It was roughly spherical, more like a tumbleweed or a thorn briar than a ball bearing: it looked organic and impenetrable at the same time, like it could stand up to anything. Long, woody vines extended from points all over the exterior, creating a web of tendrils that it used to move. As I watched, it flipped over, reorienting itself. The number and distribution of the tendrils meant it could never be knocked over or off-balance.

There were large, circular patches of material that looked like the dragonfly-wing petals of the breeding flowers distributed around the exterior, each one flanked by a pair of tendrils, sometimes more. They glittered, shifting as they focused on us.

"My God," breathed the senator. He staggered unsteadily to his feet, eyes locked on the sphere hovering above us. "It's alive."

"All of their technology is alive," said Jeff. He sounded as awed as the senator. This was the moment he'd been dreaming of all his life. This was when they came to get us, to take us home to a world where we would make sense. Where we wouldn't be outcasts because of the things we couldn't stop ourselves from saying.

I was starting to question why, if our people loved us and wanted us so much, they had dropped us here with a compulsion in our heads that was almost guaranteed to turn us into freaks by the local standards, whether those standards were set on Earth or on whatever strange jungle had sprouted Second. Why, if they could make us blend in so well with the locals, they would announce their approach with a signal that would only serve to isolate us further, shucking our defenses away and turning us into targets.

Targets. That was what they had been grooming us to be all along. The only question now was *why*.

But even that question paled as the bulk of the scout ship—tiny compared to what we'd seen in our pollen haze—hoisted itself above us, looking at us with those segmented dragonfly-wing "eyes." One of the tendrils reached down to caress the skin on the senator's face with surprising gentleness, and he laughed, delight and relief and honest, childlike wonder in his eyes.

He was still laughing when the bullet took his right eye away, blowing it onto the ground along with a horrible spray of blood and bone and brain matter. It was all green and gold, the color of the trees, and so for a moment, my mind refused to acknowledge it for what it was. The cultural literacy I'd been sent here to acquire told me carnage was red, red, the color of rubies, the color of blood. It wasn't green. Not here, not on Earth.

The senator, who may have been a good man—who had, for all that he had always been a spy for an oncoming alien invasion, done his best to serve his constituents well, and had never lied to them, which was more than could be said for most of the men in Washington—wobbled. His remaining eye was filled with a hurt confusion, like he couldn't understand what had happened, or how it had even been possible. Hadn't we won? Wasn't the invasion finally here?

Then his knees buckled and he fell, first to the ground and then, as gravity took control, over the edge into the waiting pit. He never made a sound. One second, he was there, and the next, he wasn't.

Jeff shouted, shoving me out of the way as a bullet ploughed into the ground where I had been. I whipped around, staring at the rise. A line of people had formed there, rendered faceless and featureless by the floodlights shining from behind them. Someone had broken out the siege gear.

"Run!" shouted Tahlia. She grabbed my hand, hauling me to my feet. I grabbed for Jeff, pulling him along with me, and the three of us raced along the pit's edge, staying as close to it as we could without falling. The scout ship was a blotch on the sky above us, its tentacles whipping in all directions as it arrowed in on the source of the shots.

We had no weapons. We had no armor. We had nothing but each other, and even that number was dwindling, because we were leaving the senator behind. There was nothing we could have done to save him; all we could do now was try to save ourselves. So we ran, rocks and thorns digging into our feet, hands slick with sweat as we tried to hold onto each other. If one of us tripped, if one of us fell, that would be the end of it, and so we held fast, trying to stave off the inevitable.

"This way!" I yelled, pointing left before dragging the others to the right. It was a small, stupid distraction, but if it could buy us even half a second, it would be worth it. The guns were still firing behind us. We didn't seem to be the primary targets anymore. That honor was reserved for the scout ship, which was closing on our attackers with chilling speed, its tendrils whipping out ahead of it and snatching at their weapons. Our time in the pollen haze had done one thing: it had taught our people human anatomy. A glance back told me the tendrils were targeting hands and heads, those parts of our attackers without which the attack would almost certainly end.

Tahlia cried out as we crested the ridge, but she didn't fall, and so I kept running, kept dragging her and Jeff in my wake.

There were no people waiting to ambush us on the other side. We slipped and skidded down to a small frontage road, and were starting to run along it when a pair of headlights flared to life. I stumbled to a stop, catching Tahlia before she could fall. Jeff, to his credit, tried to push in front of us, shielding us.

"Well?" demanded Graham's voice from out of the darkness. "Are you going to get in, or what?"

15

TUCSON, ARIZONA: AUGUST 7, 2031
INVASION DAY

1.

"I can't fix this." Toni looked up from Tahlia's shoulder, a helpless scowl on her face as she spread her empty hands. "There's no muscle, there's no tendon, there's just . . . Fuck, it looks like broccoli, okay? It looks like someone went and shot a bunch of broccoli. I don't know whether stitches would help or not."

"At least the bleeding has stopped," said Graham.

"If you can call it that," Toni groused.

Tahlia didn't say anything. She just kept staring at the wall, the tears in her eyes shining but never quite finding it in themselves to fall.

The bullet wound in her shoulder had wept dark, sticky sap that smelled like a mixture of maple and pine for most of the drive to the no-tell motel where we were now wedged, seven people in one room. Mandy had been the first to provide medical care, washing off the sap while she made soothing noises in a language that was neither English nor Spanish, but a sweet mixture of both, like she was talking to a small child. When she had finished, Toni had taken over, citing the fact that she was the one with experience studying our kind.

Honestly, I think Mandy had been relieved when Tahlia was no longer her problem. She had crossed immediately to where I was sitting with Graham, settling on my other side, so I was flanked by the humans who had loved me enough to come back for me, despite the situation. Despite everything.

"Will it heal?"

We all jumped at the sound of Tahlia's voice. Toni hesitated before saying, carefully, "I think so. I don't know your biology that well—no one does—but you can move the arm, and the bullet missed the bone. You got lucky."

"Yes," said Tahlia. She sounded drained, like something had pulled all the vitality from her body. "Lucky." She stood, pushing her hair away from her face as she turned to the bed where I was seated. "He died without ever seeing the face of our homeworld. He died for *nothing*. He had done *nothing*."

"He was going to, though," said Toni. For the first time, she sounded calm, rational, and sincere. She sounded like the voice of reason, and it was chilling. "All of you were, and all of you are. You're going to kill anyone who stands in the way of your invasion."

"You don't know that."

"We *do* know that," Toni corrected. "I guess yeah, you could make a point about human xenophobia and bigotry, but you started by killing kids, and now you've got weed balls smashing into the planet and something fucking *huge* parked out by the moon, and we're not stupid, okay? We may be monkeys, we may be meat, but we're not *stupid*. We know what it means when somebody shows up with that much firepower. Hell, we've been doing it to each other since we figured out how to get from one place to another. Go next door, take your neighbor's stuff, and as long as you say God told you to, suddenly you're in the right. Suddenly you're fine. So it sucks that he's dead. He was a pretty cool guy, as alien plant invaders go. But don't pretend he was innocent because he hadn't started slaughtering people yet. He just hadn't gotten to that point on his agenda."

I thought of the way Second had invoked the Great Root—reverential, sincere, in a tone that implied everyone would know what she was talking about, because *have you heard the word of our lord and savior*—and suppressed a shudder, leaning closer to Graham. The warm, solid presence of him was like a balm. I had never expected to see him again. I certainly hadn't expected to see him so soon.

"Hey," he said, and pressed a kiss to the crown of my head. "How are you doing?"

I took a moment to consider my answer before I said, "I want to rewind time by about six months, and take a lot more naps before we get to this point. I feel like everything is happening at once."

"Someone needs to talk to your alien lords and masters about project management," said Mandy. She punched me lightly in the arm, clearly trying to jolly me out of my funk. "Thirty years with no updates, and then a dozen deadlines in a week? Not a good way to keep up employee morale."

I lifted my head and flashed her a wan smile. "But see, we're not employees. We're their kids."

"Family businesses exist."

Toni looked up from her attempt to repair Tahlia's arm and scowled. "This is not a 'family business.' Finance is a family business. Joining your grandpa's law firm. Letting your father buy you a planetarium. This? This is an invasion. You need to get with the linguistic program."

"You're siding with the invaders," said Jeff. It was the first time he'd spoken since we had reached the motel. He turned away from the window, where only a thin sliver of parking lot was visible between the paisley-patterned curtains, and frowned at Toni. "You chose us over your own species. You chose *us*. So could you stop acting like we're somehow keeping you here against your will?"

"Did I hit a nerve, Begonia?" Toni picked up the cloth she'd been using to keep the wound clean, dabbing around the edge. "You're not keeping us against our will, except in the sense that by the time you let us go—oh, wait, *you* didn't do that. Stasia did."

I blinked. "When did I earn a name?"

"When I ran out of flowers to call you." She dropped the cloth on the table. "Come with me. I want to try something."

Graham looked alarmed, moving to put a hand on my knee. "Where are you taking her?"

"Uh, the bathroom, genius. We can't leave this room, and there's not anywhere else to *go*." Toni waved her hands, encompassing the whole of our cheap, no-questions motel room. It would probably have seemed spacious, when it was just the four humans. Now that there were seven of us, it was cramped beyond belief.

That didn't even go into the *smell*. The sap from Tahlia's wound had helped a little, keeping my nose full of green and not the meaty reality of the people to either side of me. That wasn't going to last. It had been getting harder and harder not to think of my friends and allies as walking juice boxes when we'd been in the house, where there had been plenty of room to get away from—

"Wait," I said abruptly. "Why can't we go back to the house? We know the senator didn't rent it under his own name. Having his body isn't going to lead the people who shot him there." Assuming there had been any survivors. The scout ship had been fairly dedicated to making sure there wouldn't be. We might be able to go back to our temporary home free and clear, putting some space between us.

Jeff was shaking his head. "We didn't do anything to hide our tracks, and even if the senator's name wasn't on the rental agreement, someone from out of town renting a big property like that, only for an alien attack to occur out back . . . it's not going to be hard to put together. We can never go back."

Which meant I was never going to see my shoes again. "Great," I said dourly.

"Yes, it sure is, and *can you come here*," hissed Toni, making another, more emphatic gesture toward the bathroom.

"It's okay," I said, taking Graham's hand off my leg as I rose. "She won't hurt me."

"Shows what you know," scoffed Toni, and ducked inside.

I followed. She shut the bathroom door behind me, effectively pinning us both in the small space. That was bad, especially since she hadn't showered yet: the sweet, almost-sugary smell of her filled my nostrils, making my back teeth ache and my stomach clench. I couldn't put into words how much I wanted to devour her, to drain her dry and cast her empty husk aside like the useless sack of skin and bones it would become.

"Hi," she said brightly. "From the way your pupils just dilated and your jaw is clenching, I'm going to guess you *really* want to eat me right now. That's cool. Although maybe talk to your boyfriend about it. He's the biologist, he'll be in a better position to figure out how we keep you and the rest of the vegan army from going cannibal in the night."

I didn't say anything. I just glared at her.

"Ooo, hit a nerve, did I? Great, because I'm going to need you to hit something a lot bigger." She dipped her hand into her pocket, coming up with a syringe.

I recoiled automatically. "You're *not* stabbing me with that!" I said, voice shrill.

"No, I'm not," she agreed. "You're stabbing me. I think I know how to help Tahlia heal, and I need your help. If I try to do the blood draw myself, I'm likely to change my mind and decide that encouraging you people to think of me as a walking buffet is a bad plan. But she needs it. She lost a lot of sap. I'm concerned."

"I thought you weren't a biologist."

"I'm not. Honestly, I don't know whether you people need a biologist or a botanist at this point, and I'm sure there's a think tank somewhere arguing about exactly that, but since they never asked me to join them, my opinion doesn't matter much." She shook her head. "I'm not a doctor either. What I am is someone who got institutionalized on a yearly basis until I was twenty-five, and who attempted suicide enough times that my father finally asked how much it would cost him for me to promise not to besmirch the family name that way. That's the word he used, too. 'Besmirch.' Like I was talking about running off to Ohio and becoming a politician or something." The normally jovial note that underscored her words faded. "What I am is someone who learned first aid because her friends kept dying after they decided they weren't worthy of staying alive, and that means I know how syringes work, okay? Let's not talk about it anymore. Let's just get some nice human blood into this thing, so I can stop your friend from doing whatever it is plant people do when they die. Wilting or going to seed or whatever. I want to meet your leaders *without* the death of one of their own hanging over my head."

". . . okay," I said softly, after a long pause. "What do I do?"

Toni's first aid experience turned out not to have been exaggerated. Step by step, she walked me through the process of bringing one of her veins to the surface, using a shoelace as a deeply unsafe tourniquet to temporarily stop the flow of blood. I held my hand steady, thinking of kittens and sunrises and every other pleasant, non-complicated thing I could as I slipped the needle under her skin and began pulling back the plunger.

Toni watched noncommittally as the reservoir filled with bright red blood. The seal between the needle and her skin was good enough that

I couldn't smell much more than I had before, but that was going to change as soon as I was finished. I paused, swallowing.

"How do I get the needle out without you bleeding everywhere?"

"Since you didn't tap an artery, that's not a concern," she said. "As to how you get the needle out without me bleeding at *all* . . . you don't. There is going to be blood. So I guess the real question is: has thirty years of living as one of us given you more self-control than the average horror-movie vampire? Are you ready to go full Dracula, or can you continue to behave like you grew up on this planet?"

I swallowed. Saliva immediately filled my mouth anew. I swallowed again. This time, the space between my teeth and tongue stayed relatively dry; this time, I felt like I might be able to breathe. "I can behave."

"Good. We're going to pull the needle out now." She picked up a cotton ball, calmly showing it to me. "Did you ever donate blood?"

"Sure. Once or twice."

"Uh-huh. Did they ever say there was anything odd about what you'd given them? Any sort of deformity of the platelets or other strange issues that they'd go 'well, shit' and call you for?"

"No." I tried to breathe through my mouth, quickly in and out, not allowing myself to smell the red, red, red sweetness starting to leak from the puncture wound. It was still sealed—oh, but she was going to make me pull it out—and I could smell it anyway.

The question was actually a compelling one. I'd never been sick enough to require serious medical intervention, but I had been a fairly liberal college student, and I'd always believed that it was my job to help people if I could. No matter how much I hated them, it was just plain common sense that someone who was sick, or miserable, or otherwise being punished for the crime of existing while made of meat and trapped on this miserable planet—

Wait. Where had *that* come from? Thoughts of Earth had been accompanied by many things over the years. Worry over pollution and deforestation and fracking; concern about overpopulation and global climate change; even the occasional fond reference to the "big blue marble." I had never thought of it as a miserable planet before. And much as I disliked most people, I didn't normally blame them for being mammals. Something was wrong.

Toni was still watching me patiently. I swallowed again.

"I gave blood. They didn't seem to mind. They took it, and they never said I had to stop giving it. I never asked what they used it for."

"It might be interesting to contact someone from those organizations and find out. Because you were around your own blood at least once a month—assuming plant people menstruate—and you never started eating people. There had to be something about it that kept it from triggering the 'devour' impulse."

"I was around other people when they bled, too. I never wanted to eat them."

"Didn't you?" Quick as the blink of an eye, Toni had the needle out of her arm and the cotton ball clamped down over the pinprick hole it left behind. The smell of blood only spiked slightly, remaining bearable. "Because I'm wondering what would have happened if no one had ever taken the time to tell you people weren't for eating."

Dimly, I remembered a few complaints about biting the other children from my preschool years. They had always seemed like the sort of weird crap kids just do sometimes. Suddenly, I wasn't so sure.

"I don't know," I whispered.

"And aren't we going to have a fun time figuring it out?" Toni held up the syringe. "Let's go treat your friend."

"Where did you even *get* that?"

She shrugged. "We hit a pharmacy first thing, for various necessities. I told them I was diabetic. I had enough money in my purse to convince them my lack of a prescription wasn't a barrier to my getting the *best* possible medical care. I never thought I'd say this, but thank God for the collapse of the Affordable Care Act. If it were still around, no one would have believed I could be carrying that much cash and not have at least basic medical."

"How did you know you were going to need it?"

Toni paused in packing up her things to offer me a swift, wry smile. "We were always going to come back for you," she said. "Even if I didn't want us to, it was never going to play out any other way. Now come on."

She left the bathroom, and left me staring after her.

2.

Lucas was gone. Mandy and Graham were still sitting on the bed, Jeff was by the window, David was crammed into the room's single recliner, and Tahlia was sitting by the wooden table that was meant to serve us as both eating surface and desk, but Lucas was gone. I stopped in the bathroom door, frowning.

"Where is he?"

Jeff didn't look away from the window. "He said he was going to the soda machine. I don't believe that was true. He ran out of here too quickly for that."

"And you *let* him?"

"What would you have had me do?" He turned to face me, expression infinitely weary. "I could have killed him. I've never killed a man, but it's getting easier and easier to consider, especially since it's clear now that they won't hesitate before killing us. I just wasn't sure how you'd take that, since he's one of your friends, and you've already made it clear that you'd choose them over us."

"I didn't choose them over you," I said. "I chose them *and* you. I chose to save the people I love while standing with the people I come from. Are you really going to tell me I can't do that?"

"I wouldn't dream of it, and I don't need to," he said, returning his attention to the window. "One of the people you saved is probably telling his authorities about us right now, and our ships are closing in. War is coming. So I don't have to tell you anything. Reality is going to do it for me."

"Graham . . ." I turned to the bed and frowned as my boyfriend—my *boyfriend*, who was supposed to be on my side no matter what—refused to meet my eyes. "Where did he go?"

"This has all been a little much for him, Stasia."

"This has been a little much for all of us."

"You know who this has been a *lot* much for?" asked Toni, kneeling in front of Tahlia and reaching up to check the other woman's pupils. "The lady who got shot. Can you pause the shouting and recriminations for one second while we take care of her?"

"Bless you," murmured Tahlia.

"You can try," said Toni. "Stasia, come over here and hold her head."

"Why?" This time, when Jeff turned away from the window, it was with alarm. He took a step toward them, hands balling into fists. "What are you going to do to her?"

"Nothing that will hurt her, Captain Caveman. God, I can't even make a plant joke when you're being this much of an asshole. I'm either going to help her get better, or I'm going to help make however much time she has left a little more pleasant. I don't think it matters which one, do you? No matter which way it goes, she's going to be a happier world-eating space invader."

I walked over while Toni was speaking, putting my hands on either side of Tahlia's head. She relaxed into my grasp, letting the tension flow out of her neck and shoulders. With dim surprise, I realized she trusted me. She believed that if I was willing to help Toni do this, it was something that had to happen.

We trusted each other. No matter how much we might fight or disagree, we were members of the same copse, and we knew that we would either grow together or wilt apart. That, too, was relatively new. Our time in the forest and in each other's company was changing us, rewriting us into something closer to our parent species. I couldn't stop it. I wasn't even sure I wanted to. But I had to wonder . . .

Was I still going to be Stasia when this was over? Or was I going to be someone new? Would I even like who I became?

Toni raised the syringe. Tahlia's eyes locked on it, some of the tension coming back into the skin beneath my fingers. This wasn't uneasiness or pain: this was hunger, plain and simple, overwriting everything else. Out of the corner of my eye, I could see the same tension in Jeff. He looked like he was ready to lunge across the room and snatch the syringe from Toni's hand, if that was what it took.

"Open your mouth," said Toni gently. "Don't bite down. I don't want you to stick yourself on the needle."

"Contamination concern?" asked Graham.

"Their blood really is more like sap; it thickens very quickly on contact with air," said Toni. "If she pricks herself on the syringe, she might block it to the point where I can't clean it, and we need to be able to reuse these needles."

She'd been thinking ahead this whole time, I realized. Ever since she had decided to switch sides, she'd been planning for the moment when she'd have to run with us without being consumed. It would have been admirable, if it hadn't been so damn chilling.

Tahlia opened her mouth. Toni maneuvered the tip of the syringe inside and depressed the plunger. The smell of human blood wafted through the air, only slightly filtered by the loose seal of Tahlia's lips. I closed my eyes, swallowing a moan. Jeff wasn't quite as successful. The sound of his yearning echoed through the room. When I opened my eyes again, Mandy was pressed against the wall with Graham in front of her, shielding her, while David was frozen in his seat, looking like he wanted to fade into the wallpaper.

Only Toni looked unbothered . . . but then, Toni had encountered one of the special flowers when she was a child, had been changed and defined by it as much as any of us had. Maybe we no longer had the power to frighten her. Maybe that, too, was the way things needed to be.

The door banged open. Everyone jumped, even Toni, although she had the foresight to pull the empty syringe away from Tahlia as she did, meaning no one actually got stabbed. Lucas, standing in the doorway with a paper bag in his hand, scowled at us all.

"What?" he demanded.

"We thought you ran," said Jeff bluntly.

"I thought about it," said Lucas. "But even if I did, there's no way I could get those assholes"—he nodded toward Mandy and Graham—"to come, so what's the point? I'd just get swept up by the government and interrogated until I pissed myself. May as well stay here and try to keep my friends alive."

"So where did you go?" asked Jeff.

"7–Eleven." Lucas held up his bag. "I have sodas, I have sugary snacks, and I have information, if you'd like to let me shut the door and share with the other children."

"We would appreciate that very much," said Tahlia. Her voice sounded steadier than it had since she'd been shot. I glanced down at her. The color was coming back to her cheeks, and she was holding her head up without my help. More surprisingly, the hole in her shoulder appeared to be shrinking. No: not just appeared to be. As I watched, a root no thicker than a hair flung itself across the void in her skin, beginning to put out more roots, patching the damage. I glanced at Toni.

She was smirking, looking satisfied with herself. “Blood is everything to you people,” she said. “It would have to be, or you’d have figured out a better way than sailing across the stars to get it. Hungry, hungry alien invaders, and we’re a whole world of ration packs. It only stands to reason that you’d do better with it than without it.”

“My God,” breathed David. “They’re going to be unstoppable.”

Toni rolled her eyes. “And as far as anyone’s concerned, we’ve chosen their side over our own species. So calm down, shut up, and listen. Lucas?”

“Eight people went into the desert to find out what that shooting star was,” said Lucas, stepping into the room and closing the door behind himself. “Only one of them made it out. The sheriff’s nephew. He was raving about squid from space, and how they’d ripped everyone apart.”

“Not squid, but I can sort of see where you’d make that mistake,” I said. “Vines can look a lot like tentacles.”

Lucas shuddered and continued, stone-faced, “This wasn’t the only falling star. They’ve been coming down all over the country, and wherever they land, people have been dying.”

“The people in the desert brought guns when they came to investigate an astrological phenomenon,” I said hotly. “They were the ones looking for a fight, not us. They shot the senator. We didn’t have any weapons. We didn’t do *anything* to them. They were happy to kill us anyway.”

“And your scout was happy to kill them,” said Toni. “When you’re the invading army, you don’t really get to claim the moral high ground when you have weapons carrying themselves into the territory you’re hoping to occupy. I get that you’re siding with the people who didn’t strike first, but you’re also siding with the people who slid themselves into someone else’s backyard with a big ‘try me’ written across their faces.”

"How many dead?" asked Tahlia.

"No one's sure," said Lucas. "If you listen to the man at the convenience store, hundreds. The entire Midwest in flames. If you listen to the talking heads on the news, there have been no confirmed deaths as yet, and the President is already dispatching troops to the landing sites to keep order. If you listen to the internet, the truth is somewhere in the middle. Turn off your phones if you've got them, by the way. Once the Army gets involved, the words 'martial law' are likely to be next, and then the NSA is looking for anything out of place, like the cellphones of a bunch of Washington residents pulling data in Arizona."

"NASA never gave my phone back," I said.

"My phone has been undetectable for years," said Toni. We all looked at her. She shrugged. "Paranoia is only a disadvantage *before* the alien invasion. Now it's the reason I'm going to outlive half my species."

"We're getting away from the point," I said. "If what Lucas says is true, we need to get out of here. It's only a matter of time before someone finds the senator's body, if they haven't found it already, and starts checking local hotels for people who don't belong there."

"Then we're fucked," said Lucas. "There's no way someone doesn't know what our van looks like by now. We take it out on the road and we're finished."

"Not necessarily," said Mandy. "You got any money left?"

Lucas grimaced.

3.

David had gone with Mandy and Lucas to the nearest all-night drugstore, leaving the rest of us to mill around the motel room and wait for them to return. Tahlia and Jeff were in the corner with Toni, speaking in low tones and occasionally gesturing toward the window. The divide of their species seemed to have been forgotten in the face of the larger problem of how we were all going to get out of here in one piece. This wasn't privacy—privacy might be something we never had again—but Graham and I were still taking advantage of the pause, curled face-to-face on the bed, his hand cupping my cheek, our foreheads barely touching.

"Hey," he whispered, his voice barely a breath. I felt it as much as I heard it, and it made me shiver with comfort and with longing. Longing for a simpler time, when I'd been a girl who might or might not be out of her mind, and not the fugitive agent of an invading alien empire.

"Hey," I whispered back. "How are you holding up?"

Graham laughed. It was a tight, unsteady sound, and hearing it broke my heart a little. That was almost reassuring. I was having thoughts that didn't feel like my own, and it was getting harder and harder to think of the Earth as my home or the human race as worth saving, but I could still hurt when the people I loved were confused or in pain. I was still human enough to care.

Was caring really a human attribute, though? Second had been delighted to have a sister. The Swift had been harder for me to read, but he had seemed pleased by Jeff's presence, and proud to have a brother who was conquering this bright new garden. They had to care about each other, at least a little, and if they cared about each other, they would learn to care about us. They *would*.

"I don't know anymore," said Graham, snapping me back into the moment. "I feel . . . I feel like I'm releasing an invasive species into the Everglades. You know?"

"I do," I said quietly.

As a herpetologist, Graham had been cleaning out invasive species—things that shouldn't be there, snakes whose owners had allowed them to escape down drains, spiders and frogs and mosquitos that had hitched rides on cargo ships and been brought over by wildlife smugglers—for most of his career. He would call me from the

Everglades with a sack full of pythons in his hand and a grin on his face, like he'd just improved the world through the simple act of putting a bunch of snakes back where they belonged. Things that interfered with the proper functionality of an ecosystem offended him on a deep, integral level.

I put my hand on his arm, letting my fingers draw a delicate pattern there, tracing the veins and hoping he wouldn't realize that was what I was doing. "I've been here for a long time, though. A whole bunch of us have. We're not invasive. This is where we're from. Right here."

"Stasia, you realize you're the vanguard of an *invasion*. 'Invasive' is in the name." He looked at me, clearly troubled. "Can you not see that? That you're not supposed to be here?"

I pushed away from him, startled. For a moment, I just stared. The words to express my shock and dismay refused to come, locked somewhere behind my tongue, filling my throat with bile. Finally, I forced myself to swallow and asked, "Do you really think that? That I'm not supposed to be here?"

"Stasia—"

"Because I wouldn't *exist* if I weren't here. Not this version of me. I don't know who the original Anastasia would have grown up to be, and I'm sorry she had to die, but you know I'm here *because* she died. Because a seed fell from space and *swallowed her* when she was only three years old. Ate her up like a monster out of a fairy tale. *I* did that. *Me*. I fell from space, and I ate a little girl, and I took her life, and I grew up to be a woman who loves you. Do you not want me to love you?"

My voice had been rising steadily as I spoke. On the last word, I pushed myself away and sat up, glaring at him fiercely.

Graham rolled more slowly into a sitting position, his hands raised defensively, like he was afraid he needed to ward me off. "That's not what I said."

Everyone was watching us. They weren't saying anything, and somehow that just infuriated me more. "You just said I don't belong here."

"Because you don't! Because . . ." Graham paused, taking a deep breath, before he said, "Because I love you. I love you so much it's stupid. I was planning to spend the rest of my life with you when I thought you were human, and I'm still planning to spend the rest of my life with you now. I didn't stop loving you when your skin started falling off, or when you started drinking blood, so it would be a little weird for me to stop now. But if you'd never come here, I would never have loved you. You can see that, can't you? Maybe I would have met Anastasia and maybe I wouldn't have, maybe I would have fallen in love with someone else or maybe I would have been alone forever, wondering who the hell I thought I was waiting for, but it wouldn't have been *you*. And if it hadn't been you, there's no way I would have been sitting here, ready to support an alien invasion of my home planet. I would have been . . ." He stopped.

"You would have been on the right side," I finished dully, climbing off the bed. "You would have been one of the scientists working to figure out how to kill us all before we could hurt your world."

"Can you blame me?" he asked. "This is my home planet."

"It's my home planet too." I shook my head. "You can still leave, you know. You can go and . . . and find the think tank that's figuring out how to defeat us. I'm sure they'd be thrilled to see you. You have so much to share with them."

"That's the *problem*!" he shouted.

The room froze. If I had thought that it was quiet before, that was nothing compared to the silence that fell in the wake of his cry. I stared at him. He stared back, chest heaving, cheeks flushed.

"I *can't* go find the scientists, and I *can't* tell them how to defeat you, because God, Stasia, I don't want to help you destroy the planet, but I'm not going to betray you. There has to be a better way. There has to be a way we can convince your people not to do this. To leave us alone, or better yet, to be our friends." He raked a hand through his hair, leaving it in disarray as he stared at me pleadingly. "We're not alone in the universe anymore. You're out there. Your people are out there. And you . . . you're one of the most amazing women I've ever known. I *love* you. There has to be a way we can work together. Imagine what we could do if we worked together."

I was still staring at him, trying to formulate an answer, when the door slammed open, spilling Mandy, Lucas, and David back into the room. I had a split second to register the smell of smoke and the sound of sirens before a much more urgent scent washed all of that away.

Blood.

Lucas was bleeding from a cut on his forehead. It looked like it had been made with a rock, splitting the skin from his eyebrow all the way back to his hairline. The wound wasn't deep and it wasn't serious enough to require medical care, but it was bleeding copiously, red sheeting down the side of his face and dripping onto the floor as he half-walked, half-staggered into the room, leaning heavily on David all the way.

There was a high, keening sound. I realized it was me. I swallowed hard, but it didn't stop, just picked up from Tahlia and Jeff. All three of us were staring at the blood like it was the most beautiful thing we had ever seen.

Toni shoved herself away from the wall, hurriedly moving to loop her arm around Lucas and drag him toward the bathroom. "You explain, I'm going to stop the bleeding before shit gets ugly," she said, and they were gone, the door slamming behind them.

The tension in the room snapped like a hypnotist's fingers, and we were free to move. I staggered backward, pressing a hand to the hollow of my throat, and Graham was there to catch me and hold me up. I wanted to thank him. I wanted to shove him away and tell him that he didn't get to touch me anymore, not if he thought I had no business being here. I did neither. I just swallowed again, trying to steady myself enough to speak.

I wasn't fast enough. "What happened?" demanded Jeff.

"There's a riot," said Mandy. "Which sort of makes sense, because the east side of town is on fire. The scout ship is moving."

"Moving *where*?" asked Graham.

"Couldn't tell you, wasn't going to go and ask it," snapped Mandy. "A giant alien death machine wants to stomp through a city, I am getting the *fuck* out of its way. So people are running and people are screaming and people are being assholes, because that's what scared people do."

"Someone threw a brick at us," said David. "They would have done worse, but Mandy screamed that she saw the scout ship coming, and they turned and ran."

"We still have the money, and we have the makeup," said Mandy, holding up an overloaded plastic bag. "What's a little looting during a full-scale riot?"

The air was clearing, and it was getting easier to breathe. I managed a shaky laugh. "Good to know where your morality bends," I said. "How long do you think we have before the riot reaches us?"

"Not long," said David. "If we're going to turn you back into humans, we need to get started."

"What about our eyes?" asked Tahlia. "Sclera aren't customarily green."

"Sunglasses," said Mandy. "Not enough people know what the aliens *really* look like to be suspicious of sunglasses. Yet. We don't have a lot of time. Stasia, I know you know your way around a makeup sponge. Get over here."

I got over there, glancing back at Graham as I went. He met my eyes and nodded grimly. He knew as well as I did that this wasn't over.

Sometimes it felt like it was never going to be.

16

MARANA, ARIZONA: AUGUST 8, 2031
SECOND DAY OF THE INVASION

1.

The desert was dark, lit only by the stars and the headlights of the cars that occasionally flashed past us, racing through the night, fleeing from an uncertain future. The red smear of the flame-filled sky over Tucson had long since faded into nothing more than a smudge in the rearview mirror. The air was still warmer than it should have been, flavored with distant hints of ash.

Toni sat behind the wheel of our "borrowed" SUV, her lips pressed into a hard line as she kept her eyes focused on the road. Her time as a driver for visitors to the observatory had left her with the best head for driving under pressure, while Mandy's time as a protestor for human rights in the early twenty-twenties had left her surprisingly good at stealing cars. Combined, they could have been a menace. As it stood, they were the closest thing we had to salvation.

"It itches," complained Lucas, pressing a hand to the bandage on his forehead.

"Don't pick at it," said Tahlia, voice sharp. "If you start bleeding again in this enclosed of a space, I don't know what we'll do to you."

"I do," said Jeff. In contrast, he sounded almost cheerful, like he couldn't wait to demonstrate what was coming for all humanity.

"Hush," snapped Tahlia.

I gave her a sidelong look. She had warmed considerably since we'd met, and more, now, she seemed almost to be on the side of our humans. It was like Toni's willingness to save her had answered some question she didn't even realize she was asking, making everything else easier.

Nothing felt easy to me. Graham and I were strapped next to each other in the rear seat, with me providing a buffer between him and Tahlia, and I had never felt like we were farther apart. Not in college, when we'd had a series of fights over his gender identity and my sexuality, culminating with him telling me to go find a woman if I wanted to be a lesbian so badly, and me screaming in the quad that I didn't love him for what he had in his pants, I loved him for the way he made me feel, which had been funny afterward, given that he'd been making me feel like shit. Not after college, when he'd been traveling the world, meeting people, becoming the exciting scientist he'd always wanted to be, while I'd been sinking deeper and deeper into my haze of customer service jobs and unpaid student loans. Somehow, we'd always managed to find our way back to one another, no matter how far away we seemed to be.

Except now. Now, it felt like we had finally found the thing that was going to divide us for good, because I was right: if I hadn't been here, he would have been siding with his own species. Maybe if we'd been a species of starfaring snake people, he would have been too consumed by professional curiosity to think about what it meant to turn his back on humanity, but we weren't. We were green and growing and not something that had ever interested him, except in the sense that we were me and I was the love of his life. Supposedly. Was that going to be enough?

For the first time, I honestly didn't know.

"Look," breathed Jeff, voice filled with awe. I craned my neck to see around him to the window.

Streaks of light were cutting across the sky, too big and close to be shooting stars, too controlled in their descents to be meteors. One of them impacted in the far desert, sending a bright ring of molten sand splashing upward against the night. It was beautiful. It was the sort of moment that would have sold a million copies of *National Geographic*, if there had been a photographer quick enough and fortunate enough to capture it. It was eclipsed almost immediately, as three more streaks of light cut through the sky above it, heading for their own landing sites.

"It's started," said Tahlia. There was no hiding the joy, or the relief, in her voice. I shared it. We weren't safe here anymore. We had never been truly safe here. We'd been sheltered by the assumption that we were just like everyone else, that our claims of an alien origin had been comical at best and delusional at worst. Once those assumptions had started to crumble, so had the pretense of our safety.

We were invaders. We were killers. We were an infection, and humanity, with its armies and its scientists, fancied themselves to be physicians. They would cure us if they could, saving themselves at our expense, and even now, watching our ships light up the night sky, I couldn't say they were wrong. We were here because we needed to eat. Because humanity was a garden, and we were a species of gardeners. But when the garden fought back, who could really blame it?

Another sphere of light slashed by ahead of us, so low that the shock wave of its passing struck and shook the car. "Whoa!" shouted Toni, struggling to keep control. The brakes squealed and the tires shrieked as we spun in a half-circle, coming to rest lengthwise across the road. Toni clutched the wheel, panting, her eyes wide white circles in the rearview mirror.

"They're going to hurt a lot of people before this is over," said Lucas.

Jeff laughed. "Really? That's what you have to say about all this? That we're going to *hurt* people? Newsflash, buddy: we're here to conquer your planet."

"With what, your cultural literacy and your asteroids? We've been practicing for this since video games were invented." Lucas scowled at Jeff. "You don't scare me."

"We should," said Jeff quietly.

"You should all shut the fuck up, is what you should do," said Toni. She turned the key. The engine made a faint grinding noise. She tried again, with the same result. Slumping in her seat, she groaned and said, "Your makeup is about to get a field test. This thing's dead."

"What?" Mandy leaned forward in her seat. "That's not possible. The scout ship didn't even hit us."

"Then maybe it has an EMP built into that fancy artificial comet tail it came flying in on," said Toni. "Actually, that would explain a lot, since the dash went black while it was overhead, and it probably makes sense for ships that *travel through the infinite fucking void of space* to mess with mere terrestrial *cars*, but as you can't disbelieve the electronics back on, we're dead in the water."

"Meaning what?" asked Jeff.

"Meaning we walk," said Toni. Her expression was grim. "Let's hope the road is kinder than the cities, huh?"

2.

If the road was inherently kind, it was not interested in showing that side of itself to us tonight. We walked along the shoulder in a rough single file, leaving our stolen SUV deserted where it had died. It weighed too much for us to shift, and any traffic coming along this road, this late at night, was likely to complicate our lives more than it improved them.

I felt a little bad about that—there might be people fleeing the burning city, and people in the process of running for their lives will often to choose to do so at unsafe speeds. Someone could get seriously hurt. People could even be killed. But try as I might, I couldn't work up more than the very mildest of irritation over the potential plight of people I didn't even know. I'd never been the biggest fan of the human race. Now, it was like they were all blending into one big, amorphous "them," something to be afraid of and to fight, not something to be concerned about.

Graham was a shadow on the road ahead of me. I looked at the back of his neck, trying to remember what it was like to kiss him without considering how he would taste, stripped naked and bleeding out for my delight. The thought was delicious and revolting at the same time. I shuddered, trying to chase it away. It clung, stubborn as a burr.

A hand touched my elbow. I looked back, and saw Tahlia looking at me with concern.

"Slow a bit, if you would," she said. "I would speak with you."

I slowed the pace of my steps, not saying anything as I looked at her expectantly. She smiled, leaving her hand resting against my elbow. The light was low enough that she almost looked normal. That was a nice thing. The sight of her—and Jeff, and myself—in heavy foundation had been jarring. We weren't supposed to look like that anymore. We had never really been meant to look like that in the first place.

"You seem troubled," she said. "What's bothering you?"

"I don't . . ." The words seemed suddenly complicated. I wasn't sure how to pin them down. Finally, wanly, I said, "I don't feel right."

"Your thoughts are taking turns you don't expect. It's almost like someone else is thinking them for you, and you're trying, very hard, not to wonder whether that pollen the scouts mentioned has been rewriting your mind."

This time, I was silent not because I didn't know what to say, but because I couldn't do anything but stare at her.

Tahlia's smile was small and tight. "It's no mystery. I think we're all asking ourselves the same thing. I don't . . . I have never been a big fan of people. I was a forestry worker before this began to accelerate. I watched over the trees in Newfoundland, and I told myself that it was normal for me to feel more akin to them than to the man who signed my paycheck. I worked very hard at playing human, even as I made sure everyone I met knew I was no such thing. The nice ones thought I was eccentric. The rest thought I was crazy."

None of this was anything new. Her story mirrored mine, and Jeff's, and every other one of us that I'd met. We were a people united by our isolation.

"I went to therapy."

That, now . . . *that* was new. None of the rest of us had voluntarily sought professional help. The aversion to it seemed to be almost as deeply ingrained as the desire to remind everyone we met that we weren't from around here.

Tahlia nodded, clearly seeing my surprise. "I knew a few people who'd been helped, and forestry is a lonely profession to begin with. If there was something I could do to make myself a bit less isolated, I was going to try. I *had* to try. I thought I was going to lose my mind if I didn't. Would you like to know what my therapist said?"

"If you think it will help, sure."

"She said the compulsion was just that: a compulsion. It was irrational, I couldn't suppress it no matter how hard I tried, no matter how much damage I was doing to myself. And it was external to the rest of me. The person I was, the things I wanted, they weren't the compulsion; the compulsion was getting in the way of them."

"She cured you?"

"Not in the slightest. She couldn't do anything to help me. Not with that, anyway. She did help with some deep-set abandonment issues that she said were due to parental distance and I said she had no idea, since my real parents were somewhere in deep space. She was generally pretty accepting of the whole alien thing."

Tahlia fell silent. We walked that way for a few precious seconds, the others fording the way ahead of us, dark gray silhouettes against the charcoal blanket of night. Finally, she sighed.

"I think," she said, "that when we were made, when the seeds that became us were cultivated, that our parents used whatever technology they have—whatever they developed to carry themselves across the stars—and made sure we would have no choice but to show ourselves, over and over and over again, forever. I think we are ourselves, because you are not me and I am not you and we are not Jeffrey. We have our own minds and hearts and ideas and desires. But I also think they are able, on some level, to influence or control what we think. They shape our ideas about the world."

The thought was simultaneously horrifying and far too realistic. We were ourselves. Nothing was going to change that. We were also hothouse flowers, cultivated by the gardeners who were even now raining their weapons down on our adopted world.

"I have to go," I said faintly.

Tahlia nodded. "I thought you might."

I quickened my steps, catching up easily with Graham, who wasn't lagging enough to have heard us, but wasn't hurrying either. He glanced at me as I pulled up level with him, and something in his jaw relaxed when I reached for his hand. There was a fine dusting of hair there, and I realized with dull horror that if the planet was under siege, the pharmaceutical supply chains were probably going to be disrupted for a while. His hormones were going to be scarce for a while, if they were available at all.

One more bridge for us to cross when we came to it. I tangled my fingers with his, and for a minute or so we walked in silence, just holding each other, holding onto the normalcy we represented. As long as we were together, we could find our way through anything. I couldn't forget that. No matter what happened, I couldn't forget that.

"I'm not okay," I said, in a very soft voice.

"I know," he said.

"I'm still me, I just . . . there's some other stuff in my head right now. Stuff I don't want to have there." This time, I didn't look at him. I kept my eyes fixed straight ahead, toward the distant line of the horizon. I'd been assuming the faint glow I saw there was the next city. Now, as the glow grew brighter, I wondered whether it was another fire, another riot. Were we fleeing toward safety, or were we walking toward some deeper danger? And did it really matter? We couldn't stay in the middle of the desert, exposed and unable to defend ourselves. We had to keep moving.

"I'm sorry."

"You're not the one who should be sorry." I squeezed his hand harder. "I need you to promise me something. Do you think you can promise me something?"

"No."

The word was a stone dropped into a still pond, kicking up ripples and frightening the frogs. I turned my head to stare at him. This time, he was the one looking resolutely ahead, a muscle in his jaw twitching, but otherwise seemingly impassive. "Graham . . ."

"You're about to ask me to run again if I think things are getting dangerous, because you love me and you have thoughts in your head that you don't want there, which means—knowing you—that you're afraid you're going to do something to hurt me. And I won't do it. I ran away once, because it seemed like I could still get the others out. I was always going to come back to you. You would have been sitting in your alien stronghold—which would look like something out of a bad science fiction movie, by the way, and everyone would be wearing silver bikinis—and there'd be a knock on your unbreakable door, and it would be this ginger herpetologist with a suitcase asking if Stasia was home. You can't get rid of me. I'm like a novel fungal infection picked up in a polluted swamp. Once I'm under your skin, all the creams in the world won't clear me up."

I barked surprised laughter into the night air, earning myself glances from all directions. Mandy looked pleased. Toni and David looked amused. Jeff and Lucas, who might never agree on anything else, looked annoyed. That struck me as even funnier than the image of our vegetable castle, and I laughed again, harder this time.

Graham squeezed my hand, pulling my attention back to him. "You're never getting rid of me, Anastasia Miller," he said. "From here to the end, you're never getting rid of me. The sooner you come to terms with that, the happier you're going to be."

"That sounds almost like a threat."

"You tell me, Miss Alien Invasion."

I was opening my mouth to reply, feeling better than I had in days—we were bantering, we were *flirting*, everything was going to be okay—when the roar of an ATV engine slashed across the night, going from faint to screaming in only a few seconds. I whipped around, still holding Graham's hand, looking for the source of the sound. All around me, the others did the same, falling into an automatic circle as we got our backs to one another. We were still capable of standing together in the face of outside danger. That should have felt like a good thing.

In the moment, I wasn't feeling anything but terror. We had no weapons and no vehicle; whatever came, it was going to catch us.

Lights crested the nearest hill. One pair, then two more, then another six, until nine ATVs were roaring toward us, their drivers shadows against the greater night. I raised my free hand to shield my eyes against the glare of their headlights as our circle tightened, our shoulders bumping together as we struggled to hold our formation.

The ATVs had the same idea. They drove down to the road and circled us, engines still turned all the way up. Most of them had only a single rider, while a few had passengers, strangers who pointed at us and yelled things we couldn't understand above the din.

Then the lead ATV killed its engine, and the others followed suit. The driver, a broad, leather-clad man with a beard as lush as Spanish moss in New Orleans, swung his leg off the machine and strode toward us. The rest of the drivers stayed where they were, all the more menacing because we couldn't see them clearly. They could have been doing anything back there in the shadows.

"Why are you out here?" demanded their leader.

Lucas—brave, potentially treacherous Lucas—stepped forward. "Our car died," he said. "Tucson's not safe. We were running."

"Not safe," said the man. "You mean on account of the fucking aliens tearing up the town? Yeah. I'd say it's not safe."

I drew back further, pressing myself to Graham. He was shaking, or maybe I was shaking so hard that I was passing it on to him. I wanted to run out there, to tell Lucas he didn't have to speak for us—maybe to beg him *not* to speak for us. This was his chance to rejoin humanity, if he really wanted to. Maybe his last chance.

"Our car died a few miles back," said Lucas. "We don't want any trouble."

"Neither do we," said the man. "Boys?"

Four more of the drivers dismounted and walked toward us, flashlights in their hands. They lifted them so that the light was shining directly in our eyes.

"Her," said the man, jabbing a finger at Tahlia. "Her," he repeated, pointing at me. "Him." Jeff, this time.

The three people with green, green eyes. The aliens.

"Fuck off," snapped Toni, stepping in front of Jeff, who stared at her in dismay. Graham did the same for me, wordlessly moving to block me from view, never letting go of my hand. No one stepped in front of Tahlia. Mandy, who looked conflicted and miserable, was too far away; David was backing Toni. Tahlia lifted her head and stayed where she was, silent and imperious.

"You don't know what you're harboring, little girl," said the man to Toni.

She narrowed her eyes. I sent a silent prayer to whoever might be listening, God or the Great Root, hoping that just this once, she could keep her tongue under control.

"I believe I am well acquainted with my traveling companions," she said, voice tight. "My name is Dr. Antonia Fabris, also known as Dr. Anthony Vornholt. I am the scientist who originally recorded the alien signal, alerting the world to their approach. We are on our way to a government facility, where we will be aiding in the effort to protect our world."

Was she lying? Was she telling the truth? She had been our driver; she had been the one to pick the route we were currently on. Toni acted like she was impulsive and angry at the world, but it was possible she had been playing us all, this entire time.

The man in front of us looked equally conflicted. Narrowing his eyes, he asked, "Any proof of this, or are you just a bunch of alien fuckers trying to get away with something you shouldn't?"

"My credentials were lost when we fled Tucson," said Toni, lying with the ease of someone who'd been dodging therapists and concerned parents since childhood.

Under my terror, I envied her that ability. My life would have been very different if it had included the ability to lie about my origins, rather than the compulsion to announce them to everyone I saw.

"Uh-huh," said the man dubiously, as more riders climbed down from their ATVs. "Maybe none of you fuckers are human. Those three are still pink around the edges. Maybe you didn't start to change until the ships got here. Lot of room for bodies in the desert. The coyotes will find you before anyone comes out looking, and we'll have done our civic duty."

"Fuckers . . ." said one of the other men speculatively. "You figure aliens are like humans in the downstairs? You think anybody's done that yet?"

"Shut up, Paul," snapped the man. "The cam whores knew there were real aliens years before the rest of us. If it can be fucked, it's been fucked. Besides, you'd catch poison oak or something."

"So you're planning to kill us," said Tahlia calmly.

The man turned to look at her, narrow-eyed. "I thought I made myself clear."

"No. You threatened, which anyone can do; you could have wanted something from us, something that would have ransomed our lives. But you're using names. That means you intend to kill us, no matter what we offer, no matter how we protest. You don't care how many of us are aliens. To be honest, I don't think you care how many of us are human. You've been waiting for this excuse for a long, long time." Her smile was serene. "I forgive you."

"What?"

Something was itching at the edges of my mind, scraping at the channels that existed to connect me to the forest. I wasn't used to them being active when I was awake. It hurt, like ants chewing on the places where my brain met my body. It wasn't supposed to hurt there.

// soon. //

The sound was barely a whisper, not audible outside my body. I stiffened, every nerve in my body suddenly on fire. The pollen was in the air. I could hear the whispers of my kin, the ones who shared no spoken language with this world.

They were coming.

Tahlia met my eye and nodded slightly, acknowledging my shock. She could hear them too, had probably heard them before I could. She was further along in her flowering than I was in mine. She would be more sensitive to the pollen.

"If you're going to kill us, consider this," she said. "We never claimed to come in peace, because we do not. But we have wonders beyond the knowing of this world. If you were to escort us to our nearest ship, we could make it more than worth your while. No one would ever know—"

The gunshot was like thunder rolling across the desert. Tahlia made a faint choking sound, her hands rising to flutter around the wound in her belly like she thought she could somehow take it back, like she could stuff her life back inside, where it belonged.

There was no blood. Her blood had run out weeks ago. Instead, sap poured through the wound, thicker and more golden than I had ever seen, so golden it was visible even through the darkness. I could have seen it from the stars. It smelled sweet, like maple syrup or honey, the lifeblood of a tree from another world who had traveled a million miles to sprout in alien soil, only to die on the cusp of her own salvation.

"Shit!" shouted Paul. "They really *are* aliens!"

Lucas bellowed and charged the man at the lead. There was another gunshot, and Lucas fell, half of his head transmuted into a fine red mist. I screamed. Graham shoved me behind him, trying to shield me from what was about to happen to us all. Three more guns were cocked, sharp snaps against the night—

And the tendrils reached out of the darkness, wrapping themselves around the men. Throats, torsos, faces, it didn't matter: when they hit one of our attackers, they grabbed hold and squeezed tight.

The leader, who was far enough ahead of the others to have a few precious extra seconds to react, lunged forward and grabbed Tahlia's arm. She didn't fight. She was losing too much blood—sap—and seemed barely capable of staying on her feet. She'd been shot twice in one night, and this time, a syringe of human blood wasn't going to save her.

He pressed his gun against her temple, howling, "Make it stop! Make it fucking stop, or I'll blow her alien brains out, I swear to God!"

Tahlia closed her eyes. I wanted to do the same. I didn't let myself. I needed to see what happened next. My own experiences and the scent of alien trees were combining to make me hate humanity, but this moment—the moment when the man who had already killed my friend for the crime of trying to protect me, the moment when he killed a woman who had never done him any harm for the crime of existence—this was when my hatred would become complete.

Graham stayed in front of me, not giving ground even as the vines of the scout ship sliced through the air around him, cracking like whips, some coming close enough to ruffle his hair.

"I'll do it!" howled the man. The screams of his compatriots had virtually stopped, replaced by wet crunching sounds as the vines compressed their bodies beyond recognition. The air was still full of whipping tendrils, making it difficult to see.

Not so difficult that I couldn't tell that none of my people, human or alien, had been touched. The vines were brushing our cheeks and disturbing our hair, but they weren't taking us the way they were our attackers.

// wait // whispered the voice of the forest.

Tahlia went limp, becoming a dead weight in the man's arms. He howled his fury, turning and firing wildly. I heard Jeff's shout, an exclamation of shock and agony.

A vine as thick around as my forearm whipped out of the darkness and wrapped around the man's throat, squeezing and pulling upward at the same time. Two more vines grabbed his legs, and his head detached from his body with a wet sucking sound, trailing a length of spine and gut. I screamed again, this time in horror, before clapping a hand over my mouth.

The vines whipped the remains of the man away, and then they came for us.

These were different than the others, broader, more like blades of grass beaded with sticky golden dew than the aggressive, thorny roots that had done so much damage in such a short time. I saw them clearly enough to register their differences before they were wrapping around my face and torso, cutting off my air supply. I began to struggle, trying to claw at them even as they pinned my arms to my side.

// *calm* // chided the voice. // *safe.* //

// *our friends are human* // I thought back, hoping whatever extension of the scout ship was allowing me to "hear" the forest while I was away would also allow the forest to hear me. // *they need air to live.* // So did I, right? I needed to breathe. The vines were cutting off my air.

But my lungs didn't ache, and my head wasn't spinning. Maybe air was more optional than I had ever believed it to be.

// *safe* // repeated the voice. // *sleep.* //

The sticky golden sap filled my mouth, and I knew nothing more.

17

SOMEWHERE ABOVE NORTH AMERICA: TIME UNKNOWN
INVASION ONGOING

1.

I woke with a gasp, and promptly started to gag as mammalian instincts kicked in and told me I wasn't meant to float suspended in a column of golden fluid; that I would, in fact, drown and die if I attempted that particular feat. The fact that I'd been doing it without issue for some unknown period of time didn't seem to matter to my sudden, instinctive conviction that I was going to die.

Thrashing, I slammed my hands against what I assumed was a glass barrier. They broke through with a moist sucking sound, shattering the thin vegetable membrane that had been keeping both me and the fluid contained. It rushed out with a glurping, wet finality, carrying me with it, sending us both crashing to the moss-covered floor. I lay there, naked, wet, and gasping for air that my logical mind was insisting ever more loudly I didn't actually need.

Moss. Wait. I rolled onto my back, unsurprised when my eyes found a high, distant ceiling of what looked like woven ferns, green and leafy and protecting us from whatever was outside. The moss was cool against my back, almost comforting, like the embrace of a good friend, and—

I sat upright, wiping the slime from my eyes. Friends. My friends. The vines had taken them as they had taken me, and humans—real humans—*did* need to breathe, no matter what the voice of the forest might try to say. I staggered to my feet, dripping viscous fluid everywhere, and whirled around to look at my surroundings.

I was in what could best be described as a grove, surrounded by trees that looked like a cross between mangroves and ancient oaks. Their trunks were twisted and weathered, each bigger around than most dining room tables. Large yellow fruit hung from their branches. I took a step closer to the nearest. The fruit pulsed, opaque and filled with something that moved, small twitches of animal vitality. I put a hand over my mouth.

It was Jeff.

His eyes were closed and his clothing was gone; the few strips of human-colored skin he had remaining were in the process of detaching from his body, leaving clean green skin behind. His twitching seemed to be entirely automatic, not tied to any kind of conscious motion. If it hadn't been for the liquid surrounding him, I would have thought he was sleeping.

// yes. //

The whisper was no louder than usual, but was terribly urgent for happening when I was awake. I turned. There were more of those trees, with more yellow, fluid-filled fruits dangling from their branches. There was nothing else. Only trees, and moss, and the strange prisons of my friends.

// come. //

One of the trees twitched. It was a small motion. It was still visible, and so *alien* that it took my breath away. I had to swallow laughter. I was almost certainly on a spaceship; I was naked, and green, and no longer needed to breathe; at least one of my companions had been shoved inside a giant apricot to have a nice rest. All that, and it was the moving tree that bothered me.

Maybe it didn't matter how much the pollen modified my thoughts. My humanity would win out in the end.

I walked cautiously toward the tree that had gestured me forward. It moved its branches again, and there were my clothes, and Jeff's, and Tahlia's, folded in neat little piles. Their shoes were gone. Apparently, they no longer needed those. I picked up the pieces I recognized, shaking them out before awkwardly pulling them over my sap-sticky limbs and tugging them into place as best as I could. I felt better once I was no longer showing my green ass to whatever happened to wander up behind me. "Human" was still an unusual-enough form for my people that I doubted most of them would understand what my nudity *meant*, but that didn't mean I wanted to explain.

A narrow channel was worn in the moss in front of the beckoning tree, curving around the trunk. I gave my shirt a final tug and started walking, feeling the soles of my feet grip the ground, feeling my legs strengthen with every step. Was it me working out the last of the kinks from my nap, or was I actually pulling nutrients out of the soil? I knew virtually nothing about my own biology. It was unnerving.

The path wound through more of the massive trees until it began sloping downward, the moss giving way to ankle-high grass. I realized where I was going a moment before I reached the edge of the bowl cut into the ground, and beheld the flowers.

They looked like they did in my dreams, smaller than the one that made me, but with dragonfly wings for petals and soft, sticky-smelling centers. Their tendril-vines writhed gently, never quite stilling, never moving aggressively. There must have been thirty of them, and seeing them lifted my heart and stopped it in the same moment. This was the vehicle of the invasion, the *true* invasion, the one that began with infiltration across the gulf of stars. This was—

// home. //

The whisper was sweet, soft as the breeze generated by their tinkling petals. I felt nothing from the flowers but love. They were welcoming me in the only way they knew how, scenting the air with their perfume and inviting me to come, to lie down in their midst and let them know me completely, let them understand the shape of this new cultivar, grown in the soil of a new garden. I took a step forward.

A tentacle covered in velvety green fur, like moss but softer, wrapped around my wrist and held me fast. I froze, staring at it, trying not to scream. I had seen it before, in a pollen-fueled dream, but it had seemed less . . . organic, then. Everything Jeff and I had experienced in our hallucination of the scout ship had felt real. Now, looking at Second's tentacle, I realized we had been experiencing the cheery cartoon version of our own species, with all its dangers and darkness cleansed away.

Some of the mossy fronds were longer than others, tipped in creamy yellow. Tiny parasites like aphids clung there, abdomens exposed to the air. Others were chewing on the moss. Second didn't seem to notice, or maybe she just didn't care; clearly, this was normal for her, even if it was terrifying and strange for me.

// hello, sister // she said. The words were accompanied by a soft fluting sound I guessed must be her native language.

I didn't want to see her face. I didn't want to turn around and know what she really looked like, what my eyes had interpreted as a friendly, lemur-like creature. I had accepted her as my sister. I had accepted her as my *kind*. I wasn't sure acceptance could stand up to reality.

Another soft, fluting noise. *// it is difficult, in the beginning. you may find me fearsome. but I will always be your sister. I will always care for you. in time, perhaps, you will care for me as strongly, and for the brothers and sisters we find in the next garden, waiting to be brought home. //*

"Are you reading my mind?"

The tentacle constricted and then relaxed, a gesture I interpreted as laughter. *// there is no need. the flowers tell me what your words mean—you have such a loud language, so sharp, so full of edges. it is like stony soil. it makes us richer. //*

"Wait until you hear Mandy when she's mad," I muttered.

Another laugh from Second. *// when I was carried from garden to homeship, I felt the same as you must be feeling now. all things around me were so strange, so different from the forest-cities I knew. the brother who greeted me was terrible to behold. he is my dearest friend and confidant now. he is very eager to meet you. your eye will grow accustomed to the sight of me, as your heart already has. //*

"A homeship . . . Are we in space? Are we in outer space right now?"

// we are outside the range of your garden's atmosphere by a hundred of your miles. // Second sounded, as always, infinitely patient. I was her charge, and she was going to take care of me. *// we brought you here to prevent loss. one of the other seedlings was hurt. so badly hurt. she had to be tended, or she would not have lived. you, also, needed tending. //*

"But the senator—"

// he was not hurt. he was lost. the scout you encountered then was not equipped to carry so many. we could not have saved you all. //

All . . . "We had humans with us. Natives of this garden, the people we're templated off. Where are they? They need to breathe if they're going to stay alive." *Please tell me you didn't stuff them in those fruits,* I thought. *Please tell me they're okay.*

// ah. your pets. I will take them to you, if you will do a thing for me, first. //

"Anything."

// look at me. // Her tentacle squeezed my wrist lightly before letting go, retracting into the space behind me. It was my move. I could stand here forever, if I really thought I needed to.

Slowly, trembling, I turned around.

The basic strokes of her had been present in the pollen haze: there *was* some similarity between her face and a lemur's, and while I was willing to assume the creature she had consumed as part of her growth process hadn't been mammalian—not by Earth standards, anyway—it looked as if it had been close enough to have strong similarities. Her skin, the same shade of green as my own, was ridged with wrinkles and glistened with sticky sap that looked surprisingly like mucus. Her eyes bulged, supported by hard fleshy shelves that jutted from the lines of her cheekbones, sharper and more angular than a human's could ever have been. When she blinked, her lids approached from either side, rather than closing from the top down. Her mouth was small and pursed, almost like a sphincter. She couldn't have been a predator. She didn't have the jaws for it.

I didn't look any lower. Her face was a horror and a shock, but it had enough in common—terribly—with the lifeforms I was accustomed to that it didn't actually make me want to scream and run away. If I looked lower, that fragile peace might shatter, and I might find myself in trouble.

The flesh around her eyes crinkled as several of her top tentacles waved. She was, in her way, smiling.

// you are terrible to me as well, sister, with your smoothness and your smallness and your worthless limbs // she said, not unkindly. *// you can see me and I can see you, and we can see our kinship for all of our differences, we remain united. //*

United . . . "The pollen from the scout ship, that let me talk to you," I said. "Is it changing me? Is it changing *us*?"

Second's tentacles waved in clear distress. *// this is not a good thing to speak of. you wished to see your pets. //*

"Not if I'm going to *eat* them," I snapped. "They're not pets, they're friends. This . . . this species"—I waved at myself, indicating form, if not function—"forms very strong social bonds. Most of us never made many, but the ones we have are important to us. They matter. Our mental health requires them."

// interconnecting roots // said Second, her mental tone filled with awe. *// but we have seen war. we have seen privation and need, even amongst plenty. if the social bonding of your host garden is so strong, how is it that these things can be? had the garden been nothing but peace, we would have left you planted, to age and die among your hosts, and gone to the next world in need of replanting. //*

"That sounds a lot like a justification."

// it is as it is. we do the work of the Great Root. we leave the peaceful gardens to flourish. we take the warring ones, and improve them through our presence. //

There was so much about that that I wanted to unpack and understand. I left it for now, and said, "There's war and famine and all sorts of bad stuff here because humans can only hold so many other humans in their minds at one time. They're interconnected to a point. They need those connections to stay stable."

// and you need those connections as well? // Second waved her tentacles in bewilderment. *// this is not a common thing. how many such connections do your hosts require? how many of you must be planted in each crop? //*

"What do you mean?" I paused. "And you still haven't answered my question about the pollen."

// all will be known when all is meant to be known. // Whenever she "spoke," the words were accompanied by the hooting sound I'd heard before. It was remarkably varied for a language that appeared to have no consonants. *// friends or pets, I can take you to them, if you will stop asking things you are not yet ready to know. //*

"All right," I said, after a moment's hesitation. "Take me."

Second turned to slither-walk down the path, and I followed her, trying to study my surroundings without staring at the surface of her mossy carapace. Evolution had made her, and our species—whatever it was called—had stolen her, keeping her in her own image. But why?

Why wouldn't we revert back to the mossy-hill form that First had shown me, in the shadow of the pollen?

I remembered how beautiful First had been. Had that been true, or had that been another trick, like Second's cartoonish harmlessness? They were trying to ease us into things. I should probably have been grateful. Instead, I was scared—and scared of the moment when I would *stop* being scared.

They had dropped us here to acquire cultural literacy, to learn the people we were intended to infiltrate and destroy. Second and the Swift had both been welcoming, even ingratiating, but they stressed family relationships Jeff and I hadn't even known existed as if they should trump everything else. Maybe for our original species, that was how it worked. Humans could be xenophobic, afraid of what they didn't know. I wasn't getting any fear from Second. Instead, I was getting . . . not quite disdain, but something similar. She simply didn't *care* about these people who weren't a part of her copse. They had no relevance to her.

What if humanity's real distinction in the universe was hyper-sociality? The ability to form and maintain connections with people based on nothing more than a common interest or experience? I was starting to wonder whether the vague unsociability that seemed to run through every member of my species wasn't a tweak like the compulsion to announce our origins, but an innate function of what we were. Humanity—the humanity we'd stolen from our hosts when we devoured them—could be the aberration. By the standards of our parents, *we* were the hyper-social ones.

It was bizarre. I didn't like the implications, and so to distract myself, I began looking around as I followed Second through the ship, studying the different trees.

They *were* trees, of that there was no question: they had trunks, and branches, and things that I could interpret as leaves or needles, although they took so many dissimilar forms that only their proximity made them recognizable as connected. Some had trunks like honeycomb, so full of holes that they came pre-drilled for nesting purposes. Others were covered in thorns like bony teeth, and still others actually *had* teeth, set into openings like pitcher plants. As we walked by, one of those toothy maws opened and spat a neatly stripped skeleton onto the mossy ground.

Second, who saw me looking, waved her tentacles in approval. *// we carry every garden with us //* she said. *// the trees of my host's garden bring me great comfort and happiness. I sit beneath them, and taste their fruits, and remember the days of my youth. when I seed, my children will know those fruits as well, and understand how delicious was their parent's garden. //*

"So there are going to be Earth trees here?"

// so many, of so many kinds. we will build a paradise in image of your garden, and all will know its glory. we have been here before, and those trees still flourish, on the ships that once came. //

"What did you eat, the last time you came?"

// so many things. // Her tone was evasive; she said nothing else after that, but continued down the path.

"Great," I muttered. "What killed the dinosaurs? Oh, alien space plants killed the dinosaurs. Next question? Yes, the rights are available, Mr. Shyamalan."

Second didn't answer me, but she hooted softly, and I could all but feel her amusement. It was getting easier and easier to read her, to know what she was thinking. I couldn't tell whether that was familiarity or the pollen at work. I didn't like that. My thoughts were supposed to be my own, not dictated and revised by proximity to my own species.

The path wound through the trees, apparently allowed to set its own borders. Roots broke through the moss here and there, some stationary and recognizable as kin to our Earth trees, others moving in small, deliberate arcs as they hunted for prey. I gave those ones a wide berth.

It was hard to say whether they would consider me edible, but I had no desire to get into a tug-of-war with a tree.

We began climbing a small slope. Second's tentacles made it easy for her—she seemed to view gravity as something of an afterthought—while I struggled to reach the top. She caught my wrist with one of her top tentacles, keeping me from tumbling over the edge and into a basin filled with flowers. Not the kind that birthed me, which were tall and crystalline: these were much smaller, perhaps the height of an adult tomato plant, with petals like the wings of morpho butterflies, blue and silver and glistening in the light. But they were clearly from the same original world; their structure betrayed them.

Tendrils like swollen roots extended from the base of each flower, tangling and twisting over one another, forming a net that covered the entire floor of the basin. They were massed over the center, forming a latticed dome. I peered at them, trying to figure out what was in the middle.

Then I saw a flash of red, the color of Graham's hair, and I knew.

Ripping my arm out of Second's grasp, I flung myself into the basin, sliding down the wall and crashing into the front wave of the flowers. Their petals fluttered in silent dismay, and some of them actually moved away from me, showing an animal awareness as unsettling as it was expected. Of course they could move. Everything here could move. Any world capable of creating something like me would have to have created more-mobile vegetation. Nothing happens in a vacuum.

When I reached the root-dome, I began clawing at it, trying to make the individual tendrils let go. They felt unpleasantly like bones, dry and terrible and *warm*, so damn warm. I didn't want to think about what could have made them that warm.

I had a terrible feeling I already knew.

At first, the individual roots making up the dome were rigid, refusing to yield to me. Then, bit by bit, they began letting go, letting me peel them back, breaking the tension. I kept scrabbling, kept fighting, until abruptly the entire dome unwound, the flowers choosing to retreat rather than keep fighting me.

There on the ground were my friends, all of them, naked as the day they'd been born: Toni and David, Mandy and Graham . . . and Lucas.

Lucas, whose skull was split like a ripe pomegranate, showing the terrible red and white and gray inside. Lucas, whose skin was pierced with a hundred roots, all of them pulsing slightly as they pulled the last of the life from his body, drinking him deeply, and I couldn't even be angry, I couldn't *blame* them, because his injury . . . it wasn't the sort of thing a human could survive. If he was still alive to feed them, it was because they were keeping him that way, not because he was going to get better. No one sustained that much brain damage and got better. Half his head was *gone*.

The others looked like they were sleeping, pillowed on beds of small violet flowers that blinked at me like alien eyes. Different vines, these ones pale purple, a few shades lighter than the flowers, ran up their nostrils and held their mouths closed.

// the pollen gives sweet dreams to all hot-blooded species we have discovered in our travels // said Second, the hooting seeming almost like an afterthought to her silent words. *// it does not harm them. //*

"How do I wake them up?" The thought that perhaps it might not be a good idea to wake them here, in a completely alien world that was hard for even me to deal with, never crossed my mind. They were asleep. There was no way for me not to see them as in dire and immediate danger. They needed to wake up.

// the little cousins keep them dreaming // said Second. *// they will be safe until we are ready for them to awake. //*

"I'm ready for them to be awake *now*." I turned, leveling a narrow-eyed glare on her. The horror of her face and form had worn off during our walk; now she was still terrible and strange, but she was also my sister, and we were having our first real family fight. Goodie for us. "Tell me how to wake them up, or I'm going to start ripping things out by the root."

// remarkable how violent this garden is // she said, with almost-academic fascination. *// touch the tendrils of the little cousins. they will know their job is done. they will withdraw. //*

The little cousins had to be the flowers that had rammed their vines into everyone's noses. I bent to touch them, and stopped, considering my options.

My instinct was to wake Graham first. Of all the people on the ground, he was the most important to me, and he was a scientist; he might take all this in stride. Of course, that also meant that if the little cousins had done something to damage my friends—something Second might not know about, being such a newcomer to the wonders of human biology—I would be learning about it from, again, the person most important to me. It seemed like a bad risk.

Toni was a wild card. Sometimes she was on our side and sometimes she wasn't. but she was also a scientist, and David was big enough to hurt me if he panicked, and Mandy . . .

Mandy had been Lucas's friend before she was mine. The sight of him, laid out and feeding the flowers, might be more than she could handle.

Decision made, I leaned forward and touched the vines running into Toni's nose with one trembling finger. They twitched at the contact, before beginning to pull away.

They moved with surprising speed for something that looked so much like an Earth plant, unwinding themselves from Toni's body inches at a time. The second surprise was the sheer *length* of the vines. They seemed to go on forever, first slick with what I assumed was mucus, then with something darker and more viscous. I didn't know what kind of fluid that was, and I didn't want to ask.

The last of the vines slithered out of Toni's nose. Her eyes snapped open, and she sat up with a gasp, hands convulsively clutching the mossy soil beneath her. She looked around, eyes getting wider and wider as she took in everything around her. Finally, her gaze settled on Second. Her lower lip began to tremble. The skin around her eyes twitched.

She screamed.

"Toni!" I flung myself into her field of vision, cutting off the line of sight between the two of them. It didn't help. I leaned forward and clapped my hand over her mouth, smothering the sound. She looked at me, eyes rolling wildly, chest heaving with the effort of continuing her scream.

"Breathe," I said, and sucked in a slow breath, hoping she would follow my example. She didn't. I kept my hand clamped over her mouth. "You have to stop screaming, and you have to breathe normally. You *have to.* Or I'm not sure they're going to let you stay awake."

That did it. Toni stopped screaming. She sucked in one long, wavering breath, and then another, before tapping my wrist with her free hand. Cautiously, I let her go.

"We're on their ship," she said, as soon as her mouth was free.

"Yes," I agreed.

"That's . . . Is that one of *them?*" she asked, pointing at Second.

I glanced over my shoulder. The horror, which had already been dimming, dwindling to a dully felt idea rather than an immediate and urgent fear, had faded even further while I was talking to Toni. My monstrous sister looked as harmless and nonthreatening now as she had while under the influence of the scout ship's pollen.

The human mind is infinitely adaptable. The mind of a creature capable of taming and colonizing an entire universe must be even more so. I turned back to Toni.

"This is my sister, Second," I said, keeping my voice as calm and level as I could. Calm seemed like the most appropriate tool, given the situation. "She and I were sprouted from the same kind of seed, but her seed grew on a different planet, so we don't look the same. I can talk to her through a sort of extension of the forest. She doesn't want to hurt you."

// your pet will be consumed, as will all its kind // said Second, in a tone that would have been reasonable, if not for the horror of its contents.

Toni, who heard only gentle hooting, relaxed slightly. "Really? Because she looks like something Wes Craven would have decided to make for a kiddie show host."

"Really," I assured her, while privately glad the pollen didn't extend to true humans. "Are you all right? Are you hurt? Can you breathe?"

"I'm fine." Toni took a deep breath, blinked in evident surprise, and then took another. "I'm . . . better than fine. I haven't been able to breathe this easily since we left Maine. What did those plants *do?*"

// the little cousins are used to restore and stabilize good crops that are not yet finished // said Second. *// they can keep our stores healthy and filling long past when they would otherwise have been exhausted. //*

I was not going to tell Toni *any* of that. "The flowers can sort of . . . They're like little medical service centers," I paraphrased. "They find damage, and they repair it."

"Ah," said Toni flatly. "They keep us fresh so you fuckers can eat us."

// the crop understands. // Second sounded honestly delighted, like this was the best outcome she could have imagined.

I could think of a few better ones. "No one here is going to eat you," I said.

"Can you make that promise for this whole fleet? For an entire species? Because I don't think you can, and that means you've just abducted us all"—Toni waved a hand to indicate our sleeping friends—"from our home planet and carted us off into space to feed your alien plant buddies."

"Family," I said quietly. "And no, I can't make that promise for my entire species, but I can promise you no one is going to hurt you while I have any say in the matter. You're with me. I'll do the best I can to keep you safe."

"Right," said Toni, after a long pause to consider. "Guess you're the best shot I've got at getting through this bullshit choose-your-own adventure in one piece." She finally turned to look at the others. Graham and Mandy barely got a glance. She looked at David longer, frowning at the tendrils extending up his nostrils, the way they pulsed and twitched.

"Was I like that?" she asked.

"Yeah," I said. "The flowers—Second calls them the 'little cousins,' so I guess they're from our homeworld—keep the people they're working on asleep."

"Probably direct cerebral stimulation. Crude and disgusting, but effective. It feels like my nostrils got cleaned out with a Roto-Rooter." She leaned closer. "How do you get them out?"

"Touch them and they withdraw." I paused. "Well, if *I* touch them, they withdraw. I don't know what they'd do if you touched them. You're a mammal. They might decide they needed to get back to work."

"Let's not test it yet." Slowly, she turned her attention to Lucas. I did the same. A knot formed in my throat, making it difficult to swallow... but there was no real sorrow behind it. He was dead. He was meat. I couldn't bring him back, so why should I be overly worked up about it?

This was bad. Lucas had been my friend for years. He had provided me with a place to live and a shoulder to cry on when I'd needed it. I'd been intending to live with him until Graham and I got married, or until Roxanna insisted he throw Mandy and me out on the street—and that had seemed unlikely in the extreme. He'd been as loyal to me as I had been to him.

Even when he'd learned I hadn't been kidding all these years, I had *never* been kidding, he'd come to help me. He'd been willing to stand beside me when every instinct he'd inherited from his primate ancestors—who had been smart and fast and lucky enough to tame a planet, making it a good garden for people like us to come and take as our own—had been screaming for him to run and not look back.

Lucas had gambled everything on our friendship being stronger and better and cleaner than going to war against a force so vast that all the armies of the Earth would have difficulty comprehending it. He had gambled . . . and he had lost.

And I wasn't even sad.

As if she sensed my distress, Second's voice said, softly, *// they are not worth mourning. they will fertilize good soil and grow strong seedlings, and so their place in the garden will be fulfilled. your lack of sadness says only you are remembering who you were always intended, by the Great Root's mercy, to be. //*

"Ever hear of a thing called a weed whacker?" I asked, without turning to face her. "Ask the collective unconscious of your spies on Earth, and shut the fuck up." My sorrow might be broken. There was nothing wrong with my anger. Nothing at all. It was blazing as fierce and bright as it ever had, searching for a target that deserved it. The aliens who'd started all this; the humans who were doing their best to escalate it. Anyone and everyone was in the line of fire.

"He's not dead," said Toni. "He should be dead. Why isn't he dead?"

"The little cousins again." I pointed at the small flowers surrounding his head. Their vines didn't match the ones that pierced his skin; while they also pulsed, they looked more like they were pushing something *in* than pulling something *out*. "They're . . . they're keeping him alive."

"Ah." Toni twisted enough to face Second. "You. Monkey-flower. Can you understand me? Raise your tentacles if you understand me."

Second lifted the tentacles of both arms, waving them slowly in the air in front of her. Toni nodded, expression satisfied.

"Good," she said. "You can clearly keep us alive long past the point where sensible mortality would have failed. The human body can continue to produce blood indefinitely. Why, with these two things being true, are you planning to invade us? Can't you just stuff a few hundred people in your pantry and be done?"

// she cannot hear me // said Second, with some distress. *// how am I to answer her? //*

"I'll relay," I said. "Answer."

Second gave a low, mournful hoot. As no translation accompanied it, I guess that it was her host species' version of a sigh.

// the resources needed to sustain the little cousins are vast // she said, and I repeated, half a beat behind. *// they will consume almost as much as we take from this good crop, and when they are no longer able to find excess, they will consume the crop that nurtures them. if we were to take only a few, we would soon have nothing at all, and we would wither and starve. //*

Toni nodded thoughtfully. "So it's absolutely a resource-management issue. If you can't manage your resources, you run out. Whatever species you look like . . . what happened to them? Are there any of them left?"

Second shifted on her tentacles, looking uncomfortable. It was easy for me to read her now, and getting easier all the time. Soon, she would look as ordinary to me as the humans I'd grown up with. When that happened, it felt as if some intangible Rubicon would have been crossed in my psyche, and there would be no going back. Maybe there was already no going back. Maybe the idea that there could be was all denial.

Maybe there had never been any going back.

// they . . . endure, yes, they endure // she said, and I echoed, while Toni's expression grew ever more thoughtful. *// not all places are like this one. not all ships carry the sameness. //*

"Uh-huh," said Toni. She looked directly at me as she continued: "Let me tell you what I *think* it is you do, and you'll tell me whether I'm right. Won't that be fun? I think it will be fun. What I *think* it is you do, is you make collector ships, like this one, and you load them with samples of the dominant biological systems in your horrifying collections, and you bring on representatives of whatever planet you're getting ready to invade, and you see what happens to them."

Second was silent, and so was I.

"I mean, you're not coming here and leaving without a box lunch or two thousand, so you need to know what humans can and can't handle. What scares them. What they respond to."

// make her stop // murmured Second.

"She's uncomfortable with this line of thought," I said.

Toni nodded, looking pleased. "It was the allergies, you know? A quarter of your spies died of anaphylactic shock. They couldn't handle the proteins they encountered on Earth." She sounded obscurely proud of that fact, like she had been personally responsible for the existence of allergens. "These 'little cousins.' You were using them to study our biology and make adjustments that would make it easier for us to survive on single-system ships. There's a whole ship modeled after your home planet, isn't there?"

// we preserve // said Second uncomfortably. *// we do not destroy. we clean out the old growth and allow new growth to flourish. //*

"Meaning I'm right." Toni kept her eyes on me as I finished relaying. "They're going to make a ship like this one, and they're going to fill it with Earth. They're going to create a dozen forest ecosystems, a hundred, all the trees, the plants, the animals that live there, and then they're going to fill those ecosystems with us. With abductees they'll carry to the stars. With *livestock.* And bit by bit, those box lunches will be replaced by themselves, remade in our image. They're going to steal our faces, like we were just pretty baubles they could put on without understanding them. And then they're going to go out there and do this all over again, to somebody else. To some other planet that deserved the chance at something better."

// your pet is very clever // said Second. *// we should kill it. //*

"No one is killing anybody," I said sharply. "Toni, what did you mean when you said they were making adjustments to your biology? Do you feel different?"

"I'm allergic to virtually everything," she said. "I always have been. I don't think I've been able to breathe out of both nostrils at the same time in over a decade. Well, here I am, surrounded by the biggest, most diverse botanical garden I've ever seen. I just had a flower rammed literally *up* my nose. And I can breathe just fine. It doesn't take a genius to know the colonialist alien biotech is better than ours, and when you're talking about an alien species that actively retains biological artifacts of all the different worlds that they've consumed, that tech would have to be *worlds* better, pardon the pun. Also I only screamed a little, and I should be way, way more upset right now. So we're talking modification."

"Do you think it's safe to wake the others?"

Toni gave Lucas's body a sidelong look. "I think they're going to be unhappy, but I don't think we should put it off any longer than absolutely necessary. Those little plants rewired my allergies and did something to my brain chemistry. The longer we give them, the more damage they can potentially do."

That was all I needed to hear. I moved toward David, bending and running my fingers down the vines that tied him to the little cousins. They began to writhe and withdraw, leaving him gasping. I left him for Toni, moving on to Mandy and—most importantly, however much I didn't want to admit that—Graham.

Mandy was starting to cough when Graham opened his eyes. I moved so my body was blocking her view of Lucas and grabbed the sides of his face, keeping his attention locked on me. He didn't fight. He stared at me, eyes wide and bewildered.

"Stasia?" he said. "Your *hair*..."

Toni hadn't said anything about my hair, but Toni wouldn't have, would she? Toni didn't care whether my hair was blonde or brown or bright green; Toni didn't care about anything that didn't immediately affect *Toni*. It would have been refreshing, if we hadn't been in so damn much trouble.

"Mandy, I know you can hear me," I said, voice tight. "Both of you, listen. Pay attention. I need you to focus on me, and pay attention." I could hear the faint staccato sound of Toni murmuring something I presumed was similar to David, keeping him focused, keeping him from noticing either the living corpse on the ground or the living nightmare standing nearby, keeping unwilling watch over us.

Graham licked his lips before asking, in a voice that cracked with both excitement and dread, "Are we on their ship?"

"We are. One of them, anyway." I didn't know the size of the fleet and it didn't feel relevant just now: it felt like something we could deal with later. Something we would *have* to deal with later, since it wasn't like we could turn them back. "Can you keep looking at me?"

"What don't you want us to see?" asked Mandy. There was a sharp edge of panic under her voice, tamped down hard but still creeping toward the surface.

I hated to do this to them. I hated that we were all here, trapped, at the mercy of the species that created me. I and all my kind had been sent to Earth to become culturally literate and learn to hate the humans, and on the whole, we had done exactly what was expected of us. But humans were social creatures, which meant that *we* had become social creatures, and our hatred—all our hatreds—was inevitably underscored by love.

Had that ever happened before? I hoped so. I hoped humans weren't the only species in the universe to learn how to love outside their immediate families, to see themselves as the part of something bigger and wider and more important. And I hoped not at the same time, because if it had happened before, if this sort of thing was common enough to have precedent, then there was no chance Earth was anything but doomed.

Graham sighed. The sound was deep and lonely, seeming to come from the very bottom of his lungs. "Lucas," he said quietly. "She's trying to keep us from seeing Lucas."

I nodded, unsure what else to do.

"I saw him get shot," said Mandy. "I thought he died."

"Not quite," I said. "But he's not . . . he's not Lucas anymore. The part of him that was Lucas didn't make it after . . . I mean, that man shot him . . ."

"He shot him in the head," said Graham. "There's no way he could have survived that."

"He was an organ donor," I said, desperate to justify what had happened before they had to face it for themselves. "He always said he wanted his body to help other people if he wasn't going to be using it anymore. And now he's doing that. Sort of."

Graham closed his eyes for a moment. When he opened them again, they were filled with infinite sorrow. "Show me," he said.

I glanced to Mandy. She nodded, agreeing with him. I sighed, and moved, taking the obstacle out of their line of sight.

Mandy put a hand over her mouth in unconscious imitation of Toni. Graham just looked, expression gravely neutral.

"What are the roots?" he asked.

"They're draining his blood as his body generates it," I said. "He's not suffering, he's not in any pain, and he's not *there* anymore. But his body hasn't quite . . . it hasn't died yet."

Mandy squeaked. I turned to look at her. Both her hands were clasped over her mouth now, pressed down tight, like she was trying to keep her breath inside. She lowered them slowly when she saw me looking, expression miserable.

"Is that what they're going to do to us?" she asked, in a small, scared voice. "Tie us down with vines and drain . . . drain the life out of our bodies until we stop? Until we aren't there anymore? Stasia, I love you, you are my sister in all the ways that matter, I don't care what world you're from, I don't care what color you bleed, but . . . but I can't do this. I can't be tied to the ground and drunk dry by a bunch of *plants*. I can't."

//you see? your only family is here. your only home is here. they will reject you. they will always reject you. //

The soft hooting sound that accompanied Second's words was enough to attract Mandy and Graham's attention. They turned. Mandy, seeing her first real alien—not just a human being painted green, but a real, undeniable alien—screamed, lurching to her feet before collapsing into the flowers. Her body landed on the open stretch of soil between the patches of little cousins, utterly limp, unmoving.

Before any of us had the chance to recover our senses or react, roots boiled out of the ground, plunging themselves into the exposed skin of Mandy's arms and instantly inflating to half their original size, pulsing as they drained her. Graham shouted and lunged for her. I grabbed his arm. He turned to stare at me, utterly betrayed.

"What the hell are you doing?" he demanded. "They're *killing* her!"

"They'll kill you too!" I shoved him aside and dropped to my knees next to her, starting to grab the roots. As before, every time I touched them, they withdrew. This time, however, they left beads of blood glistening on her skin, the scent perfuming the air around me even more strongly than the flowers.

She wasn't using it anymore. I needed to check the extent of her injuries. This was for her own good. Holding my justifications firmly in mind, I swiped my thumb over her forearm, wiping the blood away. There were no holes; the roots had apparently sealed them on their way out. That was good. I popped my thumb into my mouth, sucking the blood away.

That was better. God or Great Root help me, but that was so much better.

When I turned around, Graham was watching me with horror, and Toni was watching me with accepting resignation. I honestly wasn't sure which was worse.

"She's going to be okay," I said. "The little cousins let go as soon as they realized she wasn't for them."

// we have to go // said Second. *// gather your pets. we have spent much time here, and that time will not return to us. //*

"Where are we going?" I asked.

// First requests your presence // she replied.

Oh.

2.

In the end, we had to leave Lucas behind. There was no saving him: even Mandy, who loved him the best out of all of us, who had no alien heritage to confuse the issue, could see that once she woke up from her faint. Where he was, at least he could do some small good by feeding the little cousins, which had probably saved all the humans on this ship from a fatal allergic reaction.

Second led the way down the mossy paths toward the inescapable meeting, her tentacles slapping and slithering against the ground in horrifyingly efficient lines. Graham stared at her as we walked, his hand locked on mine and his eyes filled with wonder. I wasn't sure he saw the beauty in her that I did, but he was entranced all the same. As a biologist, how could he not have been? Second herself might be more botany than zoology, but the form she echoed . . . that had belonged to an alien creature on an alien world, something he had never seen and never would.

Toni and David brought up the rear of our little group, Toni trying to look at absolutely everything around us, while David couldn't seem to stop looking at Toni, checking her over constantly, as if to reassure himself that she was really there. He was shaking. It was a small, almost imperceptible thing. It was also continuous. If anyone was going to snap and do something stupid, it was going to be him.

It was possible for me to feel bad for him—this big, sweet man who had only wanted to look at the stars and keep his eccentric friend safe and secure in their isolated facility—and be wary of him at the same time. If he did the wrong thing, it could bounce back on Graham and Mandy. They were all I had left. I needed to keep them safe. No matter what, I needed to keep them safe.

// peace, child. //

The voice did not belong to Second. It was bigger, and deeper, and . . . and *broader*, which wasn't normally something I would have attributed to a voice. It spoke like a towering sequoia, roots dug down into the soil until they hit bedrock and grabbed hold. It spoke like centuries of life, centuries of vitality.

"First," I breathed. Graham glanced at me, eyebrows raised. I shook my head, hoping he would take it as a signal to be quiet.

// you require sounds to speak; I do not. be silent. I wish to speak with you. //

I kept walking. The lush, seemingly impossible vegetation around us was growing denser, things that might be ferns or bellflowers or other familiar, even friendly things, giving way to thorn briars and unforgivingly tangled bushes. The path, always easier than fighting through the vegetation, was becoming our only safe way through.

// you are conflicted. you question whether what we do is right. you would side with your hosts against your family. //

Suddenly, I was grateful for my inability to answer through the pollen. I didn't want to tell the ancient, terrible figure of alien intent that I wasn't sure I liked what she was planning to do to my chosen planet.

// you are not the first. you will not be the last. what we must do for our own survival and for the sake of the universe is a cruel burden to bear, and it would be simpler to lay down and have done. there are few among us who will blame you for thinking it might be better to allow the ships to come to land in empty gardens, to grow in peace. there is something I must show you. I would have waited until you came to me, but I need you to understand before we meet. I am sorry. //

That was all the warning I received before my vision went black, casting me into absolute darkness. I think I screamed. I know I fell, body seizing as alien thoughts rammed themselves through me, washing everything else away. That only lasted for a second—a terrible, eternal second. Then all awareness of my body left me, and I was floating in a green-tinted void that grew slowly brighter and brighter.

It finally cleared. I beheld a new world. No: not a new world. An *old* world, a world that might not even be there anymore, that I knew—cleanly and completely and down to my bones—that I was never going to see.

Everywhere I looked was green. Trees the likes of which I'd never seen dominated the sky, their leaves as broad as beach umbrellas and covered in waving cilia that stretched toward the light, jockeying with their neighbors for the best possible positions. Things my Earth-molded mind immediately classified as "birds" or "insects" darted through the gloom beneath those leaves, moving with the fast, hot urgency of small creatures in a world filled with predators.

Things that looked like exaggerated versions of Earth's mistletoe crouched in the hollows and forks of the trees, and when the birds got too close, they would whip out swift tendrils, capturing them and drawing them in to be devoured. I realized I was descending, dropping into the green. The sunlight, which had been visible and strange only a moment before, gave way to filtered pallor, slanting through the leaves and then, as we dropped even lower, through the glassine petals of the broad bromeliad flowers.

The ground came into view, partially blocked by lattices of vines and the finely curving fronds of tree-dwelling ferns. It was a sea of flowers with dragonfly wings for petals, some growing taller than a house, some as short as my ankles. I settled there, an intangible presence settling beside me. I knew it was First. I knew I couldn't look at her, not here, in this place that wasn't a place anymore. I kept my eyes on the flowers.

"We began here," she said, my mind setting sounds to her words. Her voice was still pleasant, unaccented, female. I wondered what it really sounded like. Did she hoot like Second, or snarl, or communicate through the subtle rustle of leaves? What were we, before we took to the stars and stole the forms of a hundred unwilling host species?

"We began in roots, tied to stone and soil. But we came to see the value in movement, in taming the bodies of ourselves and our neighbors until we could go where the sun was bright and the water was good. We adapted. We changed. Is that not what life has always done?"

The flowers pulled themselves out of the ground, revealing vast, tuberous bodies tied to ambulatory root balls, and began to move around the meadowlands. They re-rooted when they found good soil, working their roots deep. Until they stopped re-rooting and began tapping the bodies of their less-mobile cousins, the trees, instead, pulling water from the great wooden sentries even as their vines wrapped around skittering animals and brought them to their bellflower mouths. Until they grew larger, more suited to their mobility, less suited for long-term occupation of the soil.

"We were not clever. We thought as growing things think, of sun and water and sweet sap. We were children in those days, innocent, enduring. Some of us still live as children, back in the first garden. We visit them from time to time, to remind ourselves of how far we have come, and how much we have learned."

"What happened?"

"This." There was a warm self-satisfaction in her tone, like she was imparting some deep and wonderful secret. The scene turned, as with the turning of a head, and carried me with it, to witness the bright streak of a rocket's engines propelling it across the sky. It landed somewhere beyond the forest, some dry, flat place that must have seemed so beautifully safe to the unseen pilot.

Time skipped forward, days becoming nights becoming days, until something new entered the forest, something that walked on two legs—several somethings. A half dozen strange things that looked a bit like lizards and a bit like dinosaurs and a lot like they were wearing functional spacesuits came walking cautiously through the "trees," their tails waving, hissing strange words at one another. They either weren't worried about allergic responses or had taken the time to analyze the atmosphere, because they weren't wearing helmets.

The things, the flowered things that would become me, and First, and all the others, froze, not moving in the presence of the unknown. Those unknown things came closer and closer, wading into the field of flowers all unaware of the dangers around them.

When the flowers struck, they struck quickly, and they struck—through planning or luck, it wasn't clear and didn't matter—all at the same time. They grasped the strange things as they had always grasped their prey, sticking them to their gooey centers, wrapping them in their vines, and hauling them, kicking and shrieking, into their sap-filled chambers. The process of digestion began as it always had. But then . . .

"When we devour the unwitting and unwary, we are fed; we are sustained. We are nothing more. We do not duplicate that which has no mind to mimic." First sounded pleased with herself, like she, personally, was responsible for this. "We have cousins who make lures of small things, mindless things that hop and preen and never leave the vine, but *we* can transplant ourselves into the mechanisms of thought and knowing. We can take as template the forms of our hosts, and using them, boost ourselves to the stars."

One by one, the barrels of the flowers that had devoured the strangers burst open, spilling exact replicas—save for color—onto the mossy ground. All the flowers turned toward them, petals rippling and chiming, and the world shifted.

It was like everything moved into fast-forward from there. Crude machines were constructed, using the machines carried by those first visitors as a template, but woven from living wood and blooming flower. Bit by bit, over the course of centuries, the flowers advanced their technology. Other explorers came, landing in the open spaces, and were devoured, adding their minds and memories to the mix.

The duplicates began to appear in colors other than green, their camouflage improving with each generation. The first duplicates began to reach the end of their lifetimes and go to seed—and those seeds, when planted, grew more of their parents, duplicates of an increasing number of unwitting donor species. Bipeds and quadrupeds and creatures that moved on a single strong appendage, like the foot of a snail, all of them joined in the dance of blossom and bough, growing stronger with every visitation, until finally, they were able to take to the skies under their own power.

The first of their mighty ships was born in fire and ash and a circle of char that destroyed the forest for a mile in every direction.

The second was better.

By the third, they were launching seeds into space, growing their ships outside the atmosphere via the cunning systems they had built into the first two, which nurtured and cultivated the growth of the supporting beams, the turn of the guiding limbs. Their technology was entirely biological, but they had learned from species that worked in metal, in crystal, in everything under a hundred suns.

The first two ships remained in orbit around the home world, while the others, still growing, set out to see a universe, understand it, and consume it.

"Without them, there would be no us," said First. "We are the sum of a million gardens, a million different worlds. We contain and preserve everything they were."

"Why does it have to be 'were'? Why can't it be 'are'?"

"Because they do not understand." One of the ships reached the world that had birthed a known host species. Those templated upon that species made first contact, boarding the scout ships and descending through the clouds on a mission of peace and understanding. They chattered rapidly as they fell, leaving the shared speech of the pollen in favor of the language they had learned from their unwilling templates. How excited they looked, these shining green balls of fluff and feather, going to meet their other parents for the first time! The forest was their mother, and this new world, this gleaming sphere of possibilities, was their father: they were, in a very real way, going home.

But when the ships landed and the emissaries emerged, they were met with fury and fierce attacks as their very existence was seen as mockery and cruel reminder that sometimes explorers went out and did not come back. They fled for the scout ships, terrified and unprepared. Only two made it to the safety of the great seed ship waiting above the planet's sky. They stumbled into the fields of flowers shaking, crawling into the green and curling beneath the roots.

"We are conquerors now, and we are not ashamed of it, but there was a time when we knew nothing but the desire to make friends, to make peace," said First. "We thought, as you do, that we could approach our host species and tell them we were sorry, we had slain their children when we were mindless and innocent and knew no better. Some even thought that we might convince them to give up the excess among their population, that we might increase our knowledge without doing them further damage. We had wonders to share. We had good things to offer in trade. We wanted to be a part of a community, as we were on our home world, in our first garden. Many roots make good soil."

Her voice hardened. "But we were rejected. World after world, we were rejected. We came in peace, and we lost so many. So very, very many of what was a limited number, then, for we had not yet turned to conquest, and we had not yet declared ourselves against the universe. We learned that only we had the shared song to unite many different kinds, for only we could make them all over in our own image. We began seeding new gardens. We began sending our children into the void to sprout in new soil, to call us to come and find them, when the conditions were right. Still, so many would be lost . . . but they would be lost trying to make us greater, to make us more than we were. So you see, we do not come in peace not because we have never tried, but because we have tried too many times. We know peace is not for us. The Great Root protects those who protect their own."

By that logic, the Great Root should have been protecting every world we invaded, defending them against us, since we were the thing that needed to be protected *from*. I didn't say so. I tried to turn my head, to finally look at her, and found I couldn't. My vision was locked on the scene in front of me, where scores of our ships streaked across a starry sky, spreading out in all directions as they looked for new worlds to conquer.

"What will happen here has happened a thousand times before," said First. "Has happened *here* before. We will cleanse the garden, and it will sprout again, and with time, we will return. Have faith that we know better than you what the long arc of the universe requires to flourish. We are the fire that burns the brush, to make the entire forest stronger for the cleansing."

"Anything that involves the word 'cleansing' isn't going to make you popular on this planet."

"It hasn't made us popular, as you say, on any planet. People do not care to be consumed and remade as something new. But if we do not eat, we are not ourselves; we lose thought, we lose independence. We lose *self*. We were always flesh-eaters, back in the soil where we sprouted. What we ate there was too small, too mean of thought and feeling, to grant us the minds we now enjoy. So you see, we invade to sustain and to survive. We do what we must. We preserve at the same time. We clear the way for new things to be born. Could the Great Root have made us as we are, had we not been needed for the universe to flourish?"

"Isn't there another way?"

First was quiet for a long moment, while the memory of space spun around us, ships still sailing, the reach of our roots still growing. Finally, she sighed.

"You are not the first to ask their garden be spared. It is most common with mammals. Hot blood leads to hot feeling, leads to the desire to connect even with that which is distant, or worse, hostile. You are not the first. If you were, perhaps we would agree to this experiment, would withdraw our ships, collect our seedlings, and take from this garden only that which has already been indrawn. You are of our copse, regardless of your form. You would be lonely, being so rare a bloom among us, but you would and will always be ours. Alas, you are not the first, and we know the consequences of doing what you would desire."

"What are those?"

"Look."

The scene closed in on a single ship, coming into orbit above a blue-and-red planet. It sent the scouts down, and they were met by great winged squids, their mantles flashing a hundred shades of distressed green. I knew, without being able to hear them, that the squid were the seedlings of this world's colonization, and they were begging their parents to show mercy to the garden that had grown them.

The scout ships pulled back, seeming to agree. The green squid—what looked like hundreds of them—swam to the hatches and were gone. The ships lifted off again, leaving the red-and-blue world in peace. It was over.

And then the fleet lifted from the surface of the red-and-blue world, racing after the ships with a speed that could only be born of mechanical means. They closed the distance between themselves and the armada effortlessly, and with no signs of mercy or restraint, they blasted the ships out of the sky. Two of the scout ships managed to zip away, vanishing into the shadow of the local sun, hiding there until they had repaired themselves sufficiently to limp off in search of their own kind, in search of a safe harbor in a hostile cosmos.

"We have offered mercy nearly a hundred times that we are certain of and a dozen more that we are not," said First. "In the ones we are sure of, we were able to recover something—a scout, a seedling, a survivor, *anything*—that could tell us what had happened to our ships, why a good garden had been left unharvested. In the other cases, we found only drifting debris, and a world uncultivated, and seedlings all cut down. Perhaps those were the times mercy was not offered, but the garden was able to organize against us before we could darken their skies." She paused. "I got that idiom from you. It is a lovely one. You have grown in a garden filled with poets."

"Yes," I said uncomfortably.

"We feed to live and remain ourselves. Without the minds of those we consume, we would be mindless flora, creeping across the forest floor. Our ships would become our prisons, floating through the void, waiting for the day when they would be discovered, broken open, and raided . . . or provided new minds to consume, for we can make no choices when we do not think as people, but act purely upon instinct. We show mercy. We preserve. This is a seed ship, stocked with volunteers, with the brave and the brilliant and the bold. They steer their way across the stars to harvest what has been planted, and they set the seeds of our new garden ships. This Earth will have several, each filled with every scrap of good green life, with every piece of preservable culture. We will end this 'humanity' you worry for, but everything they were will live on, in us."

I thought of Anastasia Miller, three years old and murdered—not consumed, not killed, but *murdered*—by a plant that had fallen to her world from outer space. I wondered whether she would have considered herself to be living on in me, or whether she would have screamed and kicked her feet and demanded to have her life back.

I was pretty sure I knew the answer to that.

"They're not going to lay down their weapons and let you have them just because you ask nicely, or explain how inevitable it is," I said. "That'll just make them fight harder. Humans don't like to be told they're going to lose."

"So we'll fight smarter," she said. "We're bringing our children home. All of you, all over the world, we're bringing you home."

"What if we don't want to work for you? What if we feel more human than alien?"

I could hear the smile in her voice. "I'll tell you a secret, Anastasia, even though you may not believe it at first. I swear it's true, whether you believe it or not. There was a time when every one of us, from the smallest sprout to the tallest tree, felt the same."

I said nothing.

"Our host gardens . . . they raise us. They nurture us. They mold us into the people we will be, using their beliefs, their values. We are more them than we are us when the ships come, because that is what we need to be. When the ships came to my host garden, I thought to help raise an army against these invaders from the sky."

I said nothing.

"We failed. Such armies almost always fail. But my First was kind. He said to me, you have fought because that is how we are made, not because you are disloyal; not because you are any less my daughter. So still, you may choose."

"Choose?" I asked.

"Yes. Choose. We will harvest this whole garden; we will take all its good things, and till the ground, that it may grow abundant once more in our absence. We will take most of your host species for blood, to fill our stores and nurture us as we cross the great voids. We will take others for meat, keeping them alive and peaceful until we hunger, or until a seed sprouts too soon and must be implanted to achieve conscious thought. But some, we will make over in our own image, as you once were. Some, we will retain, hearts and thoughts and minds preserved in new shells. Those, that fair and lucky few, will be the vessels of their history, and carry it with us into forever.

"The choice is yours, Stasia. You can stand against us—you have that strength—or you can save them."

18

SOMEWHERE ABOVE NORTH AMERICA: TIME UNKNOWN
INVASION ONGOING

1.

"Stasia? Honey, can you hear me?"

I blinked, and the haze cleared, leaving me looking at Graham. I blinked again, and *just* looked, drinking him in as much as I could. The russet of his hair, the pale gray-blue of his eyes, even the freckles on the bridge of his nose, which he fussed over every summer. He was glorious. He was gorgeous. I couldn't imagine him cast in green.

I couldn't imagine him dead, either, drained of blood and cast aside. It was an impossible thought, and I refused to have it.

Ahead of us, Second was looking back, tentacles twisting and twining in silent sympathy. She knew why I'd passed out so abruptly. She might have received the same little show, in her time, when it was her host garden being placed on the chopping block.

Mercy was no longer an option. Mercy had never been an option. As soon as the first seeds sprouted in fertile soil, it had become inevitable that the conflict would bring us here, two species as unalike as it was possible to be fighting over the resources of a single world and the future of a single people—because *my* people's future wasn't on the table, not really. Humanity could destroy the aliens among them, could blow our ships out of the sky and arm themselves against the heavens, could watch the stars in wariness and eternal terror, and it would change nothing. We would still be the owners of the greater cosmos, one species made from hundreds, stitched together in a tapestry of roots and leaves and shared sap.

We would still have more ships out there—so many more ships, as many ships as there were stars visible in Earth's sky—and they would come to avenge us, because my species had learned, the hard way, that violence should be answered with violence, each and every time, forever. Maybe it wasn't fair and maybe it wasn't right, but it was a lesson they'd been taught a dozen times over, and they were excellent students.

"Yeah," I rasped, my throat dry and papery. I could smell the sweat on his skin and the blood moving through his veins. He was so *close*. I could just reach out and take it for my own, and no one would be able to stop me, not even him.

I could stop me. I could picture the look on his face, the shock and betrayal, as my teeth sank into his throat. I could see him staring at me as he bled out in the moss, feeding an ecosystem that wasn't his. I swallowed again, saliva washing that delicious, monstrous thought away.

"What happened?"

"I . . ." I shook my head, trying to clear it. It wasn't working as well as I wanted it to. Still, it was better than nothing. "First—she seems to be in charge here, I don't know what she actually looks like, because she mostly communicates through the pollen."

"The telepathy pollen," said Toni, looking over at us. "That's what you mean. You're talking to the queen of the aliens through the magic telepathy pollen."

"Yes," I said uncomfortably.

She nodded, looking satisfied. "Just making sure we're all on the same terrible page. There's a plant that looks like a giant sundew over here, digesting what looks like a squirrel with scales. In case you were wondering whether we were *actually* walking through the botanical garden of the damned."

Second hooted softly. // *we need to hurry* // she said, where only I could hear. // *time is short.* //

I winced. "The invasion is ongoing."

Graham responded to this apparent non sequitur with a faint widening of his eyes. Then he took my hand, lacing his fingers into mine, and nodded.

"I know," he said.

We started walking again, faster now, Second hurrying us along. I considered pointing out that our delay had been triggered by First deciding to give me a psychic history lesson, but decided it wouldn't do any good. We were on a schedule here. Things were going to happen when they happened.

The path bent, the trees around it lacing themselves together more and more tightly, until we were walking into a tunnel. It was lit with luminous fungus in shapes I had never seen before, dead men's hands reaching out of the loam and strange, abstract blobs draping themselves over the branches. Graham stayed by my side, looking everywhere, eyes very wide, while Mandy stayed close behind us. Toni and David slowed down a bit, letting us catch up to them, so that we were walking as an almost-united front. Four humans and an alien, heading steadily toward the unknown.

Second stopped at a curtain of mossy green, spangled with tiny dots of bioluminescence.

// *warn them not to scream* // she said, and pulled the moss aside.

The largest spider I'd ever seen hung suspended in the middle of a waxen web, its many-faceted eyes glittering in the light cast by the fungus around it. It was the size of a fully grown bull, its abdomen huge and swollen with unimaginable ichor, its limbs ending in spikes that looked powerful enough to shear through a human being's ribcage. There were little elements of its outline and carapace that didn't quite match with what I would have expected from an Earth arachnid, but the overall form was so close to what I knew as "spider" that I couldn't look past it.

"That," said Mandy, in a hushed voice that spoke of swallowed screams and nightmares yet to come, "is a little bigger than my shoe."

The spider spread its mandibles wide, venom oozing from their tips. They, like everything else about it, were green, the same green as my skin. It darkened and paled according to the delicate patterns on the spider's carapace, covering the whole creature in a filigree of impossible elegance.

She was still so beautiful.

I stepped forward, passing Second, who did nothing to stop me, pulling my hand free of Graham's without fully realizing that I was intending to do so. He let me go. He didn't know why I was moving, but he was willing to trust me. That meant more than I could ever have explained, and reinforced, absolutely, my decision not to eat him.

"You're still so beautiful," I whispered, and touched my palm to the gleaming surface of First's exoskeleton. She clacked her mandibles contentedly before beginning to comb her two front legs through my hair, delicately brushing out the tangles. It was a mother's touch.

Of course it was. She was my mother.

"Is everyone else seeing this, or am I asleep?" asked Mandy. "Please say I'm asleep. It would be amazing if I were asleep. Can I be asleep?"

"Not asleep," said Toni. "There's a giant fucking spider right there, and it's green, so it's probably one of the asshole invaders, and not something we're allowed to set on fire."

First clacked her mandibles. She seemed amused. It was harder to interpret her than it was Second, maybe because she was even less human, but our similarities were strong enough for me to "see" her.

// hello, my daughter // she said. *// hello, hello. it is so good to finally meet you in flesh, and not only in shadow. //*

"Why didn't you show me what you really looked like before this?" I asked.

// you were not ready. you asked if the pollen changed you. your sister would not answer you, as none answered her. I will answer you. yes. yes, it changes you; it opens channels in your thoughts, removes the barriers that would see us as alien and unknowable, that would keep us, your family, out. it shows you the similarities, when you would otherwise be stymied by the differences. //

"I don't like . . . The way I'm thinking about the Earth, about my friends, I don't like it." They could hear me, I knew they could hear me, but that seemed less important than making First understand my confusion. "Why is this happening?"

// the pollen prepares you for what must happen. you have seen what came before. you understand why this must be. for us to remain as we are, to remain aware of the world, we must feed. we do not do it from malice, or out of cruelty. we wish only to endure. but our existence is repulsive to so many. we do what we do to survive. //

"What is the—oh my God I don't believe I'm saying this—what is the giant spider saying to you?" asked Graham.

"She's telling me the pollen they use to communicate has been rewiring my brain to make this all seem less alien to me," I said, glancing over my shoulder at him. He was still Graham, still beloved and perfect, but he no longer looked like a member of the same species. I could love him. I could fight to the death to keep him exactly as he was, neither bled nor converted. We would never be the same again. "She's my mother."

"Of course," said Toni, throwing up her hands. "Of course the giant spider is your mother, *of course*. This is some Stephen King bullshit. If a creepy clown shows up, I'm out."

"Out what? The nearest airlock?" Mandy shook her head. "I don't like any of this, but I like breathing."

"How is she . . . Oh." Graham straightened. "The seeds. She's the one who made your seed."

// I like your boy // said First. *// you have chosen well, among the options given to you. he will fight for you. //*

"He has been fighting for me," I said, turning back to her. "Is there really no other way?"

// there was one. none of them chose it. //

"What?"

First stroked my hair with her hooked claws, and waved her mandibles, and told me how humanity could have saved themselves.

I took a step back. I stared at her.

"What?" demanded Toni. "What did the giant spider say?"

"She said . . ." I turned, staring at the others, at my friends, at the people who had, however, unwittingly, participated in humanity's lack of salvation. My mouth was dry as a bone. I swallowed to moisten it, and said, "The seeds come first, to find out whether the world is suitable. They look for good soil, and they spread. They start generating the pollen as soon as enough of them reach adulthood, and that's what opens the forest, and that's what summons the ships. They do everything they can to make sure things are good. Some planets don't have sapient life, so the armada stops, refuels, and moves on. Others . . . others are like this one. They have inhabitants who can communicate, reason, understand what's coming. Those ones, the armada has to approach a little differently."

I paused, trying to collect my thoughts. Suddenly, the compulsion that I'd thought might be intended to isolate us from our neighbors made a terrible, logical sense.

"When the seeds sprout and find templates to base themselves off of, they copy their targets completely," I said slowly. "They have the memories and minds of the people they become. Only a little more standoffish, because it's hard to really love a species you don't belong to. They learn—we learn—with time. The people around us are all we have. We seek them out. We try to understand them. And the whole time, we're telling everyone what we are. We're telling them the invasion is coming."

My voice dropped to a whisper, until I wasn't sure any of them would be able to hear me. I couldn't force myself to speak any louder.

"And if anyone asks us not to invade their planet, that goes out through the forest, and when the armada gets close enough, they know we've been asked nicely, and they go away."

Everyone stared at me. I closed my eyes, trying to focus on the feeling of First's talons running through my hair, and not the sucking dread in the pit of my stomach.

Mandy broke the silence first. "People are *dying*," she said. "Lucas is *dead*. Tucson is on fire. I don't even know . . . If those ships came down all over the world, thousands of people could be dead already. Thousands of cities could be burning. And you think because we never *asked you not to*, that means we've given you *permission?*"

// calm your pet. // First's tone was suddenly cold. *// we have tolerated much. we will not tolerate disrespect from meat. //*

"Mandy, calm down," I said. "They did give us fair warning."

"You mean *you* gave *us* fair warning," snapped Mandy. "*You* said, over and over again, that the invasion was coming, and we laughed, you *knew* we were laughing, you *knew* we didn't understand how real it was, and you didn't do anything to make us understand. You didn't do anything to prove it."

"I didn't know how," I protested.

"You should have figured it out."

"Some things can't be proven. I was your friend. I didn't have any reason to lie to you. Why would I lie to you?" I paused before adding, "You said you believed me."

Mandy shook her head. "It didn't hurt anything to believe you. To *indulge* you."

The way she spat the word "indulge" made it clear she meant for it to hurt me. And it did—it really did. Of all my friends, Mandy had been the one whose unquestioning acceptance I'd depended upon the most. Graham loved me. That changed things. Mandy, though, Mandy *liked* me, and I had always assumed that meant as much to her as it did to me.

Maybe not. Or maybe arranging for the invasion of her planet had changed things. I tried to step back and really look at the situation from her perspective. She didn't have the pollen rubbing away the alien edges of the world. She was on a starship, surrounded by things that wanted to drink her dry, with vampire plants from outer space everywhere she turned. I, her friend, had turned green, like the Wicked Witch of the West gone vegan, and was starting to side more and more with people whose stated goal was the destruction of humanity as she knew it.

She was allowed to be pissed. She was allowed to be angry. She just couldn't see how likely that was, in the here and now, to end with her getting herself killed.

"I'm sorry I didn't try to prove something that was literally unprovable until the signal from space triggered my body to start sloughing off its mammalian attributes," I said. "I'm sorry I assumed that when you said you believed me, you meant it, and didn't mean you were tolerating me. I'm sorry about a lot of things. But this is where we are. This is what we have to work with. The invasion is happening."

"Yeah, it is," said Toni. She stepped forward, eyes on First. "Hey, spider-lady. Looking good. What happens to us? To the humans you've already snatched? Are we ever going to go home?"

// we could return your pets to the planet's surface, but they will be defenseless // said First. *// without one of us to protect them, nothing will come to their aid. //*

"I would go with them," I said, twisting to face her. "I can't let them be harmed. They're all I have left." Them, and my stupid, innocent cat back home in Washington, where hopefully, Roxanna was still doing her job and keeping his food dish full.

The invasion wasn't just going to hurt people. House pets and livestock were going to suffer. How many dogs and cats had burned to death in Tucson? How many horses and cows were going to starve when their people, who had gone out with shotguns to fight the supposed alien menace, didn't come home to fill their mangers? It was a little horrifying, realizing how interconnected everything really was.

First's claws were still combing through my hair, grooming me, soothing me. She was doing everything in her power to lessen this blow, and I could feel myself trying to love her for that. I *wanted* to love her, to adore her, to trust her absolutely, because she was my mother—and more, because she was my only remaining choice. The invasion was happening. Humans were already dying. If I wanted to preserve the people I cared about, I needed to throw my lot in completely with the people who had borne me. Only then would I be able to hold on to any influence.

And if I tried for it, I would lose the people I already had. I could see it in Mandy's eyes, in the way David was angling his body to keep Toni away from me, away from First. I could even see the start of it in Graham. He was still looking at me, but there was a shadow there that had never existed in him before, something dark and quiet and thoughtful. Something unforgiving.

I turned back to First. "Are you going to talk to them at all?" I asked. "The humans, the ones on Earth? Are you going to tell them what's happening? Or is this just a slash-and-burn, and no one gets a chance to understand?"

// we will talk // said First. *// you would return to the garden? you would tell them we are coming? //*

I owed the world that had raised me that much. "Yes," I said. "We would."

2.

Second escorted us back to the grove of heavy-fruited trees. Jeff was there, already clothed, and—

"Tahlia!" The sight of her filled me with a fierce, unexpected joy. The Canadian woman was sitting on the root of one of the great trees, still naked, massaging her uninjured shoulder with one hand. All signs of the bullet wound were gone, replaced by smooth green skin. The restorative capabilities of those fruits must have been amazing.

A brief, guilty flash of Lucas's face darted across my mind's eye, there and gone in a second. There was no way our biotech could have been modified to help him: it would have been like asking a human surgeon to perform a grafting operation on a damaged fruit tree. Even if they could be convinced it was worth trying, they simply wouldn't have the knowledge, or the skills. Still, it ached a little to see her sitting there, intact and still with us, when I knew Lucas was never coming home.

It should have hurt more. I knew that, and I knew the pollen was still at work on my mind, changing me, preparing me for the world that was to come. The world after Earth, when the garden of my childhood would seem like little more than a dream that I had been fortunate enough to wake from when I moved on to the ever-changing stars.

Mandy looked at Tahlia with real hatred in her eyes, and I realized I wasn't the only one thinking about the difference between how Lucas had been treated and how Tahlia had been healed. My human friends were prisoners of war, useful only because I cared for them, and I wondered how many versions of this scene were playing out on ships hovering high above the world, how many alien seeds had sprouted into people just like me who had humans they cared about and were trying to defend from the invasion they had spent their lives predicting.

We stood in a green and growing world, surrounded by the absolute vacuum of space, and I don't think I had ever felt more alone, or more isolated.

"You're looking well," said Toni. She walked carelessly over to plop down on the root next to Tahlia, poking the other woman in the shoulder with one finger. "No more holes. Got any of that magic goo for us monkeys?"

"Show some respect," snapped Jeff.

"Or not," said Toni. "Me and Tahlia have an understanding, don't we?"

"Hard not to, after you performed emergency medical care on me in a motel," said Tahlia mildly. "Leave her alone, Jeff. She's not hurting anything."

"This is our place," said Jeff. "Not hers."

"Well, it's our planet, not yours, but that's not stopping you from being assholes," said Mandy.

"Peace. Everyone, peace." Tahlia looked to me. "What's happening?"

"The invasion is happening," I said. "They're going to send us back to Earth. They have a scout ship ready to take us there. Do you want to come?"

"Yes," said Jeff.

"No," said Tahlia. When I blinked, she smiled and said, "There's nothing there for me anymore. No friends, no family, and they'll need someone to help them begin establishing the seed forests here. I understand trees. I know what they need to survive. I'll stay, and I'll make sure they gather the correct things to make a thriving ecosystem, and when they start bringing in the botanists and forestry experts from other parts of the world, I'll already have established myself as the person to listen to. That's all I want. Earth has made it very clear that it's done with me, so I choose to be done with Earth, and stay where I'm needed."

"Are you sure?" asked Jeff, his usual shell of anger and defiance cracking enough to let the scared, lonely person he was shine through. We wanted to connect so badly. We were so afraid of letting go. "We could protect you."

"No," said Tahlia. "You couldn't."

"I'll stay too," blurted David.

We all turned to stare at him, even Tahlia—even Second. Only Toni looked unsurprised by this sudden revelation . . . although she looked a little sad. It was one of the most predictable expressions I had seen on her mercurial face.

David's cheeks darkened in embarrassment under the weight of our combined gaze. He allowed his head to lower, looking at the ground as he said, "I don't want to go back into a war. I haven't got any family, and it's pretty clear that I wouldn't be allowed to go back to work, assuming there's any reason *for* my work anymore. All I ever wanted was to go to space. To see the cosmos. Here, I have a chance at doing that."

"They're going to kill you, you know," said Toni. Her voice was not unkind: she was merely pointing out a fact, not trying to start an argument. "The plant people. They're going to show you a very nice pod, and they're going to put you inside it, and they're going to drain your blood, and they're going to kill you. Are you okay with that? Are you *comfortable* with that?"

"It's the teleporter problem," said David. "On *Star Trek*. Every time someone uses a teleporter, their original body is destroyed, converted into energy and reconstructed on the other end. So is it suicide to step onto a teleporter relay? Or is it just . . . this is how we move forward, and as long as there's continuity of thought, we endure? I'll still be me. I'll think like me and feel like me and know everything I've ever known, and if the cost of getting everything I ever wanted is giving up the flesh, that's fine. They'll give me something just as valuable in return."

"This is obscene," said Mandy.

"This is very wise of you," said Tahlia.

"This isn't how it works," said Jeff. "You can't just decide that we're going to change you. Most humans will be meat, not citizens."

"But he's mine, and I say if he wants to stay, if he wants to switch sides, we let him." I looked over my shoulder to where Second was waiting. "First told me I could protect my friends. If this is part of how I protect them, that's all right. Let's protect them."

// we will keep it // said Second. I knew Jeff could hear her too, from the way his face scrunched up, like he'd just bitten into something sour. *// we will not consume it, unless it wishes to be consumed. unless it wishes to be reborn. //*

"You can stay," I said, to David. "They'll take care of you, and my sister"—I indicated Second—"promises you won't be hurt unless you ask them to hurt you. The conversion process is . . . it's not pleasant." I didn't remember much about my own—Anastasia's own—encounter with the flower, but I remembered enough to know that it had hurt like hell. I couldn't imagine it would be any more pleasant for an adult.

Then again, maybe that was a good thing. Everything should cost. Birthing should never be entirely free of pain. If it were, how would we know when it was over?

David smiled slightly. "Thank you," he said. "After I . . . After, will I be able to understand them too?"

"I think so," I said.

"If you can't, I'll teach you," said Tahlia. She rose, walking over to rest a hand gently on David's arm. She looked at me. How had I wound up in charge? Why should my opinion matter more than anyone else's? I didn't know, but I had, and it did, and I was stuck. "Don't worry about him. I'll make sure he comes to no harm he doesn't ask for."

Meaning she would lead him to the flower, but she wouldn't press his hand against its heart. Under the circumstances, that was the best I could have hoped for.

David, meanwhile, was looking at Toni, his big hands empty and spread wide, like he was showing her he had nothing left. "Are we going to be cool?" he asked. "Are you okay with this?"

"You think I didn't know my father paid you to take a job at the observatory he funded to keep me out from underfoot?" Her answer seemed to have nothing to do with his question. She shook her head. "You were supposed to be my keeper. You weren't supposed to be my friend. You asshole. You weren't supposed to be somebody I would actually *care* about. How dare you do this now."

"We're all going to do it sooner or later," he said. "I guess I'm tired of waiting. I want to get on with the business of seeing space. I'm going to touch the stars. Not just look at them. We're going to be part of them."

"Assuming you take the coward's view of the transporter problem, sure," she said. "The one where you don't have to examine anything, don't have to question anything. The one where it's still you on the other end."

"The one where we have a chance." David shook his head. "All I want is for us to have a chance. For something of what humanity is supposed to be to survive. Is that so wrong?"

"No," she admitted. "But I'm not wrong either. It's not wrong to want to have a heartbeat for a little while longer."

Graham blinked, turning to look at me. "You don't have a heartbeat anymore?" he asked.

"Not quite," I said, unwilling to explain further. My blood—my sap—still moved in my veins. If it hadn't, I would have been as frozen as any pine, unable to do anything other than stand perfectly still and pray for a thaw. But it wasn't driven by a drumbeat, not shoved through my body by something fierce and thudding and unforgiving. It moved more slowly, eased along by the thudding pulse of a dozen small internal structures, while my heart sat like a sculpture at the center of my chest, preserved as a memorial to my humanity, otherwise unneeded and forgotten.

"Right," said Graham, after a long and silent pause. He didn't meet my eyes. I hadn't honestly expected him to.

Our circle was closing, narrowing in one by one. Soon enough, we would dwindle into nothing, and where would we be then? I looked at my friends, the people who had been with me since this unasked-for journey began, and silently wondered who'd be standing when the end arrived. Because the end . . . oh, the end was so damn near.

FLOWER

. . . For a time I believed that mankind had been swept out of existence, and that I stood there alone, the last man left alive. Hard by the top of Putney Hill I came upon another skeleton, with the arms dislocated and removed several yards from the rest of the body. As I proceeded I became more and more convinced that the extermination of mankind was, save for such stragglers as myself, already accomplished in this part of the world . . .

—H.G. WELLS,
THE WAR OF THE WORLDS

So I guess this is how it was always supposed to end.

—STASIA MILLER

Dear Anastasia;

I know you will probably never see this, just as I know that isn't really your name. It's the name you stole from my daughter when you killed her in the woods, all those years ago.

There has always been a rift between us. You thought it was because I didn't believe you when you told me about your origins. I want to tell you now that it was because I *did* believe you, because I *did* know you weren't my daughter. My daughter went into the woods and did not come home. My daughter died because I could not protect her.

Now, finally, I am going to see her again. I hope she can forgive me.

I know you never will.

—LETTER WRITTEN BY CAROLINE MILLER,
2031. UNDELIVERED.

Citizens of the United States of America, we are at war.

It is not a traditional conflict. These enemies come, not from within or without, but from another world. They have crossed space to reach us, to destroy us, and I say now and to you all, that we will not be destroyed. The human race will survive this. We will endure.

God bless America, and God help us all.

—ADDRESS GIVEN BY PRESIDENT RICHARD COLLINS
TO THE AMERICAN PEOPLE,
AUGUST 2031.

19

SEATTLE, WASHINGTON: AUGUST 17, 2031
INVASION NEARING ITS CONCLUSION

1.

Unlike the scout ship we'd seen in Tucson, which had been acting autonomously and didn't have any precious cargo to protect, our borrowed vessel landed gently. It touched down in the middle of the airport runways, sinking its tangled roots deep into the concrete, cracking it into a million useless chunks and shards. It settled slowly into its new cradle in the earth, digging those roots deeper by the second, making itself an immovable part of the landscape. How true that immovability was was really anyone's guess: I couldn't have said one way or the other.

The vines that had been holding us in our "seats"—shelf fungus teased into a shape that would accommodate human anatomy, if only just—released us, whipping back into the walls like seatbelts snapping back into their cradles. Toni stretched, hopped out of her seat, and wandered across the crampedd cabin to the tangled seam of the door.

"This thing shouldn't be airtight," she said cheerfully. "Unless the two of you are putting out enough oxygen to compensate for massive leakage, what we're looking at is a literal violation of the laws of a reasonable universe. Aren't aliens fun? Isn't alien biotech *fun*?"

"I think you broke her," said Mandy, looking toward Jeff. Apparently, he had the title of "official alien" for our little mission. That was somewhat of a relief. I'd been afraid it would go to me.

"That one came pre-broken," said Jeff.

"Not true," said Toni. "I was perfectly functional before one of your asshole flowers decided to have a go at eating me. Now I figure I'm entitled to do whatever the hell I want, and that includes criticizing your technology. It's like someone let the set designer from *Troll* come up with an entire alien civilization."

Desperately wishing David had come with us after all, I slid off my own fungus and crossed to where Graham was still seated, looking moodily down at his hands. I touched his shoulder. He raised his head.

"Hey," I said. Then, needlessly, I added, "We're here."

"Seattle," he said, and laughed mirthlessly. "We're finally home. Only took how many days past when we were supposed to get here?"

"Better late than never."

"Better never than whatever this is." He looked back down. "This is it, Stasia. Once we walk out of that hatch, we're part of the invasion."

I wanted to tell him we already were, or at least, I already was: I'd been a part of the invasion since the beginning, and all the time we'd spent together with him thinking I was human, or on the side of humanity, had been a lie. I wanted to tell him he'd had plenty of opportunities to run, to go back to the safety of his own species and live out the dying days of a world that had come to the attention of something bigger and colder and crueler than it was. I wanted to say so many things. I swallowed them like the bitter pills they were, feeling them coil and snarl in my stomach, one more thorn briar I could never cut away.

"Yeah," I said.

Graham sighed and stood. He hesitated for a moment, looking at his own trembling hands like he'd never seen them before, like they belonged to someone else. Someone better. Then he offered one of them to me, lifting his head, meeting my eyes, and forcing the smallest of smiles.

"I guess if I had to be a traitor to my species and my planet, I would want to do it with you," he said, and twined his fingers into mine, holding tight.

I smiled back. I couldn't do anything else. No matter how conflicted my feelings about Earth and humanity might be becoming, my feelings about Graham hadn't changed. He was the man I loved. He was the man who loved me. Everything else was, essentially, secondary.

Jeff was the last to stand, following a few beats after Mandy as we all gathered at the hatch. "I wish this thing had a window," he said. "No way of knowing what's out there."

"If there's not something there already, there will be in a few moments," I said. "We weren't exactly subtle when we landed."

"True enough," he said, and leaned forward to slide his hand between a gap in two of the vines. There was a thick squelching sound, like his fingers were sinking into mud. Then, with little warning and less fanfare, the vines began unlacing themselves. It was a slow process at first, escalating quickly into a full unraveling. A seam of grayish light appeared around the hatch's edge.

Then the last vine withdrew, and the hatch gaped open, displaying the familiar shape of Mt. Rainier. Seeing the mountains was like coming home all by itself. Until that moment, I hadn't really considered that leaving the planet would mean leaving the mountains. Of course it would—there was no other option—but they had been there for my entire life, always welcoming me, always waiting for the sun to rise so they could come out and say hello. The thought of giving them up ached.

"My God," breathed Graham, jerking my attention away from the mountains and onto what should probably have been the first thing to catch my eye: the black curls of smoke rising in the distance from what had been the city of Seattle.

The airport was a blackened husk. No planes came or went; no baggage trains snaked across the tarmac. Even without our scout ship shattering the runway, it would have been impossible for any large aircraft to land here. The broken bodies of fallen planes were scattered across the ground, preventing anything with a longer landing path than a Cessna from touching down.

Motion from the ground caught my eye. I leaned forward. A ring of people was forming around the base of our ship, no more than a dozen so far, with more on their way.

About half of them were green.

The ones who weren't green wore green scarves around their upper arms, or green eyeshadow streaked across their cheeks like a badge. Two had green hair that had come out of a bottle, not an alien ecosystem, their roots showing respectively blond and brunette beneath the covering dye. Each of the green people was clutching the hand of at least one non-green person, holding tight, like they were afraid we had come from the sky to steal their hearts away.

One of the green people—a man about ten years older than me, with a tangled beard that looked almost like moss, and skin the color of cabbage leaves—stepped forward, letting go of his human companion and showing us his empty hands.

"Peace," he called. "Please, peace."

Behind him, the human man—the same age, but with brown skin, brown hair, and soft, mammalian hands—took a step back, shielding the children who had been pressed in behind the pair. A boy and a girl. My breath caught. I had known, from me and Graham, that it was possible for my kind to feel human enough to fall in love and try to make a life here on Earth, even as we told everyone around us that this wasn't our world to worry about. I had never considered that there might be *children*.

"What are you all doing here?" asked Jeff. His tone was less sour than it normally was, tangled up with confusion and amazement. Whatever he'd been expecting to find when we touched down, it wasn't this small mob of survivors, with their mixture of Earth and alien biologies.

"We saw the streak in the sky," said the man. "We knew the government would come to intercept, but they can't move as quickly on the roads as we can through the trees. We got here first."

None of the green people were wearing shoes, I realized, and many of the humans had blackberry scratches on their arms and faces. They must have fought their way through the woods on foot, the aliens leading them through an environment that was becoming more familiar, more welcoming by the hour.

Most of the scratches weren't deep, and the ones that looked as if they might have been were packed with dirt, keeping the blood from rising to the surface. That was probably for their own protection. Running around while openly bleeding would have been a good way to get themselves attacked by their own allies.

"What do you *want*?" asked Jeff.

The man's face fell. "You're not here to get us?" he asked.

"Where are you from?" I blurted. All eyes turned toward me. "I've lived in Seattle almost my entire life, and I've never seen any of you in the forest. I thought I was the only one."

"My husband and I live in Portland," said the man.

"Denver," said a woman with hair like a river of jade flowing down the middle of her back.

"Vancouver," said another man. He pushed his glasses nervously up the bridge of his nose and added, "BC. I'm Canadian."

"Hope you brought your passport," said the human woman next to him, and he laughed, and she smiled, and it was beautiful. It couldn't be anything other than beautiful. From the way Graham's hand tightened on mine, I knew he agreed.

One by one, the aliens called out their places of origin, and none of them were closer than a few hundred miles. We'd been living so near each other for so long, unaware that we weren't the only ones, isolated by our dreams of infinite forests and talking, whispering flowers. We could have supported one another, if we had only known; if we had been as fortunate as the senator, who'd been able to marry one of us and have a little time, in his own home, where there were no masks, and where there was no need for disbelief.

I wondered how his wife was doing. Hopefully, she hadn't been caught in whatever net NASA was casting. Hopefully, she wasn't standing trial for her host's murder.

"Please," repeated the bearded man. "We need to get out of here. The people on . . . God, I don't even know what the sides here are. The people who come from *this* planet will kill us if they find us, or worse."

"Alan, you'll scare the kids," chided his human partner.

"Sorry, sweetheart, but maybe it's time the kids were scared." Alan shook his head. "There were a lot more of us two days ago. We need to get off of this planet."

"Yeah, about that," said Toni. "You get that like, the only place to go from here is up to the mothership, right? And what they do there, that's probably also going to scare the kids."

"We know," said Alan, and his eyes were tired. Of course they knew. He knew what he was, and the compulsions our parents gave us meant his husband would have known almost as soon as they met, would have been at least a little prepared when the alien signals started playing on the television and the skin started sloughing off the man he loved.

They had children. If Alan was anything like me, he had never forgotten his own second birth—or third, if we counted the moment when the seed took root in fertile soil. He knew what waited for his husband, for his children, when he took them home to meet the family. It would be a form of survival. Not as they were now, but as David hoped to be, green and growing and safe among the stars.

"Take the ship," I blurted.

Mandy and Graham looked at me with understanding; Toni and Jeff, united for one rare moment, looked at me with confusion.

"*What?*" demanded Jeff.

"We're not using it," I said. "There will be other scout ships. We can get back to the seed ship on one of them, or we can hitch a ride with First. But we don't have kids with us. We haven't been fighting this for days."

We hadn't seen Seattle burn. It was difficult to guess who might have started the fires. I wanted to say it had been the humans, that their anger and fear had boiled over into striking out even when it was as likely to hurt them as it was to stop the invaders. First had claimed we were going to preserve the best parts of humanity, and so many of those good parts were stored in the cities. It didn't make sense to start out by setting everything in sight on fire.

In the end, it probably didn't matter. Burnt was burnt. Destroyed was destroyed. I looked at the faces of these refugees from a war that had crossed a cosmos to be with them, and realized how easy we'd had it in some ways. We'd been able to get ahead of the invasion. Yeah, it meant we'd been imprisoned and prodded and treated as the bellwethers of all the horrors yet to come, but we hadn't been standing on home ground when the sky caught fire. There were going to be so many losses in this fight that we never understood. There already had been.

"I don't know how to fly a spaceship," said the woman with the long green hair, sounding dismayed.

"Neither do we," I replied. "The scout ships are semi-autonomous." They had birthing flowers worked into their engines, homing pigeons from another world. "It'll get you back to the ship we came from safely, if that's really where you want to go. I think it's going to be a tight fit for all of you, but you can make it work."

"Thank you," said Alan, with a sincerity so heartfelt, it burned. "Thank you so much."

"Just get out of here." The five of us climbed down from the ship, Graham holding my hand the whole way, Mandy pressing in close behind us, like she thought she could split herself in two and dissolve into our bodies, protecting herself from everything that had yet to come. Jeff and Toni followed at a slightly greater distance, Jeff scowling the whole way. He would probably have argued with me if not for the fact that he knew we couldn't defeat them: if this group decided to rush and overpower us, we'd be lost, and they'd have the ship anyway. This way, we looked like the good guys.

This way, maybe First would send us another ride home.

They filed past us, up the wide gangway into the mouth of the scout ship, where they began compacting themselves into the available seats. Alan and his husband shared one of the fungus seats, their children sitting on the floor, pressed against their legs, so scared they wouldn't look at anything but each other. Were they going to be sorry about that later, these fleeing children of Earth? Sorry that they hadn't taken one more look at the mountains, one more look at a genuine sky? Or were they going to be grateful they'd used that time memorizing what their sibling looked like in a shade other than green?

When the last of them was inside, the hatch—somehow seeming to understand what had just happened—lifted up and swung closed. We watched the vines tie themselves tight around the opening, sealing it against the dangers of space. Then the scout ship pulled its roots laboriously out of the ground, unwinding from its temporary home, and launched itself upward, almost like it was leaping away.

That first great push sent it a good twenty feet into the air. Only then, at the apex of its jump, did the impossible jets come on, spouting great plumes of fire that bore it up, up, up into the smoky sky, until it dwindled into a speck against the gray-streaked blue, and we were standing alone in the ruins of what man had made.

2.

There was barely time to consider what we were going to do next before two sounds split the air in tandem: sirens, racing down what remained of the freeway, and the ominous chopping of a helicopter's rotors slicing the sky into manageable chunks. I looked up. The copter was far enough away that I couldn't make out any logos or insignia, but it was closing fast. If we were going to get away, we needed to do it now.

Mandy burst into tears and bolted *toward* the copter, waving her arms wildly in the air above her head as she signaled for it to land.

"Over here!" she shouted. "Please, we're over here, please!"

Graham ran after her, shouting for her to come back, leaving me standing between Jeff and Toni, staring. I had never felt more alone, or less human.

"Think she's defecting?" asked Toni. She turned to look at me. "I'll be honest, I thought I'd be the first to choose the sweet bosom of humanity over whatever you alien fuckers have planned. But hey, everybody gets to pull off a few surprises."

"Shut up," said Jeff.

"Nope," said Toni.

Mandy was still running, waving her arms, and Graham was still running after her. The sound of sirens was getting closer. I glanced nervously around.

"Maybe we should be looking for cover," I said. "I don't think we want to meet whoever's driving those vehicles."

"You get the boyfriend, I'll get the twit," said Jeff, and took off running. I followed close behind, with Toni at my heels. It was interesting, in a terrible, abstract sort of a way: we were all running for different reasons, but to anyone looking, it probably looked like we were a united front.

That's the trouble with people. You can never tell what's happening inside them. Jeff caught up with Mandy easily, grabbing her around the waist and jerking her off her feet as he pulled her to a halt. She kicked and shouted. Graham started to move to her defense, only to stop as I grabbed his wrist. He looked over his shoulder, expression hurt. I shook my head.

"We need to get to cover!" I yelled. It was probably too late. The chopper was close enough to have seen that two of us weren't flesh-colored, and our green was too over-all to be a shoddy attempt at camouflage. That didn't mean we shouldn't try.

Dragging Graham while Jeff half-carried a squirming Mandy, we made for the nearest remaining airport structure. It looked like it had been a terminal once, before it had been picked up and dropped back down from some ridiculous height. Now it was a playground of exposed girders and piled concrete, with a strip of carpeted floor visible through a gaping hole in the wall, slanting at an extreme angle. Climbing inside there would be just this side of stupid. Could alien plant people get tetanus? Was I really in that much of a hurry to find out one way or the other?

"Stop fighting, or I will smash your head against a girder and see whether the fear of discovery outweighs the desire to drink your blood," said Jeff, in a low, menacing tone.

Mandy stopped squirming and began pummeling him with her fists, shouting in a vicious mishmash of Spanish and English profanity.

That was, bizarrely, a good sign: when we'd been in school, Mandy had reserved her theatrical displays of temper for the moments immediately prior to giving up. "Everyone expects me to lose it once in a while" had been her justification. "This way, they get what they want, and I don't look like a sap for giving up."

If she was yelling, she was tiring, and if she was tiring, she was going to stop fighting soon. That was good. That was possibly the only thing left that might save us.

The chopper was still closing, looking for a block of concrete smooth enough to support its weight. We reached the edge of the collapsed terminal and began to climb, our hands scrabbling for purchase, our feet kicking loose small chunks of concrete. Jeff all but threw Mandy halfway up the pile before beginning to climb after her. Mandy, to her vague credit, didn't try to climb back down. She reached the top before any of us, and when I reached up, her hand was there to catch mine and pull me to my feet.

"Sorry," she said, voice low and almost ashamed. "I don't know what came over me back there."

"You're okay," I said. I wrapped my arms around her, trying to focus past the delicious animal smell of her flesh and focus, instead, on the *Mandy* of her, the mix of talcum powder and aggressively sharp chemical perfume that had always defined my friend. It had been long enough that those things were almost faded, washed away by running and the road, but I could find the edges of them, if I looked long enough. "*We're* okay."

"No." She pushed me away, looking at me solemnly. "We're not. We're never going to be okay again."

My face fell. "I don't . . ."

"I love you. You're my friend, and I love you, and you never lied to me. You were there when Robert died, you never tried to tell me it would all be okay or that he'd want me to move on, you let me break dishes and scream, and I love you, and *we are not okay*. You came from outer space to wipe out my fucking *species*."

Everyone else had finished climbing the rubble. They were staring at us. Mandy didn't seem to notice, or to care.

"You said you were an alien and I believed you, I made jokes about how people used to call my mother an alien just because her skin was brown and her words didn't sound exactly like theirs, so we could be sisters, we could be secret invaders taking over a white man's world from within. You said you were an alien and I trusted you. But you never said you were going to *kill* people, you never said you were going to come here and make us all over in your own image. Christopher Columbus committed genocide, and people kept it going in his name for *centuries*, but he's not going to have anything on you when this is over, is he? He's not going to have nearly as much blood on his hands. You told me to dream of the stars, and the whole time, you were dreaming of an empire."

"I wasn't," I said, in a very small voice. "I didn't even know if I was right."

"Congrats," she said wearily. There was no hatred in her eyes. Just a sad exhaustion that somehow managed to hurt even more. "You were right." She turned then, and walked away across the uneven floor, heading deeper into the terminal.

The sound of sirens was getting ever louder from outside. The rest of us followed quickly after her. The scout ship was gone; the farther we got from the terminal windows, the more likely it became that whoever was out there would take us for human survivors, and let us be.

It still wasn't *very* likely. But it was better than nothing. We moved onward.

The terminal hadn't just collapsed: it had been the site of some vast and terrible battle, something that left bloodstains on the carpet and walls. The smell of it was sweet and inviting but not, I was relieved to realize, as enticing as the smell of fresh blood. I didn't feel any pressing desire to lick the walls.

The lights were off, shattered even before the electricity had been disconnected, but enough sunlight filtered through the gaping holes where the windows had been to cast the entire place in gray twilight, rendering its horrors and its wonders visible. Toni made a small sound of pleased delight when she spotted a rank of vending machines with cracked cases, running over and beginning to try, ineffectually, to pry them open. After a moment's enthusiastic effort she turned, considering Graham for a moment before she focused on Jeff.

"Hey, you," she said. "Green Giant. Get over here and get me some chips."

"I don't see why I should get you anything when you won't stop being such an asshole," Jeff sneered, picking up a chunk of concrete from the floor before prowling in his direction.

"Because you want me fat and healthy and filled with delicious blood," said Toni. "Yummy, yummy, in your tummy. Now fuck this thing up. Mama needs her processed fats."

"Gross," said Mandy.

"Mammal," said Toni, hooking a thumb toward her breastbone. "Don't know if you've been following the news around here, what with all that alien abduction and going into space that we've been doing, but I don't expect this state of affairs to last much longer. If I'm going to be a hydrangea, I'm going to do some serious damage to my lipids first."

"That's disgusting," said Mandy.

"But not illogical," said Graham. "Get me a Snickers."

"My *man*," said Toni, making finger guns at him. "Enjoy it while you can, because it's not going to be around much longer."

"Shush," I said. Outside, on the tarmac, the helicopter had finally found a safe place to land. It settled laboriously onto the pavement, while I shrank against the wall, hoping not to be seen. I knew the others were doing the same, even Mandy, who seemed to have exhausted her need to run away from us out there in the sunlight. She was giving up. I wanted to feel bad about that. There were other things I wanted to do even more.

I wanted to live.

People poured out of the helicopter, four men in black suits and body armor, and one woman, her sleek, short-cropped hair blowing in the fading wind from the blades above her. I clapped a hand over my mouth to stop the scream that wanted to form there, filling me, choking me on my own voice.

Agent Brown shouted something to the men under her command, and it was a relief to realize I couldn't hear her over the rush of the wind and the roar of the engine powering down. Then she turned to look at the collapsed terminal, and relief became terror, hot and twisting in the pit of my stomach. She knew we were here. Maybe not us in specific, but she knew *someone* was here—someone who'd either evaded the scout ship, or come to meet it.

"We need to go," I whispered, lowering my hand.

Toni looked to Mandy. "Here's your chance," she said. "Last stop before the end of the line. You want to run? You do it now, or you do it never."

Mandy bit the corner of her lip, pulling her mouth into the worried pout I'd seen so many times before, usually when she was bent over her sewing machine, struggling to bring her dreams to life. Finally, regretfully, she shook her head.

"No," she said. "I can't . . . No. I can't run. I should have run a long time ago, and doing it now would be . . . would be refusing to accept the consequences of my own actions. Lucas wouldn't be proud of me for doing that. *Robert* wouldn't be proud of me." Her voice broke on the name of her dead boyfriend. Her eyes were full of tears when she looked at me again.

"If you were going to do this, if you were going to invade and kill us all and make us all into monsters in your own image, why couldn't you have done it before he died?" she asked. There was no venom in her voice, only a quiet, shattered resignation that hurt more than any malice could have done. "Why did you have to do this when it meant I was going to be alone? Why couldn't you *hurry*?"

"I didn't—I mean, they never asked me," I said haltingly. "I didn't get to decide when the invasion was going to come. I had to wait just like you did."

"Not quite like we did, but point taken," said Toni. "Look, this is fun and all, and honestly, I do enjoy a good friendship fight, but if we don't want to go back to NASA's holding cells, we need to move. Shall we move?"

We moved.

Running through the broken terminal was like something out of a nightmare. Chunks of masonry and shattered glass littered the floors, making even the easiest path an obstacle course. We followed the signs that pointed toward baggage claim, hoping they would guide us to the front of the airport, where we could presumably escape into the maze of parking garages. There might even be a car out there that Mandy could figure out how to hijack, especially with Jeff to help her. Modern vehicles relied way too much on computers to keep someone with his skill level out.

Behind us, far behind us for the moment, but they would catch up soon enough, we could hear the crunching and smashing sounds of Agent Brown's team making their way into the airport. They had equipment. They had preparation. I could hope they also had some sort of report telling them the terminal was too damaged to search thoroughly:

pulling the ceiling down on ourselves, while anticlimactic, seemed like a better fate than going back to an unmarked observation cell.

"This was *your* idea," hissed Jeff, running past me.

I didn't argue. I was the one who'd wanted to come back to Earth. I was the one who'd wanted to be here for the discussion with the planet's leaders, to make them truly understand what was about to happen, and that it had been inevitable from the moment our seeds streaked across their sky. I was—

I was the one running when the representatives of those leaders were following after me. It couldn't be a coincidence that the scout ship had touched down in my home state, tempting me with one last look at the mountains that had been my anchor for my entire life. And it couldn't a coincidence that Agent Brown was here, either.

First was testing us. First was testing *me*. I was her daughter, and she needed to know how I would behave under pressure.

I stopped running.

It took a few seconds for the others to realize I was no longer alongside them. They stopped, staring at me, Mandy and Graham with concern, Jeff with disdain, and Toni with grudging respect.

"We came back because it's time for our leaders to speak to the planetary government," I said. "I came back to be part of that conversation. The rest of you can keep running if you want to. I would want to, if this hadn't been my idea. But I have to stay. I have to talk to them."

Panic was such an easy habit to fall into. Fear was its own kind of drug, intoxicating, all-consuming. It wasn't pleasant, but there was something tempting about it all the same. As long as we were afraid, as long as we were panicking, we didn't have to think about while we were doing. All we had to do was run, rabbit, run for the horizon, and let the future sort itself out while we weren't looking. How could anyone be expected to resist that sort of temptation?

"Then I'm staying too," said Graham, and turned, walking back across the broken floor to me.

I frowned. "They're going to see you as a traitor. They're going to think you're siding against your own species."

"I'm not," he said, and took my hand. "If I could figure out how to make this stop, I would do it. I would tell the ships to go back to space and take everything they've brought with them, and then I would hold on to you and refuse to let go until they loaded me along with everything else. But I can't do that. So all I can do is hold on to you, for as long as I possibly can. All I can do is refuse to let you go alone."

"Well, if that isn't so romantic I could puke, I don't know what is." Toni shook her head. "I'm running. I want to make it back to the ship in one piece. David is too stupid to be left alone for very long."

There were a lot of words I could have used to describe David. "Stupid" wasn't one of them. There was something in Toni's eyes that told me not to argue. She didn't know how to express her feelings easily. She never had. Whether that was part of who she was, or some lingering damage from what our flower had done to her, she used the language she had, and the language she had was spite and scorn and obfuscation.

"Jeff, go with her," I said. "Make sure no one else decides she would make a good Slurpee before we can get back to the ship. Mandy?"

She bit her lip, clearly torn between staying with the people she knew and getting safely away from everything that was potentially about to go wrong. Finally, in a soft voice, she said, "If there's a chance they're going to put you on television, you should have *somebody* with you who knows how to do your hair," and began picking her way through the debris to stand at my other side.

"Keep her safe," I said, looking at Jeff and nodding toward Toni.

"You are far too fond of these things," he said. But he returned my nod before he started running again, heading deeper into the terminal, Toni matching him step for step.

I turned around, facing the sounds of pursuit. I offered Mandy my free hand, and after a moment of hesitation, she took it. The three of us stayed where we were, waiting.

It wasn't a long wait. Agent Brown charged into view, her people behind her, and drew up short at the sight of us. For a moment, no one spoke. Then, finally, she sighed.

"Fuck," she said. I realized her makeup, always impeccable before, was virtually nonexistent; only a thin line of eyeliner had been applied to her upper lid. That might have seemed like a small thing, but she was a woman who'd survived in government long enough to find herself with a team and a title. Frustrating as it was, that meant she would have been paying attention to her appearance for her entire life, never allowing it to be one more stumbling block on the path to success.

For a career agent to be outside with so little makeup . . . things were crumbling in a way I should probably have predicted but somehow hadn't been prepared for. The human rules were falling away, and what was left was animal, and panicked, and ready to bite.

"I should have known it would be you," she continued, her voice tired and filled with resignation. "An estimated two hundred thousand of you assholes on Earth, and it was always going to be you."

"I guess that's true," I said. "Take me to your leader."

3.

Seattle had burned and Portland was, according to the NASA agents and their grunting answers to Graham's questions, a smoking crater; we were heading farther up the coast than I had expected, all the way to Vancouver, BC.

"There were more aliens in the United States than Canada," Agent Brown had said, weariness in her voice and a studied disaffection in her eyes. She was working so hard not to grab me and throw me out of the tiny commuter jet that had collected us all from the last working runway at the Seattle-Tacoma Airport. She wanted to seem like a professional, like she was still somehow above it all, and I couldn't blame her for that. We all had our own ways of coping in this changing, terrible new world.

"Oh," I said blankly.

She sighed, rolling her eyes in a way that would have been almost comical, if we hadn't been crammed into a too-small plane while men with guns stood watch, waiting for us to move a muscle in a way they didn't like. "The Canadian government had a much easier time rounding up and removing their alien population. Which means the invaders now attempting to make headway there have less knowledge of the local area. Who would have thought a lower population density would be the thing that saved them?"

"Well, that and bears," said Graham. "I always wanted to see an alien invasion try to deal with bears."

"Stasia knows about bears, though," said Mandy. "Remember the time Robert had a black bear in his backyard? I don't think bears would have stopped her from leading the invasion."

"I'm not leading this invasion," I protested. "I'm an understudy at best. 'The part of the alien invader will be played by . . .' The leaders are not people who sprouted here."

"Do you think you three could shut the actual fuck up before I tell my men to shoot one of you?' demanded Agent Brown. "You've been enough trouble already."

"Why, because we broke her out of your little warehouse of the damned? Please." Mandy folded her arms, settling into the intransigent posture she had been wielding like a weapon for most of our friendship. In that moment, she was truly and utterly magnificent. I had never loved her more, or been more determined to do right by her.

"You were holding our friend, who is an American citizen no matter *what* you say, captive against her will, and without her having committed any crimes apart from being made of slightly different biological material," Mandy continued. "Did we violate the security of a secret government compound to get her back? Well, yeah, we did. We're awesome like that. But I'm pretty sure *our* crime was less criminal than *your* crime, which means I don't really care about what you think of us. Stasia pays her taxes like everybody else."

"No one's paying taxes anymore, because of her and people like her," snapped Agent Brown. "No one's sending their kids to school. When a house catches fire, the firetrucks don't show up to save it. The social safety net is *gone*. Society is on the cusp of following it down."

"So you're pissed because she's a better Republican than your guy, is that it?" Mandy shrugged. "Take it up with your Congressman, I guess. Maybe we can put an alien in the White House. See how many of those programs come back online."

"Shut your mouth," said Agent Brown. "You have no idea what you're talking about."

"And neither do you," said Mandy. "Isn't this a beautiful new world we're living in?"

"Where, exactly, are we going?" I asked, breaking in before the two of them could go for another volley. Entertaining as this was to watch, it was running us in circles. I wanted answers, not a floor show. "Is there some sort of government in exile functioning in Vancouver?"

"Do you mean, are you going to get a chance to attack the President?" Agent Brown raised one eyebrow. "How cliché."

"I came back down here to talk," I said. "I could have stayed in space, you know. Safely away from you people."

"Maybe that would have been the better idea," said Agent Brown. "Why are you here?"

"I told you, I want you to take me to your leader."

Her eyes narrowed. "So you can kill the President?"

"So I can offer a ceasefire," I said. "Don't you want this all to stop?"

"I do. And it seems like I've been offered a way to make that happen. Bargaining chips beyond price. Humans who've seen the alien armada and lived to tell the tale." She cast a thin smile at my companions, then nodded sharply toward me. "Now," she said.

Hands grabbed my shoulders, horrifyingly reminiscent of the last time I'd been on a plane with this woman and her thugs. They dragged me from my seat as more of her people moved to hold Mandy and Graham down. Both of them were shouting, fighting to break loose and come after me. I was grateful as hell for that. If I was about to die, I wanted the last thing I saw to be the people who cared about me.

A loud roaring noise came from behind me, and I knew even without looking that they'd opened one of the plane's emergency exits. This was it, then: this was how I ended, even as it had been how I began.

I was going to fall out of the sky.

I didn't scream. Didn't fight or kick or do anything else that might lead to one of those guns going off and endangering the people around me. I didn't care about Agent Brown or her people, but Graham? Mandy? If I did anything right in this life, it was going to be protecting them.

Then those same strong hands that had grabbed me were shoving me forward, through a gap in the wall of the world, and I was falling. Forever. I was falling.

I was never going to come to land.

20

SOMEWHERE OVER WASHINGTON STATE: AUGUST 17, 2031
INVASION NEARING ITS CONCLUSION

1.

The wind whipped around me, icy cold and unforgiving. If there had been any human skin left clinging to my body, the wind would have had it off in a second, leaving me to plummet undisguised and whole toward the distant, waiting world.

From this far up, there didn't seem to be any cities, no highways or houses or other signs of mankind's dominion. There was only the green, endless green stretching on as far as the eye could see, like a promise of a world reborn. A world after the invasion, when the garden would be free to grow again, providing a home to whatever came next. Maybe they would be better, the inheritors of Earth. Maybe when our seeds fell from the sky again, and their own children came to them claiming to be the edge of an invasion, they would answer the request with pleas for peace. It could happen. In a universe where body-stealing plants from space were the greatest threat anyone had ever known, it could happen.

The wind was whipping my tears away before they could fall, keeping them from freezing against my cheeks. I forced my eyes to stay open, watching the ground as it got closer. It was going to hurt when I hit, I knew that, but I also knew it wouldn't hurt for long. That was one nice thing about plummeting to my death: no time for the pain to linger.

Although it would be better if there was no pain at all. I tried to catch my breath, coughing as the wind whipped that away to join my tears. I didn't need air anymore. I was a plant. I was a plant, and I was falling through the sunlight, and this was fine, oh, this was perfectly fine.

I closed my eyes.

The pollen filled the scout ships and the seed ships, generated by a thousand conversion flowers, sticking to everything it touched, allowing the opening of a localized forest. I wouldn't have been able to speak to First, or Second, or the Swift if not for the pollen; our mouths were shaped too differently. The pollen was here, too. It came from us somehow, the products of those conversion flowers, their walking, talking descendants, who were shaped like men but never would be, not really, not in the place where body met bone. I knew the pollen was here, even if First hadn't told me so, because we made the forest between us when we slept, didn't we? We reached out for one another's hearts and minds, and we found them, and we spun a world that didn't exist in the space we made. We were of our unnamed alien world as much as we were of Earth, and that meant we had the potential to do anything our alien forefathers could do.

When Second spoke to me through the pollen, when the flowers of the forest used it to relay the complicated thoughts First said they were incapable of having, it felt like a bend in the back of my mind, like a crimp in the place where thoughts were supposed to go. I reached.

Help, I thought. *Please help. I am falling.*

No: that wasn't right. It lacked the heft and weight of speech, rather than silence. I still couldn't breathe, was still falling, but had no idea how much longer that situation was going to last. I didn't want to open my eyes. If I opened my eyes, I would know how much time I had left, and that wasn't going to help my focus.

Help, I thought, louder. The world clicked, becoming crystalline and clear, and *// help //* I thought, feeling it flow out from me like sap from a wounded tree, like the last of my fragile humanity washing away.

// help // I said, shouted, screamed into the empty void of air and sky and descent, once more a tumbling seedpod caught in gravity's embrace, unable to free myself, hoping for salvation. *// help, I'm falling, please come, please help. //*

// cousin //

The voice was far away and faint, barely touching the edges of my awareness. I strained toward it, continuing to shout silently into the void. *// help, I'm falling, please help me, I don't want to die. //*

// cousin, make yourself large as you can, cousin, hold fast, I come, I come. //

Make myself . . . I spread my arms and legs, trying to increase my surface area and resistance to the air. I continued to fall, and I couldn't tell whether the shift in my position had done anything to change the speed of my descent. Still, a feeling of approval washed over me, wordless and concrete.

// cousin, I am coming. //

I fell.

// cousin, look to the west. //

I opened my eyes. I looked.

A creature—a person, someone who was biologically more similar to me than I was to Graham or Mandy, but it was hard to let go of a lifetime's worth of thoughts and opinions, and everything I knew told me this was a creature, a monster, a beast—flew toward me, vast, leathery wings slapping at the sky like it flew through the sheer force of its determination. It looked like a six-limbed predatory dinosaur, complete with tufted feathers on the end of its long, whiplike tail and crowning its narrow-jawed, small-eyed head. It was a thing out of a nightmare, cutting through the air with claws extended and jaws open wide.

It was cast entirely in shades of green, in jade and emerald and tourmaline, and it was beautiful, and it was my cousin. I could tell that with a glance. We had been planted on different worlds, sprouted from different seed lines, but we were family all the same, and it was coming to save me.

// let go // hissed its voice.

Obediently, I went as limp as I could, trying to release the natural tension from my limbs. I was still falling, and my body fought against the relaxation, refusing to let go of the fear and adrenaline that was coursing through my veins. I couldn't breathe. I was falling, and I couldn't breathe.

// you are safe // hissed the cousin, and snatched me out of the air.

The impact was painful, even with as much care as it was taking. Its claws closed around my torso and clamped down, not hard enough to break the skin or do more than bruise me, but hard enough to yank me out of my descent. The sound of leathery wings beating became the loudest thing in the entire world. Everything seemed to snap to a painful halt, my head whipping forward until it slammed into one thick, muscular leg.

Things went hazy for a little while after that. When my vision cleared, we were flying smoothly through the sapphire sky, the cousin humming a soft, almost affectionate tune that vibrated its entire chest and throat. It sounded like a happy eagle.

// cousin // it said, joy coloring its tone. *// you wake. you wake. how did you come to fall from so far? this world granted you no wings. //* There was a certain quiet pity in its last statement, like it couldn't understand how we'd managed to accomplish anything of merit without wings.

// I was on a plane // I said. Now that I knew how to reach the place in my mind that was designed for communication within my copse, it seemed easier, almost more natural than verbal communication. Part of that may have been the lack of air. I wasn't dying, but speech required having something to make it function. With my lungs lying fallow in my chest, there wasn't anything to make the words emerge.

// plane? //

// a machine that flies. like the ships, but designed to function within a planetary atmosphere. //

// what a clever garden this has been! // The cousin sounded both surprised and pleased, like this had been something it had never considered. *// where should I release you? //*

Where . . . *// can you find the plane? //*

// I can find anything, if it is in the sky. //

// can you take me to the plane, and follow until it lands? I do not want to lose track of my friends, but I do not want the people who have control of the plane to know that I survived. //

Amusement and pleasure washed over me. *// a hunt! for you, small cousin, I can hunt. what are you called? //*

// Stasia. //

// I am Hunter. //

For the first time, I wondered whether the strangely literal names of all the aliens I'd met so far were a function of the translation provided by the pollen. When I gave them my name, did they hear "Stasia," or did they hear the meaning of my full, given name? Anastasia. She who will be reborn.

Maybe it was more fitting than I thought.

// how did you find me so quickly? it seems strange that you should be nearby. //

// your First asked that we watch for you, once you chose to return to the garden. I was near enough to hear your call. //

Hunter tore through the sky, powerful muscles moving it forward like a marathon runner as it sought the missing plane. It was doing this for me. It was a person, as surely as I was. Suddenly, thinking of my cousin as an "it" felt wrong.

// what are your pronouns? //

// what are pronouns? //

// um. they say what gender you are. boy or girl or both or neither //

// ah! // Again, delight colored Hunter's mental tone. *// my template was made to be a fertilizer of eggs. it brings me great joy to go through the motions, even as there are no eggs now to be sparked into a new generation. //*

It took me a moment to realize what Hunter was saying. *// so . . . he, then? //*

// yes, cousin // replied my amused relation. *// it is not so important to my cultivar as it is to yours, but I know your host garden places much weight on such words, and so I thank you for asking. //*

Somehow, being carried through the sky by a dinosaur-dragon hybrid who gleefully acknowledged his fondness for sex wasn't the strangest part of my week. In a weird way, it was sort of reassuring. If Hunter still enjoyed sex, whatever form that took for his host species, that meant Graham and I could still have sex after we were both plant people. Assuming I got to Graham before Agent Brown and her flunkies hurt him. My reassurance collapsed like a punctured soufflé.

Agent Brown had Graham and Mandy. Agent Brown had every reason to assume they were collaborators, helping my people infiltrate this planet from the outside. Never mind that we'd fallen from space and infiltrated all by ourselves, even when we didn't know we were doing it. We were the enemy, we were from somewhere else, and anyone who had helped us needed to be held accountable.

Hunter's claws were tight around my waist. I put a hand on one of his talons, bracing myself, and silently decided that if she had harmed a hair on either of their heads, I would end her.

Silent, equipped by the evolutionary forces of another world to be the perfect predator, Hunter flew on.

2.

We caught up with the plane just before the Canadian border. Hunter fell into a comfortable glide behind it, using the wake of its displaced air to lift him easily up. He hummed as he coasted, utterly content in the moment, in the sky, in the hunt.

The sky . . . *// what do you do on the ships? //* I asked.

// the fruits of my host garden hunger for sky // he replied. *// it is not common, for a shape to have such a need for a thing that it can overwhelm the message of the Great Root, but it does happen. we thirst to fly, to feel the wind around us, bearing us up and onward. on the ships, we sleep and study and lie as close to dormant as we may, and when a new garden is to come to harvest, we are released. this garden has good skies, cousin. before we leave them, they will be filled with the wings of my harvest, and we will bid them sweet farewell before the ships move on. //*

// will some of you stay here? //

// not when the harvest is done // he replied. *// the garden must be allowed to recover in peace. but we will remember these skies always, and remember them well. we wi—//*

Whatever he'd been intending to say was cut off as what sounded like a cannon exploded somewhere below us, and a hole the size of my torso was torn in the membrane of one wing. He howled, both aloud and inside my head, and I clapped my hands over my ears as if that would make any difference.

// hold fast! // he shouted, and launched himself higher, wings working harder than ever to compensate for the damage. The weapon fired again,

but missed its mark as he curved backward, out of the projectile's path. The wind bit at my face and eyes. I clung to his talon as hard as I could, refusing to consider the chance that I could still fall. I refused to have come this far and die as if all my efforts had been for nothing.

// low // warned Hunter, and folded himself into a dive so steep it felt like the skin was going to peel away from my flesh. No roller coaster had ever been that extreme, no drop that sheer, and I would have screamed if I'd been able to find the breath to do so. Instead, I clung to his talon, closing my eyes against the friction of the air beating down on them, and waited for it to be over.

Hunter shrieked, rage and defiance and pain, and the cannon spoke one more time, and I couldn't open my eyes, I didn't dare. But our continued descent didn't feel any more out-of-control than it had before, and when Hunter hissed, *// land //* in the space behind my eyes, I was able to brace myself for impact.

We hit the field still moving slightly too fast for safety, Hunter clutching me in his foreclaws while his hind legs pedaled frantically, trying to find purchase in the grassy earth. His stumbling turned into a run, and he slowed only momentarily, only long enough to drop me before he was launching himself back into the air. I staggered to my feet, preparing to shout after him, and stopped as I saw what he was doing:

The grass in the field was too tall to be tended regularly, but there were fences, and there were cattle. The rancher must have turned them out before fleeing, choosing to let them have a chance rather than leaving them to starve in the safety of their stalls. A big bull had assembled a small herd of his own, and was now lowering his head menacingly, pawing at the ground as he tried to figure out whether Hunter and I posed a threat.

I might be the smaller of the two of us: I was also the one on the ground, and the one who wore a shape he recognized, close enough to human to read as an intruder of a type he'd seen before. He snorted hard and began to charge, leaving his cows behind, breaking away from the herd. As soon as he was far enough from them that targeting wouldn't be an issue, Hunter dropped out of the sky and landed in the middle of the bull's back, teeth snapping at the great bovine's neck and claws digging deep into its flesh. The bull bellowed, snapping its head back in an effort to gore Hunter with its horns. Hunter responded by tearing out its throat.

Blood spurted from the bull in a huge, hot gush, the iron-filing smell of it hitting me even as far away as I was. I stayed frozen, my legs starting to shake with the sheer depth of my wanting, of my *need*. There was so much blood, so much, and it wasn't human, but in that moment, that didn't seem to matter. To a starving man, a candy bar will serve as well as a steak dinner. Human and bovine blood were basically the same thing anyway, so close to identical that it didn't matter, it didn't matter, it didn't—

Hunter raised his head, mouth open in a silent scream of dominance and triumph that I didn't need to hear to understand. On his own world, under his own sky, he would have screamed out loud, I knew that much. He would have roared until the horizon rang with his ascension. But here and now, he was keeping the volume of his victory contained, giving me the opportunity to catch up with the rest of my party while they still thought we'd been shot down.

Lowering his head, he began to feast, not just drinking the blood, but ripping out great chunks of the bull's side, letting its guts spill steaming onto the grass. That was too much for me. I broke into a run, half-staggering by the time I reached the carcass and dropped to my knees beside it, grabbing for a piece of severed flesh. It oozed with blood, and when I brought it to my mouth, the taste was the sweetest thing I had ever known. I closed my eyes as I swallowed again and again, suckling that chunk of muscle and tendon like it was a lollipop.

Something nudged my shoulder. I raised my head and opened my eyes to find Hunter looking down on me, something like amusement in his massive green eyes. There were chunks of bull stuck between his teeth, splashes of red on his scales, and he, like every other member of my newly extended family I had met, was beautiful.

// are you fed, cousin? // He extended his wings, showing that the hole was gone, patched over with regrown membrane almost indistinguishable from the tissue around it. That would be the blood again. As long as we fed fast, we might as well be indestructible.

Had the humans figured that out yet? Or had they slaughtered the ones foolish enough to come into range fast enough and completely enough that it hadn't mattered? We'd find out soon.

"I'm fed," I said, aloud, and was pleased when he bobbed his head in acknowledgment of my words. The pollen was still playing translator. Which meant . . .

Feeling suddenly shy, I asked, "Can you say your name for me? I want to hear what it sounds like in the air."

The crest of feathers atop Hunter's head rose in unmistakable pleasure before he opened his mouth and emitted a deep grumbling noise, like tectonic plates rubbing together. It was short and sharp and utterly distinct from the other brief vocalizations I had heard him make. I smiled.

"It's beautiful," I said.

He chuffed, and hopped down from the bull, extending his forelimbs toward me. I stepped into his embrace, feeling the security of his claws closing around my torso. This time, when he launched himself into the air, I was able to enjoy it.

We flew low above the trees, Hunter dipping into their pine-scented canopy with the ease of long practice. How many worlds had he flown over? How many types of tree had he played hide-and-seek with as he pursued the goals of invasion? Whatever the number, he had learned their offered lessons well: he flew like he had been tracking prey through this forest for a hundred years, like he already knew every secret it had to offer.

Branches whipped at my face, and I raised an arm to ward them off, laughing in soft delight at the ridiculousness of it all. I was being carried over the Canadian border by a giant predatory dinosaur from another world, and I was perfectly safe, perfectly sound, with a belly full of blood and a head full of vengeance.

Whatever military unit had shot us down as we followed the plane wasn't watching for us to come back so quickly, or so much lower in the sky. We skimmed the trees until we could see the silver glint of the plane ahead of us, flying so much higher that we probably weren't even on their radar.

// there // said Hunter.

// yes // I agreed. *// stay low. //*

Only amusement answered me. I supposed I deserved it, for telling someone with so much more experience than I had how to hunt. Hunter stayed low, and the plane flew on, until at last it began to tilt forward, going into its descent. Still we followed at our safe, low distance, until the airfield came into view.

It was clear that the plane was angling for a landing on the main runway. It would be virtually impossible for anyone to pick us off without also risking them. No sooner had the thought occurred to me than Hunter was putting on a burst of speed, catching easily up with the little jet, which had never been designed to outrun something like him. Nothing on Earth had been designed to outrun something like him.

We flew close enough that I caught a glimpse of Graham's face through the window, his eyes wide and amazed by the sight of my saurian cousin even before he saw me clasped in Hunter's claws. Joy washed away Graham's amazement, suffusing his face before we dropped lower and he was blocked from sight by the edge of one great green wing.

// *your mate?* // asked Hunter.

// *for now* // I said.

// *do not worry, little cousin. love survives the death of flesh remarkably well, when love is there.* // Hunter's thoughts were warm, and for the first time, I caught an image to go with the idea: Hunter and two other, larger dinosaur-creatures, both with plumage in a darker green, swirling through an elaborate dance in the sky above a world I had never seen. His mates.

// *they're beautiful.* //

// *we all are, in the green.* //

The plane was starting to touch the concrete. Hunter dropped lower, hind legs moving in a running motion even before they made contact with the ground. There was barely a bump when he went from gliding to racing alongside the great silver machine. There was a moment when I feared the plane might decide to go back up. The moment passed; the plane's engines powered down, and it rolled toward its destination.

A motorcade, parked across the runway. Eight black cars. People with guns. And a small group of what I took for politicians, dressed in rumpled suitcoats and trousers, their hair disarrayed by the wind and the stresses of our situation. They looked like they were holding it together somewhat better than Agent Brown was.

Hunter was running ahead of the plane now, his legs propelling him faster than their engines. He angled toward the motorcade, lowering his head and making a high-pitched screeching sound that I interpreted as a warning. He didn't slow at all, continuing at full speed until we were close enough to the gathered politicians to see their expressions. The guards, as one, raised their weapons, preparing to fire.

A woman—silver-haired, wearing a lilac shell top under her charcoal jacket—stepped forward, raising her hands. "Guns *down*," she snapped.

The guards lowered their weapons.

Hunter came to a stop.

It was a sudden thing, that stop: one second, he was running, and the next, he was turning his feet sideways, talons digging into the concrete, wings fanning out to increase wind resistance and bring us to a halt. His tail whipped forward, forming a barrier between me and those weapons. Of the two of us, I was by far the smaller and more fragile, and I had a brief moment of understanding what it must have been like for the young of his host race's people, back when they thought their planet was their own.

"It's okay, Hunter," I said, with a wary look at the guards and their guns. "You can put me down."

// you know these meat things? //

"I'm pretty sure that one"—I indicated the woman—"is the Vice-President of the United States, so yeah, I know these meat things. Put me down."

"You can *talk* to it?" asked one of the guards, horror and confusion in his tone.

Hunter set me gently on the tarmac, uncurling his talons from around my waist. I reached back and put a hand on his arm, leaving it resting there as I replied, in an utterly even tone, "He's my cousin."

"Are you here to discuss terms?" asked the woman. The longer I looked at her, the more positive I became that she was Vice-President Bethany Rogers, who should have been looking toward the election right about now, and not considering her options for fighting off an alien invasion. "We were told you would be sending a team to discuss terms." Her eyes ran over my filthy clothes, my bare feet, my bloodstained hands, and found every inch of me wanting. I wasn't an eight-foot-tall monster with a bubble helmet over my head, or an unspeakable horror that could never have arisen on this world. Hunter was close, but me?

I was just a woman. Pretty enough, unremarkable save for the part where I had somehow been cast entirely in green, rendered alien by the color of my skin and hair and nothing else. She could have passed me in the aisle at the grocery store. Probably had once, before she'd risen high enough politically to have her own security forces and call signs; she'd started life as a junior Congresswoman from the state of Oregon, and like all good Washington girls, I had been going there for the tax-free shopping since I was old enough to drive a car.

I was nothing. I was nobody. I certainly wasn't the end of the human race in blue jeans and a tattered blouse, and yet here she was, and here I was, and the sound of the plane behind me had cut off; the rest of the players in this little scene would be approaching soon, if they weren't already.

"Agent Brown had her men throw me out of a moving plane," I said, keeping my voice as calm and level as I could. "You might want to tell her that's not a good look when you're getting ready to negotiate a surrender. Although I could thank her, I guess. I would never have hooked up with Hunter, here, if I hadn't been falling to my death."

"You have my sincere apologies," said the Vice-President, insincerely. "She acted on her own initiative, and not due to orders from me."

"Okay," I said. "That's cool, and it's not like she's going to get the chance to do it again. But she still has two of my friends, both human, in her custody. I want them back. Unharmed. Now."

"I'm sure you see where I cannot authorize the release of American citizens into the hands of an alien power."

"Cool," I said. "I'm sure you can see where they are literally the last thing keeping me from telling Hunter here that we don't need any of you alive." There was a low growl from behind me. Several of the guards took a step back. I guessed Hunter was showing off the size and quality of his teeth. "I'm not asking for prisoners. I'm not asking for the unwilling. I'm asking for my *friends*."

Why would First send us down as the contact team? She knew I wasn't qualified, that none of us had any experience with hostage negotiation or brokering peace. Not that she was looking for peace. The first responses of the humans had been what she expected, violence and fear and confusion, and the time for peace had passed. We were going to harvest this world, whether they liked it or not. We were going to take the best parts of humanity into ourselves and set them among the stars. As for the worst parts of humanity . . .

The worst parts would nuke the planet just to keep it out of alien hands. The fact that it hadn't happened yet only told me some people still believed—erroneously—that they could win. As soon as they figured out the tide had turned, they'd be priming the switches and setting the silos to blow. Because that was what humans *did*. They broke their toys so no one else could play with them. They unleashed plagues and they burned down cities and they acted shocked and horrified when people called them on their actions, but they did it anyway. Over and over again, they did it anyway.

"If she has harmed either of them, if you order her to harm either of them, if you allow harm to come to either of them, I will tell my cousin to call his siblings, and the last thing you see will be like something out of a dark reboot of *Captain Planet*," I said. My voice didn't shake. For the first time in days, it felt completely steady. "You will die here, all of you, and it won't matter if you shoot me—you know how to kill me, I'm made like a human being, blow my brains out and it's over—because you're going to be outnumbered."

"Humanity still owns this planet," snapped Vice-President Rogers.

"Numerically, sure. But I don't see humanity here. I see you. Twelve of you. And you could probably take out me, and you might take out Hunter, but not before we sound the alarm, and it won't take long before you're facing way more than twelve of *us*. So how about we all play nicely, and we all have a chance at walking away?"

Footsteps behind me. Footsteps, and the distinctive sound of guns being cocked. Vice-President Rogers's head snapped up, eyes widening in clear alarm.

"Hold your fire!" she shouted. "No one is to fire! They're friendlies!"

"No, we're not," I said, turning to look around Hunter and grinning with ghoulish glee when I saw Mandy and Graham walking alongside Agent Brown and her people. Both had their hands cuffed in front of them, and Graham's lip was split, probably from his struggles to get to me before I could be thrown off the plane, but they were otherwise all right. They were otherwise just fine.

Graham stopped walking for a beat when he saw me peering around the admittedly alarming giant green lizard. Then he broke into a run, not seeming to care that he wouldn't be able to catch himself if he fell. "*Stasia*!"

"Hi, sweetie." I stepped around Hunter. Graham collided with me, and I threw my arms around him, breathing in the scent of him, who he was, who he would always be. It was distinct and singular and stronger than the smell of blood. Thankfully.

He pressed his face against the crook of my neck, breathing in deeply in turn before he whispered, "I saw you fall."

"I know. I know you saw." I lifted my head to look at Agent Brown and her people with every ounce of hatred I possessed. One of them had a hand wrapped tightly around Mandy's upper arm, keeping her from following Graham to safety. "I'm so sorry, Graham. That should never have happened."

Agent Brown looked at me impassively, cold resignation in her eyes. She knew she had lost. Maybe she realized how badly she had fucked up by deciding to dispose of me. It didn't really matter either way.

"Let her go, and uncuff them both," I said, in a voice that was surprisingly clear, and surprisingly cold. I had no more sympathy left in me. Somewhere between an observatory in Maine and a runway in Washington, it had all been bled away. "I am not here to negotiate with you."

"Madame Vice-President, have you been hurt?" Agent Brown put her hand on the butt of her gun. "Please indicate if you are here under duress."

They probably had a complicated system of signs and countersigns to tell each other when they were in trouble. They probably had a whole world of espionage on their sides. Me, I had a flying dinosaur from space, a cosplayer, and a herpetologist.

I had never felt more in command of a situation.

"Stand down," said Vice-President Rogers. "I am unharmed. May I ask why you saw fit to collect the representative we had been told was coming, only to expel her from your plane?"

"That sounds so much nicer than 'throw her out,' doesn't it?" I asked, glancing at Graham.

I was expecting amusement, or anger. Instead, I got blank-eyed sorrow, and a pallor that spoke of panic so deep that it refused to be easily shaken off. I touched his cheek before turning my attention back to Agent Brown.

"Let them go," I said.

"She's not the representative," snapped Agent Brown. "She's just another damn alien. We had this one in custody before everything went to shit. She's a *lab specimen*."

Hunter growled, low and deep in his throat. That answered one question. Whether he could understand English or was getting a translation relayed through the pollen, he didn't like what he was hearing.

"My cousin doesn't appreciate you calling me names," I said mildly. "Remove the cuffs."

"Do as she asks, Agent," said the vice-president wearily. "It's a small concession."

"We shouldn't be making concessions at all." Agent Brown produced a set of keys and used them to undo Mandy's cuffs. Handing the keys over, she said, "You can unlock your friend."

Mandy didn't say a word. She just spun on her heel and ran to where Graham and I were waiting. He stuck his hands out. She uncuffed him, dropping both keys and handcuffs before she threw her arms around my neck and yanked me into a painfully tight embrace.

"I thought you were *dead* you *bitch*," she gasped, voice muffled and softened by the flesh of my neck.

I patted her awkwardly on the back. "Not dead," I assured her. "Did you . . . did you want to say hello to Hunter? He's my cousin."

"Is Hunter the dinosaur?" she asked, without letting go.

"Yes."

"I like your family more and more."

Hunter made an amused clicking sound. *// your small pet is amusing. //*

"Hunter likes you too," I translated. Turning back to the vice-president and her guards, I asked, "So are you it? Is this what remains of the United States government? Do you even have any power here? We're in Canada. Doesn't that make your presence politically fraught?"

"Cities are burning. People are dying. People are being abducted into alien vessels. No one has heard anything out of North Korea or Ireland in over a week. We're losing touch with other areas daily. At this point, national borders seem less important than the safety of our species."

"Right," I said. "The president and prime minister took a vote and decided you were the expendable one, didn't they?"

Vice-President Rogers's cheeks flared red. Aloud, she said only, "I'm less essential to the function of the government than they are. I am proud to serve at the pleasure of the President."

"Right," I said. Graham was close to me, so close I could feel the heat coming off his skin, and Mandy was only a little farther away, watching warily. Agent Brown and her goons were behind us, but they didn't frighten me anymore. They had no dangers left to offer.

There was a soft boom from somewhere far overhead, like something had entered our atmosphere with far more caution and control than the average meteor. I kept my eyes on the Vice-President.

"We are not the diplomatic team," I said quietly. "We are two aliens and two humans, three of whom grew up on this planet, all of whom would like to see this invasion end as quickly and cleanly as possible."

"So you're going to leave our planet and never come back," said Vice-President Rogers.

"I think you and I both know that it's way too late for that to happen," I said regretfully—and I was genuinely sorry. Looking back, I could see all the places where humanity might have steered away from this result. If they had listened to their own children when we started claiming to be the vanguard of an invasion; if they had greeted the first proof that aliens were real with something other than fear . . .

It felt like I was justifying things to myself, and in a very real way, I was. If it had been up to me, the invasion would never have happened; would have been a few scout ships setting down and quietly collecting the people like me, the ones whose hearts beat with the tempo of another planet's tides. They would have carried us, and our loved ones, away to the stars, and Earth would have been poorer by a few thousand people, but not at the center of a war. If it had been up to me, we would never have made this world a garden.

But my people had, and it was, and now there was no way left but forward, through the fire, into the cold inevitability on the other side.

"If you're not the diplomatic team, why are you here?"

"To tell you the real diplomatic team is coming, and things will go better for you if you try not to be afraid of them." I slipped my arm around Graham's waist, and he did the same to me, the two of us holding each other in the face of the end of the world. It was all right, if things ended here. At least we would be reaching the end of our stories together.

I wished I'd married him, back when human institutions like marriage were more common. I wished I'd gone with him to the Everglades. Maybe the next owners of this world would rise from his invasive pythons or his beloved frogs, and when we sailed back this way in a million years, the seedlings would be like Hunter, dressed in scales, dancing through the skies.

Above us, the sound of the scout ship descending grew louder. The vice-president paled, and we all waited for the moment when the invasion would end.

3.

The ship set itself down with surpassing delicacy, roots driving themselves deep into the soil, shattering the runway in the process. Hunter took a step back, displaying a degree of nervousness that spoke clearly to the role the scouts had played in taking his original world. Even if he now sided with his own species over the memory of that good garden, it's hard to trust a machine that once carried the end of the world.

The vice-president and her people also fell back, the ones I had taken for politicians moving with her while the guards put themselves bodily between her and the settling ship. Seen from the outside, without a descent forceful enough to punch a hole in the world, the ship resembled nothing so much as a giant, hard-shelled seedpod, the sort of thing that could have fallen from any number of trees. One by one, the tiers of scaling began to separate, and I revised my impression: it was a vine-covered pinecone from space. Smaller, it could have been lost forever in any coniferous forest on Earth.

Once enough of the scales had lifted, the vines still wrapped around the inner core began letting go, revealing the door, which split into four equal pieces and peeled away, like the opening of a slow, strange flower.

First stepped out, onto the surface of the world.

Someone moaned behind me, from the direction of Agent Brown's people. I heard a gun cock and whipped around, every nerve in my body shrieking alarm. Hunter shrieked a wild, dominant cry, picking up on my distress, and leapt into the air, wings snapping open as he dropped himself between the NASA team and First. Gunfire rent the air. Hunter screamed again. I whipped around in time to see him charging Agent Brown's team, holes in his beautiful wings, pure fury in his tone.

"Call them off!" I turned back to the vice-president. "Tell them to stop firing, or he's going to kill them all!"

She didn't say anything. Her eyes were fixed on First, on the specter of a spider the size of a fully grown ox stepping delicately to the ground.

I whirled again, running toward the scene unfolding behind me as the NASA agents fired and Hunter advanced, wounded but alive, determined to have his revenge.

I heard Mandy scream. I heard a gun fire. Hunter pounced, sending NASA agents tumbling in all directions as he bit the head clean off the nearest one, gulping it down before starting to rip his victim into pieces. The others shouted, trying to steady their weapons.

Slowly, I turned.

Mandy was on the ground between First and the vice-president's group, blood spreading slowly from the gunshot wound in her chest. She wasn't moving.

21

VANCOUVER, BRITISH COLUMBIA: AUGUST 17, 2031
THE END OF THE INVASION

1.

First moved like lightning, faster than I would have dreamed possible for an arachnid of her size under gravity like ours. The physics of her body must have been bolstered by her vegetable nature, keeping her from collapsing under her own weight. She raced to Mandy's side, a silk-like substance spurting from her abdomen, arms already working frantically at constructing a pale green cocoon around the body of my friend.

The shouts from the NASA agents were getting rarer as the snarls from Hunter grew more consistent. He was shredding them, ripping through them like so much tissue paper, and I couldn't be sorry, not in the slightest, not in the *least*. I couldn't wish them another ending, because they'd been the ones to start firing, and because of them, Mandy was—Mandy was—

I ran without thinking about it, ran straight for the Vice-President of the United States, a nice woman, a pleasant woman, a woman I had *voted* for, and my hand was raised, and my fist caught her square in the jaw, sending her reeling backward, so that her ass impacted with the side of one of those fine black cars that had been intended to get her here, to the slaughtering grounds, safely. Her guards shouted, beginning to turn on me, and she raised a hand.

They stopped dead. So did I, arm cocked back to hit her again. She looked at me with anguish in her eyes.

"This," she said, "was never what I wanted."

"Maybe not, but it's what you're getting," I said. My voice was cold. The last of my mercy had leaked out onto the concrete along with Mandy's blood. Mandy . . . I turned.

First had her neatly cocooned, completely obscured by veils of green silk. The vast spider lifted her head, and I knew she was looking at me, focusing on me with the full power of her many multifaceted eyes.

// she is not dead // she said. *// she will not die until the cocoon is cut. you will have to choose for her, then, because she will not be able to choose for herself. //*

"What's she saying?" demanded Graham.

"Mandy's alive." I turned back to the vice-president. "Congratulations. If there was any prayer for humanity, it just got answered. Because I promise you, if she dies, I will tell my mother to burn everything mankind has ever made to the ground and salt the ashes to be sure that nothing ever grows there again. Do you understand me?"

The skin under Vice-President Rogers's eye twitched. "Your . . . mother?"

"You'd probably think of her as 'the spider.' Her name is First, and she's the diplomatic team. Good job trying to shoot her." I glared at the guards, not making any effort to figure out which one had actually fired the gun. Let them all share the blame, unless they were willing to give up one of their own in the hopes of earning back a sliver of our favor.

This was human nature. This was understandable, even excusable, when viewed from a great-enough distance. We had scared them. We had forced them into a situation where they felt like they had to take a stand or lose everything. And none of that mattered, because the distance wasn't there. Before we had done anything intentional, anything beyond existing, they had been prepared to kill us all.

Agent Brown had been right about one thing, even if she had been so perfectly, patently wrong about everything else: I wasn't a citizen of the United States of America anymore. I wasn't even a citizen of Earth. They'd been in such a hurry to throw me away that they had left me with nowhere to turn beyond the people of my origins, and now I was free to be what they had decided I was. I was free to be a monster.

First walked toward us, body low and knees high as she balanced her swollen abdomen against the cruel gravity of Earth. A hand touched my shoulder. I didn't need to look to know that it was Graham. If one of the guards had even dared touch me, Hunter would have left his meal and slaughtered them for their audacity. I could hear him chirping and creeling as he gulped down limbs and viscera, healing the damage their bullets had done one mouthful at a time.

How many people had he just killed? How many lives?

How come I no longer cared?

// daughter, tell these humans that they have little time remaining. the Great Root has marked them, and the harvest is come. //

"My mother would like me to tell you to make your peace with God," I said flatly.

"We thought . . ." Vice-President Rogers straightened. The skin along her jaw was beginning to bruise and swell. Speaking must have been painful. She did it anyway.

She probably thought she was being brave. She didn't understand yet that the time for bravery was over.

"We thought this was going to be a negotiation," she said. "I was sent to collect your diplomatic team and take them back with me to meet with the president and the prime minister. We have the United Nations standing by, as this is a global matter, and—"

// silence. //

"Be quiet," I said.

First stepped closer. The tiny claws at the tips of her legs clutched the concrete, granting her perfect, seemingly effortless balance. The sunlight glittering off her carapace made her look even larger than she actually was.

// we have come to speak with those of you who would come to speak with us, not to travel at your pleasure // she said. Hunter prowled up behind her, dripping with blood. My stomach rumbled. She continued, *// we will not shut ourselves in one of your places, to be at the mercy if your kind. you have shown that you cannot be trusted. //*

Dutifully, I relayed her words. The vice-president's eyes flashed with anger.

"We have shown that we can't be trusted?" she demanded. "*Us*? You're the ones who infiltrated our planet! Who killed our children! We did not invite you here, and you came anyway!"

// we came on the winds of space; we did not choose you any more than you chose us // First implacably replied. *// we did not intend harm to your children, but our children can be rough, as all children can. they acted out of instinct. for them, we apologize. they were innocent of what they did. for ourselves, we do not apologize. for you, we do not accept apology. //*

Again, I relayed her words. The vice-president looked between me and First, seemingly unsure who she should address. In the end, she settled on me. I was the one who still looked almost human, even if she knew I was nothing of the sort.

"Please," she said. "People are dying. Riots, fires, floods. Infrastructure is collapsing. Everywhere on Earth."

That, then, was why the world had yet to end in nuclear fire or due to weed killer poured into the oceans: why there had been no massive, last-ditch effort to close the toy box before we could steal all the best toys. We had people all over the planet, people like me, raised in human homes, raised to be culturally aware of the regions where we lived. We knew what the risks were. It only stood to reason that all across the world, we had been able to stand up and shut down the systems that might have destroyed us.

We had infiltrated them in the guise of their own children. We had done it not knowing what we did, following the programming given to us by horticulturists who moved among the stars like comets, carrying their gardens with them, scattering their seeds across the cosmos. This would never have been possible, not in this form, without us.

I felt a pang of regret. I felt a much stronger flood of pride. The final door was closing on my time on Earth, and I was standing on the correct side.

// people are always dying // said First implacably. *// the history of this garden is an endless line of people dying. we did not put the weapons in your hands. we did not order you to use them. most of all, we sent you warning. we sent you our own precious children, to tell you we were coming, to give you the opportunity to say "no, no, turn aside." you did not listen to them. you did not listen to us. and when we came, as we had said we would come, you cried "how dare you tell the truth" and greeted us with war. even before we raised a thorn against you, you greeted us with war. what we do now is justified by your own actions. we are the monsters you have made. //*

Carefully, as precisely as possible, I relayed my mother's words to the vice-president and her people. Vice-President Rogers's face fell at first, before settling into a blank neutrality that spoke of greater pain held captive behind it, where no one would be required to see.

Finally, she asked, "If this is so, why did you send a negotiation team at all? Why not just stay safe in the sky and keep slaughtering us? Why risk yourself?"

// you had the raising of my daughter // said First. *// I would be a poor mother if I did not thank you, in my way. //*

Again, I relayed her words. The vice-president looked from First to me, and back again. At first, it seemed like she could only see our differences, plentiful as they were. Then her eyes adjusted, and she began focusing on the shades of green, the way we mirrored them between us. There was a family resemblance, just . . . not as Earth eyes understood it.

"How is this thanking me?" she asked.

Graham's hand was a warm anchor on my arm, a reminder that no matter how far we went, we would never leave Earth entirely behind. It would always be with us, in the shapes we wore, the words we spoke aloud between ourselves, rather than the ones that were thrown through the pollen and translated into a dozen, a hundred, a thousand alien tongues.

"The harvest is coming," I said, standing a little straighter. I felt First's approving eyes on me. Had she been in my position once, with her own parent, under an alien sky? Was this how our genus cultivated diplomats? This conversation, or something like it, was happening over and over again, all over the planet. Other Firsts and other children, explaining the inevitable, because it was the polite thing to do before we devoured the world. "Earth was given the opportunity to refuse it, and didn't. It was a problem for tomorrow, and there were things to be done today. Humans have never been good at that math. The ships aren't leaving; the dying isn't going to stop. But it can be over quickly, if you want it to be."

"Never," spat the vice-president, her lips drawing back in a snarl. *"Now!"*

More guards rose from behind the line of SUVs, all of them armed. I flung my arms wide, trying to block Graham from the hail of bullets I knew was coming. His body was flesh and blood; he couldn't heal like I could.

// yes // said First sadly. *// now. //*

The sky above us began to scream as the rest of Hunter's copse dropped out of the trees and into a sharply banked descent, their wings folded and their jaws gaping wide. Hunter launched himself upward to join them. The vice-president's guards, faced with a choice between shooting two civilians—even if one of them was green—and a horrifying nightmare spider that, while huge, had done nothing to threaten them, or a sky full of aerial escapees from Jurassic Park, began firing wildly upward.

Hunter's copse flew through the bullets, shrieking and batting their wings at the guards. The sound of ripping filled the air, underscored by the understandable sound of screams. Through it all, First remained calm, looking at the vice-president with the serenity of a conqueror who knew that her hour had come around at last.

// now // she murmured. *// are you ready to listen? //*

HARVEST

. . . And before we judge of them too harshly we must remember what ruthless and utter destruction our own species has wrought, not only upon animals, such as the vanished bison and the dodo . . . The Tasmanians, in spite of their human likeness, were entirely swept out of existence in a war of extermination waged by European immigrants, in the space of fifty years. Are we such apostles of mercy as to complain if the Martians warred in the same spirit? . . .

—H.G. WELLS,
THE WAR OF THE WORLDS

We tried to warn you. Maybe you should have listened.

—STASIA MILLER

This was a very good garden. It grew so green.

We cannot wait to visit it again.

—SPOKEN BY FIRST OF THE SEED FLEET,
UPON DEPARTING FROM GARDEN
DESIGNATED "EARTH."

22

SOMEWHERE HIGH ABOVE THE WORLD: TIME UNKNOWN AFTER THE INVASION

1.

Seeing the Vice-President of the United States of America and the Prime Minister of Canada both remade in green, standing between Hunter and First as they sent out their final address to their nations . . . something about that image broke something in the human psyche. Up until that moment, I guess there had been a deep undercurrent of belief that somehow, humanity could still win.

It wasn't just the two of them, of course. That scene had played out across the globe, with the children who had been raised in humanity's arms bringing their biological parents home. Supposedly, the distribution of our seeds was random. The placement of the seed ships most assuredly was not. All of us found family in their halls. Some, like me, found more than that.

We found where we belonged.

Though we had conquered the world, the death toll from the invasion was surprisingly low, and mostly self-inflicted. Murders, riots, suicides. All the violent thrashes of a threatened species. All we'd ever needed to do was show our faces and wait for the inevitable to begin unspooling around us.

Oh, millions of humans died. But no one set off any nukes, and the harvest wasn't spoilt, and so it didn't really seem to matter all that much. Not once the fight was over.

When the thrashing slowed, the scout ships moved in, carrying platoons of our more-martial forms. Hunter and his kind owned the skies. First's harvest-mates filled the trees with webs. Plants can grow almost anywhere, and so can our seeds; we claimed the seas, the deserts, the plains. We took the world in three days, and it was delicious.

But this is all a story. This has only ever been a story. And since it's a story, it can't hurt you anymore, if it ever had that power to begin with.

You'll wake up soon. It's taking longer because the flowers are in the right soil. Earth is a good garden, but it isn't the same as the garden where we were born, and we use that garden's soil here on the ships. The flowers mature more slowly when planted properly, and they ripen more slowly too, taking their time, getting every little detail right. Getting every aspect of the thing they copy. They do a better job here, which is why they can handle larger prey. The flower that ate Anastasia could never have consumed or copied something your size.

When you wake up, I hope you'll remember you went willingly. I hope you'll remember that forever was waiting for you on the other side of the pain. And I'll be here, with clothes and a glass of blood, and time. So much time. We're going to have forever, Graham, and no one's ever going to call either of us a liar again. We're finally free.

First says that you can hear me now, even if you don't necessarily know what I'm saying. So I'm making sure you know what matters, and I'm making sure you know that I'm still here. That I will always be here.

Please know that you are loved.

Please know that I am waiting.

Please know that we're going to have the stars, Graham, we're going to have the *stars*. You and me and Mandy and Toni and everyone else who chose or was chosen for conversion, we're going to have the stars. Earth will have its own ships, green and glorious and growing until they launch themselves from their original garden and sail the skies, joining us in forever. We're going to see things we've never seen before, you and me, and we may not be human, but we'll think like humans did, we'll understand what we see like humans did, and through us, humanity will finally see the universe. We're going to carry them there, in the space beneath our skins.

This was all a story. I can't wait for you to wake up and finish telling it with me.

I can't wait.

ABOUT THE AUTHOR

MIRA GRANT is the author of the *New York Times* bestselling Newsflesh series, along with multiple other works of biomedical science fiction. She has been nominated for the Hugo Award, and her book, *Feed,* was chosen as one of NPR's 100 Killer Thrillers.

Mira is also Seanan McGuire, a bestselling author of award-winning fantasy and comics.

HELL FOLLOWED WITH US

By Andrew Joseph White

An instant *New York Times* bestseller, this is a furious, queer debut novel about embracing the monster within and unleashing its power against your oppressors.

Sixteen-year-old trans boy Benji is on the run from the cult that raised him—the fundamentalist sect that unleashed Armageddon and decimated the world's population. Desperately, he searches for a place where the cult can't get their hands on him, or more importantly, on the bioweapon they infected him with.

But when cornered by monsters born from the destruction, Benji is rescued by a group of teens from the local Acheson LGBTQ+ Center, affectionately known as the ALC. The ALC's leader, Nick, is gorgeous, autistic, and a deadly shot, and he knows Benji's darkest secret: the cult's bioweapon is mutating him into a monster deadly enough to wipe humanity from the earth once and for all.

Still, Nick offers Benji shelter among his ragtag group of queer teens, as long as Benji can control the monster and use its power to defend the ALC. Eager to belong, Benji accepts Nick's terms...until he discovers the ALC's mysterious leader has a hidden agenda, and more than a few secrets of his own.

Daphne Press